Willis Fletcher Johnson

History of the Johnstown Flood

With full accounts also of the destruction on the Susquehanna and Juniata rivers,

and the Bald Eagle Creek - Vol. 1

Willis Fletcher Johnson

History of the Johnstown Flood
With full accounts also of the destruction on the Susquehanna and Juniata rivers, and the Bald Eagle Creek - Vol. 1

ISBN/EAN: 9783337302092

Printed in Europe, USA, Canada, Australia, Japan

Cover: Foto ©Andreas Hilbeck / pixelio.de

More available books at **www.hansebooks.com**

HISTORY

OF

THE JOHNSTOWN FLOOD.

INCLUDING

ALL THE FEARFUL RECORD; THE BREAKING OF THE SOUTH FORK DAM;
THE SWEEPING OUT OF THE CONEMAUGH VALLEY; THE OVER-
THROW OF JOHNSTOWN; THE MASSING OF THE WRECK AT
THE RAILROAD BRIDGE; ESCAPES, RESCUES, SEARCHES
FOR SURVIVORS AND THE DEAD; RELIEF
ORGANIZATIONS, STUPENDOUS CHARI-
TIES, ETC., ETC.

WITH FULL ACCOUNTS ALSO OF THE

DESTRUCTION ON THE SUSQUEHANNA AND JUNIATA RIVERS, AND THE
BALD EAGLE CREEK.

BY

WILLIS FLETCHER JOHNSON.

ILLUSTRATED.

EDGEWOOD PUBLISHING CO.,

1889.

ous. Conemaugh nestles at the very foot of the
Alleghenies; all railroad trains eastward bound
stop there to catch their breath before beginning
the long climb up to Altoona. Sang Hollow
nestles by the river amid almost tropical luxuri-
ance of vegetation ; yon little wooded islet in mid-
stream a favorite haunt of fishermen. Nineveh is
rich in bog iron and coal, and the whirr of the
mill-wheel is heard. Johnstown, between the two
creeks at their junction, is the queen city of the
valley. On either side the creek, and beyond, the
steep mountain sides ; behind, the narrow valley
reaching twenty miles back to the lake ; before,
the Conemaugh river just beginning its romantic
course. Broken hillsides streaked with torrents
encompass it. Just a century ago was Johnstown
founded by one Joseph Johns, a German settler.
Before then its beauteous site was occupied by an
Indian village, Kickenapawling. Below this was
the head of navigation on the Conemaugh. Hither
came the wagoners of the Alleghenies, with huge
wains piled high with merchandise from seaboard
cities, and placed it on flat-bottomed boats and
started it down the river-way to the western mar-
kets. The merchandise came up from Philadelphia and Baltimore by river, too ; up the Susquehanna and Juniata, to the eastern foot-hills, and
there was a great portage from the Juniata to the
Conemaugh; the Kittanning Trail, then the Franks

CHAPTER I.

Springtime in the mountains. Graceful slopes
and frowning precipices robed in darkest green of
hemlock and spruce. Open fields here and there
verdant with young grass and springing grain, or
moist and brown beneath the plow for the plant-
ing time. Hedgerow and underwood fragrant
with honeysuckle and wild blackberry bloom;
violets and geraniums purpling the forest floor.
Conemaugh creek and Stony creek dash and
plunge and foam along their rocky channels to
where they unite their waters and form the Conemaugh river, hastening down to the Ohio, to the
Mississippi, to the Mexican Gulf. Trout and pick-
erel and bass flash their bronze and silver armor
in the sparkling shallows of the streams and in
the sombre and placid depths of the lake up
yonder behind the old mud dam. Along the valley of the Conemaugh are ranged villages, towns,
cities: Conemaugh, Johnstown, Cambria, Sang
Hollow, Nineveh, and others, happy and prosper-

PAGE

250,000,000 FEET OF LOGS AFLOAT IN THE SUSQUEHANNA, ... 307

LAST TRAINS IN AND OUT OF HARRISBURG, ... 325

COLUMBIA, PA., UNDER THE FLOOD, ... 343

PENNSYLVANIA AVENUE AT SIXTH STREET, WASHINGTON, D. C., . 361

SEVENTH STREET, WASHINGTON, D. C., IN THE FLOOD, ... 379

FOURTEENTH STREET, WASHINGTON, D. C., IN THE FLOOD, . . . 397

THE FLOOD IN WASHINGTON, D. C., OPPOSITE HARRIS'S THEATRE, . 415

LIST OF ILLUSTRATIONS.

	PAGE
MAP OF THE DELUGED CONEMAUGH DISTRICT, ...	1
JOHNSTOWN AS LEFT BY THE FLOOD, ...	19
RUINS OF JOHNSTOWN VIEWED FROM PROSPECT HILL, ...	37
GENERAL VIEW OF THE RUINS, LOOKING UP STONY CREEK, . . . ·55
RUINS, SHOWING THE PATH OF THE FLOOD, ... 73
TYPICAL SCENE IN JOHNSTOWN, ... 91
JOHNSTOWN—VIEW CORNER OF MAIN AND CLINTON STREETS, . . 109
VIEW ON CLINTON STREET, JOHNSTOWN, ... 127
MAIN AND CLINTON STREETS, LOOKING SOUTHWEST, ... 145
RUINS, CORNER OF CLINTON AND MAIN STREETS, ... 163
RUINS, FROM SITE OF THE HULBURT HOUSE, ... 181
THE DÉBRIS ABOVE THE PENNSYLVANIA RAILROAD BRIDGE, . . . 199
RUINS OF THE CAMBRIA IRON WORKS, ... 217
RUINS OF THE CAMBRIA IRON COMPANY'S STORE, ... 235
THIRD STREET, WILLIAMSPORT, PA., DURING THE FLOOD, ... 253
WRECK OF THE IRON BRIDGE AT WILLIAMSPORT, PA., ... 271
WRECK OF THE LUMBER YARDS AT WILLIAMSPORT, PA., ... 289

CHAPTER XXXIV.   PAGE

Plans for the Future of Johnstown—The City to be Rebuilt on a Finer
Scale than Ever Before—A Real Estate Boom Looked For—Enlarging the Conemaugh—Views of Capitalists, : 387

CHAPTER XXXV.

Well-known People who Narrowly Escaped the Flood—Mrs. Halford's Experience—Mrs. Childs Storm-bound—Tales Related by
Travelers—A Theatrical Company's Plight, ... 393

CHAPTER XXXVI.

The Ubiquitous Reporter Getting There—Desperate Traveling through
a Storm-swept Country—Special Trains and Special Teams—Climbing Across the Mountains—Rest for the Weary in a Hay Mow, . . 402

CHAPTER XXXVII.

The Reporter's Life at Johnstown—Nothing to Eat, but Much to Do—
Kindly Remembrances of a Kindly Friend—Driven from Bed by
Rats—Three Hours of Sleep in Seventy-two—A Picturesque Group, 410

CHAPTER XXXVIII.

Williamsport's Great Losses—Flooded with Thirty-four Feet of Water
—Hundreds of Millions of Feet of Lumber Swept Away—Loss of
Life—Incidents of Rescue and of Death—The Story of Garret
Crouse and his Gray Horse, ... 421

CHAPTER XXXIX.

The Juniata Valley Ravaged by the Storm—Losses at Tyrone, Huntingdon and Lewistown—Destruction at Lock Haven—A Baby's
Voyage Down Stream—Romantic Story of a Wedding, ... 435

CHAPTER XL.

The Floods along the Potomac—The National Capital Submerged—
A Terrible Record in Maryland—Gettysburg a Sufferer—Tidings
of Devastation from Many Points in Several States, ... 444

CHAPTER XXVI.

Breaking up the Ruins and Burying the Dead—Innumerable Funerals
—The Use of Dynamite—The Holocaust at the Bridge—The Cambria Iron Works—Pulling out Trees with Locomotives, ... 299

CHAPTER XXVII.

Caring for the Sufferers—Noble Work of Miss Clara Barton and the Red Cross Society—A Peep into a Hospital—Finding Homes for the Orphans—Johnstown Generous in its Woe—A Benevolent Eating House, 309

CHAPTER XXVIII.

Recovering from the Blow—The Voice of the Locomotive Heard again—Scenes Day by Day amid the Ruins and at the Morgue—Strange Salvage from the Flood—A Family of Little Children, . . 319

CHAPTER XXIX.

The City Filled with Life Again—Work and Bustle on Every Hand—Railroad Trains Coming In—Pathetic Meetings of Friends—Persistent Use of Dynamite to Break Up the Masses of Wreckage—The Daily Record of Work Amid the Dead, ... 341

CHAPTER XXX.

Scenes at the Relief Stations—The Grand Army of the Republic in Command—Imposing Scenes at the Railroad Station—Cars Loaded with Goods for the Relief of the Destitute, ... 353

CHAPTER XXXI.

General Hastings' Headquarters—Duties of the Military Staff—A Flood of Telegrams of Inquiry Pouring In—Getting the Post-office to Work Again—Wholesale Embalming—The Morgue in the Presbyterian Church.—The Record of the Unknown Dead—A Commemorative Newspaper Club, ... 358

CHAPTER XXXII.

A Cross between a Military and a Mining Camp—Work of the Army Engineers.—Equipping Constables—Pressure on the Telegraph Lines —Photographers not Encouraged—Sight-seers Turned Away—Strange Uses for Coffins, ... 370

CHAPTER XXXIII.

Sunday Amid the Ruins—Services in One Church and in the Open Air—The Miracle at the Church of the Immaculate Conception—Few Women and Children Seen—Disastrous Work of Dynamite—A Happy Family in the Wreck, ... 378

CHAPTER XIX.

Newspaper Correspondents Making their Way in—The Railroads
Helpless—Hiring a Special Train—Making Desperate Speed—
First faces of the Flood—Through to Johnstown at Last, ... 216

CHAPTER XX.

The Work of the Reporters—Strange Chronicles of Heroism and of
Woe—Deadly Work of the Telegraph Wires—A Baby's Strange
Voyage—Prayer wonderfully Answered—Steam against Torrent, 228

CHAPTER XXI.

Human Ghouls and Vampires on the Scene—A Short Shrift for
Marauders—Vigilance Committees Enforcing Order—Plunderers of
the Dead Relentlessly Dispatched—Outbursts of Righteous Indignation, ... 238

CHAPTER XXII.

The Cry for Help and the Nation's Answer—President Harrison's
Eloquent and Effective Appeal—Governor Beaver's Message—A
Proclamation by the Governor of New York—Action of the Com-
missioner of Pensions—Help from over the Sea, ... 249

CHAPTER XXIII.

The American Heart and Purse Opened Wide—A Flood of Gold
against the Flood of Water—Contributions from every Part of the
Country, in Sums Large and Small, ... 265

CHAPTER XXIV.

Benefactions of Philadelphia—Organization of Charity—Train loads
of Food and Clothing—Generous spirit of Convicts in the Penitentiary—Contributions from over the Sea—Queen Victoria's sympathy—Letter from Florence Nightingale, ... 281

CHAPTER XXV.

Raising a Great Relief Fund in New York—Where the Money came
from—Churches, Theatres and Prisons join in the good work—
More than One Hundred Thousand Dollars a Day—A few Names
from the Great Roll of Honor, ... 292

CHAPTER XII.

A Desperate Voyage—Scenes like those after a Great Battle—Mother and Babe Dead together—Praying as they Drifted to Destruction—Children Telling the Story of Death—Significant Greetings between Friends—Prepared for any News, ... 154

CHAPTER XIII.

Salutations in the City of the Dead—Crowds at the Morgues—Endless Trains of Wagons with Ghastly Freight—Registering the Survivors—Minds Unsettled by the Tragedy—Horrible Fragments of Humanity Scattered through Piles of Rubbish, ... 161

CHAPTER XIV.

Recognizing the Dead—Food and Clothing for Destitute Survivors—Looking for the Lost—The Bereaved Burying their Dead—Drowned Close by a Place of Safety—A Heroic Editor—One who would not be Comforted, ... 171

CHAPTER XV.

A Bird'seye View of the Ruined City—Conspicuous Features of the Disaster—The Railroad Lines—Stones and Iron Tossed about like Driftwood—An Army Officer's Valuable Services in Restoring and Maintaining Order, ... 179

CHAPTER XVI.

Clearing a Road up the Creek—Fantastic Forms of Ruin—An Abandoned Locomotive with no Rail to Run on—Iron Beams Bent like Willow Twigs—Night in the Valley—Scenes and Sounds of an Inferno, ... 188

CHAPTER XVII.

Sights that Greeted Visitors—Wreckage Along the Valley—Ruins of the Cambria Iron Works—A Carnival of Drink—Violence and Robbery—Camping on the Hillsides—Rich and Poor alike Benefit, ... 198

CHAPTER XVIII.

The First Train Load of Anxious Seekers—Hoping against Hope—Many Instances of Heroism—Victims Seen Drifting down beyond the Reach of Help—Unavailing Efforts to Rescue the Prey of the Flood, ... 207

CHAPTER VI.

Pictures of the Flood Drawn by Eye-witnesses—A Score of Loco-motives Swallowed up—Railroad Cars Swept away—Engineers who would not Abandon their Posts—Awful Scenes from a Car Window—A Race for Life—Victims of the Flood, ... 81

CHAPTER VII.

Some Heroes of the Flood—The Ride of Collins Graves at Williams-burg Recalled—John G. Parke's Heroic Warning—Gallant Self-sacrifice of Daniel Peyton—Mrs. Ogle, the Intrepid Telegraph Operator—Wholesale Life Saving by Miss Nina Speck, ... 97

CHAPTER VIII.

Stories of Suffering—A Family Swept away at a Stroke—Beside a Sister's Corpse—A Bride Driven Mad—The Unidentified Dead—Courage in the Face of Death—Thanking God his Child had not Suffered—One Saved out of a Household of Thirteen—Five Saved out of Fifty-Five, ... 108

CHAPTER IX.

Stories of Railroad Men and Travelers who were in the Midst of the Catastrophe—A Train's Race with the Wave—Houses Crushed like Eggshells—Relics of the Dead in the Tree tops—A Night of Horrors —Fire and Flood Commingled—Lives Lost for the Sake of a Pair of Shoes, ... 119

CHAPTER X.

Scenes in a House of Refuge—Stealing from the Dead—A Thousand Bodies seen Passing over the Bridge—" Kill us, or Rescue us!"—Thrilling Escapes and Agonizing Losses—Children Born amid the Flood—A Night in Alma Hall—Saved through Fear, ... 135

CHAPTER XI.

The Flight to the Mountains—Saving a Mother and her Babe—The Hillsides Black with Refugees—An Engineer's Story—How the Dam gave away—Great Trees Snapped off like Pipe-stems by the Torrent, ... 147

CONTENTS.

CHAPTER I.

The Conemaugh Valley in Springtime—Johnstown and its Suburbs—Founded a Hundred Years ago—The Cambria Iron Works—History of a Famous Industry—American Manufacturing Enterprise Exemplified—Making Bessemer Steel—Social and Educational Features—The Busiest City of its Size in the State, ... 15

CHAPTER II.

Conemaugh Lake—Remains of an Old-time Canal System—Used for the Pleasure of Sportsmen—The Hunting and Fishing Club—Popular Distrust Growing into Indifference—The Old Cry of " Wolf!"—Building a Dam of Straw and Mud—Neglect Ripening into Fitness for a Catastrophe, ... 31

CHAPTER III.

Dawning of the Fatal Day—Darkness and Rain—Rumors of Evil—The Warning Voice Unheeded—A Whirlwind of Watery Death—Fate of a Faithful Telegrapher—What an Eye-Witness Saw—A Solid Wall of Water Rushing Down the Valley, ... 42

CHAPTER IV.

The Pathway of the Torrent—Human Beings Swept away like Chaff—The Twilight of Terror—The Wreck of East Conemaugh—Annihilation of Woodvale—Locomotives Tossed about like Cockle-shells by the mighty Maelstrom, ... 51

CHAPTER V.

" Johnstown is Annihilated"—Appearance of the Wreck—An Awful Sabbath Spectacle—A Sea of Mud and Corpses—The City in a Gigantic Whirlpool—Strange Tokens of the Fury of the Flood—Scene from the Bridge—Sixty Acres of Débris—A Carnival of Slaughter, ... 66

PREFACE.

The summer of 1889 will ever be memorable for its appalling disasters by flood and flame. In that period fell the heaviest blow of the nineteenth century—a blow scarcely paralleled in the histories of civilized lands. Central Pennsylvania, a centre of industry, thrift and comfort, was desolated by floods unprecedented in the records of the great waters. On both sides of the Alleghenies these ravages were felt in terrific power, but on the western slope their terrors were infinitely multiplied by the bursting of the South Fork Reservoir, letting out millions of tons of water, which, rushing madly down the rapid descent of the Conemaugh Valley, washed out all its busy villages and hurled itself in a deadly torrent on the happy borough of Johnstown. The frightful aggravations which followed the coming of this torrent have waked the deepest sympathies of this nation and of the world, and the history is demanded in permanent form, for those of the present day, and for the generation to come.

town Turnpike. Later came the great trunk railroad whose express trains now go roaring down the valley.

Johnstown is—nay, Johnstown was!—a busy and industrious place. The people of the town were the employees of the Cambria Iron and Steel Company, their families, and small storekeepers. There was not one rich man in the town. Three-quarters of the 28,000 people lived in small frame tenement houses on the flats by the river around the works of the Cambria Company. The Cambria Company owns almost all the land, and the business and professional men and the superintendents of the company live on the hills away up from the creeks. The creeks become the Conemaugh river right at the end of the town, near where the big stone Pennsylvania Railroad bridge crosses the river.

The borough of Johnstown was on the south bank of Conemaugh creek, and the east bank of Stony creek, right in the fork. It had only about a third of the population of the place. It had never been incorporated with the surrounding villages, as the Cambria Company, which owned most of the villages and only part of Johnstown, did not wish to have them consolidated into one city.

Conemaugh was the largest village on the creek between the lake and Johnstown. It is often

spoken of as part of Johnstown, though its railroad station is two or three miles up the creek from
the Johnstown station. The streets of the two
towns run into each other, and the space between
the two stations is well built up along the creek.
Part of the Cambria Iron and Steel Company's
works are at Conemaugh, and five or six thousand of the workingmen and their families lived
there. The business was done in Johnstown
borough, where almost all the stores of Johnstown city were.

The works of the Cambria Company were
strung along from here down into Johnstown
proper. They were slightly isolated to prevent a
fire in one spreading to the others, and because
there was not much flat land to build on. The
Pennsylvania road runs along the river, and the
works were built beside it.

Between Conemaugh and Johnstown borough
was a string of tenements along the river which
was called Woodvale. Possibly 3000 workmen
lived in them. They were slightly built of wood,
many of them without cellars or stone foundations.
There were some substantially built houses in the
borough at the fork. Here the flats widen out
somewhat, and they had been still further increased
in extent by the Cambria Company, which filled
up part of the creek beds with refuse and the
ashes from their works. This narrowed the beds

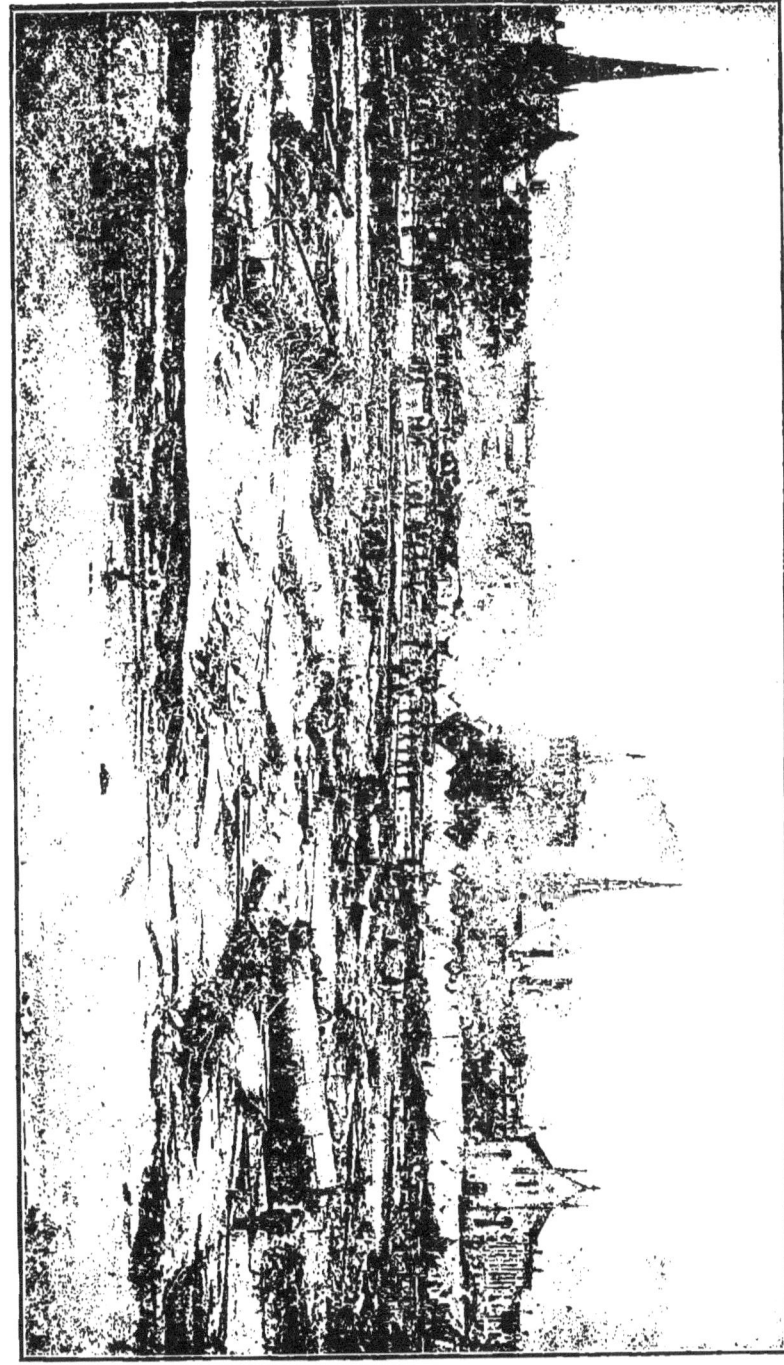

of the creeks. The made land was not far above the water at ordinary times. Even during the ordinary spring floods the waters rose so high that it flowed into the cellars of the tenements, and at times into the works. The natural land was occupied by the business part of the town, where the stores were and the storekeepers had their residences. The borough had a population of about 9000. On the north bank of the river were a third as many more people living in tenements built and owned by the Cambria Company. Further down, below the junction of the two creeks, along both banks of the Conemaugh river, were about 4000 employees of the Cambria Company and their families. The place where they lived was called Cambria or Cambria City. All these villages and boroughs made up what is known as the city of Johnstown.

The Cambria Company employed about 4000 men in its works and mines. Besides these were some railroad shops, planing mills, flour mills, several banks and newspapers. Only the men employed by the Cambria Company and their families lived on the flats and made ground. The Cambria Company owned all this land, and made it a rule not to sell it, but to lease it. The company put rows of two-story frame tenements close together, on their land close to the works, the cheaper class of tenements in solid blocks, to

2

cheapen their construction. The better tenements were separate buildings, with two families to the house. The tenements rented for from $5 to $15 a month, and cost possibly, on the average, $500 to build. They were all of wood, many of them without cellars, and were built as cheaply as possible. The timbers were mostly pine, light and inflammable. It was not an uncommon thing for a fire to break out and to burn one or two rows of tenements. But the different rows were not closely bunched, but were sprinkled around in patches near the separate works, and it was cheaper for the company to rebuild occasionally than to put up brick houses.

Besides owning the flats, the Cambria Company owned the surrounding hills. In one of the hills is limestone, in another coal, and there is iron ore not far away. The company has narrow-gauge roads running from its mines down to the works. The city was at the foot of these three hills, which meet in a double V shape. Conemaugh creek flowing down one and Stony creek flowing down the other. The hills are not so far distant that a man with a rifle on any one could not shoot to either of the others. They are several hundred feet high and so steep that roads run up them by a series of zigzag grades. Few people live on these hills except on a small rise of ground across the river from Johnstown. In some places the company has leased the land for dwelling houses, but it retains the ownership of the land and of the coal, iron and limestone in it. The flats having all been occupied, the company in recent years had put up some tenements of a better class on the north bank of the river, higher up than the flood reached. The business part of the town also was higher up than the works and the tenements of the company.

In normal times the river is but a few hundred feet wide. The bottom is stony. The current is so fast that there is little deposit along the bank. It is navigable at no time, though in the spring a good canoeist might go down it if he could steer clear of the rocks. In the summer the volume of water diminishes so much that a boy with a pair of rubber boots on can wade across without getting his feet wet, and there have been times when a good jumper could cross the river on the dry stones. Below Johnstown, after Stony creek has joined the Conemaugh creek, the volume of water increases, but the Conemaugh throughout its whole length is nothing but a mountain stream, dry in the summer and roaring in the spring. It runs down into the Kiskiminitas river and into the Allegheny river, and then on to Pittsburgh. It is over 100 miles from Johnstown to Pittsburgh following the windings of the river, twice as far as the straight line.

Johnstown was one of the busiest towns of its size in the State. Its tonnage over the Pennsylvania and Baltimore and Ohio roads was larger than the tonnage of many cities three times its size. The Iron and Steel Company is one of the largest iron and steel corporations in the world. It had its main rolling mills, Bessemer steel works, and wire works at Johnstown, though it also has works in other places, and owns ore and coal mines and leases in the South, in Michigan, and in Spain, besides its Pennsylvania works. It had in Johnstown and the surrounding villages 4000 or 5000 men usually at work. In flush times it has employed more than 6000. So important was the town from a railroad point of view that the Baltimore and Ohio ran a branch from Rockwood, on its main line to Pittsburgh, up to Johnstown, forty-five miles. It was one of the main freight stations on the Pennsylvania road, though the passenger business was so small in proportion that some express trains do not stop there. The Pennsylvania road recently put up a large brick station, which was one of the few brick buildings on the flats. Some of the Cambria Company's offices were also of brick, and there was a brick lodging house for young men in the employ of the company. The Pennsylvania road had repair shops there, which employed a few hundred men, and the Baltimore and Ohio branch had some smaller shops.

Johnstown had several Catholic and Presbyterian, Methodist, Baptist, and Lutheran churches. It had several daily and weekly papers. The chief were the *Tribune*, the *Democrat*, and the *Freie Presse*.

The Cambria Iron Works, the great industry of Johnstown, originated in a few widely separated charcoal furnaces built by pioneer iron workers in the early years of the century. As early as 1803 General Arthur St. Clair engaged in the iron business, and erected the Hermitage furnace about sixteen miles from the present site of Johnstown. In 1809 the working of ores was begun near Johnstown. These were primitive furnaces, where charcoal was the only fuel employed, and the raw material and product were transported entirely on wagons, but they marked the beginning of the manufacture of iron in this country.

The Cambria Iron Company was chartered under the general law in 1852, for the operation of four old-fashioned charcoal furnaces in and near Johnstown, which was then a village of 1300 inhabitants, to which the Pennsylvania railroad had just been extended. In 1853 the construction of four coke furnaces was begun, but it was two years before the first was finished. England was then shipping rails into this country under a low duty, and the iron industry here was struggling for existence. The company at Johnstown was

aided by a number of Philadelphia merchants, but
was unable to continue in business, and suspended
in 1854. At a meeting of the creditors in Philadelphia soon afterward a committee was appointed,
with Daniel J. Morrell as Chairman, to visit the
works at Johnstown and recommend the best
means, if any, to save themselves from loss. In
his report, Mr. Morrell strongly urged the Philadelphia creditors to invest more money and continue the business. They did so, and Matthew
Newkirk was made President of the company.
The company again failed in 1855, and Mr. Morrell then associated a number of gentlemen with
him, and formed the firm of Wood, Morrell &
Co., leasing the works for seven years. The year
1856 was one of great financial depression, and
1857 was worse, and, as a further discouragement,
the large furnace was destroyed by fire in June,
1857. In one week, however, the works were
in operation again, and a brick building was soon
constructed. When the war came, and with it the
Morrill tariff of 1861, a broader field was opened
up, and in 1862 the present company was formed.

The years following the close of the war brought
about an unprecedented revival in railroad building. In 1864 there were but 33,908 miles of railroad in the United States, while in 1874 there were
72,741 miles, or more than double. There was a
great demand for English steel rails, which ad-

vanced to $170 per ton. Congress imposed a
duty of $28 a ton on foreign rails, and encour-
aged American manufacturers to go into the business. The Cambria Company began the erection
of Bessemer steel works in 1869, and sold the
first steel rails in 1871, at $104 a ton.

The company had 700 dwelling-houses, rented
to employees. The works and rolling mills of the
company were situated upon what was originally
a river flat, where the valley of the Conemaugh
expanded somewhat, just below Johnstown, and
now part of Millville. The Johnstown furnaces,
Nos. 1, 2, 3 and 4, formed one complete plant,
with stacks 75 feet high and 16 feet in diameter at
the base. Steam was generated in forty boilers
fired by furnace gas, for eight vertical, direct-acting
blowing engines. Nos. 5 and 6 blast furnaces
formed together a second plant, with stacks 75
feet high and 19 feet in diameter. The Bessemer
plant was the sixth started in the United States
(July, 1871). The main building was 102 feet in
width by 165 feet in length. The cupolas were
six in number. Blast was supplied from eight
Baker rotary pressure blowers, driven by engines
16 x 24 inches at 110 revolutions per minute.
The Bessemer works were supplied with steam by
a battery of twenty-one tubular boilers. The best
average, although not the very highest work
done in the Bessemer department, was 103 heats

of 8½ tons each for each twenty-four hours. The best weekly record reached 4847 tons of ingots, and the best monthly record 20,304 tons. The best daily output was 900 tons of ingots. All grades of steel were made in the converters, from the softest wire and bridge stock to spring stock. The open-hearth building, 120 x 155 feet, containing three Pernot revolving hearth furnaces of fifteen tons capacity each, supplied with natural gas. The rolling mill was 100 feet in width by 1900 feet in length, and contained a 24-inch train of two stands of three-high rolls, and a ten-ton traveling crane for changing rolls. The product of the mill was 80,000 pounds per turn. The bolt and nut works produced 1000 kegs of finished track bolts per month, besides machine bolts. The capacity of the axle shop was 100 finished steel axles per day. The "Gautier steel department" consisted of a brick building 200 x 50 feet, where the wire was annealed, drawn and finished; a brick warehouse 373 x 43 feet, many shops, offices, etc.; the barb-wire mill, 50 x 250 feet, where the celebrated Cambria link barb wire was made, and the main merchant mill, 725 x 250 feet. These mills produced wire, shafting, springs, ploughshares, rake and harrow teeth, and other kinds of agricultural implement steel. In 1887 they produced 50,000 tons of this material, which was marketed mainly in the Western States. Grouped with the principal mills thus described were the foundries, pattern and other shops, draughting offices and time offices, etc., all structures of a firm and substantial character.

The company operated about thirty-five miles of railroad tracks, employing in this service twenty-four locomotives, and owned 1500 cars. To the large bodies of mountain land connected with the old charcoal furnaces additions have been made of ores and coking coals, and the company now owns in fee simple 54,423 acres of mineral lands. It has 600 beehive coke ovens in the Connellsville district, and the coal producing capacity of the mines in Pennsylvania owned by the company is 815,000 tons per year.

In continuation of the policy of Daniel J. Morrell, the Cambria Iron Company has done a great deal for its employees. The Cambria Library was erected by the Iron Company and presented to the town. The building was 43 x 68½ feet, and contained a library of 6914 volumes. It contained a large and valuable collection of reports of the United States and the State, and it is feared that they have been greatly damaged. The Cambria Mutual Benefit Association is composed of employees of the company, and is supported by it. The employees receive benefits when sick or injured, and in case of death their families are provided for. The Board of Directors of this association also controls the Cambria Hospital, which was erected by the Iron Company in 1866, on Prospect Hill, in the northern part of the town. The company also maintained a club house, and a store which was patronized by others, as well as by its employees.

CHAPTER II.

Twenty miles up Conemaugh creek, beyond the workingmen's villages of South Fork and Mineral Point, was Conemaugh lake. It was a part of the old and long disused Pennsylvania Canal system. At the head of Conemaugh creek, back among the hills, three hundred feet or more above the level of Johnstown streets, was a small, natural lake. When the canal was building, the engineers took this lake to supply the western division of the canal which ran from there to Pittsburgh. The Eastern division ended at Hollidaysburgh east of the summit of the Alleghanies, where there was a similar reservoir. Between the two was the old Portage road, one of the first railroads constructed in the State. The canal was abandoned some years ago, as the Pennsylvania road destroyed its traffic. The Pennsylvania Company got a grant of the canal from the State. Some years after the canal was abandoned the Hollidaysburgh reservoir was torn down, the water gradually escaping into the Frankstown branch of the Juniata river. The people of the neighborhood objected to the existence of the reservoir after the canal was abandoned, as little attention was paid to the structure, and the farmers in the valley below feared that the dam would break and drown them. The water was all let out of that reservoir about three years ago.

The dam above Johnstown greatly increased the small natural lake there. It was a pleasant drive from Johnstown to the reservoir. Boating and fishing parties often went out there. Near the reservoir is Cresson, a summer resort owned by the Pennsylvania road. Excursion parties are made up in the summer time by the Pennsylvania Company, and special trains are run for them from various points to Cresson. A club called the South Fork Fishing and Hunting Club was organized some years ago, and got the use of the lake from the Pennsylvania Company. Most of the members of the club live in Pittsburgh, and are prominent iron and coal men. Besides them there are some of the officials of the Pennsylvania road among the members. They increased the size of the dam until it was not far from a hundred feet in height, and its entire length, from side to side at the top, was not far from nine hundred feet. This increased the size of the lake to three miles in length and a mile and a quarter in width. It was an irregular oval in shape. The volume of water in it depended on the time of the year.

Some of the people of Johnstown had thought for years that the dam might break, but they did not think that its breaking would do more than flood the flats and damage the works of the Cambria Company.

When the Hunting and Fishing Club bought the site of the old reservoir a section of 150 feet had been washed out of the middle. This was rebuilt at an expense of $17,000 and the work was thought to be very strong. At the base it was 380 feet thick and gradually tapered until at the top it was about 35 feet thick. It was considered amply secure, and such faith had the members of the club in its stability that the top of the dam was utilized as a driveway. It took two years to complete the work, men being engaged from '79 to '81. While it was under process of construction the residents of Johnstown expressed some fears as to the solidity of the work, and requested that it be examined by experts. An engineer of the Cambria Iron Works, secured through Mr. Morrell, of that institution, one provided by Mr. Pitcairn, of the Pennsylvania Railroad, and Nathan McDowell, chosen by the club itself, made a thorough examination. They pronounced the structure perfectly safe, but suggested some precautionary measures as to the stopping

of leaks, that were faithfully carried out. The
members of the club themselves discovered that
the sewer that carried away the surplus or overflow from the lake was not large enough in times
of storm. So five feet of solid rock were cut
away in order to increase the mouth of the lake.
Usually the surface of the water was 15 feet below
the top of the dam, and never in recent years did
it rise to more than eight feet. In 1881, when
work was going on, a sudden rise occurred, and
then the water threatened to do what it did on
this occasion. The workmen hastened to the
scene and piled débris of all sorts on the top and
thus prevented a washout.

For more than a year there had been fears of a
disaster. The foundations of the dam at South
Fork were considered shaky early in 1888, and
many increasing leakages were reported from
time to time.

"We were afraid of that lake," said a gentleman who had lived in Johnstown for years; "We
were afraid of that lake seven years ago. No
one could see the immense height to which that
artificial dam had been built without fearing the
tremendous power of the water behind it. The
dam must have had a sheer height of 100 feet,
thus forcing the water that high above its natural
bed, and making a lake at least three miles long
and a mile wide, out of what could scarcely be

called a pond. I doubt if there is a man or woman in Johnstown who at some time or other had not feared and spoken of the terrible disaster that has now come.

"People wondered, and asked why the dam was not strengthened, as it certainly had become weak; but nothing was done, and by and by they talked less and less about it, as nothing happened, though now and then some would shake their heads as if conscious the fearful day would come some time when their worst fears would be transcended by the horror of the actual occurrence."

There is not a shadow of doubt but that the citizens of Cambria County frequently complained, and that at the time the dam was constructed a vigorous effort was made to put a stop to the work. It is true that the leader in this movement was not a citizen of Johnstown, but he was and is a large mine owner in Cambria County. His mine adjoins the reservoir property. He was frequently on the spot, and his own engineer inspected the work. He says the embankment was principally of shale and clay, and that straw was used to stop the leaking of water while the work was going on. He called on the sheriff of Cambria County and told him it was his duty to apply to the court for an injunction. The sheriff promised to give the matter his attention, but, instead of going before court, went to the Cambria Company for consultation.   An employee was sent up to make an inspection, and as his report was favorable to the reservoir work the sheriff went no further.   But the gentleman referred to said that he had not failed to make public his protest at the time and to renew it frequently.   This recommendation for an injunction and protest were spoken of by citizens of Altoona as a hackneyed subject.

Confirmation has certainly been had at South Fork, Conemaugh, Millvale and Johnstown.   The rumor of an expected break was prevalent at these places, but citizens remarked that the rumor was a familiar incident of the annual freshets.   It was the old classic story of " Wolf, wolf."   They gave up the first floors to the water and retired upstairs to wait until the river should recede, as they had done often before, scouting the oft-told story of the breaking of the reservoir.

An interesting story, involving the construction and history of the Conemaugh lake dam, was related by J. B. Montgomery, who formerly lived in Western Pennsylvania, and is now well known in the West as a railroad contractor.   " The dam," said he, " was built about thirty-five years ago by the State of Pennsylvania, as a feeder for the western division of the Pennsylvania Canal.   The plans and specifications for the dam were furnished by the Chief Engineer of the State.   I am not sure, but it is my impression, that Colonel William Mil-

GENERAL VIEW OF THE RUINS, LOOKING UP STONY CREEK.

nor Roberts held the office at the time. Colonel
Roberts was one of the most famous engineers in
the country. He died several years ago in Chili.
The contractors for the construction of the dam
were General J. K. Moorhead and Judge H. B.
Packer, of Williamsport, a brother of Governor
Packer. General Moorhead had built many dams
before this on the rivers of Pennsylvania, and his
work was always known to be of the very best.
In this case, however, all that he had to do was to
build the dam according to the specifications furnished by the State. The dam was built of stone
and wood throughout, and was of particularly
solid construction. There is no significance in the
discovery of straw and dirt among the ruins of
the dam. Both are freely used when dams are
being built, to stop the numerous leaks.

" The dam had three waste-gates at the bottom,
so arranged that they could be raised when there
was too much water in the lake, and permit the
escape of the surplus. These gates were in big
stone arches, through which the water passed to
the canal when the lake was used as a feeder.

" In 1859 the Pennsylvania Railroad Company
purchased the canal from the State, and the dam
and lake went into the possession of that company.
Shortly afterward the Pennsylvania Company
abandoned the western division of the canal, and
the dam became useless as a feeder. For twenty-

3

five years the lake was used only as a fish-pond,
and the dam and the gates were forgotten. Five
years ago the lake was leased to a number of
Pittsburgh men, who stocked it with bass, trout,
and other game fish. I have heard it said that the
waste-gates had not been opened for a great many
years. If this is so, no wonder the dam broke.
Naturally the fishermen did not want to open the
gates after the lake was stocked, for the fish would
have run out. A sluiceway should have been
built on the side of the dam, so that when the water
reached a certain height the surplus could escape.
The dam was not built with the intention that the
water should flow over the top of it under any
circumstances, and if allowed to escape in that
way the water was bound to undermine it in a
short time. With a dam the height of this the
pressure of a quantity of water great enough to
overflow it must be something tremendous.

"If it is true that the waste-gates were never
opened after the Pittsburgh men had leased the
lake, the explanation of the bursting of the dam
is to be found right there. It may be that the
dam had not been looked after and strengthened
of late years, and it was undoubtedly weakened
in the period of twenty-five years during which
the lake was not used. After the construction of
the dam the lake was called the Western Reservoir.
The south fork of the Conemaugh, which fed the

lake, is a little stream not over ten feet wide, but even when there were no unusual storms it carried enough water to fill the lake full within a year, showing how important it was that the gates should be opened occasionally to run off the surplus."

Mr. Montgomery was one of a party of engineers who inspected the dam when it was leased by the Pennsylvania Company, five years ago. It then needed repairs, but was in a perfectly safe condition if the water was not allowed to flow over it.

CHAPTER III.

Friday, May 31st, 1889. The day before had been a solemn holiday. In every village veterans of the War for the Union had gathered ; in every cemetery flowers had been strewn upon the grave-mounds of the heroic dead. Now the people were resuming the every-day toil. The weather was rainy. It had been wet for some days. Stony Creek and Conemaugh were turbid and noisy. The little South Fork, which ran into the upper end of the lake, was swollen into a raging torrent. The lake was higher than usual; higher than ever. But the valley below lay in fancied security, and all the varied activities of life pursued their wonted round.

Friday, May 31st, 1889. Record that awful date in characters of funereal hue. It was a dark and stormy day, and amid the darkness and the storm the angel of death spread his wings over the fated valley, unseen, unknown. Midday comes. Disquieting rumors rush down the valley. There is a roar of an approaching storm—

approaching doom! The water swiftly rises. A horseman thunders down the valley: "To the hills, for God's sake! To the hills, for your lives!" They stare at him as at a madman, and their hesitating feet linger in the valley of the shadow of death, and the shadow swiftly darkens, and the everlasting hills veil their faces with rain and mist before the scene that greets them.

This is what happened: —

The heavy rainfall raised the lake until its water began to pour over the top of the dam. The dam itself—wretchedly built of mud and boulders—saturated through and through, began to leak copiously here and there Each watery sapper and miner burrowed on, followers swiftly enlarging the murderous tunnels. The whole mass became honeycombed. And still the rain poured down, and still the South Fork and a hundred minor streams sent in their swelling floods, until, with a roar like that of the opening gates of the Inferno belching forth the legions of the damned, the wall gave way, and with the rush of a famished tiger into a sheepfold, the whirlwind of water swept down the valley on its errand of destruction—

> " And like a horse unbroken,
> When first he feels the rein,
> The furious river struggled hard,
> And tossed his tawny mane,

And burst the curb, and bounded,
　　Rejoicing to be free,
And, whirling down in mad career,
Battlement and plank and pier,
　　Rushed headlong to the sea!"

According to the statements of people who lived in Johnstown and other towns on the line of the river, ample time was given to the inhabitants of Johnstown by the railroad officials and by other gentlemen of standing and reputation. In hundreds of cases this warning was utterly disregarded, and those who heeded it early in the day were looked upon as cowards, and many jeers were uttered by lips that now are cold. The people of Johnstown also had a special warning in the fact that the dam in Stony Creek, just above the town, broke about noon, and thousands of feet of lumber passed down the river. Yet they hesitated, and even when the wall of water, almost forty feet high, was at their doors, one man is said by a survivor to have told his family that the stream would not rise very high.

How sudden the calamity is illustrated by an incident which Mr. Bender, the night chief operator of the Western Union in Pittsburgh, relates: "At 3 o'clock that Friday afternoon," said he, " the girl operator at Johnstown was cheerfully ticking away that she had to abandon the office on the first floor, because the water was three feet deep there. She said she was telegraphing from the second story and the water was gaining steadily. She was frightened, and said many houses were flooded. This was evidently before the dam broke, for our man here said something encouraging to her, and she was talking back as only a cheerful girl operator can, when the receiver's skilled ear caught a sound on the wire made by no human hand, which told him that the wires had grounded, or that the house had been swept away in the flood from the lake, no one knows which now. At 3 o'clock the girl was there, and at 3.07 we might as well have asked the grave to answer us."

The water passed over the dam about a foot above its top, beginning at about half-past 2. Whatever happened in the way of a cloud-burst took place in the night. There had been little rain up to dark. When the workmen woke in the morning the lake was full, and rising at the rate of a foot an hour. It kept on rising until 2 P. M., when it began breaking over the dam and undermining it. Men were sent three or four times during the day to warn people below of their danger. When the final break came at 3 o'clock, there was a sound like tremendous and continued peals of thunder. Trees, rocks and earth shot up into mid-air in great columns and then started down the ravine. A farmer who escaped said that the water did not come down like a wave, but jumped on his house and beat it to fragments in an instant. He was safe on the hillside, but his wife and two children were killed.

Herbert Webber, who was employed by the Sportsmen's Club at the lake, tells that for three days previous to the final outburst, the water of the lake forced itself out through the interstices of the masonry, so that the front of the dam resembled a large watering pot. The force of the water was so great that one of these jets squirted full thirty feet horizontally from the stone wall. All this time, too, the feeders of the lake, particularly three of them, more nearly resembled torrents than mountain streams, and were supplying the dammed up body of water with quite 3,000,-000 gallons of water hourly.

At 11 o'clock that Friday morning, Webber says he was attending to a camp about a mile back from the dam, when he noticed that the surface of the lake seemed to be lowering. He doubted his eyes, and made a mark on the shore, and then found that his suspicions were undoubtedly well founded. He ran across the country to the dam, and there saw, he declares, the water of the lake welling out from beneath the foundation stones of the dam. Absolutely helpless, he was compelled to stand there and watch the gradual development of what was to be the most disastrous flood of this continent.

According to his reckoning it was 2.45 when the stones in the centre of the dam began to sink because of the undermining, and within eight minutes a gap of twenty feet was made in the lower half of the wall face, through which the water poured as though forced by machinery of stupendous power. By 3 o'clock the toppling masonry, which before had partaken somewhat of the form of an arch, fell in, and then the remainder of the wall opened outward like twin gates, and the great storage lake was foaming and thundering down the valley of the Conemaugh.

Webber became so awestruck at the catastrophe that he declares he was unable to leave the spot until the lake had fallen so low that it showed bottom fifty feet below him. How long a time elapsed he says he does not know before he recovered sufficient power of observation to notice this, but he does not think that more than five minutes passed. Webber says that had the dam been repaired after the spring freshet of 1888 the disaster would not have occurred. Had it been given ordinary attention in the spring of 1887 the probabilities are that thousands of lives would have been saved.

Imagine, if you can, a solid piece of ground, thirty-five feet wide and over one hundred feet high, and then, again, that a space of two hundred feet is cut out of it, through which is rushing over seven hundred acres of water, and you can have only a faint conception of the terrible force of the blow that came upon the people of this vicinity like a clap of thunder out of a clear sky. It was irresistible in its power and carried everything before it. After seeing the lake and the opening through the dam it can be readily understood how that outbreak came to be so destructive in its character.

The lake had been leaking, and a couple of Italians were at work just over the point where the break occurred, and in an instant, without warning, it gave way and they went down in the whirling mass of water, and were swept into eternity.

Mr. Crouse, proprietor of the South Fork Fishing Club Hotel, says: "When the dam of Conemaugh lake broke the water seemed to leap, scarcely touching the ground. It bounded down the valley, crashing and roaring, carrying everything before it. For a mile its front seemed like a solid wall twenty feet high." The only warning given to Johnstown was sent from South Fork village by Freight Agent Dechert. *When the great wall that held the body of water began to crumble at the top he sent a message begging the people of Johnstown for God's sake to take to the hills.* He reports no serious accidents at South Fork.

Richard Davis ran to Prospect Hill when the water raised. As to Mr. Dechert's message, he says just such have been sent down at each flood since the lake was made. *The warning so often proved useless that little attention was paid to it this time.* "I cannot describe the mad rush," he said. "At first it looked like dust. That must have been the spray. I could see houses going down before it like a child's play blocks set on edge in a row. As it came nearer I could see houses totter for a moment, then rise and the next moment be crushed like egg shells, against each other."

Mr. John G. Parke, of Philadelphia, a civil engineer, was at the dam superintending some improvements in the drainage system at the lake. He did all he could with the help of a gang of laborers to avert the catastrophe and to warn those in danger. His story of the calamity is this :—

" For several days prior to the breaking of the dam, storm after storm swept over the mountains and flooded every creek and rivulet. The waters from these varied sources flowed into the lake, which finally was not able to stand the pressure forced upon it. Friday morning I realized the danger that was threatened, and although from that time until three o'clock every human effort was made to prevent a flood, they were of no avail. When I at last found that the dam was bound to go, I started out to tell the people, and by twelve o'clock everybody in the Conemaugh region did or should have known of their danger. Three hours later my gravest fears were more than realized. It is an erroneous idea, however, that the dam burst. It simply moved away. The water gradually ate into the embankment until there was nothing left but a frail bulwark of wood. This finally split asunder and sent the waters howling down the mountains."

CHAPTER IV.

The course of the torrent from the broken dam at the foot of the lake to Johnstown is almost eighteen miles, and with the exception of one point, the water passed through a narrow V-shaped valley. Four miles below the dam lay the town of South Fork, where the South Fork itself empties into the Conemaugh river. The town contained about 2000 inhabitants. About four-fifths of it has been swept away. Four miles further down on the Conemaugh river, which runs parallel with the main line of the Pennsylvania Railroad, was the town of Mineral Point. It had 800 inhabitants, 90 per cent. of the houses being on a flat and close to the river. Terrible as it may seem, very few of them have escaped. Six miles further down was the town of Conemaugh, and here alone there was a topographical possibility—the spreading of the flood and the breaking of its force. It contained 2500 inhabitants, and has been almost wholly devastated. Woodvale, with 2000 people, lay a

mile below Conemaugh in the flat, and one mile
further down were Johnstown and its suburbs—
Cambria City and Conemaugh borough, with a
population of 30,000. On made ground, and
stretched along right at the river's verge, were the
immense iron works of the Cambria Iron and
Steel Company, who have $5,000,000 invested in
their plant. Besides this there are many other
large industrial establishments on the bank of the
river.

The stream of human beings that was swept
before the angry floods was something most pitiful to behold. Men, women and children were
carried along frantically shrieking for help, but
their cries availed them nothing. Rescue was
impossible. Husbands were swept past their
wives, and children were borne along, at a terrible speed, to certain death, before the eyes of
their terrorized and frantic parents. Houses, out-
buildings, trees and barns were carried on the
angry flood of waters as so much chaff. Cattle
standing in the fields were overwhelmed, and their
carcasses strewed the tide. The railroad tracks
converging on the town were washed out, and
wires in all directions were prostrated.

Down through the Packsaddle came the rushing
waters. Clinging to improvised rafts, constructed
in the death battle from floating boards and timbers, were agonized men, women and children,

their heart-rending shrieks for help striking horror to the breasts of the onlookers. Their cries were of no avail. Carried along at a railway speed on the breast of this rushing torrent, no human ingenuity could devise a means of rescue.

It is impossible to describe briefly the suddenness with which the disaster came. A warning sound was heard at Conemaugh a few minutes before the rush of water came, but it was attributed to some meteorological disturbance, and no trouble was borrowed because of the thing unseen. As the low, rumbling noise increased in volume, however, and came nearer, a suspicion of danger began to force itself even upon the bravest, which was increased to a certainty a few minutes later, when, with a rush, the mighty stream spread out in width, and when there was no time to do anything to save themselves. Many of the unfortunates were whirled into the middle of the stream before they could turn around; men, women and children were struggling in the streets, and it is thought that many of them never reached Johnstown, only a mile or two below.

At Johnstown a similar scene was enacted, only on a much larger scale. The population is greater and the sweeping whirlpool rushed into a denser mass of humanity. The imagination of the reader can better depict the spectacle than the pen of the writer can give it. It was a twilight of terror, and the gathering shades of evening closed in on a panorama of horrors that has few parallels in the history of casualties.

When the great wave from Conemaugh lake, behind the dam, came down the Conemaugh Valley, the first obstacle it struck was the great viaduct over the South Fork. This viaduct was a State work, built to carry the old Portage road across the Fork. The Pennsylvania Railroad parallels the Portage road for a long distance, and runs over the Fork. Besides sweeping the viaduct down, the bore, or smaller bores on its wings, washed out the Portage road for miles. One of the small bores went down the bed of a brook which comes into the Conemaugh at the village of South Fork, which is some distance above the viaduct. The big bore backed the river above the village. The small bore was thus checked in its course and flowed into the village.

The obstruction below being removed, the backed-up water swept the village of South Fork away. The flood came down. It moved steadily, but with a velocity never yet attained by an engine moved by power controllable by man. It accommodated itself to the character of the breaks in the hill. It filled every one, whether narrow or broad. Its thrust was sideways and downward as well as forward. By side thrusts it scoured every cave and bend in the line of the mountains,

RUINS OF JOHNSTOWN, VIEWED FROM PROSPECT HILL.

lessening its direct force to exert power laterally, but at the same time moving its centre straight on Johnstown. It is well to state that the Conemaugh river is tortuous, like most streams of its kind. Wherever the mountains retreat, flats make out from them to the channel of the stream. It was on such flats that South Fork and Mineral Point villages and the boroughs of Conemaugh, Franklin, Woodvale, East Conemaugh and Johnstown were built.

After emerging from the South Fork, with the ruins of the great viaduct in its maw, it swept down a narrow valley until just above the village of Mineral Point. There it widened, and, thrusting its right wing into the hollow where the village nestled, it swept away every house on the flat. These were soon welded into a compact mass, with trees and logs and general drift stuff. This mass followed the bore. What the bore could not budge, its follower took up and carried.

The first great feat at carrying and lifting was done at East Conemaugh. It tore up every building in the yard of the Pennsylvania Railroad. It took locomotives and carried them down and dug holes for their burials. It has been said that the flood had a downward thrust. There was proof of this on the banks of the river, where there was a sort of breakwater of concreted cinders, slag, and other things, making a combination harder than stone.

4

Unable to get a grip directly on these banks, the· flood jumped over them, threw the whole weight of the mass of logs and broken buildings down on the sand behind them, scooped this sand out, and then, by backward blows, knocked the concrete to ⸌pieces. In this it displayed almost the uttermost skill of human malice.

After crossing the flat of East Conemaugh and scooping out of their situations sixty-five houses in two streets, as well as tearing passenger trains to pieces, drowning an unknown number of persons, and picking up others to dash against whatever obstacles it encountered, it sent a force to the left, which cut across the flat of Franklin borough, ripped thirty-two houses to pieces, and cut a second channel for the Conemaugh river, leaving an island to mark the place of division of the forces of the flood. The strength of the eastern wing can be estimated from the fact that the iron bars piled in heaps in the stock yard of the Cambria Iron Company were swept away, and that some of them may be found all along the river as far as Johnstown.

After this came the utter wiping out of the borough of Woodvale, on the flat to the northeast of Johnstown and diagonally opposite it. Woodvale had a population of nearly 3000 people. It requires a large number of houses to shelter so many. Estimating 10 to a family, which is a big estimate, there were 300 houses in Woodvale. There were also a woolen mill, a flour mill, the Gautier Barb Wire Mills of the Cambria Iron Company, and the tannery of W. H. Rosenthal & Co. Only the flour mill and the middle section of the bridge remain. The flat is bare otherwise. The stables of the Woodvale Horse Railroad Company went out with the water; every horse and car in them went also.

The change was wrought in five minutes. Robert Miller, who lost two of his children and his mother-in-law, thus describes the scene: "I was standing near the Woodvale Bridge, between Maple avenue and Portage street, in Johnstown. The river was high, and David Lucas and I were speculating about the bridges, whether they would go down or not. Lucas said, 'I guess this bridge will stand; it does not seem to be weakened.' Just then we saw a dark object up the river. Over it was a white mist. It was high and somehow dreadful, though we could not make it out. Dark smoke seemed to form a background for the mist. We did not wait for more. By instinct we knew the big dam had burst and its water was coming upon us. Lucas jumped on a car horse, rode across the bridge, and went yelling into Johnstown. The flood overtook him, and he had to abandon his horse and climb a high hill.

"I went straight to my house in Woodvale, warning everybody as I ran. My wife and mother-in-law were ready to move, with my five children, so we went for the hillside, but we were not speedy enough. The water had come over the flat at its base and cut us off. I and my wife climbed into a coal car with one of the children, to get out of the water. I put two more children into the car and looked around for my other children and my mother-in-law. My mother-in-law was a stout woman, weighing about two hundred and twelve pounds. She could not climb into a car. The train was too long for her to go around it, so she tried to crawl under, leading the children.

"The train was suddenly pushed forward by the flood, and she was knocked down and crushed, so were my children, by the same shock. My wife and children in the car were thrown down and covered with coal. I was taken off by the water, but I swam to the car and pulled them from under a lot of coal. A second blow to the train threw our car against the hillside and us out of it to firm earth. I never saw my two children and mother-in-law after the flood first struck the train of coal cars. I have often heard it said that the dam might break, but I never paid any attention to it before. It was common talk whenever there was a freshet or a big pack of ice."

The principal street of Woodvale was Maple

avenue. The Conemaugh river now rushes through it from one side of the flat to the other. Its pavement is beautifully clean. It is doubtful that it will ever be cleared by mortal agency again.

Breaking down the barbed steel wire mill and the tannery at the bridge, the flood went across the regular channel of the river and struck the Gautier Steel Works, made up of numerous stanch brick buildings and one immense structure of iron, filled with enormous boilers, fly wheels, and machinery generally. The buildings are strewn through Johnstown. Near their sites are some bricks, twisted iron beams, boilers, wheels, and engine bodies, bound together with logs, driftwood, tree branches, and various other things, woven in and out of one another marvelously. These aggregations are of enormous size and weight. They were not too strong for the immense power of the destroying agent, for a twenty-ton locomotive, taken from the Gautier Works, now lies in Main street, three-quarters of a mile away. It did not simply take a good grip upon them ; it was spreading out its line for a force by its left wing, and hit simultaneously upon Johnstown flat, its people and houses, while its right wing did whatever it could in the way of helping the destructive work. The left wing scoured the flat to the base of the mountain. With a portion of the centre it then rushed across

Stony creek. The remainder of the central force cleared several paths in diverging directions through the town.

While the left and centre were tearing houses to pieces and drowning untold lives, the right had been hurrying along the base of the northern hills, in the channel of the Conemaugh river, carrying down the houses, bridges, human beings and other drift that had been picked up on the way from South Fork.

Thus far the destruction at Johnstown had not been one-quarter what it is now. But the bed of the Conemaugh beyond Johnstown is between high hills that come close together. The cut is bridged by a viaduct. The right wing, with its plunder, was stopped by the bridge and the bend. The left and centre came tearing down Stony creek. There was a collision of forces. The men, women, children, horses, other domestic animals, houses, bridges, railroad cars, logs and tree branches were jammed together in a solid mass, which only dynamite can break up. The outlet of Stony creek was almost completely closed and the channel of the Conemaugh was also choked. The water in both surged back. In Stony creek it went along the curve of the base of the hill in front of which Kernville is built. Dividing its strength, one part of the flood went up Stony creek a short distance and moved around again into Johnstown. It swept before it many more houses than before and carried them around in a circle, until they met and crashed against other houses, torn from the point of Johnstown flat by a similar wave moving in a circle from the Conemaugh.

The two waves and their burdens went around and around in slowly-diminishing circles, until most of the houses had been ground to pieces. There are living men, women and children who circled in these frightful vortices for an hour. Lawyer Rose, his wife, his two brothers and his two sisters are among those. They were drawn out of their house by the suction of the retreating water, and thus were started on a frightful journey. Three times they went from the Kernville side of the creek to the centre of the Johnstown flat and past their own dwelling. They were dropped at last on the Kernville shore. Mr. Rose had his collar bone broken, but the others were hurt only by fright, wetting and some bruises.

Some of the back water went up the creek and did damage at Grubtown and Hornerstown. More of it, following the line of the mountain, rushed in at the back of Kernville. It cut a clear path for itself from the lower end of the village to the upper end, diagonally opposite, passing through the centre. It sent little streams to topple homes over in side places and went on a round trip into the higher part of Johnstown, between the creek and the hill. It carried houses from Kernville to the Johnstown bank of the creek, and left them there. Then it coursed down the bank, overturning trains of the Baltimore and Ohio railroad, and also houses, and keeping on until it had made the journey several times.

How so marvelous a force was exerted is illustrated in the following statement from Jacob Reese, of Pittsburg, the inventor of the basic process for manufacturing steel. Mr. Reese says :—

"When the South Fork dam gave way, 16,000,000 tons of water rushed down the mountain side, carrying thousands of tons of rocks, logs and trees with it. When the flood reached the Conemaugh Valley it struck the Pennsylvania Railroad at a point where they make up the trains for ascending the Allegheny Mountains. Several trains with their locomotives and loaded cars were swept down the valley before the flood wave, which is said to have been fifty feet high. Cars loaded with iron, cattle, and freight of all kinds, with those mighty locomotives, weighing from seventy to one hundred tons each, were pushed ahead of the flood, trucks and engines rolling over and over like mere toys.

" Sixteen million tons of water gathering fences, barns, houses, mills and shops into its maw. Down the valley for three miles or more rushed this mighty avalanche of death, sweeping everything before it, and leaving nothing but death and destruction behind it. When it struck the railroad bridge at Johnstown, and not being able to force its way through that stone structure, the débris was gorged and the water dammed up fifty feet in ten minutes.

"This avalanche was composed of more than 100,000 tons of rocks, locomotives, freight cars, car trucks, iron, logs, trees and other material pushed forward by 16,000,000 tons of water falling 500 feet, and it was this that, sliding over the ground, mowed down the houses, mills and factories as a mowing machine does a field of grain. It swept down with a roaring, crushing, sound, at the rate of a mile a minute, and hurled 10,000 people into the jaws of death in less than half an hour. And so the people called it the avalanche of death."

CHAPTER V.

"Johnstown is annihilated," telegraphed Superintendent Pitcairn to Pittsburg on Friday night. "He came," says one who visited the place on Sunday, "very close to the facts of the case. Nothing like it was ever seen in this country. Where long rows of dwelling-houses and business blocks stood forty-eight hours ago, ruin and desolation now reign supreme. Probably 1500 houses have been swept from the face of the earth as completely as if they had never been erected. Main street, from end to end, is piled fifteen and twenty feet high with débris, and in some instances it is as high as the roofs of the houses. This great mass of wreckage fills the street from curb to curb, and frequently has crushed the buildings in and filled the space with reminders of the terrible calamity. There is not a man in the place who can give any reliable estimate of the number of houses that have been swept away. City Solicitor Kuehn, who should be very good authority in this matter, places the number at

1500. From the woolen mill above the island to the bridge, a distance of probably two miles, a strip of territory nearly a half mile in width has been swept clean, not a stick of timber or one brick on top of another being left to tell the story. It is the most complete wreck that imagination could portray.

"All day long men, women, and children were plodding about the desolate waste looking in vain to locate the boundaries of their former homes. Nothing but a wide expanse of mud, ornamented here and there with heaps of driftwood, remained, however, for their contemplation. It is perfectly safe to say that every house in the city that was not located well up on the hillside was either swept completely away or wrecked so badly that rebuilding will be absolutely necessary. These losses, however, are nothing compared to the frightful sacrifice of precious human lives to be seen on every hand.

"During all this solemn Sunday Johnstown has been drenched with the tears of stricken mortals, and the air is filled with sobs and sighs that come from breaking hearts. There are scenes enacted here every hour and every minute that affect all beholders profoundly. When homes are thus torn asunder in an instant, and the loved ones hurled from the arms of loving and devoted mothers,

there is an element of sadness in the tragedy that
overwhelms every heart.

"A slide, a series of frightful tosses from side
to side, a run, and you have crossed the narrow
rope bridge which spanned the chasm dug by the
waters between the stone bridge and Johnstown.
Crossing the bridge is an exciting task, yet many
women accomplished it rather than remain in
Johnstown. The bridge pitched like a ship in a
storm. Within two inches of your feet rushed the
muddy waters of the Conemaugh. There were
no ropes to easily guide, and creeping was more
convenient than walking. One had to cross the
Conemaugh at a second point in order to reach
Johnstown proper. This was accomplished by a
skiff ferry. The ferryman clung to a rope and
pulled the boat over.

"After landing one walks across a desolate sea
of mud, in which there are interred many human
bodies. It was once the handsome portion of the
town. The cellars are filled up with mud, so that
a person who has never seen the city can hardly
imagine that houses ever stood where they did.
Four streets solidly built up with houses have been
swept away. Nothing but a small, two-story frame
house remains. It was near the edge of the wave
and thus escaped, although one side was torn off.
The walk up to wrecks of houses was interrupted
in many places by small branch streams. Occa-

sionally across the flats could be seen the remains of a victim. The stench arising from the mud is sickening. Along the route were strewn tin utensils, pieces of machinery, iron pipes, and wares of every conceivable kind. In the midst of the wreck a clothing store dummy, with a hand in the position of beckoning to a person, stands erect and uninjured.

" It is impossible to describe the appearance of Main street. Whole houses have been swept down this one street and become lodged. The wreck is piled as high as the second-story windows. The reporter could step from the wreck into the auditorium of the opera house. The ruins consist of parts of houses, trees, saw logs and reels from the wire factory. Many houses have their side walls and roofs torn up, and one can walk directly into what had been second-story bed-rooms, or go in by way of the top. Further up town a raft of logs lodged in the street, and did great damage. At the beginning of the wreckage, which is at the opening of the valley of the Conemaugh, one can look up the valley for miles and not see a house. Nothing stands but an old woolen mill.

"Charles Luther is the name of the boy who stood on an adjacent elevation and saw the whole flood. He said he heard a grinding noise far up the valley, and looking up he could see a dark line moving slowly toward him. He saw that it was houses. On they came, like the hand of a giant clearing off his table. High in the air would be tossed a log or beam, which fell back with a crash. Down the valley it moved and across the little mountain city. For ten minutes nothing but moving houses were seen, and then the waters came with a roar and a rush. This lasted for two hours, and then it began to flow more steadily."

Seen from the high hill across the river from Johnstown, the Conemaugh Valley gives an easy explanation of the terrible destruction which it has suffered. This valley, stretching back almost in a straight line for miles, suddenly narrows near Johnstown. The wall of water which came tearing down toward the town, picking up all the houses and mills in the villages along its way, suddenly rose in height as it came to the narrow pass. It swept over the nearest part of the town and met the waters of Stony creek, swollen by rains, rushing along with the speed of a torrent. The two forces coming together, each turned aside and started away again in a half-circle, seeking an outlet in the lower Conemaugh Valley. The massive stone bridge of the Pennsylvania Railroad Company, at the lower base of the triangle, was almost instantly choked up with the great mass of wreckage dashed against it, and became a dam that could not be swept away, and proved to be the ruin of the town and the villages above. The waters checked here, formed a vast whirlpool, which destroyed everything within its circle. It backed up on the other side of the triangle, and devastated the village of Kernville, across the river from Johnstown.

The force of the current was truly appalling. The best evidence of its force is exhibited in the mass of débris south of the Pennsylvania bridge. Persons on the hillsides declare that houses, solid from their foundation stones, were rushed on to destruction at the rate of thirty miles an hour. On one house forty persons were counted; their cries for help were heard far above the roaring waters. At the railroad bridge the house parted in the middle, and the cries of the unfortunate people were smothered in the engulfing waters.

At the Cambria Iron Works a huge hickory struck the south brick wall of the rolling mill at an angle, went through it and the west wall, where it remains. A still more extraordinary incident is seen at the foot-bridge of the Pennsylvania station, on the freight track built for the Cambria Iron Works. The sunken track and bridge are built in a curve. In clearing out the track the Cambria workmen discovered two huge bridge trusses intact, the larger one 30 feet long and 10 feet high. It lay close to the top of the bridge and had been driven into the cut at least fifty feet.

It was with an impulse to the right side of the

mountain that the great mass of water came down
the Conemaugh river.   It was a mass of water
with a front forty feet high, and an eighth of a
mile wide.   Its velocity was so great that its first
sweep did little damage on either side.   It had no
time to spread.   Where it burst from the gap it
swept south until it struck the bridge, and, although
it was ten feet or more deep over the top of the
bridge, the obstruction of the mass of masonry
was so great that the head of the rush of water
was turned back along the Pennsylvania Railroad
bluff on the left, and, sweeping up to where it met
the first stream again, licked up the portion of the
town on the left side of the triangular plain.   A
great eddy was thus formed.   Through the Stony
Creek Gap to the right there was a rush of surplus
water.   In two minutes after the current first burst
through, forty feet deep, with a solid mass of water
whirling around with a current of tremendous velocity, it was a whirlpool vastly greater than that
of ten Niagaras.   The only outlet was under and
over the railroad bridge, and the continuing rush
of the waters into the valley from the gap was
greater for some time than the means of escape
at the bridge.

   "Standing now at the bridge," says a visitor on
Monday, "where this vast whirlpool struggled for
exit, the air is heavy with smoke and foul with
nameless odors from a mass of wreckage.   The

RUINS SHOWING THE PATH OF THE FLOOD.

area of the triangular space where the awful whirlpool revolved is said to be about four square
miles. The area of the space covered by this
smoking mass is sixty acres. The surface of this
mass is now fifteen feet below the top of the
bridge and about thirty below the point on the
bluff where the surface of the whirlpool lashed
the banks. One ragged mass some distance
above the bridge rises several feet above the
general level, but with that exception the surface
of the débris is level. It has burned off until it
reached the water, and is smouldering on as the
water gradually lowers. On the right bank, at
about where was the highest water level, a detach-
ment of the Pittsburg Fire Department is throwing two fitful streams of water down into the
smoke, with the idea of gradually extinguishing
the fire. In the immensity of the disaster with
which they combat their feeble efforts seem like
those of boys with squirt guns dampening a bon-
fire. About the sixty acres of burning débris, and
to the left of it from where it begins to narrow
toward Stony Creek Gap, there is a large area of
level mud, with muddy streams wandering about
in it. This tract of mud comprises all of the triangle except a thin fringe of buildings along the
bluff on the Pennsylvania Railroad. A considerable number of houses stand on the high ground
on the lower face of the central mountain and off

to the right into Stony Creek Gap. The fringe
along the Pennsylvania Railroad is mostly of
stores and other large brick buildings that are
completely wrecked, though not swept away. The
houses on the higher ground are unharmed; but
down toward the edge they fade away by degrees
of completeness in their wreckage into the yellow
level of the huge tract over which the mighty whirlpool swept. Off out of sight, in Stony Creek Gap,
are fringes of houses on either side of the muddy
flat.

"This flat is a peculiar thing. It is level and
uninteresting as a piece of waste ground. Too
poor to grow grass, there is nothing to indicate
that it had ever been anything else than what it is.
It is as clean of débris and wreckage as though
there had never been a building on it. In reality
it was the central and busiest part of Johnstown.
Buildings, both dwellings and stores, covered it
thickly. Its streets were paved, and its sidewalks
of substantial stone. It had street-car lines, gas
and electric lights, and all the other improvements
of a substantial city of 15,000 or 20,000 inhabitants.
Iron bridges spanned the streams, and the buildings were of substantial character. Not a brick
remains, not a stone nor a stick of timber in all
this territory. There are not even hummocks and
mounds to show where wreckage might be covered
with a layer of mud. They are not there, they are

gone—every building, every street, every sidewalk and pavement, the street railways, and everything else that covered the surface of the earth has vanished as utterly as though it had never been there. The ground was swept as clean as though some mighty scraper had been dragged over it again and again. Not even the lines of the streets can be remotely traced.

" ' I have visited Johnstown a dozen times a year for a long time,' said a business man to-day, 'and I know it thoroughly, but I haven't the least idea now of what part of it this is. I can't even tell the direction the streets used to run.'

" His bewilderment is hardly greater than, that of the citizens themselves. They wander about in the mud for hours trying to find the spot where the house of some friend or relative used to stand. It takes a whole family to locate the site of their friend's house with any reasonable certainty.

"Wandering over this muddy plain one can realize something of what must have been the gigantic force of that vast whirlpool. It pressed upon the town like some huge millstone, weighing tens of thousands of tons and revolving with awful velocity, pounding to powder everything beneath. But the conception of the power of that horrible eddy of the flood must remain feeble until that sixty acres of burning débris is inspected. It seems from a little distance like any other mass of wreckage, though vastly longer than any ever before seen in this country. It must have been many times more tremendous when it was heaped up twenty feet higher over its whole area and before the fire leveled it off. But neither then nor now can the full terror of the flood that piled it there be adequately realized until a trip across parts where the fire has been extinguished shows the manner in which the stuff composing it is packed together. It is not a heap of broken timbers lying loosely thrown together in all directions. It is a solid mass. The boards and timbers which made up the frame buildings are laid together as closely as sticks of wood in a pile—more closely, for they are welded into one another until each stick is as solidly fixed in place as though all were one. A curious thing is that wherever there are a few boards together they are edge up, and never standing on end or flat. The terrible force of the whirlpool that ground four square miles of buildings into this sixty acres of wreckage left no opportunity for gaps or holes between pieces in the river. Everything was packed together as solidly as though by sledge-hammer blows.

" But the boards and timber of four square miles of buildings are not all that is in that sixty-acre mass. An immense amount of débris from further up the valley lies there. Twenty-seven locomotives, several Pullman cars and probably a hundred other cars, or all that is left of them, are in that mass. Fragments of iron bridges can be seen sticking out occasionally above the wreckage. They are about the only things the fire has not leveled, except the curious hillock spoken of, which is an eighth of a mile back from the bridge, where the flames apparently raged less fiercely. Scattered over the area, also, are many blackened logs that were too big to be entirely burned, and that stick up now like spar buoys in a sea of ruin. Little jets of flame, almost unseen by daylight, but appearing as evening falls, are scattered thickly over the surface of the wreckage.

"Of the rest of Johnstown, and the collection of towns within sight of the bridge, not much is to be said. They are, to a greater or less extent, gone, as Johnstown is gone. Far up the gap through which came the flood a large brick building remains standing, but ruined. It is all that is left of one of the biggest wire mills and steel works in the country. Turning around below the bridge are the works of the Cambria Iron Company. The buildings are still standing, but they are pretty well ruined, and the machinery with which they were filled is either totally destroyed or damaged almost beyond repair. High up on the hill at the left and scattered up on other hills in sight are many dwellings, neat, well kept, and attractive places apparently, and looking as bright and fresh now as before the awful torrent wiped out of existence everything in the valley below.

"This is Johnstown and its immediate vicinity as nearly as words can paint it. It is a single feature, one section out of fifteen miles of horror that stretches through this once lovely valley of the Allegheny. What is true of Johnstown is true of every town for miles up and down. The desolation of one town may differ from the desolation in others as one death may differ from another; but it is desolation and death everywhere—desolation so complete, so relentless, so dreadful that it is absolutely beyond the power of language fairly to tell the tale."

CHAPTER VI.

MR. WILLIAM HENRY SMITH, General Manager of the Associated Press, was a passenger on a railroad train which reached the Conemaugh Valley on the very day of the disaster. He writes as follows of what he saw:

"The fast line trains that leave Chicago at quarter past three and Cincinnati at seven P. M. constitute the day-express eastward from Pittsburg; which runs in two sections. This train left Pittsburg on time Friday morning, but was stopped for an hour at Johnstown by reports of a wash-out ahead. It had been raining hard for over sixteen hours, and the sides of the mountains were covered with water descending into the valleys. The Conemaugh River, whose bank is followed by the Pennsylvania Railroad for many miles, looked an angry flood nearly bankfull. Passengers were interested in seeing hundreds of saw-logs and an enormous amount of driftwood shoot rapidly by, and the train pursued its way eastward. At

81

Johnstown there was a long wait, as before stated. The lower stories of many houses were submerged by the slack-water, and the inhabitants were looking out of the second-story windows. Horses were standing up to their knees in water in the streets; a side-track of the railroad had been washed out; loaded cars were on the bridge to keep it steady, and the huge poles of the Western Union Telegraph Company, carrying fifteen wires, swayed badly, and several soon went down. The two sections ran to Conemaugh, about two miles eastward of Johnstown, and lay there about three hours, when they were moved on to the highest ground and placed side by side. The mail train was placed in the rear of the first section, and a freight train was run onto a side track on the bank of the Conemaugh. The report was that a bridge had been washed out, carrying away one track and that the other track was unsafe. There was a rumor also that the reservoir at South Fork might break. This made most of the passengers uneasy, and they kept a pretty good look-out for information. The porters of the Pullman cars remained at their posts, and comforted the passengers with the assurance that the Pennsylvania Railroad Company always took care of its patrons. A few gentlemen and some ladies and children quietly seated themselves, apparently contented.

One gentleman, who was ill, had his berth made up and retired, although advised not to do so.

"Soon the cry came that the water in the reservoir had broken down the barrier and was sweeping down the valley. Instantly there was a panic and a rush for the mountain side. Children were carried and women assisted by a few who kept cool heads. It was a race for life. There was seen the black head of the flood, now the monster Destruction, whose crest was high raised in the air, and with this in view even the weak found wings for their feet. No words can adequately describe the terror that filled every breast, or the awful power manifested by the flood. The round-house had stalls for twenty-three locomotives. There were eighteen or twenty of these standing there at this time. There was an ominous crash, and the round-house and locomotives disappeared. Everything in the main track of the flood was first lifted in air and then swallowed up by the waters. A hundred houses were swept away in a few minutes. These included the hotel, stores, and saloons on the front street and residences adjacent. The locomotive of one of the trains was struck by a house and demolished. The side of another house stopped in front of another locomotive and served as a shield. The rear car of the mail train swung around in the rear of the second section of the express and turned over on its side. Three men were observed standing upon it as it floated. The coupling broke, and the car moved out upon the bosom of the waters. As it would roll the men would shift their position. The situation was desperate, and they were given up for lost. Two or three hardy men seized ropes and ran along the mountain side to give them aid. Later it was reported that the men escaped over some driftwood as their car was carried near a bank. It is believed there were several women and children inside the car. Of course they were drowned. As the fugitives on the mountain side witnessed the awful devastation they were moved as never before in their lives. They were powerless to help those seized upon by the waters ; the despair of those who had lost everything in life and the wailing of those whose relatives or friends were missing filled their breasts with unutterable sorrow.

" The rain continued to fall steadily, but shelter was not thought of. Few passengers saved anything from the train, so sudden was the cry 'Run for your lives, the reservoir has broken !'

" Many were without hats, and as their baggage was left on the trains, they were without the means of relieving their unhappy condition. The occupants of the houses still standing on the high ground threw them open to those who had lost all, and to the passengers of the train.

" During the height of the flood, the spectators were startled by the sound of two locomotive whistles from the very midst of the waters. Two engineers, with characteristic courage, had remained at their posts, and while there was destruction on every hand, and apparently no escape for them, they sounded their whistles. This they repeated at intervals, the last time with triumphant vigor, as the waters were receding from the sides of their locomotives. By half-past five the force of the reservoir water had been spent on the village of Conemaugh, and the Pullman cars and locomotive of the second section remained unmoved. This was because, being on the highest and hardest ground, the destructive current of the reservoir flood had passed between that and the mountain, while the current of the river did not eat it away. But the other trains had been destroyed. A solitary locomotive was seen embedded in the mud where the round-house had stood.

" As the greatest danger had passed, the people of Conemaugh gave their thoughts to their neighbors of the city of Johnstown. Here was centred the great steel and iron industries, the pride of Western Pennsylvania, the Cambria Iron Works being known everywhere. Here were churches, daily newspapers, banks, dry-goods houses, warehouses, and the comfortable and well-built homes of twelve thousand people. In the contemplation of the irresistible force of that awful flood, gathering additional momentum as it swept on toward the Gulf, it became clear that the city must be destroyed, and that unless the inhabitants had telegraphic notice of the breaking of the reservoir they must perish. A cry of horror went up from the hundreds on the mountain-side, and a few instinctively turned their steps toward Johnstown. The city was destroyed. All the mills, furnaces, manufactories, the many and varied industries, the banks, the residences, all, all were swallowed up before the shadows of night had settled down upon the earth. Those who came back by daybreak said that from five thousand to eight thousand had been drowned. Our hope is that this is an exaggeration, and when the roll is called most will respond. In the light of this calamity, the destruction at Conemaugh sinks into insignificance."

Mr. George Johnston, a lumber merchant of Pittsburg, was another witness. "I had gone to Johnstown," he says, "to place a couple of orders. I had scarcely reached the town, about three o'clock in the afternoon, when I saw a bulletin posted up in front of the telegraph office, around which quite a crowd of men had congregated. I pushed my way up, and read that the waters were so high in the Conemaugh that it was feared the three-mile dam, as it was called, would give way. I know enough about Johnstown to feel that my life was not worth a snap once that dam gave way. Although the Johnstown people did not seem to pay much attention to the warning, I was nervous and apprehensive. I had several parties to see, but concluded to let all but one go until some later day. So I hurried through with my most urgent transactions and started for the depot. The Conemaugh had then gotten so high that the residents of the low-lying districts had moved into upper stories. I noticed a number of wagons filled with furniture hurrying through the streets. A few families, either apprehensive of the impending calamity or driven from their houses by the rising waters, had started for the surrounding hills. Johnstown, you know, lies in a narrow valley, and lies principally on the V-shaped point between the converging river and Stony Creek.

"I was just walking up the steps to the depot when I heard a fearful roar up the valley. It sounded at first like a heavy train of cars, but soon became too loud and terrible for that. I boarded a train, and as I sat at the car window a sight broke before my view that I will remember to my dying day. Away up the Conemaugh came a yellow wall, whose crest was white and frothy. I rushed for the platform of the car, not knowing what I did, and just then the train began to move. Terrified as I was, I remember feeling that I was in the safest place and I sank back in a seat. When I looked out again what had been the busy mill yards of the Cambria Iron Company was a yellow, turbulent sea, on whose churned currents houses and barns were riding like ships in a brook. The water rushing in upon the molten metal in the mills had caused deafening explosions, which, coupled with the roar and grinding of the flood, made a terrifying din. Turning to the other side and looking on down the valley, I saw the muddy water rushing through the main streets of the town. I could see men and horses floundering about almost within call. House-tops were being filled with white-faced people who clung to each other and looked terror-stricken upon the rising flood.

"It had all come so quickly that none of them seemed to realize what had happened. The conductor of my train had been pulling frantically at the bell-rope, and the train went spinning across the bridge. I sat in my seat transfixed with horror. Houses were spinning through beneath the bridge, and I did not know at what moment the structure would melt away under the train. The conductor kept tugging at the bell-rope and the train shot ahead again. We seemed to fairly leap over the yellow torrents, and I wondered for an instant whether we had not left the rails and were flying through the air. My heart gave a bound of relief when we dashed into the forest on the hillside opposite the doomed town. As the train sped along at a rate of speed that made me think the engineer had gone mad, I took one look back upon the valley. What a sight it was! The populous valley for miles either way was a seething, roaring cauldron, through whose boiling surface roofs of houses and the stand-pipes of mills protruded. The water was fairly piling up in a well farther up, and I saw the worst had not yet come. Then I turned my eyes away from the awful sight and tried not to even think until Pittsburg was reached.

"I cannot see how it is possible for less than five thousand lives to have been sacrificed in Johnstown alone. At least two-thirds of the town was swept away. The water came so quickly that escape from the low districts was impossible. People retreated to the upper floors of their residences and stores until the water had gotten too deep to allow their escape. When the big flood came the houses were picked up like pasteboard boxes or collapsed like egg-shells. The advance of the flood was black with houses, logs, and other debris, so that it struck Johnstown with the solid force of a battering-ram. None but eye-witnesses of the flood can comprehend its size and awfulness as it came tumbling, roaring down upon the unprotected town."

The appearance of the flood at Sang Hollow, some miles below Johnstown, is thus pictured by C. W. Linthicum, of Baltimore:

"My train left Pittsburg on Friday morning for Johnstown. The train was due at Sang Hollow at two minutes after four, but was five minutes late. At Sang Hollow, just as we were about to pull out, we heard that the flood was coming. Looking ahead, up the valley, we saw an immense wall of water thirty feet high, raging, roaring, rushing toward us. The engineer reversed his engine and rushed back to the hills at full speed, and we barely escaped the waters. We ran back three hundred yards, and the flood swept by, tearing up track, telegraph poles, trees, and houses. Superintendent Pitcairn was on the train. We all got out and tried to save the floating people. Taking the bell cord we formed a line and threw the rope out, thus saving seven persons. We could have saved more, but many were afraid to let go of the debris. It was an awful sight. The immense volume of water was roaring along, whirling over huge rocks, dashing against the banks and leaping high into the air, and this seething flood was strewn with timber, trunks of trees, parts of houses, and hundreds of human beings, cattle, and

TYPICAL SCENE IN JOHNSTOWN.

almost every living animal. The fearful peril of the living was not more awful than the horrors of hundreds of distorted, bleeding corpses whirling along the avalanche of death. We counted one hundred and seven people floating by and dead without number. A section of roof came by on which were sitting a woman and girl. A man named C. W. Heppenstall, of Pittsburg, waded and swam to the roof. He brought the girl in first and then the woman. They told us they were not relatives. The woman had lost her husband and four children, and the girl her father and mother, and entire family. A little boy came by with his mother. Both were as calm as could be, and the boy was apparently trying to comfort the mother. They passed unheeding our proffered help, and striking the bridge below, went down into the vortex like lead.

" One beautiful girl came by with her hands raised in prayer, and, although we shouted to her and ran along the bank, she paid no attention. We could have saved her if she had caught the rope. An old man and his wife whom we saved said that eleven persons started from Cambria City on the roof with him, but that the others had dropped off.

" At about eight P. M. we started for New Florence. All along the river we saw corpses without number caught in the branches of trees and wedged in corners in the banks. A large sycamore tree in the river between Sang Hollow and New Florence seemed to draw into it nearly all who floated down, and they went under the surface at its roots like lead. When the waters subsided two hundred and nine bodies were found at the root of this tree. All night the living and the dead floated by New Florence. At Pittsburg seventy-eight bodies were found on Saturday, and as many more were seen floating by. Hundreds of people from ill-fated Johnstown are wandering homeless and starving on the mountain-side. . Very few saved anything, and I saw numbers going down the stream naked. The suffering within the next few days will be fearful unless prompt relief is extended."

H. M. Bennett and S. W. Keltz, engineer and conductor of engine No. 1,165, an extra freight, which happened to be lying at South Fork when the dam broke, tell a graphic story of their wonderful flight and escape on the locomotive before the advancing flood. At the time mentioned Bennett and Keltz were in the signal tower at that point awaiting orders. The fireman and flagman were on the engine, and two brakemen were asleep in the caboose. Suddenly the men in the tower heard a loud booming roar in the valley above them. They looked in the direction of the sound. and were almost transfixed with horror to see two miles above them a huge black wall of water, at least one hundred and fifty feet in height, rushing down the valley upon them.

One look the fear-stricken men gave the awful sight, and then they made a rush for the locomotive, at the same time giving the alarm to the sleeping brakemen in the caboose with loud cries, but with no avail. It was impossible to aid them further, however, so they cut the engine loose from the train, and the engineer, with one wild wrench, threw the lever wide open, and they were away on a mad race for life. For a moment it seemed that they would not receive momentum enough to keep ahead of the flood, and they cast one despairing glance back. Then they could see the awful deluge approaching in its might. On it came, rolling and roaring like some Titanic monster, tossing and tearing houses, sheds, and trees in its awful speed as if they were mere toys. As they looked they saw the two brakemen rush out of the cab, but they had not time to gather the slightest idea of the cause of their doom before they, the car, and signal tower were tossed high in the air, to disappear forever in engulfing water.

Then with a shudder, as if at last it comprehended its peril, the engine leaped forward like a thing of life, and speeded down the valley. But fast as it went, the flood gained upon them. Hope,

however, was in the ascendant, for if they could
but get across the bridge below the track would
lean toward the hillside in such a manner that they
would be comparatively safe. In a few breathless
moments the shrieking locomotive whizzed around
the curve and they were in sight of the bridge.
Horror upon horrors! Ahead of them was a
freight train, with the rear end almost on the
bridge, and to get across was simply impossible!
Engineer Bennett then reversed the lever and
succeeded in checking the engine as they glided
across the bridge, and then they jumped and ran
for their lives up the hillside, as the bridge and
tender of the locomotive they had been on were
swept away like a bundle of matches in the torrent.

CHAPTER VII.

THERE have been many famous rides in history. Longfellow has celebrated that of Paul Revere. Read has sung of Sheridan's. John Boyle O'Reilly has commemorated in graceful verse the splendid achievement of Collins Graves, who, when the Williamsburg dam in Massachusetts broke, dashed down the valley on horseback in the van of the flood, warning the people and saving countless lives:

" He draws no rein, but he shakes the street
With a shout and a ring of the galloping feet,
And this the cry that he flings to the wind:
To the hills for your lives ! The flood is behind !'

" In front of the roaring flood is heard
The galloping horse and the warning word.
Thank God ! The brave man's life is spared !
From Williamsburg town he nobly dared
To race with the flood and take the road
In front of the terrible swath it mowed.
For miles it thundered and crashed behind,
But he looked ahead with a steadfast mind :
'They must be warned,' was all he said,
As away on his terrible ride he sped.''

There were two such heroes in the Conemaugh Valley. Let their deeds be told and their names held in everlasting honor. One was John G. Parke, a young civil engineer of Philadelphia, a nephew of the General John G. Parke who commanded a corps of the Union Army. He was the first to discover the impending break in the South Fork dam, and jumping into the saddle he started at breakneck speed down the valley shouting: "The dam; the dam is breaking; run for your lives!" Hundreds of people were saved by this timely warning. Reaching South Fork Station, young Parke telegraphed tidings of the coming inundation to Johnstown, ten miles below, fully an hour before the flood came in "a solid wall of water thirty feet high" to drown the mountain-bound town.

Some heeded the note of alarm at Johnstown; others had heard it before, doubted, and waited until death overtook them. Young Parke climbed up into the mountains when the water was almost at his horse's heels, and saw the deluge pass.

Less fortunate was Daniel Peyton, a rich young man of Johnstown. He heard at Conemaugh the message sent down from South Fork by the gallant Parke. In a moment he sprang into the saddle. Mounted on a grand, big, bay horse, he came riding down the pike which passes through Conemaugh to Johnstown, like some angel of wrath of old, shouting his warning:

"Run for your lives to the hills! Run to the hills!"

The people crowded out of their houses along the thickly settled streets awe-struck and wondering. No one knew the man, and some thought he was a maniac and laughed. On and on, at a deadly pace, he rode, and shrilly rang out his awful cry. In a few moments, however, there came a cloud of ruin down the broad streets, down the narrow alleys, grinding, twisting, hurling, overturning, crashing—annihilating the weak and the strong. It was the charge of the flood, wearing its coronet of ruin and devastation, which grew at every instant of its progress. Forty feet high, some say, thirty according to others, was this sea, and it travelled with a swiftness like that which lay in the heels of Mercury.

On and on raced the rider, on and on rushed the wave. Dozens of people took heed of the warning and ran up to the hills.

Poor, faithful rider! It was an unequal contest. Just as he turned to cross the railroad bridge the mighty wall fell upon him, and horse, rider, and bridge all went out into chaos together.

A few feet further on several cars of the Pennsylvania Railroad train from Pittsburg were caught up and hurried into the cauldron, and the heart of the town was reached.

The hero had turned neither to the right nor left for himself, but rode on to death for his townsmen. When found Peyton was lying face upward beneath the remnants of massive oaks, while hard by lay the gallant horse that had so nobly done all in his power for humanity before he started to seek a place of safety for himself.

Mrs. Ogle, the manager of the Western Union telegraph office, who died at her post, will go down in history as a heroine of the highest order. Notwithstanding the repeated notifications which she received to get out of reach of the approaching danger, she stood by the instruments with unflinching loyalty and undaunted courage, sending words of warning to those in danger in the valley below. When every station in the path of the coming torrent had been warned, she wired her companion at South Fork: "This is my last message," and as such it shall always be remembered as her last words on earth, for at that very moment the torrent engulfed her and bore her from her post on earth to her post of honor in the great beyond.

Miss Nina Speck, daughter of the Rev. David Speck, pastor of the First United Brethren Church, of Chambersburg, was in Johnstown visiting her brother and narrowly escaped death in the flood. She arrived home clad in nondescript clothing, which had been furnished by an old colored washerwoman, and told the following story of the flood:

" Our house was in Kernsville, a part of Johnstown through which Stony Creek ran. Although we were a square from the creek, the back-water from the stream had flooded the streets in the morning and was up to our front porch. At four o'clock on Friday afternoon we were sitting on the front porch watching the flood, when we heard a roar as of a tornado or mighty conflagration.

" We rushed up-stairs and got out upon the bay-window. There an awful sight met our eyes. Down the Conemaugh Valley was advancing a mighty wall of water and mist with a terrible roar. Before it were rolling houses and buildings of all kinds, tossing over and over. We thought it was a cyclone, the roar sounding like a tempest among forest trees. We started down-stairs and out through the rear of the house to escape to the hillside near by. But before we could get there the water was up to our necks and we could make no progress. We turned back and were literally dashed by the current into the house, which began to move off as soon as were in it again. From the second-story window I saw a young man drifting toward us. I broke the glass from the frames with my hands and helped him in, and in

a few minutes more I pulled in an old man, a
neighbor, who had been sick.

"Our house moved rapidly down the stream
and fortunately lodged against a strong building.
The water forced us out of the second-story up
into the attic. Then we heard a lot of people on
our roof begging us for God's sake to let them in.
I broke through the roof with a bed-slat and
pulled them in. Soon we had thirteen in all
crouched in the attic.

"Our house was rocking, and every now and
then a building would crash against us. Every
moment we thought we would go down. The
roofs of all the houses drifting by us were covered
with people, nearly all praying and some singing
hymns, and now and then a house would break
apart and all would go down. On Saturday at
noon we were rescued, making our way from one
building to the next by crawling on narrow planks.
I counted hundreds of bodies lying in the
debris, most of them covered over with earth and
showing only the outlines of the form."

Opposite the northern wall of the Methodist
Church the flood struck the new Queen Anne
house of John Fronheiser, a superintendent in the
Cambria Works. He was at home, as most men
were that day, trying to calm the fears of the
women and children of the family during the ear-
lier flood. Down went the front of the new Queen

Anne house, and into the wreck of it fell the Superintendent, two elder children, a girl and a boy. As the flood passed he heard the boy cry: "Don't let me drown, papa; break my arms first!" and the girl: "Cut off my legs, but don't let me drown!"

And as he heard them, came a wilder cry from his wife drifting down with the current, to "Save the baby." But neither wife nor baby could be saved, and boy and girl stayed in the wreck until the water went down and they were extricated.

Horror piled on horror is the story from Johnstown down to the viaduct. Horror shot through with intense lights of heroism, and here and there pervaded with gleams of humor. It is known that one girl sang as she was whirled through the flood, "Jesus, lover of my soul," until the water stopped her singing forever. It is known that Elvie Duncan, daughter of the Superintendent of the Street Car Company, when her family was separated and she was swept away with her baby sister, kept the little thing alive by chewing bread and feeding it to her. It is known that John Dibart, banker, died as helplessly in his splendid house as John McKee the prisoner in his cell; that the pleasant park, with the chain fence about it, was so completely annihilated that not even one root of the many shade trees within its boundaries remains. It is known also that to a leaden-footed

messenger boy, who was ambling along Main
Street, fear lent wings to lift him into the *Tribune*
office in the second story of the Post Office, and
that the Rosensteels, general storekeepers of
Woodvale, were swept into the windows of their
friends, the Cohens, retail storekeepers of Main
Street, Johnstown, two miles from where they
started. It is known that the Episcopal Church, at
Locust and Market Streets, went down like a
house of cards, or as the German Lutheran had
gone, in the path of the flood, and that Rector
Diller, his wife and child, and adopted daughter
went with it, while of their next-door neighbors,
Frank Daly, of the Cambria Company, and his
mother, the son was drowned and the mother, not
so badly hurt in body as in spirit, died three nights
after in the Mercy Hospital, Pittsburg.

But while the flood was driving people to silent
death down the valley, there was a sound of lam-
entation on the hills. Hundreds who had climbed
there to be out of reach during the morning's
freshet saw the city in the valley disappearing,
and their cries rose high above the crash and the
roar. Little time had eyes to watch or lips to cry.
O'Brien, the disabled Millville storekeeper, was
one of the crowd in the park. He saw a town
before him, then a mountain of timber approaching, then a dizzy swirl of men at the viaduct, a
breaking of the embankment to the east of it, the

forming of a whirlpool there that ate up homes and those that dwelt in them, as a cauldron of molten iron eats up the metal scraps that are thrown in to cool it, and then a silence and a subsidence.

It was a quarter of four o'clock. At half-past three there had been a Johnstown. Now there was none.

CHAPTER VIII.

VOLUMES might be written of the sufferings endured and valor exhibited by the survivors of the flood, or of the heart-rending grief with which so many were stricken. At Johnstown an utterly wretched woman named Mrs. Fenn stood by a muddy pool of water trying to find some trace of a once happy home. She was half crazed with grief, and her eyes were red and swollen. As a correspondent stepped to her side she raised her pale, haggard face and remarked:

"They are all gone. O God! be merciful to them! My husband and my seven dear little children have been swept down with the flood, and I am left alone. We were driven by the awful flood into the garret, but the water followed us there. Inch by inch it kept rising, until our heads were crushing against the roof. It was death to remain. So I raised a window, and one by one, placed my darlings on some driftwood, trusting to the great Creator. As I liberated the last one, my sweet little boy, he looked at me and said:

' Mamma, you always told me that the Lord would
care for me; will He look after me now ?' I saw
him drift away with his loving face turned toward
me, and, with a prayer on my lips for his deliver-
ance, he passed from sight forever. The next
moment the roof crashed in, and I floated outside,
to be rescued fifteen hours later from the roof of
a house in Kernsville. If I could only find one of
my darlings I could bow to the will of God, but
they are all gone. I have lost everything on earth
now but my life, and I will return to my old Virginia home and lay me down for my last great
sleep."

A handsome woman, with hair as black as a
raven's wing, walked through the depot where a
dozen or more bodies were awaiting burial. Passing from one to another, she finally lifted the
paper covering from the face of a woman, young,
and with traces of beauty showing through the
stains of muddy water, and with a cry of anguish
she reeled backward to be caught by a rugged
man who chanced to be passing. In a moment
or so she had calmed herself sufficiently to take
one more look at the features of her dead. She
stood gazing at the corpse as if dumb. Finally,
turning away with another wild burst of grief, she
said: "And her beautiful hair all matted and her
sweet face so bruised and stained with mud and
water!" The dead woman was the sister of the

mourner. The body was placed in a coffin a few minutes later and sent away to its narrow house.

A woman was seen to smile, one morning just after the catastrophe, as she came down the steps of Prospect Hill, at Johnstown. She ran down lightly, turning up toward the stone bridge. She passed the little railroad station where the undertakers were at work embalming the dead, and walked slowly until she got opposite the station. Then she stopped and danced a few steps. There was but a small crowd there. The woman raised her hands above her head and sang. She became quiet and then suddenly burst into a frenzied fit of weeping and beat her forehead with her hands. She tore her dress, which was already in rags.

"I shall go crazy," she screamed, "if they do not find his body."

The poor woman could not go crazy, as her mind had been already shattered.

"He was a good man," she went on, while the onlookers listened pityingly. "I loved him and he loved me."

"Where is he?" she screamed. "I must find him."

And she started at the top of her speed down the track toward the river. Some men caught her. She struggled desperately for a few moments, and then fainted.

JOHNSTOWN—VIEW COR. MAIN AND CLINTON STS.

Her name was Eliza Adams, and she was a bride of but two months. Her husband was a foreman at the Cambria Iron Works and was drowned.

The body of a beautiful young girl of twenty was found wedged in a mass of ruins just below the Cambria Iron Works. She was taken out and laid on the damp grass. She was tall, slender, of well-rounded form, clad in a long red wrapper, with lace at her throat and wrists. Her feet were encased in pretty embroidered slippers. Her face was a study for an artist. Features clear cut as though chiseled from Parian marble; and, strangely enough, they bore not the slightest disfigurement, and had not the swelled and puffed appearance that was present in nearly all the other drowned victims. A smile rested on her lips. Her hair, which had evidently been golden, was matted with mud and fell in heavy masses to her waist.

" Does any one know her?" was asked of the silent group that had gathered around.

No one did, and she was carried to the improvised morgue in the school-house, and now fills a grave as one of the " unidentified dead."

Miss Rose Clark was fastened in the debris at the railroad bridge, at Johnstown. The force of the water had torn all of her garments off and pinned her left leg below the water between two beams. She was more calm than the men who were trying to rescue her. The flames were coming nearer, and the intense heat scorching her bare skin. She begged the men to cut off the imprisoned leg. Finally half of the men turned and fought the fire, while the rest endeavored to rescue Miss Clark. After six hours of hard work, and untold suffering by the brave little lady she was taken from the ruins in a dead faint. She was one mass of bruises, from her breast to her knees, and her left arm and leg were broken.

Just below Johnstown, on the Conemaugh, three women were working on the ruins of what had been their home. An old arm-chair was taken from the ruins by the men. When one of the women saw the chair, it brought back a wealth of memory, probably the first since the flood occurred, and throwing herself on her knees on the wreck she gave way to a flood of tears.

"Where in the name of God," she sobbed, "did you get that chair? It was mine—no, I don't want it. Keep it and find for me, if you can, my album. In it are the faces of my husband and little girl."

Patrick Downs was a worker in one of the mills of the Cambria Iron Works. He had a wife and a fourteen-year-old daughter, Jessie Downs, who was a great favorite with the sturdy, hard-handed fellow-workmen of her father.

She was of rare beauty and sweetness. Her waving, golden-yellow hair, brushed away from a face of wondrous whiteness, was confined by a ribbon at the neck. Lustrous Irish blue eyes lighted up the lovely face and ripe, red lips parted in smiles for the workmen in the mills, every one of whom was her lover.

Jessie was in the mill when the flood struck the town, and had not been seen since till the work of cleaning up the Cambria plant was begun in earnest. Then, in the cellar of the building a workman spied a little shoe protruding from a closely packed bed of sandy mud. In a few moments the body of Jessie Downs was uncovered.

The workmen who had been in such scenes as this for six days stood about with uncovered heads and sobbed like babies. The body had not been bruised nor hurt in any way, the features being composed as if in sleep.

The men gathered up the body of their little sweetheart and were carrying it through the town on a stretcher when they met poor Patrick Downs. He gazed upon the form of his baby, but never a tear was in his eye, and he only thanked God that she had not suffered in contest with the angry waves.

He had but a moment before identified the body of his wife among the dead recovered, and the mother and child were laid away together in one grave on Grove Hill, and the father resumed work with the others.

Dr. Lowman is one of the most prominent physicians of Western Pennsylvania. His residence in Johnstown was protected partially from the avalanche of water by the Methodist Church, which is a large stone structure. Glancing upstream, the Doctor saw advancing what seemed to be a huge mountain. Grasping the situation, he ran in and told the family to get to the top floors as quickly as possible. They had scarcely reached the second floor when the water was pouring into the windows. They went higher up, and the water followed them, but it soon reached its extreme height.

While the family were huddled in the third story the Doctor looked out and saw a young girl floating toward the window on a door. He smashed the glass, and, at the great risk of his own life, succeeded in hauling the door toward him and lifting the girl through the window. She had not been there long when one corner of the building gave way and she became frightened. She insisted on taking a shutter and floating downstream. In vain did the Doctor try to persuade her to forego such a suicidal attempt. She said that she was a good swimmer, and that, once out in the water, she had no fears for her ultimate safety. Resisting all entreaties and taking a shutter from the window, she plunged out into the surging waters, and has not since been heard from.

When the girl deserted the house, Dr. Lowman and his family made their way to the roof. While up there another corner of the house gave way. After waiting for several hours, the intervening space between the bank building and the dwelling became filled with drift. The Doctor gathered his family around him, and after a perilous walk they all reached the objective point in safety. Dr. Lowman's aged father was one of the party. When his family was safe Dr. Lowman started to rescue other unfortunates. All day Saturday he worked like a beaver in water to his neck, and he saved the lives of many.

No man returns from the valley of death with more horrible remembrance of the flood than Dr. Henry H. Phillips, of Pittsburg. He is the only one known to be saved out of a household of thirteen, among whom was his feeble old mother and other near and dear friends. His own life was saved by his happening to step out upon the portico of the house just as the deluge came. Dr. Phillips had gone to Johnstown to bring his mother, who was an invalid, to his home in the East End. They had intended starting for Pittsburg Friday morning, but Mrs. Phillips did not

feel able to make the journey, and it was post-
poned until the next day.   In the meantime the
flood began to come, and during the afternoon of
Friday the family retired to the upper floors of
the house for safety.   There were thirteen in the
house, including little Susan McWilliams, the
twelve-year-old daughter of Mr. W. H. Mc-
Williams, of Pittsburg, who was visiting her aunt,
Mrs. Phillips ; Dr. L. T. Beam, son-in-law of Mrs.
Phillips ; another niece, and Mrs. Dowling, a
neighbor.   The latter had come there with her
children because the Phillips house was a brick
structure while her own was frame.   Its destruction proved to be the more sudden and complete
on account of the material.

The water was a foot deep on the first floor,
and the family were congratulating themselves
that they were so comfortably situated in the
upper story, when Dr. Phillips heard a roaring
up toward the Cambria Iron Works.   Without a
thought of the awful truth, he stepped out upon
the portico of the house to see what it meant.
A wall of water and wreckage loomed up before
him like a roaring cloud.   Before he could turn
back or cry out he saw a house, that rode the
flood like a chip, come between him and his vision
of the window.   Then all was dark, and the cold
water seemed to wrap him up and toss him to a
house-top three hundred yards from where that

of his mother had stood. Gathering his shattered wits together the Doctor saw he was floating about in the midst of a black pool. Dark objects were moving all about him, and although there was some light, he could not recognize any of the surroundings. For seventeen hours he drifted about upon the wreckage where fate had tossed him. Then rescuers came, and he was taken to safe quarters. A long search has so far failed to elicit any tidings of the twelve persons in the Phillips' house.

Mr. G. B. Hartley, of Philadelphia, was one of the five out of fifty-five guests of the Hurlburt House who survived.

"The experience I passed through at Johnstown on that dreadful Friday night," said Mr. Hartley to a correspondent, "is like a horrible nightmare in a picture before me. When the great rush of water came I was sitting in the parlors of the Hurlburt House. Suddenly we were startled to hear several loud shouts on the streets. These cries were accompanied by a loud, crashing noise. At the first sound we all rushed from the room panic-stricken. There was a crash and I found myself pinned down by broken boards and debris of different kinds. The next moment I felt the water surging in. I knew it went higher than my head because I felt it. The water must have passed like a flash or I would not have come out alive. After the shock I could see that the entire roof of the hotel had been carried off. Catching hold of something I manged to pull myself up on to the roof. The roof had slid off and lay across the street. On the roof I had a chance to observe my surroundings. Down on the extreme edge of the roof I espied the proprietor of the hotel, Mr. Benford. He was nearly exhausted, and it required every effort for him to hold to the roof. Cautiously advancing, I managed to creep down to where he was holding. I tried to pull him up, but found I was utterly powerless. Mr. Benford was nearly as weak as myself, and could do very little toward helping himself. We did not give up, however, and in a few minutes, by dint of struggling and putting forth every bit of strength, Mr. Benford managed to crawl upon the roof. Crouching and shivering on another part of the roof were two girls, one a chamber-maid of the hotel, and the other a clerk in a store that was next to it. The latter was in a pitiable plight. Her arm had been torn from its socket. I took off my overcoat and gave it to her. Mr. Benford did the same thing for the other, for it was quite chilly. A young man was nursing his mother, who had had her scalp completely torn off. He asked me to hold her head until he could make a bandage. He tore a thick strip of cloth and placed it round her head. The blood saturated it before it was well on. Soon after this I was rescued more dead than alive."

CHAPTER IX.

MANY of the most thrilling sights and experiences were those of railroad employees and passengers. Mr. Henry, the engineer of the second section of express train No. 8, which runs between Pittsburg and Altoona, was at Conemaugh when the great flood came sweeping down the valley. He was able to escape to a place of safety. His was the only train that was not injured, even though it was in the midst of the great wave. The story as related by Mr. Henry is most graphic.

"It was an awful sight," he said. "I have often seen pictures of flood scenes and I thought they were exaggerations, but what I witnessed last Friday changes my former belief. To see that immense volume of water, fully fifty feet high, rushing madly down the valley, sweeping everything before it, was a thrilling sight. It is engraved indelibly on my memory. Even now I can see that mad torrent carrying death and destruction before it.

"The second section of No. 8, on which I was,

was due at Johnstown about quarter past ten in the morning. We arrived there safely and were told to follow the first section. When we arrived at Conemaugh the first section and the mail were there. Washouts further up the mountain prevented our going on, so we could do nothing but sit around and discuss the situation. The creek at Conemaugh was swollen high, almost overflowing. The heavens were pouring rain, but this did not prevent nearly all the inhabitants of the town from gathering along its banks. They watched the waters go dashing by and wondered whether the creek would get much higher. But a few inches more and it would overflow its banks. There seemed to be a feeling of uneasiness among the people. They seemed to fear that something awful was going to happen. Their suspicions were strengthened by the fact that warning had come down the valley for the people to be on the lookout. The rains had swollen everything to the bursting point. The day passed slowly, however. Noon came and went, and still nothing happened. We could not proceed, nor could we go back, as the tracks about a mile below Conemaugh had been washed away, so there was nothing for us to do but to wait and see what would come next.

"Some time after three o'clock Friday afternoon I went into the train dispatcher's office to learn the latest news. I had not been there long when

I heard a fierce whistling from an engine away up the mountain. Rushing out I found dozens of men standing around. Fear had blanched every cheek. The loud and continued whistling had made every one feel that something serious was going to happen. In a few moments I could hear a train rattling down the mountain. About five hundred yards above Conemaugh the tracks make a slight curve and we could not see beyond this. The suspense was something awful. We did not know what was coming, but no one could get rid of the thought that something was wrong at the dam.

"Our suspense was not very long, however. Nearer and nearer the train came, the thundering sound still accompanying it. There seemed to be something behind the train, as there was a dull, rumbling sound which I knew did not come from the train. Nearer and nearer it came; a moment more and it would reach the curve. The next instant there burst upon our eyes a sight that made every heart stand still. Rushing around the curve, snorting and tearing, came an engine and several gravel cars. The train appeared to be putting forth every effort to go faster. Nearer it came, belching forth smoke and whistling long and loud. But the most terrible sight was to follow. Twenty feet behind came surging along a mad rush of water fully fifty feet high. Like the train,

it seemed to be putting forth every effort to push
along faster. Such an awful race we never before
witnessed. For an instant the people seemed
paralyzed with horror. They knew not what to
do, but in a moment they realized that a second's
delay meant death to them. With one accord they
rushed to the high lands a few hundred feet away.
Most of them succeeded in reaching that place
and were safe.

"I thought of the passengers in my train. The
second section of No. 8 had three sleepers. In
these three cars were about thirty people, who
rushed through the train crying to the others
'Save yourselves!' Then came a scene of the
wildest confusion. Ladies and children shrieked
and the men seemed terror-stricken. I succeeded
in helping some ladies and children off the train
and up to the high lands. Running back, I
caught up two children and ran for my life to a
higher place. Thank God, I was quicker than the
flood! I deposited my load in safety on the high
land just as it swept past us.

"For nearly an hour we stood watching the
mad flood go rushing by. The water was full of
debris. When the flood caught Conemaugh it
dashed against the little town with a mighty
crash. The water did not lift the houses up and
carry them off, but crushed them up one against
the other and broke them up like so many egg-

shells. Before the flood came there was a pretty little town. When the waters passed on there was nothing but a few broken boards to mark the central portion of the city. It was swept as clean as a newly-brushed floor. When the flood passed onward down the valley I went over to my train. It had been moved back about twenty yards, but it was not damaged. About fifteen persons had remained in the train and they were safe. Of the three trains ours was the luckiest. The engines of both the others had been swept off the track, and one or two cars in each train had met the same fate. What saved our train was the fact that just at the curve which I mentioned the valley spread out. The valley is six or seven hundred yards broad where our train was standing. This, of course, let the floods pass out. It was only about twenty feet high when it struck our train, which was about in the middle of the valley. This fact, together with the elevation of the track, was all that saved us. We stayed that night in the houses in Conemaugh that had not been destroyed. The next morning I started down the valley and by four o'clock in the afternoon had reached Conemaugh furnace, eight miles west of Johnstown. Then I got a team and came home.

"In my tramp down the valley I saw some awful sights. On the tree branches hung shreds of clothing torn from the unfortunates as they were whirled along in the terrible rush of the torrent. Dead bodies were lying by scores along the banks of the creeks. One woman I helped drag from the mud had tightly clutched in her hand a paper. We tore it out of her hand and found it to be a badly water-soaked photograph. It was probably a picture of the drowned woman."

Pemberton Smith is a civil engineer employed by the Pennsylvania Railroad. On Friday, when the disaster occurred, he was at Johnstown, stopping at the Merchants' Hotel. What happened he described as follows:

" In the afternoon, with four associates, I spent the time playing checkers in the hotel, the streets being flooded during the day. At half-past four we were startled by shrill whistles. Thinking a fire was the cause, we looked out of the window. Great masses of people were rushing through the water in the street, which had been there all day, and still we thought the alarm was fire. All of a sudden the roar of the water burst upon our ears, and in an instant more the streets were filled with debris. Great houses and business blocks began to topple and crash into each other and go down as if they were toy-block houses. People in the streets were drowning on all sides. One of our company started down-stairs and was drowned.

The other four, including myself, started up-stairs, for the water was fast rising. When we got on the roof we could see whole blocks swept away as if by magic. Hundreds of people were floating by, clinging to roofs of houses, rafts, timbers, or anything they could get a hold of. The hotel began to tremble, and we made our way to an adjoining roof. Soon afterward part of the hotel went down. The brick structures seemed to fare worse than frame buildings, as the latter would float, while the brick would crash and tumble into one great mass of ruins. We finally climbed into a room of the last building in reach and stayed there all night, in company with one hundred and sixteen other people, among the number being a crazy man. His wife and family had all been drowned only a few hours before, and he was a raving maniac. And what a night! Sleep! Yes, I did a little, but every now and then a building near by would crash against us, and we would all jump, fearing that at last our time had come.

"Finally morning dawned. In company with one of my associates we climbed across the tops of houses and floating debris, built a raft, and poled ourselves ashore to the hillside. I don't know how the others escaped. This was seven o'clock on Saturday morning. We started on foot for South Fork, arriving there at three P. M. Here we found that all communication by telegraph and

railroad was cut off by the flood, and we had
naught to do but retrace our steps. Tired and
footsore! Well, I should say so. My gum-boots
had chafed my feet so I could hardly walk at all.
The distance we covered on foot was over fifty
miles. On Sunday we got a train to Altoona.
Here we found the railroad connections all cut off,
so we came back to Johnstown again on Monday.
And what a desolate place! I had to obtain a pass
to go over into the city. Here it is:

"Pass Pemberton Smith through all the streets.
"ALEC. HART, Chief of Police.
"A. J. MAXHAM, Acting Mayor."

"The tragic pen-pictures of the scenes in the
press dispatches have not been exaggerated.
They cannot be. The worse sight of all was to
see the great fire at the railroad-bridge. It makes
my blood fairly curdle to think of it. I could see
the lurid flames shoot heavenward all night Friday,
and at the same time hundreds of people were
floating right toward them on top of houses, etc.,
and to meet a worse death than drowning. To
look at a sight like this and not be able to render
a particle of assistance seemed awful to bear. I
had a narrow escape, truly. In my mind I can
hear the shrieks of men, women, and children, the
maniac's ravings, and the wild roar of a sea of
water sweeping everything before it."

VIEW ON FRANKLIN ST., JOHNSTOWN.

Among the lost was Miss Jennie Paulson, a passenger on a railroad train, whose fate is thus described by one of her comrades :

"We had been making but slow progress all the day. Our train lay at Johnstown nearly the whole day of Friday. We then proceeded as far as Conemaugh, and had stopped from some cause or other, probably on account of the flood. Miss Paulson and a Miss Bryan were seated in front of me. Miss Paulson had on a plaid dress, with shirred waist of red cloth goods. Her companion was dressed in black. Both had lovely corsage bouquets of roses. I had heard that they had been attending a wedding before they left Pittsburg. The Pitttsburg lady was reading a novel entitled *Miss Lou.* Miss Bryan was looking out of the window. When the alarm came we all sprang toward the door, leaving everything behind us. I had just reached the door when poor Miss Paulson and her friend, who were behind me, decided to return for their rubbers, which they did. I sprang from the car into a ditch next the hillside, in which the water was already a foot and a-half deep, and, with the others, climbed up the mountain side for our very lives. We had to do so, as the water glided up after us like a huge serpent. Any one ten feet behind us would have been lost beyond a doubt. I glanced back at the train when I had reached a place of safety,

8

but the water already covered it, and the Pullman
car in which the ladies were was already rolling
down the valley in the grasp of the angry waters."

Mr. William Scheerer, the teller of the State
Banking Company, of Newark, N. J., was among
the passengers on the ill-fated day express on the
Pennsylvania Railroad that left Pittsburg at
eight o'clock A. M., on the now historic Friday,
bound for New York.

There was some delays incidental to the floods
in the Conemaugh Valley before the train reached
Johnstown, and a further delay at that point, and
the train was considerably behind time when it
left Johnstown. Said Mr. Scheerer: "The parlor
car was fully occupied when I went aboard the
train, and a seat was accordingly given me in the
sleeper at the rear end of the train. There were
several passengers in this car, how many I cannot
say exactly, among them some ladies. It was raining hard all the time and we were not a very excited nor a happy crowd, but were whiling away
the time in reading and in looking at the swollen
torrent of the river. Very few of the people were
apprehensive of any danger in the situation, even
after we had been held up at Conemaugh for
nearly five hours.

"The railroad tracks where our train stopped
were full fourteen feet above the level of the
river, and there was a large number of freight

and passenger cars and locomotives standing on
the tracks near us and strung along up the road
for a considerable distance. Between the road
and the hill that lay at our left there was a ditch,
through which the water that came down from the
hill was running like a mill-race. It was a monot-
onous wait to all of us, and after a time many inquiries were made as to why we did not go ahead.
Some of the passengers who made the inquiry
were answered laconically—' Wash-out,' and with
this they had to be satisfied. I had been over the
road several times before, and knew of the existence of the dangerous and threatening dam up
in the South Fork gorge, and could not help connecting it in my mind with the cause of our delay.
But neither was I apprehensive of danger, for the
possibility of the dam giving away had been often
discussed by passengers in my presence, and
everybody supposed that the utmost damage it
would do when it broke, as everybody believed it
sometime would, would be to swell a little higher
the current that tore down through the Conemaugh Valley.

"Such a possibility as the carrying away of a
train of cars on the great Pennsylvania road was
never seriously entertained by anybody. We had
stood stationary until about four o'clock, when
two colored porters went through the car within
a short time of each other, looking and acting

rather excited. I asked the first one what the
matter was, and he replied that he did not know.
I inferred from his reply that if there was any
thing serious up, the passengers would be informed, and so I went on reading. When the
next man came along I asked him if the reservoir
had given way, and he said he thought it had.

"I put down my book and stepped out quickly
to the rear platform, and was horrified at the sight
that met my gaze up the valley. It seemed as if
a forest was coming down upon us. There was
a great wall of water roaring and grinding swiftly
along, so thickly studded with the trees from
along the mountain sides that it looked like a
gigantic avalanche of trees. Of course I lingered
but an instant, for the mortal danger we all were
in flashed upon me at the first sight of that terrible on-coming torrent. But in that instant I saw
an engine lifted bodily off the track and thrown
over backward into the whirlpool, where it disappeared, and houses crushed and broken up in the
flash of an eye.

"The noise was like incessant thunder. I turned
back into the car and shouted to the ladies, three
of whom alone were in the car at the moment, to
fly for their lives. I helped them out of the car
on the side toward the hill, and urged them to
jump across the ditch and run for their lives. Two
of them did so, but the third, a rather heavy lady,

a missionary, who was on her way to a foreign station, hesitated for an instant, doubtful if she could make the jump. That instant cost her her life. While I was holding out my hand to her and urging her to jump, the rush of waters came down and swept her, like a doll, down into the torrent. In the same instant an engine was thrown from the track into the ditch at my feet. The water was about my knees as I turned and scrambled up the hill, and when I looked back, ten seconds later, it was surging and grinding ten feet deep over the track I had just left.

"The rush of waters lasted three-quarters of an hour, while we stood rapt and spell-bound in the rain, looking at the ruin no human agency could avert. The scene was beyond the power of language to describe. You would see a building standing in apparent security above the swollen banks of the river, the people rushing about the doors, some seeming to think that safety lay indoors, while others rushed toward higher ground, stumbling and falling in the muddy streets, and then the flood rolled over them, crushing in the house with a crash like thunder, and burying house and people out of sight entirely. That, of course, was the scene of only an instant, for our range of vision was only over a small portion of the city.

"We sought shelter from the rain in the home of a farmer who lived high up on the side-hill,

and the next morning walked down to Johnstown
and viewed the ruins. It seemed as if the city
was utterly destroyed. The water was deep
over all the city and few people were visible. We
returned to Conemaugh and were driven over
the mountains to Ebensburg, where we took the
train for Altoona, but finding we could get no
further in that direction we turned back to Ebensburg, and from there went by wagon to Johnstown, where we found a train that took us to
Pittsburg. I got home by the New York
Central."

CHAPTER X.

EDWARD H. JACKSON, who worked in the Cambria Iron Works, told the following story:

"When we were going to work Friday morning at seven o'clock, May 31st, the water in the river was about six inches below the top of the banks, the rains during the night having swollen it. We were used to floods about this time of the year, the water always washing the streets and running into the cellars, so we we did not pay much attention to this fact. It continued rising, and about nine o'clock we left work in order to go back to our homes and take our furniture and carpets to the upper floors, as we had formerly done on similar occasions. At noon the water was on our first floors, and kept rising until there was five feet of water in our homes. It was still raining hard. We were all in the upper stories about half-past four, when the first intimation we had of anything unusual was a frightful crash, and the same moment our house toppled over.

135

Jumping to the windows, we saw the water rushing down the streets in immense volumes, carrying with it houses, barns, and, worst of all, screaming, terrified men, women, and children. In my house were Colonel A. N. Hart, who is my uncle, his wife, sister, and two children. They watched their chance, and when a slowly moving house passed by they jumped to the roof and by careful manœuvring managed to reach Dr. S. M. Swan's house, a three-story brick building, where there were about two hundred other people. I jumped on to a tender of an engine as it floated down and reached the same house. All the women and children were hysterical, most of the men were paralyzed by terror, and to describe the scene is simply impossible. From the windows of this house we threw ropes to persons who floated by on the roofs of houses, and in this way we saved several.

"Our condition in the house was none of the pleasantest. There was nothing to eat; it was impossible to sleep, even had any one desired to do so; when thirsty we were compelled to catch the rain-water as it fell from the roof and drink it. Other people had gone for safety in the same manner as we had to two other brick houses, H. Y. Hawse's residence and Alma Hall's, and they went through precisely the same experience as we did. Many of our people were badly injured and cut, and they were tended bravely and well by Dr. W. E. Matthews, although he himself was badly injured. During the evening we saved by ropes W. Forrest Rose, his wife, daughter, and four boys. Mr. Rose's collar-bone and one rib were broken. After a fearful night we found, when day broke, that the water had subsided, and I and some others of the men crawled out upon the rubbish and debris to search for food, for our people were starving. All we could find were water-soaked crackers and some bananas, and these were eagerly eaten by the famished sufferers.

"Then, during the morning, began the thieving. I saw men bursting open trunks, putting valuables in their pockets, and then looking for more. I did not know these people, but I am sure they must have lived in the town, for surely no others could have got there at this time. A meeting was held, Colonel Hart was made Chief of Police, and he at once gave orders that any one caught stealing should be shot without warning. Notwithstanding this we afterward found scores of bodies, the fingers of which were cut off, the fiends not wishing to waste time to take off the rings. Many corpses of women were seen from which the ears had been cut, in order to secure the diamond earrings.

" Then, to add to our horrors, the debris piled

up against the bridge caught fire, and as the streets were full of oil, it was feared that the flames would extend backwards, but happily for us this was not the case. It was pitiful to hear the cries of those who had been caught in the rubbish, and, after having been half drowned, had to face death as inevitable as though bound to a stake. The bodies of those burned to death will never be recognized, and of those drowned many were so badly disfigured by being battered against the floating houses that they also will be unrecognizable. It is said that Charles Butler, the assistant treasurer of the Cambria Iron Works, who was in the Hurlburt House, convinced that he could not escape and wishing his body to be recognized, pinned his photograph and a letter to the lapel of his coat, where they were found when his body was recovered. I have lost everything I owned in the world," said Mr. Jackson, in conclusion, "and hundreds of others are in the same condition. The money in the banks is all right, however, for it was stowed away in the vaults."

Frank McDonald, a railroad conductor, says:

"I certainly think I saw one thousand bodies go over the bridge. The first house that came down struck the bridge and at once took fire, and as fast as the others came down they were consumed. I believe I am safe in saying I saw one thousand bodies burn. It reminded me of a lot of flies on fly-paper struggling to get away, with no hope and no chance to save them. I have no idea that had the bridge been blown up the loss of life would have been any less. They would have floated a little further with the same certain death. Then, again, it was impossible for any one to have reached the bridge in order to blow it up, for the waters came so fast that no one could have done it."

Michael Renesen tells a wonderful story of his escape. He says he was walking down Main Street when he heard a rumbling noise, and, looking around, he imagined it was cloud, but in a minute the water was upon him. He floated with the tide for some time, when he was struck with some floating timber and borne underneath the water. When he came up he was struck again, and at last he was caught by a lightning rod and held there for over two hours, when he was finally rescued.

Mrs. Anne Williams was sitting sewing when the flood came on. She heard some people crying and jumped out of the window and succeeded in getting on the roof of an adjoining house. Under the roof she heard the cries of men and women, and saw two men and a woman with their heads just above the water, crying "For God's sake, either kill us outright or rescue us!"

Mrs. Williams cried for help for the drowning

people, but none came, and she saw them give up one by one.

James F. McCanagher had a thrilling experience in the water. He saw his wife was safe on land, and thought his only daughter, a girl aged about twenty-one, was also saved, but just as he was making for the shore he saw her and went to rescue her. He succeeded in getting within about ten feet of land, when the girl said, " Good-bye, father," and expired in his arms before he reached the shore.

James M. Walters, an attorney, spent Friday night in Alma Hall, and relates a thrilling story. One of the most curious occurrences of the whole disaster was how Mr. Walters got to the hall. He has his office on the second floor. His home is at No. 135 Walnut Street. He says he was in the house with his family when the waters struck it. All was carried away. Mr. Walters' family drifted on a roof in another direction ; he passed down several streets and alleys until he came to the hall. His dwelling struck that edifice and he was thrown into his own office. About three hundred persons had taken refuge in the hall and were on the second, third, and fourth stories. The men held a meeting and drew up some rules which all were bound to respect.

Mr. Walters was chosen president, and Rev. Mr. Beale was put in charge of the first floor, A.

M. Hart of the second floor, Dr. Matthews of the fourth floor. No lights were allowed, and the whole night was spent in darkness. The sick were cared for, the weaker women and children had the best accommodation that could be had, while the others had to wait. The scenes were most agonizing. Heartrending shrieks, sobs, and moans pierced the gloomy darkness. The crying of children mingled with the suppressed sobs of the women. Under the guardianship of the men all took more hope. No one slept during all the long, dark night. Many knelt for hours in prayer, their supplications mingling with the roar of the waters and the shrieks of the dying in the surrounding houses.

In all this misery two women gave premature birth to children. Dr. Matthews is a hero— several of his ribs were crushed by a falling timber, and his pains were most severe. Yet through all he attended the sick. When two women in a house across the street shouted for help, he, with two other brave young men, climbed across the drift and ministered to their wants. No one died during the night, but a woman and children surrendered their lives on the succeeding day as a result of terror and fatigue. Miss Rose Young, one of the young ladies in the hall, was frightfully cut and bruised. Mrs. Young had a leg broken. All of Mr. Walters' family were saved.

Mrs. J. F. Moore, wife of a Western Union Telegraph employee in Pittsburg, escaped with her two children from the devastated city just one hour before the flood had covered their dwelling-place. Mr. Moore had arranged to have his family move Thursday from Johnstown and join him in Pittsburg. Their household goods were shipped on Thursday and Friday. The little party caught the last train which made the trip between Johnstown and Pittsburg.

Mrs. Moore told her story. " Oh ! it was terrible," she said. " The reservoir had not yet burst when we left, but the boom had broken, and before we got out of the house the water filled the cellar. On the way to the depot the water was high up on the carriage wheels. Our train left at quarter to two P. M., and at that time the flood had begun to rise with terrible rapidity. Houses and sheds were carried away and two men were drowned almost before our eyes. People gathered on the roofs to take refuge from the water, which poured into the lower rooms of their dwellings, and many families took flight and became scattered. Just as the train pulled out I saw a woman crying bitterly. Her house had been flooded and she had escaped, leaving her husband behind, and her fears for his safety made her almost crazy. Our house was in the lower part of the town, and it makes me shudder to

think what would have happened had we remained in it an hour longer. So far as I know,
we were the only passengers from Johnstown on
the train."

, Mrs. Moore's little son told the reporter that
he had seen the rats driven out of their holes by
the flood and running along the tops of the
fences.

One old man named Parsons, with his wife and
children, as soon as the water struck their house,
took to the roof and were carried down to the
stone bridge, where the back wash of the Stony
Creek took them back up along the banks and
out of harm's way, but not before a daughter-in-
law became a prey to the torrent. He has lived
here for thirty-five years, and had acquired a nice,
comfortable home. To-day all is gone, and as he
told the story he pointed to a rather seedy-looking
coat he had on. " I had to ask a man for it. It's
hard, but I am ruined, and I am too old to begin
over again."

Mr. Lewis was a well-to-do young man, and
owned a good property where now is a barren
waste. When the flood came the entire family of
eight took to the roof, and were carried along on
the water. Before they reached the stone bridge,
a family of four that had floated down from
Woodvale, two and a half miles distant, on a raft,
got off to the roof of the Lewis House, where the

entire twelve persons were pushed to the bank of
the river above the bridge, and all were saved.
When Mr. Lewis was telling his story he seemed
grateful to the Almighty for his safety while thousands were lost to him.

Another young man who had also taken to a
friendly roof, became paralyzed with fear, and
stripping himself of his clothes flung himself from
the housetop into the stream and tried to swim.
The force of the water rushed him over to the
west bank of the river, where he was picked up
soon after.

A baby's cradle was fished out of a ruin and
the neatly tucked-in sheets and clothes, although
soiled with mud, gave evidence of luxury. The
entire family was lost, and no one is here to lay
claim to baby's crib. In the ruin of the Penn
House the library that occupied the extension was
entirely gone, while the brick front was taken out
and laid bare the parlor floor, in which the piano,
turned upside down, was noticeable, while several
chandeliers were scattered on top.

MAIN AND CLINTON STREETS, LOOKING SOUTHWEST.

CHAPTER XI.

THE first survivors of the Johnstown wreck who arrived at Pittsburg were Joseph and Henry Lauffer and Lew Dalmeyer. They endured considerable hardship and had several narrow escapes with their lives. Their story of the disaster can best be told in their own language. Joe, the youngest of the Lauffer brothers, said :

" My brother and I left on Thursday for Johnstown. The night we arrived there it rained continually, and on Friday morning it began to flood. I started for the Cambria store at a quarter-past eight on Friday, and in fifteen minutes afterward I had to get out of the store in a wagon, the water was running so rapidly. We then arrived at the station and took the day express and went as far as Conemaugh, where we had to stop. The limited, however, got through, and just as we were about to start the bridge at South Fork gave way with a terrific crash, and we had to stay there. We then went to Johnstown. This

9   147

was at a quarter to ten in the morning, when the flood was just beginning. The whole city of Johnstown was inundated and the people all moved up to the second floor.

"Now this is where the trouble occurred. These poor unfortunates did not know the reservoir would burst, and there are no skiffs in Johnstown to escape in. When the South Fork basin gave way mountains of water twenty feet high came rushing down the Conemaugh River, carrying before them death and destruction. I shall never forget the harrowing scene. Just think of it! thousands of people, men, and women, and children, struggling and weeping and wailing as they were being carried suddenly away in the raging current. Houses were picked up as if they were but a feather, and their inmates were all carried away with them, while cries of 'God help me!' 'Save me!' 'I am drowning!' 'My child!' and the like were heard on all sides. Those who were lucky enough to escape went to the mountains, and there they beheld the poor unfortunates being crushed to death among the debris without any chance of being rescued. Here and there a body was seen to make a wild leap into the air and then sink to the bottom.

"At the stone bridge of the Pennsylvania Railroad people were dashed to death against the piers. When the fire started there hundreds of bodies were burned. Many lookers-on up on the mountains, especially the woman, fainted."

Mr. Lauffer's brother, Harry, then told his part of the tale, which was not less interesting. He said: "We had a series of narrow escapes, and I tell you we don't want to be around when anything of that kind occurs again.

" The scenes at Johnstown have not in the least been exaggerated, and, indeed, the worst is to be heard. When we got to Conemaugh and just as we were about to start the bridge gave way. This left the day express, the accommodation, a special train, and a freight train at the station. Above was the South Fork water basin, and all of the trains were well filled. We were discussing the situation when suddenly, without any warning, the whistles of every engine began to shriek, and in the noise could be heard the warning of the first engineer, 'Fly for your lives! Rush to the mountains, the reservoir has burst.' Then with a thundering peal came the mad rush of waters. No sooner had the cry been heard than those who could rushed from the train with a wild leap and up the mountains. To tell this story takes some time, but the moments in which the horrible scene was enacted were few. Then came the avalanche of water, leaping and rushing with tremendous force. The waves had angry crests of white, and their roar was something deafening. In one terrible swath they caught the four trains and lifted three of them right off the track, as if they were only a cork. There they floated in the river. Think of it, three large locomotives and finely finished Pullmans floating around, and above all the hundreds of poor unfortunates who were unable to escape from the car swiftly drifting toward death. Just as we were about to leap from the car I saw a mother, with a smiling, blue-eyed baby in her arms. I snatched it from her and leaped from the train just as it was lifted off the track. The mother and child were saved, but if one more minute had elapsed we all would have perished.

"During all of this time the waters kept rushing down the Conemaugh and through the beautiful town of Johnstown, picking up everything and sparing nothing.

"The mountains by this time were black with people, and the moans and sighs from those below brought tears to the eyes of the most stony-hearted. There in that terrible rampage were brothers, sisters, wives and husbands, and from the mountain could be seen the panic-stricken marks in the faces of those who were struggling between life and death. I really am unable to do justice to the scene, and its details are almost beyond my power to relate. Then came the burning of the debris near the Pennsylvania Railroad bridge. The scene was too sickening to endure. We left the spot and journeyed across country and delivered many notes, letters, etc., that were intrusted to us.

The gallant young engineer, John G. Parke, whose ride of warning has already been described, relates the following:

"On Thursday night I noticed that the dam was in good order and the water was nearly seven feet from the top. When the water is at this height the lake is then nearly three miles in length. It rained hard on Thursday night and I rode up to the end of the lake on the eventful day and saw that the woods around there was teeming with a seething cauldron of water. Colonel Unger, the president of the fishing club that owns the property, put twenty-five Italians to work to fix the dam. A farmer in the vicinity also lent a willing hand. To strengthen the dam a plow was run along the top of it, and earth was then thrown into the furrows. On the west side a channel was dug and a sluice was constructed. We cut through about four feet of shale rock, when we came to solid rock which was impossible to cut without blasting. Once we got the channel open the water leaped down to the bed-rock, and a stream fully twenty feet wide and three feet deep rushed out on that end of the dam, while great quantities of water were coming in by the pier at the other end. And then in the face of this great escape of water from the dam, it kept rising at the rate of ten inches an hour.

"At noon I fully believed that it was practically impossible to save the dam, and I got on a horse and galloped down to South Fork, and gave the alarm, telling the people at the same time of their danger, and advising them to get to a place of safety. I also sent a couple of men to the telegraph tower, two miles away, to send messages to Johnstown and Cambria and to the other points on the way. The young girl at the instrument fainted when the news reached her, and was carried away. Then, by the timely warning given, the people at South Fork had an opportunity to move their household goods and betake themselves to a place of safety. Only one person was drowned in that place, and he was trying to save an old washtub that was floating downstream.

"It was noon when the messages were sent out, so that the people of Johnstown had just three hours to fly to a place of safety. Why they did not heed the warning will never be told. I then remounted my horse and rode to the dam, expecting at every moment to meet the lake rushing down the mountain-side, but when I reached there I found the dam still intact, although the water had then reached the top of it. At one p. m. I walked over the dam, and then the water was about three inches on it, and was gradually gnawing away its face. As the stream leaped down the outer face, the water was rapidly wearing down the edge of the embankment, and I knew that it was a question of but a few hours. From my knowledge I should say there was fully ten million tons of water in the lake at one o'clock, while the pressure was largely increased by the swollen streams that flowed into it, but even then the dam could have stood it if the level of the water had been kept below the top. But, coupled with this, there was the constantly trickling of the water over the sides, which was slowly but surely wearing the banks away.

"The big break took place at just three o'clock, and it was about ten feet wide at first and shallow; but when the opening was made the fearful rushing waters opened the gap with such increasing rapidity that soon after the entire lake leaped out and started on its fearful march of death down the Valley of the Conemaugh. It took but forty minutes to drain that three miles of water, and the downpour of millions of tons of water was irresistible. The big boulders and great rafters and logs that were in the bed of the river were picked up, like so much chaff, and carried down the torrent for miles. Trees that stood fully seventy-five feet in height and four feet through were snapped off like pipe-stems."

CHAPTER XII.

ONE of the most thrilling incidents of the disaster was the performance of A. J. Leonard, whose family reside in Morrellville. He was
at work, and hearing that his house had been
swept away, determined at all hazards to ascertain
the fate of his family. The bridges having been
carried away, he constructed a temporary raft, and
clinging to it as close as a cat to the side of a
fence, he pushed his frail craft out in the raging
torrent and started on a chase which, to all who
were watching, seemed to mean an embrace in
death.

Heedless of cries "For God's sake, go back,
you will be drowned," and "Don't attempt it,"
he persevered. As the raft struck the current he
threw off his coat and in his shirt sleeves braved
the stream. Down plungèd the boards and down
went Leonard, but as it rose he was seen still
clinging. A mighty shout arose from the throats
of the hundreds on the banks, who were now

154

deeply interested, earnestly hoping he would suc-
cessfully ford the stream.

Down again went his bark, but nothing, it
seemed, could shake Leonard off. The craft shot
up in the air apparently ten or twelve feet, and
Leonard stuck to it tenaciously. Slowly but surely
he worked his boat to the other side of the stream,
and after what seemed an awful suspense he
finally landed, amid ringing cheers of men, women,
and children.

The scenes at Heanemyer's planing-mill at
Nineveh, where the dead bodies are lying, are
never to be forgotten. The torn, bruised, and
mutilated bodies of the victims are lying in a row
on the floor of the planing-mill, which looks more
like the field of Bull Run after that disastrous
battle than a workshop. The majority of the
bodies are nude, their clothing having been torn
off. All along the river bits of clothing—a tiny
shoe, a baby dress, a mother's evening wrapper, a
father's coat—and, in fact, every article of wearing
apparel imaginable, may be seen hanging to
stumps of trees and scattered on the bank.

One of the most pitiful sights of this terrible
disaster came to notice when the body of a young
lady was taken out of the Conemaugh River. The
woman was apparently quite young, though her
features were terribly disfigured. Nearly all the
clothing excepting the shoes was torn off the

body. The corpse was that of a mother, for, although cold in death, she clasped a young male babe, apparently not more than a year old, tightly in her arms. The little one was huddled close up to the face of the mother, who, when she realized their terrible fate, had evidently raised it to her lips to imprint upon its lips the last kiss it was to receive in this world. The sight forced many a stout heart to shed tears. The limp bodies, with matted hair, some with holes in their heads, eyes knocked out, and all bespattered with blood were a ghastly spectacle.

Mr. J. M. Fronheiser, one of the Superintendents in the Cambria Iron Works, lived on Main Street. His house was one of the first to go, and he himself, his wife, two daughters, son, and baby were thrown into the raging torrent. His wife and eldest daughter were lost. He, with the baby, reached a place of safety, and his ten-year-old boy and twelve-year-old girl floated near enough to be reached. He caught the little girl, but she cried:

"Let me go, papa, and save brother; my leg is broken and my foot is caught below."

When he told her he was determined to rescue her, she exclaimed:.

"Then, papa, get a sharp knife and cut my leg off. I can stand it.".

The little fellow cried to his father: " You can't

save me, papa. Both my feet are caught fast, and I can't hold out any longer. Please get a pistol and shoot me."

Captain Gageby, of the army, and some neighbors helped to rescue both children. The girl displayed Spartan fortitude and pluck. All night long she lay in a bed without a mattress or medical attention in a garret, the water reaching to the floor below, without a murmur or a whimper. In the morning she was carried down-stairs, her leg dangling under her, but when she saw her father at the foot of the stairs, she whispered to Captain Gageby:

"Poor papa; he is so sad." Then, turning to her father, she threw a kiss with her hands and laughingly said, "Good morning, papa; I'm all right."

The Pennsylvania Railroad Company's operators at Switch Corner, "S. Q.," which is near Sang Hollow, tell thrilling stories of the scenes witnessed by them on Friday afternoon and evening. Said one of them:

"In order to give you an idea of how the tidal wave rose and fell, let me say that I kept a measure and timed the rise and fall of the water, and in forty-eight minutes it fell four and a half feet.

"I believe that when the water goes down about seventy-five children and fifty grown persons will be found among the weeds and bushes in the bend of the river just below the tower.

"There the current was very strong, and we saw dozens of people swept under the trees, and I don't believe that more than one in twenty came out on the other side."

"They found a little girl in white just now," said one of the other operators.

"O God!" said the chief operator. "She isn't dead, is she?"

"Yes; they found her in a clump of willow bushes, kneeling on a board, just about the way we saw her when she went down the river." Turning to me he said:

"That was the saddest thing we saw all day yesterday. Two men came down on a little raft, with a little girl kneeling between them, and her hands raised and praying. She came so close to us we could see her face and that she was crying. She had on a white dress and looked like a little angel. She went under that cursed shoot in the willow bushes at the bend like all the rest, but we did hope she would get through alive."

"And so she was still kneeling?" he said to his companion, who had brought the unwelcome news.

"She sat there," was the reply, "as if she was still praying, and there was a smile on her poor little face, though her mouth was full of mud."

Driving through the mountains a correspondent picked up a ragged little chap not much more than big enough to walk. From his clothing he was evidently a refugee.

"Where are your folks?" he was asked.

"We're living at Aunty's now."

"Did you all get out?"

"Oh! we're all right—that is, all except two of sister's babies. Mother and little sister wasn't home, and they got out all right."

"Where were you?"

"Oh! I was at sister's house. We was all in the water and fire. Sister's man—her husband, you know—took us up-stairs, and he punched a hole through the roof, and we all climbed out and got saved."

"How about the babies?"

"Oh! sister was carrying two of them in her arms, and the bureau hit her and knocked them out, so they went down."

The child had unconsciously caught one of the oddest and most significant tricks of speech that have arisen from the calamity. Nobody here speaks of a person's having been drowned, or killed, or lost, or uses any other of the general expressions for sudden death. They have simply "gone down." Everybody here seems to avoid harsh words in referring to the possible affliction of another. Euphonistic phrases are substituted for plain questions. Two old friends met for the first time since the disaster.

"I'm glad to see you," exclaimed the first. "Are you all right?"

"Yes, I'm doing first rate," was the reply.

The first friend looked awkwardly about a moment, and then asked with suppressed eagerness:

"And—and your family—are they all—well?"

There was a world of significance in the hesitation before the last word.

"Yes. Thank God! not one of them went down."

A man who looked like a prosperous banker, and who had evidently come from a distance drove through the mountains toward South Fork. On the way he met a handsome young man in a silk hat, mounted on a mule. The two shook hands eagerly.

"Have you anything?"

"Nothing. What have you?"

"Nothing."

The younger man turned about and the two rode on silently through the forest road. Inquiry later developed the fact that the banker-looking man was really a banker whose daughter had been lost from one of the overwhelmed trains. The young man was his son. Both had been searching for some clue to the young woman's fate.

CHAPTER XIII.

IT was not "good morning" in Johnstown nor "good night" that passed as a salutation between neighbors who meet for the first time since the deluge, but "How many of your folks gone?" It is always "folks," always "gone." You heard it everywhere among the crowds that thronged the viaduct and looked down upon the ghastly twenty acres of unburied dead, from which dynamite was making a terrible exhumation of the corpses of two thousand mortals and five hundred houses. You heard it at the rope bridge, where the crowds waited the passage of the incessant file of empty coffins. You heard it upon the steep hillside beyond the valley of devastation, where the citizens of Johnstown had fled into the borough of Conemaugh for shelter. You heard it again, the first salutation, whenever a friend, who had been searching for *his* dead, met a neighbor: "Are any of your friends gone?"

It was not said in tears or even seemingly in madness. It had simply come to be the "how-d'ye-do" of the eleven thousand people who survived the twenty-nine thousand five hundred people of the valley of the Conemaugh.

Still finding bodies by scores in the debris; still burying the dead and caring for the wounded; still feeding the famishing and housing the homeless, was the record for days following the one on which Johnstown was swept away. A perfect stream of wagons bearing the dead as fast as they were discovered was constantly filing to the various improvised morgues where the bodies were taken for identification. Hundreds of people were constantly crowding to these temporary houses, one of which was located in each of the suburban boroughs that surround Johnstown. Men armed with muskets, uniformed sentinels, constituting the force that guarded the city while it was practically under martial law, stood at the doors and admitted the crowd by tens.

In the central dead-house in Johnstown proper there lay two rows of ghastly dead. To the right were twenty bodies that had been identified. They were mostly women and children, and they were entirely covered with white sheets, and a piece of paper bearing the name was pinned at the feet. To the left were eighteen bodies of the unknown dead. As the people passed they were hurried along by an attendant and gazed at the uncovered faces seeking to identify them. All

RUINS, CORNER MAIN AND CLINTON STS.

applicants for admission, if it was thought they were prompted by idle curiosity, were not allowed to enter. The central morgue was formerly a school-house, and the desks were used as biers for the dead bodies. Three of the former pupils lay on the desks dead, with white pieces of paper pinned on the white sheets that covered them, giving their names.

But what touching scenes are enacted every hour about this mournful building! Outside the sharp voices of the sentinels are constantly shouting: " Move on." Inside weeping women and sad-faced, hollow-eyed men are bending over loved and familiar faces. Back on the steep grassy hill which rises abruptly on the other side of the street are crowds of curious people who have come in from the country round about to look at the wreckage strewn around where Johnstown was.

" Oh! Mr. Jones," a pale-faced woman asks, walking up, sobbing, " can't you tell me where we can get a coffin to bury Johnnie's body?"

" Do you know," asks a tottering old man, as the pale-faced woman turns away, " whether they have found Jennie and the children ?"

" Jennie's body has just been found at the bridge," is the answer, " but the children can't be found."

Jennie is the old man's widowed daughter, and was drowned, with her two children, while her

10

husband was at work over at the Cambria Mills.

Just a few doors below the school-house morgue is the central office of the "Registry Bureau." This was organized by Dr. Buchanan and H. G. Connaugh, for the purpose of having a registry made of all those who had escaped. They real- ized that it would be impossible to secure a com- plete list of dead, and that the only practicable thing was to get a complete list of the living. Then they would get all the Johnstown names, and by that means secure a list of the dead. That estimate will be based on figures secured by the subtraction of the total registry saved from total population of Johnstown and surrounding boroughs.

"I have been around *trying to find my sister- in-law, Mrs. Laura R. Jones, who is lost," said David L. Rogers.

"How do you know she is lost?" he was asked.

"Because I can't find her."

When persons can't be found it is taken as conclusive evidence that they have been drowned. It is believed that the flood has buried a great many people below the bridge in the ground lying just below the Cambria Works. Here the rush of waters covered the railroad tracks ten feet deep with a coating of stones. Whether they will ever be dug for remains to be seen. Meantime, those who are easier to reach will be hunted for. There are many corpses in the area of rubbish that drifted down and lodged against the stone bridge of the Pennsylvania Railroad. Out of this rubbish one thousand bodies have already been taken. The fire that was started by the driftwood touching against the burning Catholic Church as it floated down was still burning.

Walk almost anywhere through the devastated district and you will hear expressions like this: "Why, you see that pile of wreckage there. There are three bodies buried beneath that pile. I know them, for I lived next door. They are Mrs. Charles E. Kast and her daughter, who kept a tavern, and her bartender, C. S. Noble."

Henry Rogers, of Pittsburg, is here caring for his relatives. "I am scarcely in a condition to talk," he says. "The awful scenes I have just witnessed and the troubles of my relatives have almost unnerved me. My poor aunt, Mrs. William Slick, is now a raving maniac. Her husband was formerly the County Surveyor. He felt that the warning about the dam should not be disregarded. Accordingly he made preparations to go to a place of safety. His wife was just recovering from an illness, but he had to take her on horseback, and there was no time to get a carriage. They escaped, but all their property was washed away. Mrs. Slick for a time talked cheerfully enough, and said they should be thankful they had escaped with their lives. But on Sunday it was noticed that she was acting strangely. By night she was insane. I suppose the news that some relatives had perished was what turned her mind. I am much afraid that Mrs. Slick is not the only one in Johnstown whose reason has been dethroned by the calamity. I have talked with many citizens, and they certainly seem crazy to me. When the excitement passes off I suppose they will regain their reason. The escape of my uncle, George R. Slick, and his wife, I think was really providential. They, too, had determined to heed the warning that the dam was unsafe. When the flood came they had a carriage waiting at the front door. Just as they were entering it, the water came. How it was, my aunt cannot tell me, but they both managed to catch on to some debris, and were thus floated along. My aunt says she has an indistinct recollection of some one having helped her upon the roof of a house. The person who did her this service was lost. All night they floated along on the roof. They suffered greatly from exposure, as the weather was extremely chilly. Next morning they were fortunately landed safely. My uncle, however, is now lying at the point of death. I have noticed a singular coincidence here. Down in the lower end of the city stood the United Presbyterian parsonage. The waters carried it two miles and a half, and landed it in Sandy Vale Cemetery. Strange as it may seem, the sexton's house in the cemetery was swept away and landed near the foundations of the parsonage. I have seen this myself, and it is commented on by many others."

In one place the roofs of forty frame houses were packed in together just as you would place forty bended cards one on top of another. The iron rods of a bridge were twisted into a perfect spiral six times around one of the girders. Just beneath it was a woman's trunk, broken up and half filled with sand, with silk dresses and a veil streaming out of it. From under the trunk men were lifting the body of its owner, perhaps, so burned, so horribly mutilated, so torn limb from limb that even the workmen, who have seen so many of these frightful sights that they have begun to get used to them, turned away sick at heart. In one place was a wrecked grocery store —bins of coffee and tea, flour, spices and nuts, parts of the counter and the safe mingled together. Near it was the pantry of a house, still partly intact, the plates and saucers regularly piled up, a waiter and a teapot, but not a sign of the wood-work, not a recognizable outline of a house.

In another place was a human foot, and crumbling indications of a boot, but no signs of a body.

A hay-rick, half ashes, stood near the centre of the gorge. Workmen who dug about it to-day found a chicken coop, and in it two chickens, not only alive but clucking happily when they were released. A woman's hat, half burned; a reticule, with part of a hand still clinging to it; two shoes and part of a dress told the story of one unfortunate's death. Close at hand a commercial traveler had perished. There was his broken valise, still full of samples, fragments of his shoes, and some pieces of his clothing.

Scenes like these were occurring all over the charred field where men were working with pick and axe and lifting out the poor, shattered remains of human beings, nearly always past recognition or identification, except by guess-work, or the locality where they were found. Articles of domestic use scattered through the rubbish helped to tell who some of the bodies were. Part of a set of dinner plates told one man where in the intangible mass his house was. In one place was a photograph album with one picture still recognizable. From this the body of a child near by was identified. A man who had spent a day and all night looking for the body of his wife, was directed to her remains by part of a trunk lid.

CHAPTER XIV.

THE language of pathos is too weak to describe the scenes where the living were searching for their loved and lost ones among the dead.

"That's Emma," said an old man before one of the bodies. He said it as coolly as though he spoke of his daughter in life, not in death, and as if it were not the fifth dead child of his that he had identified.

"Is that you, Mrs. James," said one woman to another on the foot-bridge over Stony Creek.

"Yes, it is, and we are all well," said Mrs. James.

"Oh, have you heard from Mrs. Fenton?"

"She's left," said the first woman, "but Mr. Fenton and the children are gone."

The scenes at the different relief agencies, where food, clothing, and provisions were given out on the order of the Citizens Committee, were extremely interesting. These were established at the Pennsylvania Railroad depot, at Peter's Hotel, in Adams Street, and in each of the suburbs.

At the depot, where there was a large force of police, the people were kept in files, and the relief articles were given out with some regularity, but at such a place as Kernsville, in the suburbs, the relief station was in the upper story of a partly wrecked house.

The yard was filled with boxes and barrels of bread, crackers, biscuit, and bales of blankets. The people crowded outside the yard in the street, and the provisions were handed to them over the fence, while the clothing was thrown to them from the upper windows. There was apparently great destitution in Kernsville.

"I don't care what it is, only so long as it will keep me warm," said one woman, whose ragged clothing was still damp.

The stronger women pushed to the front of the fence and tried to grab the best pieces of clothing which came from the windows, but the people in the house saw the game and tossed the clothing to those in the rear of the crowd. A man stood on a barrel of flour and yelled out what each piece of clothing was as it came down.

At each yell there was a universal cry of "That's just what I want. My boy is dying; he must have that. Throw me that for my poor wife," and the likes of that. Finally the clothing was all gone, and there were some people who didn't get any. They went away bewailing their misfortune.

A reporter was piloted to Kernsville by Kellog, a man who had lost his wife and baby in the flood.

"She stood right thar, sir," said the man, pointing to a house whose roof and front were gone. "She climbed up thar when the water came first and almost smashed the house. She had the baby in her arms. Then another house came down and dashed against ours, and my wife went down with the baby raised above her head. I saw it all from a tree thar. I couldn't move a step to help 'em."

Coming back, the same reporter met a man whose face was radiant. He fairly beamed good nature and kindness.

"You look happy," said the reporter.

"Yes, sir; I've found my boy," said the man.

"Is your house gone?" asked the reporter.

"Oh, of course," answered the man. "I've lost all I've got except my little boy," and he went on his way rejoicing.

A wealthy young Philadelphian named Ogle had become engaged to a Johnstown lady, Miss Carrie Diehl. They were to be wedded in the middle of June, and were preparing for the ceremony.

The lover heard of the terrible flood, but, knowing that the residence of his dear one was up in the hills, felt little fear for her safety. To make sure, however, he started for Johnstown. Near the Fourth Street morgue he met Mr. Diehl.

"Thank God! you are safe," he exclaimed, and then added : "Is Carrie well?"

"She was visiting in the valley when the wave came," was the mournful reply. Then he beckoned the young man to enter the chamber of death.

A moment later Mr. Ogle was kneeling beside the rough bier and was kissing the cold, white face. From the lifeless finger he slipped a ring and in its place put one of his own. Then he stole quietly out.

"Mamma! mamma!" cried a child. She had recognized a body that no one else could, and in a moment the corpse was ticketed, boxed, and delivered to laborers, who bore it away to join the long funeral procession.

A mother recognized a baby boy. "Keep it a few minutes," she asked the undertaker in charge. In a few moments she returned, carrying in her arms a little white casket. Then she hired two men to bear it to a cemetery. No hearses were seen in Johnstown. Relatives recognized their dead, secured the coffins, got them carried the best way they could to the morgues, then to the graveyards. A prayer, some tears, and a few more of the dead thousands were buried in mother earth.

A frequent visitor at these horrible places was David John Lewis. All over Johnstown he rode a powerful gray horse, and to each one he met whom he knew he exclaimed : "Have you seen my sisters?" Hardly waiting for a reply, he galloped away, either to seek ingress into a morgue or to ride along the river banks. One week before Mr. Lewis was worth $60,000, his all being invested in a large commission business. After the flood he owned the horse he rode, the clothes on his back, and that was all. In the fierce wave were buried five of his near relatives, sons, and his sisters Anna, Louise, and Maggie. The latter was married, and her little boy and babe were also drowned. They were all dearly loved by the merchant, who, crazed with grief and mounted on his horse, was a conspicuous figure in the ruined city.

. William Gaffney, an insurance agent, had a very pitiful duty to perform. On his father's and wife's side he lost fourteen relatives, among them his wife and family. He had a man to take the bodies to the grave, and he himself dug graves for his wife and children, and buried them. In speaking of the matter he said : "I never thought that I could perform such a sad duty, but I had to do it, and I did it. No one has any idea of the feelings of a man who acts as undertaker, grave-digger, and pall-bearer for his own family."

The saddest sight on the river bank was Mr. Gilmore, who lost his wife and family of five children. Ever since the calamity this old man was seen on the river bank looking for his family. He insisted on the firemen playing a stream of water on the place where the house formerly stood, and where he supposed the bodies lay. The firemen, recognizing his feelings, played the stream on the place, at intervals, for several hours, and at last the rescuers got to the spot where the old man said his house formerly stood. "I know the bodies are there, and you must find them." When at last one of the men picked up a charred skull, evidently that of a child, the old man exclaimed : "That is my child. There lies my family ; go on and get the rest of them." The workmen continued, and in a few minutes they came to the remains of the mother and three other children. There was only enough of their clothing left to recognize them by.

On the floor of William Mancarro's house, groaning with pain and grief, lay Patrick Madden, a furnaceman of the Cambria Iron Company. He told of his terrible experience in a voice broken with emotion. He said : "When the Cambria Iron Company's bridge gave way I was in the house of a neighbor, Edward Garvey. We were caught through our own neglect, like a great many others, and a few minutes before the houses were struck Garvey remarked that he was a good swimmer, and could get away no matter how high the water rose. Ten minutes later I saw him and his son-in-law drowned.

"No human being could swim in that terrible torrent of débris. After the South Fork Reservoir broke I was flung out of the building, and saw, when I rose to the surface of the water, my wife hanging upon a piece of scantling. She let it go and was drowned almost within reach of my arm, and I could not help or save her. I caught a log and floated with it five or six miles, but it was knocked from under me when I went over the dam. I then caught a bale of hay and was taken out by Mr. Morenrow.

"My wife is certainly drowned, and six children. Four of them were: James Madden, twenty-three years old; John, twenty-one years; Kate, seventeen years; and Mary, nineteen years.

A spring wagon came slowly from the ruins of what was once Cambria. In it, on a board and covered by a muddy cloth, were the remains of Editor C. T. Schubert, of the Johnstown *Free Press*, German. Behind the wagon walked his friend Benjamin Gribble. Editor Schubert was one of the most popular and well-known Germans in the city. He sent his three sons to Conemaugh Borough on Thursday, and on Friday afternoon he and his wife and six other children called at Mr. Gribble's residence. They noticed the rise of the water, but not until the flood from the burst dam washed the city did they anticipate danger. All fled from the first to the second floor. Then, as the water rose, they went to the attic, and Mr. Schubert hastily prepared a raft, upon which all embarked. Just as the raft reached the bridge, a heavy piece of timber swept the editor beneath the surface. The raft then glided through, and all the rest were rescued. Mr. Schubert's body was found beneath a pile of broken timbers.

A pitiful sight was that of an old, gray-haired man named Norn. He was walking around among the mass of débris, looking for his family. He had just sat down to eat his supper when the crash came, and the whole family, consisting of wife and eight children, were buried beneath the collapsed house. He was carried down the river to the railroad bridge on a plank. Just at the bridge a cross-tie struck him with such force that he was shot clear upon the pier, and was safe. But he is a mass of bruises and cuts from head to foot. He refused to go to the hospital until he found the bodies of his loved ones.

CHAPTER XV.

FIVE days after the disaster a bird's-eye view was taken of Johnstown from the top of a precipitous mountain which almost overhangs it. The first thing that impresses the eye, wrote the observer, is the fact that the proportion of the town that remains uninjured is much smaller than it seems to be from lower-down points of view. Besides the part of the town that is utterly wiped out, there are two great swaths cut through that portion which from lower down seems almost uninjured. Beginning at Conemaugh, two miles above the railroad bridge, along the right side of the valley looking down, there is a strip of an eighth by a quarter of a mile wide, which constituted the heart of a chain of continuous towns, and which was thickly built over for the whole distance, upon which now not a solitary building stands except the gutted walls of the Wood, Morrell & Co. general store in Johnstown, and of the Gautier wire mill and Woodvale flour mill at Woodvale. Except for these buildings, the whole two-mile strip is swept clean, not only of buildings, but of everything. It is a tract of mud, rocks, and such other miscellaneous débris as might follow the workings of a huge hydraulic placer mining system in the gold regions. In Johnstown itself, besides the total destruction upon this strip, extending at the end to cover the whole lower end of the city, there is a swath branching off from the main strip above the general store and running straight to the bluff. It is three blocks wide and makes a huge "Y," with the gap through which the flood came for the base and main strip and the swaths for branches. Between the branches there is a triangular block of buildings that are still standing, although most of them are damaged. At a point exactly opposite the corner where the branches of the "Y" meet, and distant from it by about fifty yards, is one of the freaks of the flood. The Baltimore and Ohio Railroad station, a square, two-story brick building, with a little cupola at the apex of its slanting roof, is apparently uninjured, but really one corner is knocked in and the whole interior is a total wreck. How it stood when everything anywhere near it was swept away is a mystery. Above the "Y"-shaped tract of ruin there is another still wider swath, bending around in Stony Creek, save on the left, where the flood

RUINS FROM SITE OF THE HULBURT HOUSE.

surged when it was checked and thrown back by
the railroad bridge. It swept things clean before
it through Johnstown and made a track of ruin
among the light frame houses for nearly two miles
up the gap. The Roman Catholic Church was
just at its upper edge. It is still standing, and
from its tower the bell strikes the hours regularly
as before, although everybody now is noticing that
it always sounds like a funeral. Nobody ever
noticed it before, but from the upper side it can be
seen that a huge hole has been knocked through
the side of the building. A train of cars could be
run through it. Inside the church is filled with
all sorts of rubbish and ruin. A little further on
is another church, which curiously illustrates the
manner in which fire and flood seemed determined
to unite in completing the ruin of the city. Just
before the flood came down the valley there was
a terrific explosion in this church, supposed to
have been caused by natural gas. Amid all the
terrors of the flood, with the water surging thirty
feet deep all around and through it, the flames
blazed through the roof and tower, and its fire-
stained walls arise from the debris of the flood,
which covers its foundations. Its ruins are one
of the most conspicuous and picturesque sights
in the city.

Next to Adams Street, the road most traveled
in Johnstown now is the Pennsylvania Railroad

track, or rather bed, across the Stony Creek, and
at a culvert crossing just west of the creek. More
people have been injured here since the calamity
than at any other place. The railroad ties which
hold the track across the culvert are big ones,
and their strength has not been weakened by the
flood, but between the ties and between the
freight and passenger tracks there is a wide
space. The Pennsylvania trains from Johnstown
have to stop, of course, at the eastern end of the
bridge, and the thousands of people whom they
daily bring to Johnstown from Pittsburgh have to
get into Johnstown by walking across the track
to the Pennsylvania Railroad depot, and then
crossing the pontoon foot-bridge that has been
built across the Stony Creek. All day long there
is a black line of people going back and forth
across this course. Every now and then there is
a yell, a plunge, a rush of people to the culvert,
a call for a doctor, and cries of "Help" from underneath the culvert. Some one, of course, has
fallen between the freight and passenger tracks,
or between the ties of the tracks themselves. In
the night it is particularly dangerous traveling to
the Pennsylvania depot this way, and people falling then have little chance of a rescue. So far at
least thirty persons have fallen down the culvert,
and a dozen of them, who have descended entirely to the ground, have escaped in some mar-

velous manner with their lives. Several Pitts-
burghers have had their legs and arms broken,
and one man cracked his collar-bone. It is to be
hoped that these accidents will keep off the flock
of curiosity-seekers, in some degree at least. The
presence of these crowds seriously interferes with
the work of clearing up the town, and affects the
residents here in even a graver manner, for
though many of those coming to Johnstown to
spend a day and see the ruins bring something
to eat with them, many do not do so, and invade
the relief stands, taking the food which is lavishly
dealt out to the suffering. Though the Pennsylvania Railroad bridge is as strong as ever, apparently, beyond the bridge, the embankment on
which the track is built is washed away, and people therefore do not cross the bridge, but leave
the track on the western side, and, clambering
down the abutments, cross the creek on a rude
foot-bridge hastily erected, and then through the
yard of the Open-Hearth Works and of the railroad
up to the depot. This yard altogether is about
three-quarters of a mile long, but so deceptive are
distances in the valley that it does not look one-
third that. The bed of this yard, three-quarters
of a mile long, and about the same distance wide,
is the most desolate place here. The yard itself
is fringed with the crumbling ruins of the iron
works and of the railroad shops. The iron works

were great, high brick buildings, with steep-iron
roofs. The ends of these buildings were smashed
in, and the roofs bend over where the flood struck
them, in a curve.

But it is the bed of the yard itself that is desolate. In appearance it is a mass of stones and
rocks and huge boulders, so that it seems a vast
quarry hewn and uncovered by the wind. There
is comparatively little débris here, all this having
been washed away over to the sides of the buildings, in one or two instances filling the buildings
completely. There is no soft earth or mud on
the rocks at all, this part of Johnstown being
much in contrast with the great stretch of sand
along the river. In some instances the dirt is
washed away to such a depth that the bed-rock is
uncovered.

The fury of the waters here may be gathered
from this fact: piled up outside the works of the
Open-Hearth Company were several heaps of
massive blooms—long, solid blocks of pig iron,
weighing fifteen tons each. The blooms, though
they were not carried down the river, were scattered about the yard like so many logs of wood.
They will have to be piled up again by the use of
a derrick. The Open-Hearth Iron Works people
are making vigorous efforts to clear their buildings. The yards of the company were blazing
last night with the burning débris, but it will

be weeks before the company can start operations.

In the Pennsylvania Railroad yard all is activity and bustle. At the relief station, and at the headquarters of General Hastings, in the signal tower, the man who is the head of all operations there, and the directing genius of the place, is Lieutenant George Miller, of the Fifth United States Infantry. Lieutenant Miller was near here on his vacation when the flood came. He was one of the first on the spot, and was about the only man in Johnstown who showed some ability as an organizer and a disciplinarian. A reporter who groped his way across the railroad track, the footbridge, and the quarries and yards at reveille found Lieutenant Miller in a group of the soldiers of the Fourteenth Pennsylvania Regiment telling them just what to do.

CHAPTER XVI.

TRAVEL was resumed up the valley of Conemaugh Creek for a few miles about five days
after the flood, and a weird sight was presented
to the visitor. No pen can do justice to it, yet
some impressions of it must be recorded. Every
one has seen the light iron beams, shafts, and
rods in a factory lying in twisted, broken, and
criss-cross shape after a fire has destroyed the
building. In the gap above Johnstown water has
picked up a four-track railroad covered with
trains, freight, and passengers, and with machine
shops, a round-house, and other heavy buildings
with heavy contents, and it has torn the track
to pieces, twisted, turned, and crossed it as fire
never could. It has tossed huge freight locomotives about like barrels, and cars like packing-
boxes, torn them to pieces, and scattered them
over miles of territory. It has in one place put
a stream of deep water, a city block wide, be-

tween the railroad and the bluff, and in another
place it has changed the course of the river as
far in the other direction and left a hundred
yards inland the tracks that formerly skirted the
banks.

Add to this that in the midst of all this devastation, fire, with the singular fatality that has made
it everywhere the companion of the flood in this
catastrophe, has destroyed a train of vestibule
cars that the flood had wrecked; that the passengers who remained in the cars through the
flood and until the fire were saved, while their
companions who attempted to flee were overwhelmed and drowned; and that through it all
one locomotive stood and still stands comparatively uninjured in the heart of this disaster, and
the story of one of the most marvelous freaks
of this marvelous flood is barely outlined. That
locomotive stands there on its track now with its
fires burning, smoke curling from the stack, and
steam from its safety valve, all ready to go ahead
as soon as they will build a track down to it. It
is No. 1309, a fifty-four ton, eight driver, class R,
Pennsylvania Railroad locomotive. George Hudson was its engineer, and Conductor Sheely had
charge of its train. They, with all the rest of the
crew, escaped by flight when they saw the flood.

The wonders of this playground, where a giant
force played with masses of iron, weighing scores

of tons each, as a child might play with pebbles, begins with a bridge, or a piece of a bridge, about thirty feet long, that stands high and dry upon two ordinary stone abutments at Woodvale. The part of the bridge that remains spanned the Pennsylvania tracks. The tracks are gone, the bridge is gone on either side, the river is gone to a new channel, the very earth for a hundred yards around has been scraped off and swept away, but this little span remains perched up there, twenty feet above everything, in the midst of a desert of ruins—the only piece of a bridge that is standing from the railroad bridge to South Forks. It is a light iron structure, and the abutments are not unusually heavy. That it should be kept there, when everything else was twisted and torn to pieces, is one other queer freak of this flood. Near by are the wrecks of two freight trains that were standing side by side when the flood caught them. The lower ends of both trains are torn to pieces, the cars tossed around in every direction, and many of them carried away. The whole of the train on the track nearest the river was smashed into kindling wood. Its locomotive is gone entirely, perhaps because this other train acted as a sort of buffer for the second one. The latter has twenty-five or thirty cars that are uninjured, apparently. They could move off as soon as that wonderful engine, No. 1309, that stands with steam up at their head, gets ready to pull out. A second look, however, shows that the track is in many places literally washed from beneath the cars. Some of the trucks also are turned half way around and standing with wheels running across the track. But the force that did this left the light wood box cars themselves unharmed. They were loaded with dressed beef and provisions. They have been emptied to supply the hungry in Johnstown.

In front of engine 1309 and this train the water played one of its most fantastic tricks with the rails. The débris of trees, logs, planks, and every description of wreckage is heaped up in front of the engine to the headlight, and is packed in so tightly that twenty men with ropes and axes worked all day without clearing all away. The track is absolutely gone from the front of the engine clear up to beyond Conemaugh. Parts of it lie about everywhere, twisted into odd shapes, turned upside down, stacked crosswise one above the other, and in one place a section of the west track has been lifted clear over the right track, runs along there for a ways, and then twists back into its proper place. Even stranger are the tricks the water has played with the rails where they have been torn loose from the ties. The rails are steel and of the heaviest weight used. They were twisted as easily as willow branches in

a spring freshet in a country brook. One rail
lies in the sand in the shape of a letter "S."
More are broken squarely in two. Many times
rails have been broken within a few feet of a fish-
plate, coupling them to the next rail, and the
fragments are still united by the comparatively
weak plates. Every natural law would seem to
show that the first place where they should have
broken was at the joints.

There is little to indicate the recent presence
of a railroad in the stretch from this spot up to
the upper part of Conemaugh. The little plain
into which the gap widened here, and in which
stood the bulk of the town, is wiped out. The
river has changed its course from one side of the
valley to the other. There is not the slightest
indication that the central part of the plain was
ever anything but a flood-washed gulch in some
mountain region. At the upper end of the plain,
surrounded by a desert of mud and rock, stands a
fantastic collection of ruined railroad equipments.
Three trains stood there when the flood swept down
the valley. On the outside was a local passenger
train with three cars and a locomotive. It stands
there yet, the cars tilted by the washing of the
tracks, but comparatively uninjured. Somehow
a couple more locomotives have been run into
the sand bank. In the centre a freight train
stood on the track, and a large collection of

smashed cars has its place now. It was broken all to pieces. Inside of all was the day express, with its baggage and express cars, and at the end three vestibule cars. It was from this train that a number of passengers—fifteen certainly, and no one knows how many more—were lost. When the alarm came most of the passengers fled for the high ground. Many reached it; others hesitated on the way, tried to run back to the cars, and were lost. Others stayed on the cars, and, after the first rush of the flood, were rescued alive. Some of the freight cars were loaded with lime, and this leaped over the vestibule cars and set them on fire. All three of the vestibule cars were burned down to the trucks. These and the peculiar-shaped iron frames of the vestibules are all that show where the cars stood.

The reason the flood, that twisted heavy steel rails like twigs just below, did not wipe out these three trains entirely is supposed to be that just in front of them, and between them and the flood, was the round-house, filled with engines. It was a large building, probably forty feet high to the top of the ventilators in the roof. The wave of wrath, eye-witnesses say, was so high that these ventilators were beneath it. The round-house was swept away to its very foundations, and the flood played jackstraws with the two dozen locomotives lodged in it, but it split the torrent, and a part of it went down each side of the three trains, saving them from the worst of its force. Thirty-three locomotives were in and about the round-house and the repair shops near by. Of these, twenty-six have been found, or at least traced, part of them being found scattered down into Johnstown, and one tender was found up in Stony Creek. The other seven locomotives are gone, and not a trace of them has been found up to this time. It is supposed that some of them are in the sixty acres of débris above the bridge at Johnstown. All the locomotives that remain anywhere within sight of the round-house, all except those attached to the trains, are thrown about in every direction, every side up, smashed, broken, and useless except for old iron. The tenders are all gone. Being lighter than the locomotives, they floated easier, and were quickly torn off and carried away. The engines themselves were apparently rolled over and over in whichever direction the current that had hold of them ran, and occasionally were picked up bodily and slammed down again, wheels up, or whichever way chanced to be most convenient to the flood. Most of them lie in five feet of sand and gravel, with only a part showing above the surface. Some are out in the bed of the river.

A strange but very pleasant feature of the disaster in Conemaugh itself is the comparatively small loss of life. As the townspeople figure it out, there are only thirty-eight persons there positively known to have perished besides those on the train. This was partly because the buildings in the centre of the valley were mostly stores and factories, and also because more heed appears to have been paid to the warnings that came from up the valley. At noon the workmen in the shops were notified that there was danger, and that they had better go home. At one o'clock word was given that the dam was likely to go, and that everybody must get on high ground. Few remained in the central part of the valley when the high wave came through the gap.

Doré never dreamed a weirder, ghastlier picture than night in the Conemaugh Valley since the flood desolated it. Darkness falls early from the rain-dropping, gray sky that has palled the valley ever since it became a vast bier, a charnel-house fifteen miles long. The smoke and steam from the placers of smouldering débris above the bridge aid to hasten the night. Few lights gleam out, except those of the scattered fires that still flicker fitfully in the mass of wreckage. Gas went out with the flood, and oil has been almost entirely lacking since the disaster. Candles are used in those places where people think it worth while to stay up after dark. Up on the hills around the town bright sparks gleam out like lovely stars from the few homes built so high. Down in the valley the gloom settles over everything, making it look, from the bluffs around, like some vast death-pit, the idea of entering which brings a shudder. The gloomy effect is not relieved, but rather deepened, by the broad beams of ghastly, pale light thrown across the gulf by two or three electric lights erected around the Pennsylvania Railroad station. They dazzle the eye and make the gloom still deeper.

Time does not accustom the eyes to this ghastly scene. The flames rising and falling over the ruins look more like witches' bale-fires the longer they are looked at. The smoke-burdened depths in the valley seem deserted by every living thing, except that occasionally, prowling ghoul-like about the edges of the mass of débris, may be seen, as they cross the beams of electric light, dark figures of men who are drawn to the spot day and night, hovering over the place where some chance movement may disclose the body of a wife, mother, or daughter gone down in the wreck. They pick listlessly away at the heaps in one spot for awhile and then wander aimlessly off, only to reappear at another spot, pulling fever-ishly at some rags that looked like a dress, or poking a stick into some hole to feel if there is anything soft at the bottom. At one or two places the electric lights show, with exaggerated and distorted shadows, firemen in big hats and long rubber coats, standing upon the edge of the bridge, steadily holding the hose, from which two streams of water shoot far out over the mass, sparkle for a moment like silver in the pale light, and then drop downward into the blackness.

For noise, there is heavy splashing of the Conemaugh over the rapids below the bridge, the petulant gasping of an unseen fire-engine, pumping water through the hose, and the even more rapid but greater puffing of the dynamo-engine that, mounted upon a flat car at one end of the bridge, furnishes electricity for the lights. There is little else heard. People who are yet about gather in little groups, and talk in low tones as they look over the dark, watchfire-beaconed gulf. Everybody in Johnstown looks over that gulf in every spare moment, day or night. Movement about is almost impossible, for the ways are only footpaths about the bluffs, irregular and slippery. Every night people are badly hurt by falls over bluffs, through the bridge, or down banks. Lying about under sheds in ruined buildings, and even in the open air, wherever one goes, are the forms, wrapped in blankets, of men who have no better place to sleep, resembling nothing so much as the corpses that men are seen always to be carrying about the streets in the daytime.

CHAPTER XVII.

One of the first to reach Johnstown from a distance was a New York *World* correspondent, who on Sunday wrote as follows :—

"I walked late yesterday afternoon from New Florence to a place opposite Johnstown, a distance of four miles. I describe what I actually saw. All along the way bodies were seen lying on the river banks. In one place a woman was half buried in the mud, only a limb showing. In another was a mother with her babe clasped to her breast. Further along lay a husband and wife, their arms wound around each other's necks. Probably fifty bodies were seen on that one side of the river; and it must be remembered that here the current was the swiftest, and consequently fewer of the dead were landed among the bushes. On the opposite side bodies could also be seen, but they were all covered with mud. As I neared Johnstown the wreckage became grand in its massive

THE DÉBRIS ABOVE THE PENNSYLVANIA RAILROAD BRIDGE.

proportions. In order to show the force of the current I will say that three miles below Johnstown I saw a grand piano lying on the bank, and not a board or key was broken. It must have been lifted on the crest of the wave and laid gently on the bank. In another place were two large iron boilers. They had evidently been treated by the torrent much as the piano had been.

"The scenes, as I neared Johnstown, were the most heart-rending that man was ever called to look upon. Probably three thousand people were scattered in groups along the Pennsylvania Railroad track and every one of them had a relative lying dead either in the wreckage above, in the river below, or in the still burning furnace. Not a house that was left standing was in plumb. Hundreds of them were turned on their sides, and in some cases three or four stood one on top of the other. Two miles from Johnstown, on the opposite side of the river from where I walked, stood one-half of the water-works of the Cambria Iron Company, a structure that had been built of massive stone. It was filled with planks from houses, and a large abutment of wreckage was piled up fully fifty feet in front of it. A little above, on the same side, could be seen what was left of the Cambria Iron Works, which was one of the finest plants in the world. Some of the walls are

12

still standing, it is true, but not a vestige of the valuable machinery remains in sight. The two upper portions of the works were swept away almost entirely, and under the pieces of fallen iron and wood could be seen the bodies of more than forty workmen.

"At this point there is a bend in the river and the fiery furnace blazing for a quarter of a mile square above the stone bridge came into view.

"'My God!' screamed a woman who was hastening up the track, 'can it be that any are in there?'

"'Yes; over a thousand,' replied a man who had just come from the neighborhood, and it is now learned that he estimated the number at one thousand too low.

"The scenes of misery and suffering and agony and despair can hardly be chronicled. One man, a clerk named Woodruff, was reeling along intoxicated. Suddenly, with a frantic shout, he threw himself over the bank into the flood and would have been carried to his death had he not been caught by some persons below.

"'Let me die,' he exclaimed, when they rescued him. 'My wife and children are gone; I have no use for my life.' An hour later I saw Woodruff lying on the ground entirely overcome by liquor. Persons who knew him said that he had never tasted liquor before.

" Probably fifty barrels of whisky were washed ashore just below Johnstown, and those men who had lost everything in this world sought solace in the fiery liquid. So it was that as early as six o'clock last night the shrieks and cries of women were intermingled with drunkards' howls and curses. What was worse than anything, however, was the fact that incoming trains from Pittsburgh brought hundreds of toughs, who joined with the Slavs and Bohemians in rifling the bodies, stealing furniture, insulting women, and endeavoring to assume control of any rescuing parties that tried to seek the bodies under the bushes and in the limbs of trees. There was no one in authority, no one to take command of even a citizens' posse could it have been organized. A lawless mob seemed to control this narrow neck of land that was the only approach to the city of Johnstown. I saw persons take watches from dead men's jackets and brutally tear finger-rings from the hands of women. The ruffians also climbed into the overturned houses and ransacked the rooms, taking whatever they thought valuable. No one dared check them in this work, and, consequently, the scene was not as riotous as it would have been if the toughs had not had sway. In fact, they became beastly drunk after a time and were seen lying around in a stupor. Unless the military is on hand

early to-morrow there may be serious trouble,
for each train pours loads of people of every
description into the vicinity, and Slavs are flock-
ing like birds of prey from the surrounding
country.

"Here I will give the latest conservative estimate of the dead—it is between seven and eight
thousand drowned and two thousand burned. The
committee at Johnstown in their last bulletin
placed the number of lives lost at eight thousand.
In doing so they are figuring the inhabitants of
their own city and the towns immediately adjoining. But it must be remembered that the tidal
wave swept ten miles through a populous district
before it even reached the locality over which this
committee has supervision. It devastated a tract
the size and shape of Manhattan Island. Here are
a few facts that will show the geographical outlines
of the terrible disaster: The Hotel Hurlbut of
Johnstown, a massive three-story building of one
hundred rooms, has vanished. There were in it
seventy-five guests at the time of the flood. Two
only are now known to be alive. The Merchants'
Hotel is leveled. How many were inside it is
not known, but as yet no one has been seen who
came from there or heard of an inmate escaping.
At the Conemaugh round-house forty-one locomotives were swept down the stream, and before they reached the stone bridge all the iron

and steel work had been torn from their boilers. It is almost impossible in this great catastrophe to go more into details.

"I stood on the stone bridge at six o'clock and looked into the seething mass of ruin below me. At one place the blackened body of a babe was seen; in another, fourteen skulls could be counted. Further along the bones became thicker and thicker, until at last at one place it seemed as if a concourse of people who had been at a ball or entertainment had been carried in a bunch and incinerated. At this time the smoke was still rising to the height of fifty feet, and it is expected that when it dies down the charred bodies will be seen dotting the entire mass.

"A cable had been run last night from the end of the stone bridge to the nearest point across—a distance of three hundred feet. Over this cable was run a trolley, and a swing was fastened under it. A man went over, and he was the first one who visited Johnstown since the awful disaster. I followed him to-day.

"I walked along the hillside and saw hundreds of persons lying on the wet grass, wrapped in blankets or quilts. It was growing cold and a misty rain had set in. Shelter was not to be had, and houses on the hillsides that had not been swept away were literally packed from top to bottom. The bare necessities of life were soon at a premium, and loaves of bread sold at fifty cents. Fortunately, however, the relief train from Pittsburgh arrived at seven o'clock. Otherwise the horrors of starvation would have been added. All provisions, however, had to be carried over a rough, rocky road a distance of four miles (as I knew, who had been compelled to walk it), and in many cases they were seized by the toughs, and the people who were in need of food did not get it.

"Rich and poor were served alike by this terrible disaster. I saw a girl standing in her bare feet on the river's bank, clad in a loose petticoat and with a shawl over her head. At first I thought she was an Italian woman, but her face showed that I was mistaken. She was the belle of the town—the daughter of a wealthy Johnstown banker—and this single petticoat and shawl were not only all that was left her, but all that was saved from the magnificent residence of her father. She had escaped to the hills not an instant too soon.

" The solicitor of Johnstown, Mr. George Martin, said to me to-day :—

" ' All my money went away in the flood. My house is gone. So are all my clothes, but, thank God, my family are safe.' "

CHAPTER XVIII.

THE first train that passed New Florence, bound east, was crowded with people from Pittsburgh and places along the line, who were going to the scene of the disaster with but little hope of finding their loved ones alive. It was a heart-rending sight. Not a dry eye was in the train. Mothers moaned for their children. Husbands paced the aisles and wrung their hands in mute agony. Fathers pressed their faces against the windows and endeavored to see something, they knew not what, that would tell them in a measure of the dreadful fate that their loved ones had met with. All along the raging Conemaugh the train stopped, and bodies were taken on the express car, being carried by the villagers who were out along the banks. Oh, the horror and infinite pity of it all! What a journey has been that of the last half hour! Swollen corpses lay here and there in piles of cross-ties, or on the river banks along the tangled greenery.

(207)

It was about nine o'clock when the first passenger train since Friday came to the New Florence depot with its load of eager passengers.
They were no idle travelers, but each had a mission.   Here and there men were staring out the
windows with red eyes.   Among them were
tough-looking Hungarians and Italians who had
lost friends near Nineveh, while many were weeping, on all sides.   Two of the passengers on the
train were man and wife from Johnstown.   He
was dignified and more or less self-possessed.
She was anxious, and tried hard to control her
feelings.   From every newcomer and possible
source of information she sought news.

"Ours is a big, new brick house," said she with
a brave effort, but with her brown eyes moist and
red lips trembling. "It is a three-story house, and
I don't think there is any trouble, do you?" said
she to me, and without waiting for my answer,
she continued with a sob, "There are my four
children in the house and their nurse, and I guess
father and mother will go over to the house, don't
you?"

In a few moments all those in the car knew the
story of the pair, and many a pitying glance was
cast at them.   Their house was one of the first to
go.

The huge wave struck Bolivar just after dark,
and in five minutes the Conemaugh rose from six

to forty feet, and the waters spread out over the whole country. Soon houses began floating down, and clinging to the débris were men, women, and children shrieking for aid. A large number of citizens gathered at the county bridge, and they were reinforced by a number from Garfield, a town on the opposite side of the river. They brought ropes, and these were thrown over into the boiling waters as persons drifted by, in efforts to save them. For half an hour all efforts were fruitless, until at last, when the rescuers were about giving up all hope, a little boy astride a shingle roof managed to catch hold of one of the ropes. He caught it under his left arm and was thrown violently against an abutment, but managed to keep hold and was pulled onto the bridge amid the cheers of the onlookers. The lad was at once taken to Garfield and cared for. The boy is about sixteen years old and his name is Hessler. His story of the calamity is as follows :—

"With my father I was spending the day at my grandfather's house in Cambria City. In the house at the time were Theodore, Edward, and John Kintz, John Kintz, Jr., Miss Mary Kintz, Mrs. Mary Kintz, wife of John Kintz, Jr.; Miss Treacy Kintz, Mrs. Rica Smith, John Hirsch and four children, my father, and myself. Shortly after five o'clock there was a noise of roaring waters and screams of people. We looked out the door

and saw persons running. My father told us to
never mind, as the waters would not rise further.
But soon we saw houses swept by, and then we
ran up to the floor above. The house was three
stories, and we were at last forced to the top one.
In my fright I jumped on the bed. It was an old-
fashioned one, with heavy posts. The water kept
rising, and my bed was soon afloat. Gradually
it was lifted up. The air in the room grew close,
and the house was moving. Still the bed kept
rising and pressed the ceiling. At last the posts
pushed the plaster. It yielded, and a section of
the roof gave way. Then I suddenly found myself on the roof and was being carried down
stream. After a little this roof commenced to
part, and I was afraid I was going to be drowned,
but just then another house with a shingle roof
floated by, and I managed to crawl on it and
floated down until nearly dead with cold, when I
was saved. After I was freed from the house I
did not see my father. My grandfather was on a
tree, but he must have been drowned, as the
waters were rising fast. John Kintz, Jr., was also
on a tree. Miss Mary Kintz and Mrs. Mary
Kintz I saw drown. Miss Smith was also drowned.
John Hirsch was in a tree, but the four children
were drowned. The scenes were terrible. Live
bodies and corpses were floating down with me
and away from me. I would see a person shriek

and then disappear. All along the line were people who were trying to save us, but they could do nothing, and only a few were caught."

An eye-witness at Bolivar Block station tells a story of heroism which occurred at the lower bridge which crosses the Conemaugh at that point. A young man, with two women, were seen coming down the river on part of a floor. At the upper bridge a rope was thrown down to them. This they all failed to catch. Between the two bridges he was noticed to point toward the elder woman, who, it is supposed, was his mother. He was then seen to instruct the women how to catch the rope which was being lowered from the other bridge.. Down came the raft with a rush. The brave man stood with his arms around the two women. As they swept under the bridge he reached up and seized the rope. He was jerked violently away from the two women, who failed to get a hold on the rope. Seeing that they would not be rescued, he dropped the rope and fell back on the raft, which floated on down the river. The current washed their frail craft in toward the bank. The young man was enabled to seize hold of a branch of a tree. He aided the two women to get up into the tree. He held on with his hands and rested his feet on a pile of drift-wood. A piece of floating débris struck the drift, sweeping it away. The man hung with his body immersed in the water. A pile of drift soon collected, and he was enabled to get another insecure footing. Up the river there was a sudden crash, and a section of the bridge was swept away and floated down the stream, striking the tree and washing it away. All three were thrown into the water and were drowned before the eyes of the horrified spectators, just opposite the town of Bolivar.

At Bolivar a man, woman, and child were seen floating down in a lot of drift. The mass soon began to part, and, by desperate efforts, the husband and father succeeded in getting his wife and little one on a floating tree. Just then the tree was washed under the bridge, and a rope was thrown out. It fell upon the man's shoulders. He saw at a glance that he could not save his dear ones, so he threw the means of safety on one side and clasped in his arms those who were with him. A moment later and the tree struck a floating house. It turned over, and in an instant the three persons were in the seething waters, being carried to their death.

An instance of a mother's love at Bolivar is told. A woman and two children were floating down the torrent. The mother caught a rope, and tried to hold it to her and her babe. It was impossible, and with a look of anguish she relinquished the rope and sank with her little ones.

A family, consisting of father and mother and nine children, were washed away in a creek at Lockport. The mother managed to reach the shore, but the husband and children were carried out into the Conemaugh to drown. The woman was crazed over the terrible event.

A little girl passed under the Bolivar bridge just before dark. She was kneeling on part of a floor, and had her hands clasped as if in prayer. Every effort was made to save her, but they all proved futile. A railroader who was standing by remarked that the piteous appearance of the little waif brought tears to his eyes. All night long the crowd stood about the ruins of the bridge which had been swept away at Bolivar. The water rushed past with a roar, carrying with it parts of houses, furniture, and trees. No more living persons are being carried past. Watchers, with lanterns, remained along the banks until daybreak, when the first view of the awful devastation of the flood was witnessed. Along the bank lay the remnants of what had once been dwelling-houses and stores; here and there was an uprooted tree. Piles of drift lay about, in some of which bodies of the victims of the flood will be found.

Harry Fisher, a young telegraph operator, who was at Bolivar when the first rush of waters began, says: "We knew nothing of the disaster until we noticed the river slowly rising, and then more rapidly. News reached us from Johnstown that the dam at South Fork had burst. Within three hours the water in the river rose at least twenty feet. Shortly before six o'clock ruins of houses, beds, household utensils, barrels, and kegs came floating past the bridges. At eight o'clock the water was within six feet of the road-bed of the bridge. The wreckage floated past, without stopping, for at least two hours. Then it began to lessen, and night coming suddenly upon us, we could see no more. The wreckage was floating by for a long time before the first living persons passed. Fifteen people that I saw were carried down by the river. One of these, a boy, was saved, and three of them were drowned just directly below the town. Hundreds of animals lost their lives. The bodies of horses, dogs, and chickens floated past in numbers that could not be counted."

Just before reaching Sang Hollow, the end of the mail line on the Pennsylvania Railroad, is "S. O." signal tower, and the men in it told piteous stories of what they saw.

A beautiful girl came down on the roof of a building, which was swung in near the tower. She screamed to the operators to save her, and one big, brawny, brave fellow walked as far into the river as he could, and shouted to her to guide herself into shore with a bit of plank. She was a plucky girl, full of nerve and energy, and stood upon her frail support in evident obedience to the command of the operator. She made two or three bold strokes, and actually stopped the course of the raft for an instant. Then it swerved, and went out from under her. She tried to swim ashore, but in a few seconds she was lost in the swirling water. Something hit her, for she lay on her back, with face pallid and expressionless.

Men and women, in dozens, in pairs, and singly; children, boys, big and little, and wee babies, were there among the awful confusion of water, drowning, gasping, struggling, and fighting desperately for life. Two men, on a tiny raft, shot into the swiftest part of the current. They crouched stolidly, looking at the shores, while between them, dressed in white, and kneeling with her face turned heavenward, was a girl six or seven years old. She seemed stricken with paralysis until she came opposite the tower, and then she turned her face to the operator. She was so close they could see big tears on her cheeks, and her pallor was as death. The helpless men on shore shouted to her to keep up her courage, and she resumed her devout attitude, and disappeared under the trees of a projecting point a short distance below. "We couldn't see her come out again," said the operator, "and that was all of it."

CHAPTER XIX.

An interesting story of endeavor was related on Monday by a correspondent of the New York *Sun*, who made his way to the scene of disaster. This is what he wrote:—

Although three days have passed since the disaster, the difficulty of reaching the desolated region is still so great that, under ordinary circumstances, no one would dream of attempting the trip. The Pennsylvania Railroad cannot get within several miles of Johnstown, and it is almost impossible to get on their trains even at that. They run one, two, or three trains a day on the time of the old through trains, and the few cars on each train are crowded with passengers in a few minutes after the gates open. Then the sale of tickets is stopped, the gates are closed, and all admission to the train denied. No extra cars will be put on, no second section sent out, and no special train run on any account, for love

(216)

RUINS OF THE CAMBRIA IRON WORKS.

or money. The scenes at the station when the gates are shut are sorrowful. Men who have come hundreds of miles to search for friends or relatives among the dead stand hopelessly before the edict of the blue-coated officials from eight in the morning until one in the afternoon. There is no later train on the Pennsylvania road out of Pittsburgh, and the agony of suspense is thus prolonged. Besides that, the one o'clock train is so late in getting to Sang Hollow that the work of beginning a search is practically delayed until the next morning.

The *Sun's* special correspondents were of a party of fifteen or twenty business men and others who had come from the East by way of Buffalo, and who reached Pittsburgh in abundant time to have taken the Pennsylvania Railroad train at eight o'clock, had the company wished to carry them. With hundreds of others they were turned away, and appeals even to the highest official of the road were useless, whether in the interest of newspaper enterprise or private business, or in the sadder but most frequent case where men prayed like beggars for an opportunity to measure the extent of their bereavement, or find if, by some happy chance, one might not be alive out of a family. The sight-seeing and curious crowd was on hand early, and had no trouble in getting on the train. Those who had come from distant

13

cities, and whose mission was of business or sorrow, were generally later, and were left. No effort was made to increase the accommodations of the train for those who most needed them. The *Sun's* men had traveled a thousand miles around to reach Pittsburgh. Their journey had covered three sides of the State of Pennsylvania, from Philadelphia at the extreme southeast, through New Jersey and New York to Buffalo by way of Albany and the New York Central, and thence by the Lake Shore to Ashtabula, O., passing through Erie at the extreme northwest corner of the State; thence down by the Pittsburgh and Lake Erie road to Youngstown, O., and so into Pittsburgh by the back door, as it were. Circumstances and the edict of the Pennsylvania Railroad were destined to carry them still further around, more than a hundred miles, nearly south of Pittsburgh, almost across the line into Maryland, and thence fifty miles up before they reached their destination.

The Baltimore and Ohio Railroad ordinarily does not attempt to compete for business from Pittsburgh into Johnstown. Its only route between those two cities leads over small branch lines among the mountains south of Johnstown, and is over double the length of the Pennsylvania main line route. The first train to reach Johnstown, however, was one over the Baltimore

and Ohio lines, and, although they made no attempt to establish a regular line, they did on Sunday get two relief trains out of Pittsburgh and
into Johnstown. Superintendent Patten, of the
Baltimore and Ohio, established headquarters in
a box car two miles south of Johnstown, and telegraphed to Acting Superintendent McIlvaine, at
Pittsburgh, to take for free transportation all
goods offered for the relief of the sufferers. No
passenger trains were run, however, except the
regular trains on the main line for Cumberland,
Md., and the branches from the main line to
Johnstown were used entirely by wildcat trains
running on special orders, with no object but to
get relief up as quickly as possible. Nothing had
left Pittsburgh for Johnstown, however, to-day
up to nine o'clock. Arrangements were made
for a relief train to go out early in the afternoon,
to pick up cars of contributed goods at the stations along the line and get them into Johnstown
some time during the night. "No specials" was
also the rule on the Baltimore and Ohio, but Acting Superintendent McIlvaine recognized in the
Sun, with its enormous possibilities in the way of
spreading throughout the country the actual situation of affairs in the devastated district, a means
of awaking the public to the extent of the disaster
that would be of more efficient relief to the suffering people than even train-loads of food and cloth-

ing. The *Sun's* case was therefore made excep
tional, and when the situation was explained to him
he consented, for a sum that appalled the representatives of some other papers who heard it, but
which was, for the distance to be covered, very
fair, to set the *Sun's* men down in Johnstown at
the earliest moment that steam and steel and iron
could do it.

In fifteen minutes one of the Baltimore and
Ohio light passenger engines, with Engineer W.
E. Scott in charge and Fireman Charles Hood for
assistant, was hitched to a single coach out in the
yard. Conductor W. B. Clancy was found somewhere about and put in command of the expedi-
tion. Brakeman Dan Lynn was captured just as
he was leaving an incoming train, and although
he had been without sleep for a day, he readily
consented to complete the crew of the *Sun's*
train. There was no disposition to be hoggish in
the matter, and at a time like this the great thing
was to get the best possible information as to affairs at Johnstown spread over the country in the
least possible time. The facilities of the train
were therefore placed at the disposal of other
newspaper men who were willing to share in the
expense. None of them, however, availed themselves of this chance to save practically a whole
day in reaching the scene, except the artist repre-
senting *Harper's Weekly*, who had accompanied

the *Sun* men this far in their race against time from the East. As far as the New York papers were concerned, there were no men except those from the *Sun* to take the train. If any other New York newspaper men had yet reached Pittsburgh at all, they were not to be found around the Baltimore and Ohio station, where the *Sun* extended its invitation to the other representatives of the press. There were a number of Western newspaper men on hand, but journalism in that section is not accustomed to big figures except in circulation affidavits, and they were staggered at the idea of paying even a share of the expense that the *Sun* was bearing practically alone.

At 9.15 A. M., therefore, when the special train pulled out of the Baltimore and Ohio station, it had for passengers only the *Sun* men and *Harper's* artist. As it started Acting Superintendent McIlvaine was asked :—

" How quickly can we make it ? "

"Well, it's one hundred and forty-six miles," he replied, "and it's all kinds of road. There's an accommodation train that you will have to look out for until you pass it, and that will delay you. It's hard to make any promise about time."

" Can we make it in five hours ? " he was asked.

"I think you can surely do that," he replied.

How much better than the acting superintendent's word was the performance of Engineer

Scott and his crew this story shows. The special, after leaving Pittsburgh, ran wild until it got to McKeesport, sixteen miles distant. At this point the regular train, which left Pittsburgh at 8.40, was overtaken. The regular train was on a sid ing, and the special passed through the city with but a minute's stop. Then the special had a clear track before it, and the engineer drove his machine to the utmost limit of speed consistent with safety. It is nineteen miles from McKeesport to West Newton, and the special made this distance in twenty minutes, the average time of over a mile a minute being much exceeded for certain periods. The curves of the road are frightful, and at times the single car which composed the train was almost swung clear off the track. The *Sun* men recalled vividly the ride of Horace Greeley with Hank Monk, and they began to reflect that there was such a thing as riding so fast that they might not be able to reach Johnstown at all. From Layton's to Dawson the seven and one-half miles were made in seven minutes, while the fourteen miles from Layton's to Connellsville were covered in fourteen minutes precisely. On the tender of the engine the cover of the water-tank flew open and the water splashed out. Coal flew from the tender in great lumps, and dashed against the end of the car. Inside the car the newspaper men's grips and belongings went flying around on the floor and over seats like mad. The Allegheny River, whose curves the rails followed, seemed to be right even with the car windows, so that one could look straight down into the water, so closely to it was the track built. In Connellsville there was a crowd to see the special. On the depot was the placard :—

" Car will leave at 3 P. M. to day with food and clothing for Johnstown."

In Connellsville the train stopped five minutes and underwent a thorough inspection. Then it shoved on again. At Confluence, twenty-seven miles from Connellsville, a bridge of a Baltimore and Ohio branch line across the river was washed away, but this didn't interfere with the progress of the special. For sixty miles on the road is up hill at a grade of sixty-five feet to the mile, and the curves, if anything, are worse, but there was no appreciable diminution in the speed of the train. Just before reaching Rockwood the first real traces of the flood were apparent. The waters of the Castlemore showed signs of having been recently right up to the railroad tracks, and driftwood and débris of all descriptions lay at the side of the rails. Nearly all bridges on the country roads over the river were washed away and their remnants scattered along the banks.

Rockwood was reached at 12.05 P. M. Rockwood is eighty-seven miles from McKeesport, and this distance, which is up an extremely steep grade, was therefore made in two hours, which includes fifteen minutes' stop. The distance covered from Pittsburgh was one hundred and two miles in two hours. Rockwood is the junction of the main line of the Baltimore and Ohio road at its Cambria branch, which runs to Johnstown. The regular local train from there to Johnstown was held to allow the *Sun's* special to pass first.

The *Sun's* special left Rockwood at 12.20 in charge of Engineer Oliver, who assumed charge at that point. He said that the branch to Johnstown was a mountain road, with steep grades, very high embankments, and damaged in spots, and that he would have to use great precaution in running. He gave the throttle a yank and the train started with a jump that almost sent the newspaper men on their heads. Things began to dance around the car furiously as the train dashed along at a great pace, and the reporters began to wonder what Engineer Oliver meant by his talk about precautions. All along the route up the valley at the stations were crowds of people, who stared in silence as the train swept by. On the station platforms were piled barrels of flour, boxes of canned goods, and bales of clothing. The roads leading in from the country to the stations were full of farmers' wagons laden with produce of all kinds for the sufferers,

The road from Rockwood to Johnstown lies in a deep gully, at the bottom of which flows little Stony Creek, now swollen to a torrent. Wooden troughs under the track carry off the water which trickles down from the hills, otherwise the track would be useless. As it is there are frequent washouts, which have been partly filled in, and for ten miles south of Johnstown all trains have to be run very slowly. The branches of trees above the bank which have been blown over graze the cars on the railroad tracks. The *Sun's* special arrived in Johnstown at two o'clock.

CHAPTER XX.

The experience of the newspaper correspondents in the Conemaugh valley was the experience of a lifetime. Few war correspondents, even, have been witnesses of such appalling scenes of horror and desolation. Day after day they were busy recording the annals of death and despair, conscious, meanwhile, that no expressions of accumulated pathos at their command could do justice to the theme. They had only to stand in the street wherever a knot of men had gathered, to hear countless stories of thrilling escapes. Hundreds of people had such narrow escapes that they hardly dared to believe that they were saved for hours after they reached solid ground. William Wise, a young man who lived at Woodvale, was walking along the road when the rush of water came down the valley. He started to rush up the side of the hills, but stopped to help a young woman, Ida Zidstein, to escape; lost too much time, and was forced to drag the young woman upon a high pile of metal near the road. They had clung there several hours, and thought that they could both escape, as the metal pile was not exposed to the full force of the torrent. A telegraph pole came dashing down the flood, its top standing above the water, from which dangled some wires. The pole was caught in an eddy opposite the pile. It shot in toward the two who were clinging there. As the pole swung around, the wires came through the air like a whip-lash, and catching in the hair of the young woman, dragged her down to instant death. The young man remained on the heap of metal for hours before the water subsided so as to allow him to escape.

One man named Homer, with his child, age six, was on one of the houses which were first carried away. He climbed to the roof and held fast there for four hours, floating all the way to Bolivar, fifteen miles below.

A young hero sat upon the roof of his father's house, holding his mother and little sister. Once the house swung in toward a brick structure which still rested on its foundation. As one house struck the other, the boy sprang into one of the windows. As he turned to rescue his mother and sister, the house swung out again, and the boy, seeing that there was no possibility of getting them off, leaped back to their side. A second time the house was stopped —this time by a tree. The boy helped his mother and sister to a place of safety in the tree, but before he could leave the roof, the house was swept on and he was drowned.

One man took his whole family to the roof of his floating house. He and one child escaped to another building, but his wife and five children were whirled around for hours, and finally carried down to the bridge where so many people perished in the flames. They were all rescued.

District Attorney Rose, his wife, two brothers and two sisters were swept across the lower portion of the town. They had been thrown into the water, and were swimming, the men assisting the women. Finally, they got into a back current, and were cast ashore at the foot of the hills back of Knoxville.

One merchant of Johnstown, after floating about upon a piece of wreckage for hours, was carried down to the stone bridge. After a miraculous escape from being burned to death, he was rescued and carried ashore. He was so dazed and terrified by his experience, however, that he walked off the bridge and broke his neck.

One man who was powerless to save his wife, after he had leaped from a burning building to a house floating by, was driven insane by her shrieks for help.

An old gentleman of Verona rescued a modern Moses from the bulrushes. Verona is on the east bank of the Allegheny river, twelve miles above

Pittsburg. Mr. McCutcheon, while standing on the river bank watching the drift floating by, was compelled by instinct to take a skiff and row out to one dense mass of timber. As he reached it, he was startled to find in the centre, out of the reach of the water, a cradle covered with the clothing. As he lifted the coverings aside a pretty five-months-old boy baby smiled on him. The little innocent, unconscious of the scenes it had passed through, crowed with delight as the old man lifted it tenderly, cradle and all, into his skiff and brought it ashore.

Among the miraculous escapes is that of George J. Lea and family. When the rush of water came there were eight people on the roof of Lea's house. The house swung around and floated for nearly half an hour before it struck the wreck above the stone bridge. A three-year-old girl, with sunny, golden hair and dimpled cheeks, prayed all the while that God would save them, and it seemed that God really answered the prayer and directed the house against the drift, enabling every one of the eight to get off.

H. M. Bennett and S. W. Keltz, engineer and conductor of engine No. 1165 and the extra freight, which happened to be lying at South Fork when the dam broke, tell a graphic story of their wonderful flight and escape on the locomotive before the advancing flood. Bennett and Keltz were in the signal tower awaiting orders. The fireman and flagman were on the engine, and two brakemen were asleep in the caboose. Suddenly the men in the tower heard a roaring sound in the valley above them. They looked in that direction and were almost transfixed with horror to see, two miles above them, a huge black wall of water, at least 150 feet in height, rushing down the valley. The fear-stricken men made a rush for the loco-motive, at the same time giving the alarm to the sleeping brakemen in the caboose, but with no avail. It was impossible to aid them further, how-ever, so Bennett and Keltz cut the engine loose from the train, and the engineer, with one wild wrench, threw the lever wide open, and they were away on a mad race for life. It seemed that they would not receive momentum enough to keep ahead of the flood, and they cast one despairing glance back. Then they could see the awful deluge approaching in its might. On it came, rolling and roaring, tossing and tearing houses, sheds and trees in its awful speed as if they were toys. As they looked, they saw the two brake-men rush out of the caboose, but they had not time to gather the slightest idea of the cause of their doom before they, the car and signal tower were tossed high in the air, to disappear forever. Then the engine leaped forward like a thing of life, and speeded down the valley. But fast as it went, the flood gained upon it. In a few moments the shrieking locomotive whizzed around a curve, and they were in sight of a bridge. Horror upon horrors! ahead of them was a freight train, with the rear end almost on the bridge, and to get across was simply impossible. Engineer Bennett then reversed the lever, and succeeded in checking the engine as they glided across the bridge. Then the men jumped and ran for their lives up the hillside. The bridge and the tender of the engine they had been on were swept away like a bundle of matches.

A young man who was a passenger on the Derry express furnishes an interesting account of his experiences. "When we reached Derry," he said, "our train was boarded by a relief committee, and no sooner was it ascertained that we were going on to Sang Hollow than the contributions of provisions and supplies of every kind were piled on board, filling an entire car. On reaching Sang Hollow the scene that presented itself to us was heart-rending. The road was lined with homeless people, some with a trunk or solitary chair, the only thing saved from their household goods, and all wearing an aspect of the most hopeless misery. Men were at work transferring from a freight car a pile of corpses at least sixty in number, and here and there a ghastly something under a covering showed where the body of some

victim of the flood lay awaiting identification or
burial in a nameless grave. Busy workers were
engaged in clearing away the piles of driftwood
and scattered articles of household use which
cumbered the tracks and the roads. These piles
told their own mournful story. There were beds,
bureaus, mattresses, chairs, tables, pictures, dead
horses and mules, overcoats, remnants of dresses
sticking on the branches of trees, and a thousand
other odd pieces of flotsam and jetsam from ruined
homes. I saw a man get off the train and pick up
an insurance policy for $30,000. Another took
away as relics a baby's chair and a confirmation
card in a battered frame. On the banks of the
Little Conemaugh creek people were delving in
the driftwood, which was piled to a depth of six or
seven feet, unearthing and carrying away whatever
could be turned to account. Under those piles, it
is thought, numbers of bodies are buried, not to
be recovered except by the labor of many days.
A woman and a little girl were brought from Johnstown by some means which I could not ascertain.
The woman was in confinement, and was carried
on a lounge, her sole remaining piece of property.
She was taken to Latrobe for hospital treatment.
I cannot understand how it is that people are
unable to make their way from Sang Hollow to
Johnstown. The distance is short, and it should
certainly be a comparatively easy task to get over

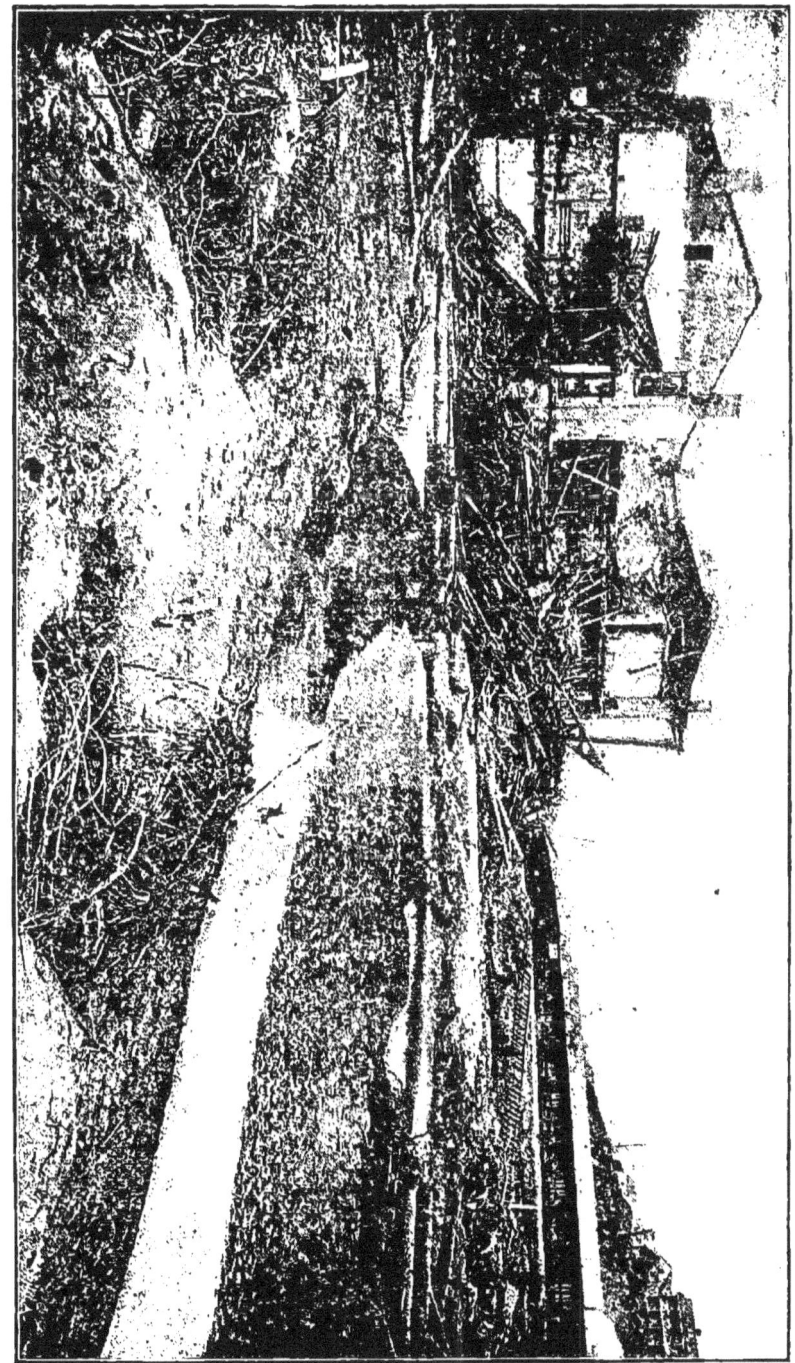

RUINS OF THE CAMBRIA IRON CO'S STORE.

it on foot or horseback. However, there seems to be some insuperable obstacle. All those who made the trip on the train with me in order to obtain tidings of their friends in Johnstown, were forced to return as I did.

"The railroad is in a terrible condition. The day express and the limited, which left Pittsburg on Friday morning, are lying between Johnstown and Conemaugh on the east, having been cut off by the flood. Linemen were sent down from our train at every station to repair the telegraph wires which are damaged. Tremendous efforts are being exerted to repair the injury sustained by the railroad, and it is only a question of a couple of days until through communication is reëstablished. Our homeward trip was marked by a succession of sad spectacles. At Blairsville intersection two little girls lay dead, and in a house taken from the river was the body of a woman. Some idea of the force of the flood may be had from the statement that freight cars, both loaded and empty, had been lifted bodily from the track, and carried a distance of several blocks, and deposited in a graveyard in the outskirts of the town, where they were lying in a mass mixed up with tombstones and monuments."

CHAPTER XXI.

Where the carcass is, there will the vultures be gathered together. It is humiliating to human nature to record it, but it is nevertheless true, that amid all the suffering and sacrifice, and heroism and generosity that was displayed in this awful time, there arose some of the basest passions of unbridled vice. The lust of gain led many skulking wretches to rob and despoil, and even to mutilate the bodies of the dead. Pockets were searched. Jewels were stolen. Finger-rings and ear-rings were torn away, the knife often being used upon the poor, dead clay to facilitate the spoliation. Against this savagery the better elements of the populace sternly revolted. For the time there was no organized government. But outraged and indignant humanity soon formulates its own code of laws. Pistol and rope and bludgeon, in the hand of honesty, did effective work. The reports of summary lynchings that at first were spread abroad were doubtless exaggerated, but they had a stern foundation of truth ; and they had abundant provocation.

238

Writing on that tragic Sunday, one correspondent says: "The way of the transgressor in the desolated valley of the Conemaugh is hard indeed. Each hour reveals some new and horrible story of suffering and outrage, and every succeeding hour brings news of swift and merited punishment meted out to the fiends who have dared to desecrate the stiff and mangled bodies in the city of the dead, and torture the already half-crazed victims of the cruelest of modern catastrophes. Last night a party of thirteen Hungarians were noticed stealthily picking their way along the banks of the Conemaugh toward Sang Hollow. Suspicious of their purpose, several farmers armed themselves and started in pursuit. Soon their most horrible fears were realized. The Hungarians were out for plunder. They came upon the dead and mangled body of a woman, lying upon the shore, upon whose person there were a number of trinkets of jewelry and two diamond rings. In their eagerness to secure the plunder, the Hungarians got into a squabble, during which one of the number severed the finger upon which were the rings, and started on a run with his fearful prize. The revolting nature of the deed so wrought upon the pursuing farmers, who by this time were close at hand, that they gave immediate chase. Some of the Hungarians showed fight, but, being outnumbered, were compelled to flee for their lives. Nine of the brutes escaped, but four were literally driven into the surging river and to their death. The thief who took the rings was among the number of the involuntary suicides."

At 8.30 o'clock this morning an old railroader, who had walked from Sang Hollow, stepped up to a number of men who were on the platform station at Curranville, and said :—

"Gentlemen, had I a shot-gun with me half an hour ago, I would now be a murderer, yet with no fear of ever having to suffer for my crime. Two miles below here I watched three men going along the banks stealing the jewels from the bodies of the dead wives and daughters of men who have been robbed of all they hold dear on earth."

He had no sooner finished the last sentence than five burly men, with looks of terrible determination written on their faces, were on their way to the scene of plunder, one with a coil of rope over his shoulder and another with a revolver in his hand. In twenty minutes, so it is stated, they had overtaken two of their victims, who were then in the act of cutting pieces from the ears and fingers from the hands of the bodies of two dead women. With revolver leveled at the scoundrels, the leader of the posse shouted :—

"Throw up your hands, or I'll blow your heads off!"

With blanched faces and trembling forms, they obeyed the order and begged for mercy. They were searched, and, as their pockets were emptied of their ghastly finds, the indignation of the crowd intensified, and when a bloody finger of an infant encircled with two tiny gold rings was found among the plunder in the leader's pocket, a cry went up, "Lynch them! Lynch them!" Without a moment's delay ropes were thrown around their necks and they were dangling to the limbs of a tree, in the branches of which an hour before were entangled the bodies of a dead father and son. After half an hour the ropes were cut and the bodies lowered and carried to a pile of rocks in the forest on the hill above. It is hinted that an Allegheny county official was one of the most prominent in this justifiable homicide.

One miserable wretch who was caught in the act of mutilating a body was chased by a crowd of citizens, and when captured was promptly strung up to a telegraph pole. A company of officers rescued him before he was dead, much to the disgust of many reputable people, whose feelings had been outraged by the treatment of their deceased relations. Shortly after midnight an attempt was made to rob the First National Bank, which, with the exception of the vaults, had been destroyed. The plunderers were discovered by the citizens' patrol, which had been established during the

night, and a lively chase ensued. A number of
the thieves—six, it is said—were shot.   It is not
known whether any were killed or not, as their
bodies would have been washed away almost immediately if such had been the case.

A number of Hungarians collected about a
number of bodies at Cambria which had been
washed up, and began rifling the trunks.   After
they had secured all the contents they turned their
attention to the dead.

The ghastly spectacle presented by the distorted
features of those who had lost their lives during
the flood had no influence upon the ghouls, who
acted more like wild beasts than human beings.
They took every article from the clothing on the
dead bodies, not leaving anything of value or anything that would serve to identify the remains.

After the miscreants had removed all their
plunder to dry ground a dispute arose over a
division of the spoils.   A pitched battle followed,
and for a time the situation was alarming. Knives
and clubs were used freely.   As a result several
of the combatants were seriously wounded and
left on the ground, their fellow-countrymen not
making any attempt to remove them from the
field of strife.

A Hungarian was caught in the act of cutting
off a dead woman's finger, on which was a costly
ring.   The infuriated spectators raised an outcry

and the fiend fled. He was hotly pursued, and after a half-hour's hard chase, was captured and hanged to a telegraph pole, but was cut down and resuscitated by officers. Liquor emboldened the ghouls, and Pittsburg was telegraphed for help, and the 18th and 14th Regiments, Battery B and the Washington Infantry were at once called out for duty, members being apprised by posters in the newspaper windows.

One correspondent wrote: " The number of drunken men is remarkable. Whiskey seems marvelously plenty. Men are actually carrying it around in pails. Barrels of the stuff are constantly located among the drifts, and *men are scrambling over each other and fighting like wild beasts* in their mad search for it. At the cemetery, at the upper end of town, I saw a sight that rivals the Inferno. A number of ghouls had found a lot of fine groceries, among them a barrel of brandy, with which they were fairly stuffing themselves. One huge fellow was standing on the strings of an upright piano singing a profane song, every little while breaking into a wild dance. A half-dozen others were engaged in a hand-to-hand fight over the possession of some treasure stolen from a ruined house, and the crowd around the barrel were yelling like wild men."

These reports were largely discredited and denied by later and probably more trustworthy authorities, but there was doubtless a considerable residue of truth in them.

There were so many contradictory stories about these horrible doings that our painstaking correspondent put to "Chall" Dick, the Deputy Sheriff, this "leading question": "Did you shoot any robbers?" Chall did not make instant reply, but finally looked up with a peculiar expression on his face and said:—

"There are some men whom their friends will never again see alive."

"Well, now, how many did you shoot?" was the next question.

"Say," said Chall. "On Saturday morning I was the first to make my way to Sang Hollow to see if I could not get some food for people made homeless by the flood. There was a car-load of provisions there, but the vandals were on hand. They broke into the car and, in spite of my protestations, carried off box after box of supplies. I only got half a wagon load. They were too many for me. I know when I have no show. There was no show there and I got out.

"As I was leaving Sang Hollow and got up the mountain road a piece, I saw two Hungarians and one woman engaged in cutting the fingers off of corpses to get some rings. Well, I got off that team and—well, there are three people who were not drowned and who are not alive."

" Where are the bodies ?"

" Ain't the river handy there ?   I went down to Sang Hollow on Sunday, but I went fixed for trouble that time.   When I got into the hollow the officers had in tow a man who claimed he was arrested because he had bummed it on the freight train.   A large crowd of men were trying to rescue the fellow.   I rode into that crowd and scattered it.   I got between the crowd and officers, who succeeded in getting their man in here.   The fellow had been robbing the dead and had a lot of jewelry on his person.   I see by the papers that Consul Max Schamberg, of Pittsburg, asserts that the Huns are a law-abiding race, and that when they were accused of robbing the dead they were simply engaged in trying to identify some of their friends.   Consul Schamberg does not know what he is talking about.   I know better, for I saw them engaged in robbing the dead.

" Those I caught at it will never do the like again.   Why, I saw them let go of their friends in the water to catch a bedstead with a mattress on it.   That's the sort of law-abiding citizens the Huns are."

Down the Cambria road, past which the dead of the river Conemaugh swept into Nineveh in awful numbers, was witnessed a wretched scene —that of a young officer of the National Guard in full uniform, and a poor deputy-sheriff, who had lost home, wife, children and all, clinched like madmen and struggling for the former's revolver. If the officer of the Guard had won, there might have been a tragedy, for he was drunk. The homeless deputy-sheriff, with his wife and babies swept to death past the place where they struggled, was sober and in the right.

The officer was a first lieutenant. His company came with that regiment into this valley of distress to protect survivors from ruffianism and maintain the peace and dignity of the State. The man with whom he fought for the weapon was almost crazy in his own woe, but singularly cool and self-possessed regarding the safety of those left living.

It was one o'clock in the afternoon when a Philadelphia *Press* correspondent noticed on the Cambria road the young officer with his long military coat cut open, leaning heavily for support upon two privates. He was crying in a maudlin way, "You just take me to a place and I'll drink soft stuff." They entreated him to return at once to the regimental headquarters, even begged him, but he cast them aside and went staggering down the road to the line, where he met the grave-faced deputy face to face. The latter looked in the white of his eyes and said: "You can't pass here, sir."

"Can't pass here?" he cried, waving his arms. "You challenge an officer?   Stand aside!"

"You can't pass here!" this time quietly, but firmly; "not while you're drunk."

"Stand aside!" yelled the lieutenant. "Do you know who I am? You talk to an officer of the National Guard."

"Yes; and listen," said the man in front of him so impatiently that it hushed his antagonist's tirade. "I talk to an 'officer' of the National Guard—I who have lost my wife, my children and all in this flood no man has yet described; we who have seen our dead with their bodies mutilated and their fingers cut from their hands by dirty foreigners for a little gold, are not afraid to talk for what is right, even to an officer of the National Guard."

While he spoke another great, dark, stout man, who looked as if he had suffered, came up, and upon taking in the situation every vein in his forehead swelled purple with rage.

"You dirty cur," he cried to the officer; "you dirty, drunken cur, if it was not for the sake of peace I'd lay you out where you stand."

"Come on," yelled the Lieutenant, with an oath.

The big man sent out a terrible blow that would have left the Lieutenant senseless had not one of the privates dashed in between, receiving part of it and warding it off. The Lieutenant got out of his military coat. The privates seized the big man and with another correspondent, who ran to the scene, held him back. The Lieutenant put his hand to his pistol pocket, the deputy seized him, and the struggle for the weapon began. For a moment it was fierce and desperate, then another private came to the deputy's assistance. The revolver was wrested from the drunken officer and he himself was pushed back panting to the ground.

The deputy seized the military coat he had thrown on the ground, and with it and the weapon started to the regimental headquarters. Then the privates got around him and begged him, one of them with tears in his eyes, not to report their officer, saying that he was a good man when he was sober. He studied a long while, standing in the road, while the officer slunk away over the hill. Then he threw the disgraced uniform to them, and said: "Here, give them to him; and, mind you, if he does not go at once to his quarters, I'll take him there, dead or alive."

CHAPTER XXII.

While yet the first wild cry of anguish was thrilling among the startled hills of the Conemaugh, the great heart of the nation answered it with a mighty throb of sympathy. On Tuesday afternoon, at Washington, the President called a gathering of eminent citizens to devise measures of relief. The meeting was held in Willard's Hall, on F street, above Fourteenth, and President Harrison made such an eloquent appeal for assistance that nearly $10,000 was raised in the hour and a half that the meeting was in session.

As presiding officer the Chief Magistrate sat in a big arm-chair on the stage. On his right were District Commissioner Douglass, Hine and Raymond, and on his left sat Postmaster-General Wanamaker and Private Secretary Halford. In the audience were Secretaries Noble, Proctor and Tracy, Attorney-General Miller, Congressman Randall and Senators and Representatives from all parts of the country.

President Harrison called the meeting to order promptly at 3 o'clock. A dead silence fell over the three hundred people as the President stepped to the front of the platform and in a clear, distinct voice appealed for aid for the thousands who had been bereft of their all by the terrible calamity. His voice trembled once or twice as he dwelt upon the scene of death and desolation, and a number of handkerchiefs were called into use at his vivid portrayal of the disaster.

Upon taking the chair the President said :—

"Every one here to-day is distressingly conscious of the circumstances which have convened this meeting. It would be impossible to state more impressively than the newspapers have already done the distressing incidents attending the calamity which has fallen upon the city of Johnstown and the neighboring hamlets, and upon a large section of Pennsylvania situated upon the Susquehanna river. The grim pencil of Doré would be inadequate to portray the horrors of this visitation. In such meetings as we have here in the national capital and other like gatherings that are taking place in all the cities of this land, we have the only rays of hope and light in the general gloom. When such a calamitous visitation falls upon any section of our country we can do no more than to put about the dark picture the golden border of love and charity. [Applause.] It is in such fires as these that the brotherhood of man is welded.

"And where is sympathy and help more appropriate than here in the national capital? I am glad to say that early this morning, from a city not long ago visited with pestilence, not long ago itself appealing to the charitable people of the whole land for relief—the city of Jacksonville, Fla.—there came the ebb of that tide of charity which flowed toward it in the time of its need, in a telegram from the Sanitary Relief Association authorizing me to draw upon them for $2000 for the relief of the Pennsylvania sufferers. [Applause.]

"But this is no time for speech. While I talk men and women are suffering for the relief which we plan to give. One word or two of practical suggestion, and I will place this meeting in your hands to give effect to your impatient benevolence. ·I have a despatch from the Governor of Pennsylvania advising me that communication has just been opened with Williamsport, on a branch of the Susquehanna river, and that the losses in that section have been appalling; that thousands of people there are homeless and penniless, and that there is an immediate call for food to relieve their necessities. He advises me that any supplies of food that can be hastily gathered here should be sent via Harrisburg to Williamsport, where they will be distributed. I suggest, therefore, that a committee be constituted having in charge the speedy collection of articles of food.

"The occasion is such that the bells might well be rung through your streets to call the attention of the thoughtless to this great exigency—in order that a train load of provisions may be despatched to-night or in the early morning to this suffering people.

"I suggest, secondly, as many of these people have had the entire furnishings of their houses swept away and have now only temporary shelter, that a committee be appointed to collect such articles of clothing, and especially bed clothing, as can be spared. Now that the summer season is on, there can hardly be a house in Washington which cannot spare a blanket or a coverlet.

"And, third, I suggest that from the substantial business men and bankers there be appointed a committee who shall collect money, for after the first exigency is past there will be found in those communities very many who have lost their all, who will need aid in the construction of their demolished homes and in furnishing them so that they may be again inhabited.

"Need I say in conclusion that, as a temporary citizen of Washington, it would give me great satisfaction if the national capital should so generously respond to this call of our distressed fellow citi-

THIRD STREET, WILLIAMSPORT, DURING THE FLOOD.

zens as to be conspicuous among the cities of our land. [Applause.] I feel that, as I am now calling for contributions, I should state that on Saturday, when first apprised of the disaster at Johnstown, I telegraphed a subscription to the Mayor of that city. I do not like to speak of anything so personal as this, but I felt it due to myself and to you that I should say so much as this."

The vice presidents elected included all the members of the Cabinet, Chief Justices Fuller, Bingham and Richardson, M. G. Emery, J. A. J. Cresswell, Dr. E. B. Clark, of the Bank of the Republic; C. L. Glover, of the Riggs Bank; Cashier James, of the Bank of Washington; B. H. Warner, Ex-Commissioners Webb and Wheatley, Jesse B. Wilson, Ex-Minister Foster and J. W. Thompson. The secretaries were S. H. Kaufmann, Beriah Wilkins, E. W. Murphy and Hallett Kilbourne; treasurer, E. Kurtz Johnson.

While subscriptions were being taken up, the President intimated that suggestions would be in order, and a prompt and generous response was the result. The Adams Express Company volunteered to transport all material for the relief of the distressed people free of charge, and the Lamont Opera Company tendered their services for a benefit, to be given in aid of the sufferers. The managers offered the use of their theatre free of charge for any performances. Numerous other

15

offers of provisions and clothing were made and accepted.

Then President Harrison read a number of telegrams from Governor Beaver, in which he gave a brief synopsis of the horrors of the situation and asked for the government pontoon bridge.

"I regret to say," added the President, "that the entire length of the pontoon bridge is only 550 feet. Governor Beaver advises me that the present horrors are not alone to be dreaded, but he fears that pestilence may come. I would therefore suggest that disinfectants be included in the donations. I think we should concentrate our efforts and work, through one channel, so that the work may be expeditiously done. In view of that fact we should have one headquarters and everything should be sent there. Then it could be shipped without delay."

The use of Willard Hall was tendered and decided upon as a central point. The District Commissioners were appointed a committee to receive and forward the contributions. When the collections had been made, the amounts were read out and included sums ranging from $500 to $1.

The President, in dismissing the meeting, said :—

" May I express the hope that this work will be earnestly and thoroughly pushed, and that every man and woman present will go from this meeting to use their influence in order that these supplies of food and clothing so much and so promptly needed may be secured, and that either to-night or to-morrow morning a train well freighted with relief may go from Washington."

In adjourning the meeting, President Harrison urged expediency in forwarding the materials for the sufferers. Just before adjournment a resolution was read, thanking the President for the interest he had taken in the matter. President Harrison stepped to the front of the platform then, and declined the resolution in a few graceful remarks.

"I appreciate the resolution," he said, "but I don't see why I should be thanked any more than the others, and I would prefer that the resolution be withdrawn."

Pension Commissioner Tanner, on Monday, sent the following telegram to the United States Pension agent at Pittsburg :—

"Make special any current vouchers from the towns in Pennsylvania ruined by floods and pay at once on their receipt. Where certificates have been lost in floods send permit to execute new voucher without presenting certificate to magistrate. Permits signed in blank forwarded to-day. Make special all original certificates of pensioners residing in those towns and pay on receipt of vouchers, regardless of my instruction of May 13th."

The Governor of Pennsylvania issued the following :—

"COMMONWEALTH OF PENNSYLVANIA,

"EXECUTIVE CHAMBER,

"HARRISBURG, PA., June 3d, 1889.

"*To the People of the United States :*—

"The Executive of the Commonwealth of Pennsylvania has refrained hitherto from making any appeal to the people for their benefactions, in order that he might receive definite and reliable information from the centres of disaster during the late floods, which have been unprecedented in the history of the State or nation. Communication by wire has been established with Johnstown to-day. The civil authorities are in control, the Adjutant General of the State coöperating with them ; order has been restored and is likely to continue. Newspaper reports as to the loss of life and property have not been exaggerated.

"The valley of the Conemaugh, which is peculiar, has been swept from one end to the other as with the besom of destruction. It contained a population of forty thousand to fifty thousand people, living for the most part along the banks of a small river confined within narrow limits. The most conservative estimates place the loss of life at 5000 human beings, and of property at twenty-five millions. Whole towns have been utterly destroyed. Not a vestige remains. In the more substantial towns the better buildings, to a certain extent, remain, but in a damaged condition. Those who are least able to bear it have suffered the loss of everything.

"The most pressing needs, so far as food is concerned, have been supplied. Shoes and clothing of all sorts for men, women and children are greatly needed. Money is also urgently required to remove the débris, bury the dead and care temporarily for the widows and orphans and for the homeless generally. Other localities have suffered to some extent in the same way, but not in the same degree.

"Late advices seem to indicate that there is great loss of life and destruction of property along the west branch of the Susquehanna and in localities from which we can get no definite information. What does come, however, is of the most appalling character, and it is expected that the details will add new horrors to the situation.

"The responses from within and without the State have been most generous and cheering. North and South, East and West, from the United States and from England, there comes the same hearty, generous response of sympathy and help. The President, Governors of States, Mayors of cities, and individuals and communities, private and municipal corporations, seem to vie with each other in their expressions of sympathy and in their contributions of substantial aid. But, gratifying as these responses are, there is no danger of their exceeding the necessities of the situation.

"A careful organization has been made upon the ground for the distribution of whatever assistance is furnished, in kind. The Adjutant General of the State is there as the representative of the State authorities, and is giving personal attention, in connection with the Chief Burgess of Johnstown and a committee of relief, to the distribution of the help which is furnished.

"Funds contributed in aid of the sufferers can be deposited with Drexel & Co., Philadelphia ; Jacob C. Bomberger, banker, Harrisburg, or William R. Thompson & Co., bankers, Pittsburg. All money contributed will be used carefully and judiciously. Present wants are fairly met.

"A large force will be employed at once to remove the débris and bury the dead, so as to avoid disease and epidemic.

"The people of the Commonwealth and others whose unselfish generosity is hereby heartily appreciated and acknowledged may be assured that their contributions will be made to bring their benefactions to the immediate and direct relief of those for whose benefit they are intended.

"JAMES A. BEAVER.

"By the Governor, CHARLES W. STONE, Secretary of the Commonwealth."

Governor Hill, of New York, also issued the following proclamation :—

STATE OF NEW YORK.

"A disaster unparalleled of its kind in the history of our nation has overtaken the inhabitants of the city of Johnstown and surrounding towns in our sister State of Pennsylvania. In consequence of a mighty flood thousands of lives have been lost, and thousands of those saved from the waters are homeless and in want. The sympathy of all the people of the State of New York is profoundly aroused in behalf of the unfortunate sufferers by the calamity. The State, in its capacity as such, has no power to aid, but the generous-hearted citizens of our State are always ready and willing to afford relief to those of their fellow countrymen who are in need, whenever just appeal has been made.

"Therefore, as the Governor of the State of New York, I hereby suggest that in each city and town in the State relief committees be formed, contributions be solicited and such other appropriate action be taken as will promptly afford material assistance and necessary aid to the unfortunate. Let the citizens of every portion of the State vie with each other in helping with liberal hand this worthy and urgent cause.

"Done at the Capitol, this third day of June, in the year of our Lord one thousand eight hundred and eighty-nine." DAVID B. HILL.

By the Governor, WILLIAM G. RICE, *Sec.*

Nor were Americans in foreign lands less prompt with their offerings. On Wednesday, in Paris, a meeting of Americans was held at the United States Legation, on a call in the morning papers by Whitelaw Reid, the United States Minister, to express the sympathy of the Americans in Paris with the sufferers by the Johnstown calamity. In spite of the short notice the rooms of the Legation were packed, and many went away unable to gain admittance. Mr. Reid was called to the chair, and Mr. Ernest Lambert was appointed secretary. The following resolutions were offered by Mr. Andrew Carnegie and seconded by Mr. James N. Otis :—

Resolved, That we send across the Atlantic to our brethren, overwhelmed by the appalling disaster at Johnstown, our most profound and heartfelt sympathy. Over their lost ones we mourn with them, and in every pang of all their misery we have our part.

Resolved, That as American citizens we congratulate them upon and thank them for the numerous acts of noble heroism displayed under circumstances calculated to unnerve the bravest. Especially do we honor and admire them for the capacity shown for local self-government, upon which the stability of republican institutions depends, the military organizations sent from distant points to preserve order during the chaos that supervened having been returned to their homes as no longer required within forty-eight hours of the calamity. In these few hours the civil power recreated and asserted itself and resumed sway without the aid of counsel from distant authorities, but solely by and from the inherent power which remains in the people of Johnstown themselves.

Resolved, That the thanks of this meeting be cordially tendered to Mr. Reid for his prompt and appropriate action in this matter, and for services as chairman of this meeting.

Resolved, That a copy of these resolutions be forwarded at once by telegraph to the Mayors of Johnstown, Pittsburg and Philadelphia.

Brief and touching speeches were made by General Lawton, late United States Minister to Austria; the Hon. Abram S. Hewitt, General Meredith Read and others.

The resolutions were then unanimously adopted, and a committee was appointed to receive subscriptions. About 40,000 francs were subscribed on the spot. The American bankers all agreed to open subscriptions the next day at their banking houses. "Buffalo Bill" subscribed the entire receipts of one entertainment, to be given under the auspices of the committee.

Besides those already named, there were present Benjamin Brewster, Louis von Hoffman, Charles A. Pratt, ex-Congressman Lloyd Bryce,

Clarence Dinsmore, Edward Tuck, Professor Chanler, the Rev. Dr. Stoddard and others from New York; Colonel Otis Ritchie, of Boston; General Franklin and Assistant Commissioner Tuck; George W. Allen, of St. Louis; Consul-General Rathbone, and a large number of the American colony in Paris. It was the largest and most earnest meeting of Americans held in Paris for many years.

The Municipal Council of Paris gave 5000 francs to the victims of the floods.

In London, the American Minister, Mr. Robert T. Lincoln, received from his countrymen there large contributions. Mr. Marshall R. Wilder, the comedian, gave an evening of recitations to swell the fund. Generous contributions also came from Berlin and other European cities.

CHAPTER XXIII.

Spontaneously as the floods descended upon the fated valley, the American people sprang to the relief of the survivors. In every city and town subscription lists were opened, and clothing and bedding and food were forwarded by the train-load. Managers gave theatrical perform-ances and baseball clubs gave benefit games to swell the fund. The Mayors of New York, Phila-delphia and other large cities took personal charge of the collection and forwarding of funds and goods. In New York a meeting of representative citizens was called by the Mayor, and a committee formed, with General Sherman as chairman, and the presidents of the Produce Exchange and the Chamber of Commerce among the vice-chairmen, while the president of the Stock Exchange acted as treasurer. The following appeal was issued :—

"*To the People of the City of New York :*—

"The undersigned have been appointed a com-mittee by a meeting held at the call of the Mayor of the city to devise means for the succor and relief of the sufferers in the Conemaugh Valley. A disaster of unparalleled magnitude has overtaken the people of that valley and elsewhere. Without warning, their homes have been swept away by an unexpected and unprecedented flood. The daily journals of this city contain long lists of the dead, and the number of those who perished is still unknown. The survivors are destitute. They are houseless and homeless, with scant food and no shelter, and the destructive waters have not yet subsided.

" In this emergency their cry for help reaches us. There has never been an occasion in our history that the appeal to our citizens to be generous in their contributions was of greater moment than the present. That generosity which has distinguished them above the citizens of every other city, and which was extended to the relief of the famishing in Ireland, to the stricken city of Charleston, to the plague-smitten city of Jacksonville, and so on through the record of every event where man was compelled to appeal to man, will not be lacking in this most recent calamity. Generous contributions have already reached the committee. Let the amount increase until they swell into a mighty river of benevolence.

" The committee earnestly request, as the want is pressing and succor to be effectual must be speedy, that all contributions be sent at as early a date as possible. Their receipt will be promptly acknowledged and they will be applied, through responsible channels, to the relief of the destitute and suffering."

All the exchanges, newspapers and other public agencies took up the work, and hundreds of thousands of dollars rolled in every day. Special collections were taken in the churches, and large sums were thus realized.

In Philadelphia the work of relief was entered into in a similar manner, with equally gratifying results. By Tuesday evening the various funds established in that city for the sufferers had reached a total of $360,000. In addition over 100,000 packages of provisions, clothing, etc., making fully twenty car-loads, had been started on the way. The leading business houses tendered the service of their delivery wagons for the collection of goods, and some of them placed donation boxes at their establishments, yielding handsome returns.

At a meeting of the Board of Directors of the Pennsylvania Railroad Company the following resolution was adopted by a unanimous vote :—

"*Resolved*, That in addition to the $5000 subscribed by this company at Pittsburg, the Pennsylvania Railroad Company hereby makes an extra donation of $25,000 for the assistance of the sufferers by the recent floods at Johnstown and other points upon the lines of the Pennsylvania Railroad and the other affiliated roads, the contribution to be expended under the direction of the Committee on Finance."

At the same time the members of the Board and executive officers added a contribution, as individuals, of $5000.

The Philadelphia and Reading Railroad Company subscribed $10,000 to the Citizens' Fund.

In pursuance of a call issued by the Citizens' Permanent Relief Association, a largely-attended meeting was held at the Mayor's office. Drexel & Co., the treasurers of the fund, started the fund with a contribution of $10,000. Several subscriptions of $1000 each were announced. Many subscriptions were sent direct to Drexel & Co.'s banking house, including $5000 from the Philadelphia brewers, $5000 from the Baldwin Locomotive Works and other individual contributors.

But the great cities had no monopoly of benefactions. How every town in the land responded to the call may be imagined from a few items clipped at random from the daily papers, items the like of which for days crowded many columns of the public press :—

Bethlehem, Penn., June 3.—The Bethlehem Iron Company to-day contributed $5000 for the relief of the sufferers.

Johnstown, Penn., June 3.—Stephen Collins, of

the Pittsburg post-office, and several other members of the Junior Order of United American
Mechanics, were here to-day to establish a relief
fund. They have informed the committees that
the members of this strong organization are ready
to do their best for their sufferers.

Buffalo, June 3.—A meeting was held at the
Mayor's office to-day to devise means for the aid
of the flood sufferers. The Mayor sent $1000 by
telegraph this afternoon. A committee was
appointed to raise funds. The Merchants' Exchange also started a relief fund this morning.
A relief train on the Western New York and
Pennsylvania Railroad left here for Pittsburg to-
night with contributions of food and clothing.

Albany, June 3.—*The Morning Express* to-day
started a subscription for the relief of the sufferers. A public meeting, presided over by Mayor
Maher, was held at noon to-day, and a number of
plans were adopted for securing funds. There is
now on hand $1000. Another meeting was held
this evening. The offertory in the city churches
will be devoted to the fund.

Poughkeepsie, June 3.—A general movement
was begun here to-day to aid the sufferers in Pennsylvania. Mayor Rowley issued a proclamation
and people have been sending money to *The
Eagle* office all day. Factory operatives are contributing, clergymen are taking hold of the matter,

and to-night the Retail Dealers' Association held a public meeting at the Court House to appoint committees to go about among the merchants with subscription lists. Mrs. Brazier, proprietress of a knitting factory, sent off sixty dozen suits of underwear to the sufferers to-day.

Troy, June 3.—Subscriptions exceeding $1500 for the relief of the Pennsylvania flood sufferers were received to-day by *The Troy Press.* The Mayor has called a public meeting for to-morrow.

Washington, June 3.—A subscription for the relief of the sufferers by the Johnstown flood was started at the Post-office Department to-day by Chief Clerk Cooley. First Assistant Postmaster-General Clarkson headed the list with $100. The indications are that nearly $1000 will be raised in this Department. Postmaster-General Wanamaker had already subscribed $1000 in Philadelphia.

The Post has started a subscription for the relief of the Johnstown sufferers. It amounts at present to $810. The largest single contribution is $250 by Allen McLane.

Trenton, June 3.—In the Board of Trade rooms to-night over $1000 was subscribed for the benefit of Johnstown sufferers. Contributions made to-day will swell the sum to double that amount. Committees were appointed to canvass the city.

Chicago, June 3.—Mayor Cregier called a pub-

WRECK OF TRUSS BRIDGE, AT WILLIAMSPORT.

lic meeting, which was held at the City Hall to-day, to take measures for the relief of the Johnstown sufferers. John B. Drake, of the Grand Pacific, headed a subscription with $500.

Hartford, Conn., June 3.—The House to-day concurred with the Senate in passing the resolution appropriating $25,000 for the flood sufferers.

Boston, June 3.—The House this afternoon admitted a bill appropriating $10,000 for the relief of the sufferers.

A citizens' committee will receive subscriptions. It was announced that $4600 had already been subscribed. Dockstader's Minstrels will give a benefit to-morrow afternoon in aid of the sufferers' fund.

Pittsfield, Mass., June 3.—A meeting was held here to-night and about $300 was raised for the Johnstown sufferers. The town will be canvassed to-morrow. Senator Dawes attended the meeting, made an address and contributed liberally.

Charleston, S. C., June 3.—At a meeting of the Charleston Cotton Exchange to-day $500 was subscribed for the relief of the flood sufferers.

Fort Worth, Texas, June 3.—The Texas Spring Palace Association to-night telegraphed to George W. Childs, of Philadelphia, that to-morrow's receipts at the Spring Palace will be given to the sufferers by the flood.

Nashville, Tenn., June 3.—*The American* to-

16

day started a fund for the relief of the Johnstown sufferers.

Utica, June 4.—Utica to-day sent $2000 to Johnstown.

Ithaca, June 4.—Cornell University has collected $800 for the sufferers.

Troy, June 4.—*The Troy Times* sent this afternoon $1200 to the Mayor of Pittsburg. *The Press* sent $1000, making $2000 forwarded by *The Press.*

Boston, June 4.—The House to-day amended its bill of yesterday and appropriated $30,000.

The Citizens' Committee has received $12,000, and Governor Ames' check for $250 was received.

New Bedford, Mass., June 4.—Mayor Clifford has sent $500 to the sufferers.

Providence, R. I., June 4.—A meeting of business men this morning raised $4000 for the sufferers.

Erie, Penn., June 4.—In mass meeting last night ex-Congressman W. L. Scott led with a $1500 subscription for Johnstown, followed by ex-Judge Galbraith with $500. The list footed up $6000 in a quarter of an hour. Ward committees were appointed to raise it to $10,000. In addition to a general subscription of $1000, which was sent forward yesterday, it is rumored that a private gift of $5000 was also sent.

Toledo, June 4.—Two thousand dollars have been obtained here for the flood sufferers.

Cleveland, June 4.—Over $16,000 was sub-scribed yesterday, which, added to the $5000 raised on Sunday, swells Cleveland's cash con-tributions to $21,000. Two car-loads of provisions and clothing and twenty-one car-loads of lumber went forward to Johnstown.

Cincinnati, June 4.—Subscriptions amounting to $10,000 were taken on 'Change yesterday.

Milwaukee, June 4.—State Grand Commander Weissert telegraphed $250 to the Pennsylvania Department yesterday.

Detroit, June 4.—The relief fund already reaches nearly $1000. Ex-Governor Alger and Senator James McMillan have each telegraphed $500 to the scene of the disaster.

Chicago, June 4.—A meeting of business men was held this morning to collect subscriptions. Several large subscriptions, including one of $1000 by Marshall Field & Co., were received. The committees expect to raise $50,000 within twenty-four hours.

Governor Fifer has issued a proclamation urging the people to take measures for render-ing aid. The Aldermen of Chicago subscribed among themselves a purse of $1000. The jew-elers raised $1500. On the Board of Trade one member obtained $5000, and another $4000.

From a citizens' meeting in Denver to-night $2500 was raised.

President Hughitt announces that the Chicago and Northwestern, the Chicago, St. Paul, Minneapolis and Omaha, and the Fremont, Elkhorn and Missouri Valley Railways will transport, free of charge, all provisions and clothing for the sufferers.

Kansas City, Mo., June 4.—At the mass meeting last night a large sum was subscribed for the sufferers.

Chattanooga, June 3.—Chattanooga to-day subscribed $500.

Wilmington, Del., June 4.—Over $2700 has been raised here for the sufferers. A carload of supplies was shipped last night. Two doctors have offered their services.

Knoxville, Tenn., June 4.—The relief committee to-day raised over $1500 in two hours for the sufferers in Johnstown and vicinity.

Saratoga, June 4.—The village of Saratoga Springs has raised $2000. Judge Henry Hilton subscribed one-half the amount. A committee was appointed to-night to solicit additional subscriptions.

Carlisle, Penn., June 4.—Aid for the sufferers has been pouring in from all sections of the Cumberland Valley. From this city $700 and a supply of clothing and provisions have been sent. Among the contributions to-day was $100 from the Indian children at the Government training school.

Charleston, S. C., June 4.—The City Council to-day voted $1000 for the relief of the Pennsylvania sufferers. The Executive Committee of the Chamber of Commerce subscribed $380 in a few minutes, and appointed three committees to canvass for subscriptions. The Merchants' Exchange is at work and general subscriptions are starting.

St. Louis, June 4.—Generous subscriptions for the Conemaugh Valley sufferers have been made here. The Merchants' Exchange has called a mass meeting for to-morrow.

Middletown, June 4.—To-day the Mayor telegraphed the Mayor of Johnstown to draw on him for $1000.

Poughkeepsie, June 4.—Mayor Rowley to-day sent $1638 to Drexel & Co., Philadelphia. As much more was subscribed to-day.

Auburn, June 5.—Auburn has subscribed $2000.

Lockport, N. Y., June 5.—The Brewers' National Convention at Niagara Falls this morning contributed $10,000.

St. Johnsbury, Vt., June 5.—Grand Master Henderson issued an invitation to-day to Odd Fellows in Vermont to contribute toward the sufferers.

Newburg, N. Y., June 5.—Newburg has raised about $2000 for the sufferers.

Worcester, Mass., June 5.—Subscriptions to the amount of $2400 were made here to-day.

Boston, June 5.—The total of the subscriptions

received through Kidder, Peabody & Co. to-day amounted to $35,400. The Fall River Line will forward supplies free of charge.

Providence, June 5.—The subscriptions here now exceed $11,000.

Minneapolis, June 5.—The Citizens' Committee to-day voted to send 2000 barrels of flour to the sufferers.

Chicago, June 5.—It is estimated that Chicago's cash contributions to date aggregate about $90,-000.

St. Louis, June 5.—The town of Desoto in this State has contributed $200. Litchfield, Ill., has also raised $200.

Los Angeles, Cal., June 5.—This city has forwarded $2000 to Governor Beaver.

Macon, June 5.—The City Council last night appropriated $200 for the sufferers.

Chattanooga, Tenn., June 5.—A. B. Forrest Camp, No. 3, Confederate Veterans. of Chattanooga, have contributed $100 to the relief fund. J. M. Duncan, general manager of the South Tredegar Iron Company, of this city, who a few years ago left Johnstown for Chattanooga as a young mechanic, sent $1000 to-day to the relief fund. Another $1000 will be sent from the proceeds of a popular subscription.

Savannah, June 5.—The Savannah Benevolent Association subscribed $1000 for the sufferers.

Binghamton, June 5.—More than $2600 will be sent to Johnstown from this city. Lieutenant-Governor Jones telegraphed that he would subscribe $100.

Albany, June 5.—Mayor Maher has telegraphed the Mayor of Pittsburg to draw on him for $3000. The fund being raised by *The Morning Express* amounts to over $1141.

Lebanon, Penn., June 5.—This city will raise $5000 for the sufferers.

Rochester, June 5.—Over $400 was subscribed to the Red Cross relief fund to-day and $119 to a newspaper fund besides.

Cleveland, June 5.—The cash collected in this city up to this evening is $38,000. Ten car-loads of merchandise were shipped to Johnstown to-day, and a special train of twenty-eight car-loads of lumber, from Cleveland dealers, left here to-night.

Fonda, N. Y., June 5.—The people of Johnstown, N. Y., instead of making an appropriation with which to celebrate the Fourth of July, will send $1000 to the sufferers at Johnstown, Pa.

New Haven, June 5.—Over $2000 has been collected here.

Wilmington, Del., June 5.—This city's fund has reached $470. The second car-load of supplies will be shipped to-morrow.

Glens Falls, N. Y., June 5.—Subscriptions here to-day amounted to $622.

Poughkeepsie, June 5.—Up to this evening $2736 have been raised in this city for Johnstown.

Washington, June 7.—The total cash contributions of the employees of the Treasury Department to date, amounting to $2070, were to-day handed to the treasurer of the Relief Fund of Washington. The officers and clerks of the several bureaus of the Interior Department have subscribed $2280. The contributions in the Government Printing Office aggregate $1275. Chief Clerk Cooley to-day transmitted to the chairman of the local committee $600 collected in the Post-office Department.

Syracuse, N. Y., June 7.—Mayor Kirk to-day sent to Governor Beaver a draft for $3000.

Utica, N. Y., June 7.—Ilion has raised $1100, and has sent six cases of clothing to Johnstown.

The Little Falls subscription is $700 thus far.

The Utica subscription is now nearly $6000.

Thus the gifts of the people flowed in, day by day, from near and from far, from rich and from poor, to make less dark the awful desolation that had set up its fearful reign in the Valley of the Conemaugh.

CHAPTER XXIV.

THE city of Philadelphia with characteristic generosity began the work of raising a relief fund on the day following the disaster, the Mayor's office and Drexel's banking house being the chief centres of receipt. Within four days six hundred thousand dollars was in hand. A most thorough organization and canvass of all trades and branches of business was made under the following committees:

Machinery and Iron—George Burnham, Daniel A. Waters, William Sellers, W. B. Bement, Hamilton Disston, Walter Wood, J. Lowber Welsh, W. C. Allison, Charles Gilpin, Jr., E. Y. Townsend, Dawson Hoopes, Alvin S. Patterson, Charles H. Cramp, and John H. Brill.

Attorneys—Mayer Sulzberger, George S. Graham, George W. Biddle, Lewis C. Cassidy, William F. Johnson, Joseph Parrish, Hampton L. Carson, John C. Bullitt, John R. Read, and Samuel B. Huey.

Physicians—William Pepper, Horatio C. Wood, Thomas G. Morton, W. H. Pancoast, D. Hayes Agnew, and William W. Keen.

Insurance—R. Dale Benson, C. J. Madeira, E. J. Durban, and John Taylor.

Chemicals—William Weightman, H. B. Rosengarten, and John Wyeth.

City Officers—John Bardsley, Henry Clay, Robert P. Dechert, S. Davis Page, and Judge R. N. Willson.

Paper—A. G. Elliott, Whitney Paper Company, W. E. & E. D. Lockwood, Alexander Balfour, and the Nescochague Paper Manufacturing Company.

Coal—Charles F. Berwind, Austin Corbin, Charles E. Barrington, and George B. Newton.

Wool Dealers—W. W. Justice, David Scull, Coates Brothers, Lewis S. Fish & Co., and Theodore C. Search.

Commercial Exchange—Walter F. Hagar and William Brice.

Board of Trade—Frederick Fraley, T. Morris Perot, John H. Michener, and Joel Cook.

Book Trade, Printing, and Newspapers—Charles Emory Smith, Walter Lippincott, A. K. McClure, Charles E. Warburton, Thomas MacKellar, William M. Singerly, Charles Heber Clark, and William V. McKean.

Furniture—Charles B. Adamson, Hale, Kilburn & Co., John H. Sanderson, and Amos Hillborn & Co.

Bakers and Confectioners—Godfrey Keebler, Carl Edelheim, Croft & Allen, and H. O. Wilbur & Sons.

China, etc.—R. J. Allen, and Tyndale, Mitchell & Co.

Lumber—Thomas P. C. Stokes, William M. Lloyd Company, Henry Bayard & Co., Geissel & Richardson, and D. A. Woelpper.

Cloth and Tailors' Trimmings—Edmund Lewis, Henry N. Steel, Joseph R. Keim, John Alburger, and Samuel Goodman.

Notions, etc.—Joel J. Baily, John Field, Samuel Clarkson, John C. Sullivan, William Super, John C. File, and W. B. Hackenberg.

Clothing—H. B. Blumenthal, William Allen, Leo Loeb, William H. Wanamaker, Alan H. Reed, Morris Newberger, Nathan Snellenburg, Samuel Goodman, and John Alburger.

Dry Goods Manufacturers—Lincoln Godfrey, Lemuel Coffin, N. Parker Shortridge, and W.H. Folwell.

Wholesale Dry Goods—Samuel B. Brown, John M. Howett, Henry H. Ellison, and Edward T. Steel.

Retail Dry Goods—Joseph G. Darlington, Isaac H. Clothier, Granville B. Haines, and Henry W. Sharpless.

Jewelers—Mr. Bailey, of Bailey, Banks & Biddle ; James E. Caldwell, and Simon Muhr.

Straw Goods, Hats, and Millinery—John Adler, C. H. Garden & Co., and Henry Tilge.

City Railways—Alexander M. Fox, William H. Kemble, E. B. Edwards, John F. Sullivan, and Charles E. Ellis.

Photography—F. Gutekunst, A. K. P. Trask, and H. C. Phillips.

Pianos and Musical—W. D. Dutton, Schomacker Piano Company, and C. J. Heppe.

Plumbers—William Harkness, Jr., J. Futhey Smith, C. A. Blessing, and Henry B. Tatham.

Liquors and Brewers—Joseph F. Sinnott, Bergner & Engel, John Gardiner, and John F. Betz.

Hotels—E. F. Kingsley, Thomas Green, L. U. Maltby, C. H. Reisser, and H. J. Crump.

Butchers—Frank Bower and Shuster Boraef.

Woolen Manufacturers—William Wood, George Campbell, Joseph P. Truitt, and John C. Watt.

Retail Grocers—George B. Woodman, George A. Fletcher, Robert Ralston, H. B. Summers, and E. J. Howlett.

Boots and Shoes—John Mundell, John G. Croxton, Henry Z. Ziegler, and A. A. Shumway.

Theatrical—J. Fred. Zimmerman, Israel Fleishman, and T. F. Kelly.

Tobacco Trade—M. J. Dohan, L. Bamberger, E. H. Frishmuth, Jr., Walter Garrett, M. E. McDowell, J. H. Baltz, Henry Weiner, and George W. Bremer.

Hosiery Manufactures—J. B. Allen and James B. Doak, Jr.

Real Estate—Adam Everly, John M. Gummey, and Lewis H. Redner.

Cordage—E. H. Fitler, John T. Bailey, and Charles Lawrence.

Patent Pavement—Dr. L. S. Filbert and James Stewart, Jr.

Bankers and Brokers—Winthrop Smith, Robert H. Glendenning, George H. Thomas, William G. Warden, Lindley Smyth, Thomas Cochran, J. L. Erringer, Charles H. Banes, Wharton Barker, and Jacob Naylor.

Wholesale Grocers and Sugar Refiners—Francis B. Reeves, Edward C. Knight, Adolph Spreckels, William Janney, and Charles C. Harrison.

Shirt Manufacturers and Dealers—Samuel Sternberger and Jacob Miller.

Carpets—James Dobson, Robert Dornan, Hugh McCallum, John F. Orne, John R. White, and Thomas Potter, Jr.

Saddlery Hardware, etc.—William T. Lloyd, of Lloyd & Supplee; Conrad B. Day, George DeB. Keim, Charles Thackara, John C. Cornelius, William Elkins, Jr., and James Peters.

By Tuesday the tide of relief was flowing strongly. On that day between eight and nine thousand packages of goods were sent to the freight depot of the Pennsylvania Railroad, to be forwarded to the sufferers. Wagons came in an apparently endless stream and the quantity of goods received far exceeded that of any previous day. Eight freight cars, tightly packed, were shipped to Johnstown, while five car-loads of provisions were sent to Williamsport, and one of provisions to Lewistown.

The largest consignment of goods from an individual was sent to Williamsport by W. M. McCormick. He was formerly a resident of Williamsport, and when he heard that the people of that city were suffering for want of provisions, he immediately went out and ordered a car-load of flour (one hundred and twenty-five barrels) and a car-load of groceries and provisions, consisting of dried and smoked meats, sugar, crackers, and a large assortment of other necessaries. Mr. McCormick said he thought that several of his friends would go in with him when they knew of the venture, but if they did not he would foot all the bills himself.

The saddest incident of the day was the visit of a handsome young lady, about twenty-three years of age. She was accompanied by an older lady, and brought three packages of clothing. It was Miss Clydia Blackford, whose home was in Johnstown. She said sobbingly that every one of her relatives and friends had been lost in the floods, and her home entirely wiped out. The gift of the packages to the sufferers of her old home seemed to give her a sort of sad pleasure. She departed with tears in her eyes.

When the convicts in the Eastern Penitentiary learned of the disaster through the weekly papers which arrived on Wednesday and Thursday—the only papers they are allowed to receive—a thing that will seem incongruous to the outside world happened. The criminal, alone in his cell, was touched with the same sympathy and desire to help fellow-men in sore distress as the good people who have been filling relief depots with supplies and coffers with money. Each as he read the story of the flood would knock on his wicket and tell the keeper he wanted to give some of his money.

The convicts, by working over and above their daily task, are allowed small pay for the extra time. Half the money so earned goes to the county from which the convict comes and half to the convict himself. The maximum amount a Cherry Hill inmate can make in a week for himself is one dollar.

The keepers told Warden Cassidy of the desire expressed all along that the authorities receive their contributions. The convicts can do what they please with their over-time money, by sending it to their friends, and several had already sent small sums out of the Penitentiary to be given to the Johnstown sufferers. The warden very promptly acceded to the general desire and gave the keepers instructions. There are about one thousand one hundred and ten men imprisoned in the institution, and of this number one hundred and forty-six persons gave five hundred and forty-two dollars and ninety-six cents. It would take one convict working all his extra time ten years to earn that sum.

There was one old man, a cripple, who had fifteen dollars to his credit. He said to the keeper: "I've been doing crooked work nearly all my life, and I want to do something square this time. I want to give all the money coming to me for these fellers out there." The warden, however, had made a rule prohibiting any individual from contributing more than five dollars. The old man was told this, but he was determined. "Look here," said he; "I'll send the rest of my money out to my folks and tell them to send it."

Chief of Police Mayer, in denying reports that there was an influx of professional thieves into the flooded regions to rob the dead, said: "The thieves wouldn't do anything like that; there is too much of the gentleman in them." But here were thieves and criminals going into their own purses out of that same "gentlemanly" part of them.

Up to Saturday, June 8th, the cash contributions in Philadelphia, amounted to $687,872,68. Meantime countless gifts and expressions of sympathy came from all over the world. The Lord Mayor of Dublin, Ireland, raised a fund of $5,000. Archbishop Walsh gave $500.

Sir Julian Pauncefote, the British Minister at Washington, called on the President on June 7th, in company with Secretary Blaine, and delivered a message from Queen Victoria expressing her deep sympathy for the sufferers by the recent floods in Pennsylvania. The President said in reply :

" Mr. Minister : This message of sympathy from Her Majesty the Queen will be accepted by our people as another expression of her own generous character, as well as of the friendliness and good-will of her people. The disasters which have fallen upon several communities in the State of Pennsylvania, while extreme and full of the most tragic and horrifying incidents, have fortunately been limited in territorial extent. The generosity of our own citizens will promptly lessen to these stricken people every loss that is not wholly irretrievable ; and these the sympathy of the Queen and the English people will help to assuage. Will you, Mr. Minister, be pleased to convey to the Queen the sincere thanks of the American people."

A newspaper correspondent called upon the illustrious Miss Florence Nightingale, at her home in London, and asked her to send a message to America regarding the floods. In response, she wrote :

" I am afraid that I cannot write such a message as I would wish to just at this moment. I

WRECK OF THE LUMBER YARDS AT WILLIAMSPORT, PA.

am so overdone. I have the deepest sympathy with the poor sufferers by the floods, and with Miss Clara Barton, of the Red Cross Societies, and the good women who are hastening to their help. I am so overworked and ill that I can feel all the more but write all the less for the crying necessity.

(Signed) " FLORENCE NIGHTINGALE."

Though Miss Nightingale is sixty-nine years old, and an invalid, this note was written in a hand indicating all the strength and vigor of a schoolgirl. She is seldom able to go out now, though when she can she dearly loves to visit the Nightingale Home for Training Nurses, which constitutes such an enduring monument and noble record of her life. But, though in feeble health, Miss Nightingale manages to do a great deal of work yet. From all parts of the world letters pour in upon her, asking advice and suggestions on matters of hospital management, of health and of education, all of which she seldom fails to answer.

Last, but not least, let it be recorded that the members of the club that owned the fatal lake sent promptly a thousand blankets and many thousands of dollars to the sufferers from the floods, which had been caused by their own lack of proper supervision of the dam.

17

CHAPTER XXV.

NEW YORK, Philadelphia, and Pittsburg were, of course, the three chief centres of charitable contributions, and the sources from which the golden flood of relief was poured into the devastated valley. One of the earliest gifts in New York city was that of $1,200, the proceeds of a collection taken on Sunday morning, June 2d, in the West Presbyterian Church, after an appeal by the Rev. Dr. John R. Paxton, the pastor. The next day a meeting of prominent New York business men was held at the Mayor's office, and a relief committee was formed. At this meeting many contributions were announced. Isidor Wormser said that the Produce Exchange had raised $15,000 for the sufferers. Ex-Mayor Grace reported that the Lackawanna Coal and Iron Company had telegraphed the Cambria Iron Company to draw upon it for $5,000 for the relief of the Cambria's employees. Mayor Grant announced that he had received letters and checks during the forenoon aggregating the sum of

$15,000, and added his own for $500. Subscriptions of $1,000 each were offered as fast as the Secretary could record them by Kuhn, Loeb & Co., Jesse Seligman, Calvin S. Brice, Winslow, Lanier & Co., Morris K. Jesup, Oswald Ottendorfer, R. H. Macy & Co., M. Schiff & Co., and O. B. Potter. Sums of $500 were subscribed with equal cheerfulness by Eugene Kelly, Sidney Dillon, the Chatham National Bank, Controller Myers, Cooper, Hewitt & Co., Frederick Gallatin, Tefft, Weller & Co., City Chamberlain Croker, and Tiffany & Co. Numerous gifts of less sums quickly followed. Elliott F. Shepard announced that the *Mail and Express* had already sent $10,000 to Johnstown. Before the Committee on Permanent Organization had time to report, the Secretary gave out the information that $27,000 had been subscribed since the meeting was called to order. Before the day was over no less than $75,000 had been received at the Mayor's office, including the following subscriptions:

Pennsylvania Relief Committee of the Maritime Association of the Port of New York, Gustav H. Schwab, Treasurer, $3,435; Chatham National Bank, $500; Morris K. Jesup, $1,000; William Steinway, $1,000; Theodore W. Myers, $500; J. G. Moore, $1,000; J. W. Gerard, $200; Platt & Bowers, $250; Henry L. Hoguet, $100; Harry Miner, $200; Tefft, Weller & Co., $500; Louis May, $200; Madison Square Bank, $200; Richard Croker, $500; Tiffany & Co., $500; John Fox, $200; Jacob H. Schiff, $1,000; Nash &

Brush, $100; Oswald Ottendorfer, $1,000; William P. St. John, $100; George Hoadly, for Hoadly, Lauterbach & Johnson, $250; Edwin Forrest Lodge, Order of Friendship, $200; W. T. Sherman, $100; W. L. Stone, $500; John R. Dos Passos, $250; G. G. Williams, $100; Coudert Bros., $250; *Staats-Zeitung*, $1,166; Cooper, Hewitt & Co., $500; Frederick Gallatin, $500; R. H. Macy & Co., $1,000; Mr. Caldwell, $100; C. N. Bliss, $500; Ward & Olyphant, $100; Eugene Kelly, $500; Lackawanna Coal and Iron Company, through Mayor Grace, $5,000; W. R. Grace, $500; G. Schwab & Bros., $300; Kuhn, Loeb & Co., $1,000; Central Trust Co., $1,000; Calvin S. Brice, $1,000; J. S. Seligman & Co., $1,000; Sidney Dillon, $500; Winslow, Lanier & Co., $1,000; Hugh J. Grant, $500; Orlando B. Potter, $1,000.

Through *The Tribune*, $319.75; through *The Sun*, $87.50; from Tammany Society, through Richard Croker, $1,000; Joseph Pulitzer, $2,000; Lazard Frères, $1,000; Arnold, Constable & Co., $1,000; D. H. King, Jr., $1,000; August Belmont & Co., $1,000; New York Life Insurance Co., $500; John D. Crimmins, $500; Nathan Manufacturing Co., $500; Hugh N. Camp, $250; National Railway Publishing Co., $200; William Openhym & Sons, $200; New York Transfer Co., $200; Warner Brothers, $100; L. J. and I. Phillips, $100; John Davel & Sons, $100; Hoole Manufacturing Co., $100; Hendricks Brothers, $100; Rice & Bijur, $100; C. A. Auffmordt, $100; Thomas C. T. Crain, $100; J. J. Wysong & Co., $100; Megroz, Portier, & Megroz & Co., $100; Foster, Paul & Co., $100; S. Stein & Co., $100; James McCreery & Co., $100; Lazell, Dalley & Co., $100; George W. Walling, $100; Thomas Garner & Co, $100; John Simpson, $100; W. H. Schieffelin & Co., $100; through A. Schwab, $1,400; H. C. F. Koch & Co., $100; George T. Hoadly, $250; G. Sidenburg & Co., $100; Ward & Oliphant, $100; Robert Bonner, $1,000;

Horace White, $100; A. H. Cridge, $250; Edward Shriever, $300; C. H. Ludington, $100; Gamewell Fire Alarm Telegraph Company of New York, $200; Warner Brothers, $100; *New York Times* (cash), $100; cash items, $321.20; Bennett Building, $105.

Shortly after the opening of the New York Stock Exchange a subscription was started for the benefit of the Johnstown sufferers. The Governing Committee of the Exchange made Albert King treasurer of the Exchange Relief Fund, and, although many leading members were absent from the floor, as is usual on Monday at this season of the year, the handsome sum of $14,520 was contributed by the brokers present at the close of business. Among the subscriptions received were:

Vermilye & Co., $1,000; Moore & Schley, $1,000; L. Von Hoffman & Co., $500; N. S. Jones, $500; Speyer & Co., $500; Homans & Co., $500; Work, Strong & Co., $250; Washington E. Connor, $250; Van Emberg & Atterbury, $250; Simon Borg & Co., $250; Chauncey & Gwynne Bros., $250; John D. Slayback, $250; Woerishoffer & Co., $250; S. V. White, $250; I. & S. Wormser, $250; Henry Clews & Co., $250; Ladenberg, Thalmann & Co., $250; John H. Davis & Co., $200; Jones, Kennett & Hopkins, $200; H. B. Goldschmidt, $200; other subscriptions, $7,170.

Generosity rose higher still on Tuesday. Early in the day $5,000 was received by cable from the London Stock Exchange. John S. Kennedy also sent $5,000 from London. John Jacob Astor subscribed $2,500 and William Astor $1,000. Other contributions received at the Mayor's office were these:

Archbishop Corrigan, $250 ; Straiton & Storm, $250; Bliss, Fabyan & Co., $500; Funk & Wagnalls, $100 ; Nathan Straus, $1,000 ; Sidney Dillon, $500; Winslow, Lanier & Co., $1,000 ; Henry Hilton, $5,000 ; R. J. Livingston, $1,000 ; Peter Marie, $100 ; The Dick & Meyer Co., Wm. Dick, President, $1,000 ; Decastro & Donner Sugar Refining Co., $1,000; Havemeyers & Elder Sugar Refining Co., $1,000 ; Frederick Gallatin, $500 ; Continental National Bank, from Directors, $1,000 ; F. O. Mattiessen & Wiechers' Sugar Refining Co., $1,000 ; Phelps, Dodge & Co., $2,500 ; Knickerbocker Ice Co., $1,000 ; First National Bank, $1,000 ; Apollinaris Water Co., London, $1,000 ; W. & J. Sloane, $1,000; Tefft, Weller & Co., $500 ; New York Stock Exchange, $20,000 ; Board of Trade, $1,000 ; Central Trust Co., $1,000 ; Samuel Sloan, $200.

The following contributions were made in ten minutes at a special meeting of the Chamber of Commerce:

Brown Brothers & Co., $2,500 ; Morton, Bliss & Co., $1,000 ; H. B. Claflin & Co., $2,000 ; Percy R. Pyne, $1,000; Fourth National Bank, $1,000 ; E. D. Morgan & Co., $1,000 ; C. S. Smith, $500 ; J. M. Ceballas, $500 ; Barbour Brothers & Co., $500 ; Naumberg, Kraus & Co., $500 ; Thos. F. Rowland, $500 ; Bliss, Fabyan & Co., $500 ; William H. Parsons & Co., $250 ; Smith, Hogg & Gardner, $250 ; Doerun Lead Company, $250 ; A. R. Whitney & Co., $250 ; Williams & Peters, $100 ; Joy, Langdon & Co., $250 ; B. L. Solomon's Sons, $100 ; D. F. Hiernan, $100 ; A. S. Rosenbaum, $100 ; Henry Rice, $100 ; Parsons & Petitt, $100 ; Thomas H. Wood & Co., $100 ; T. B. Coddington, $100 ; John I. Howe, $50 ; John Bigelow, $50 ; Morrison, Herriman & Co., $250 ; Frederick Sturges, $250 ; James O. Carpenter, $50 ; C. H. Mallory, $500 ; George A. Low, $25 ; Henry W. T. Mali & Co., $500 ; C. Adolph Low, $50 ; C. C. Peck, $20. Total, $15,295.

Thousands of dollars also came in from the Produce Exchange, Cotton Exchange, Metal Exchange, Coffee Exchange, Real Estate Exchange, etc. The Adams Express Co. gave $5,000, and free carriage of all goods for the sufferers. The Mutual Life Insurance Co., gave $10,000. And so all the week the gifts were made. Jay Gould, gave $1,000 ; the Jewish Temple Emanuel, $1,500 ; The Hide and Leather Trade, $5,000 ; the Commercial Cable Co., $500 ; the Ancient Order of Hibernians, $270 ; J. B. & J. H. Cornell, $1,000 ; the New York Health Department, $500 ; Chatham National Bank, $500 ; the boys of the House of Refuge on Randall's Island, $258.22. Many gifts came from other towns and cities.

Kansas City, $12,000 ; Cincinnati Chamber of Commerce, $22,106 ; Washington Post Office, $600 ; Boston, $94,000 ; Willard (N. Y.) Asylum for Insane, $136 ; Washington Government Printing Office, $1,275 ; Saugerties N. Y., $850; Ithaca, N. Y., $1,600 ; Cornell University, $1,100 ; Whitehall, N. Y., $600 ; Washington Interior Department, $2,280 ; Schenectady, N. Y., $3,000 ; Albany, $10,500 ;

Washington Treasury Department, $2,070 ; Augusta, Ga., $1,000 ; Charleston, S. C., $3,500 ; Utica, N. Y., $6,000 ; Little Falls, N. Y., $700 ; Ilion, N. Y., $1,100 ; Trenton, N. J., $12,000 ; Cambridge, Mass., $3,500 ; Haverhill, Mass., $1,500 ; Lawrence, Mass., $5,000 ; Salem, Mass., $1,000 ; Taunton, Mass., $1,010 ; New London, Conn., $1,120 ; Newburyport, Mass., $1,500.

No attempt has been made above to give anything more than a few random and representative names of givers. The entire roll would fill a volume. By the end of the week the cash contributions in New York city amounted to more than $600,000. Collections in churches on Sunday, June 9th, aggregated $15,000 more. Benefit performances at the theatres the next week brought up the grand total to about $700,000.

CHAPTER XXVI.

AND now begins the task of burying the dead and caring for the living. It is Wednesday morning. Scarcely has daylight broken before a thousand funerals are in progress on the green hillsides. There were no hearses, few mourners, and as little solemnity as formality. The majority of the coffins were of rough pine. The pall-bearers were strong ox-teams, and instead of six pall-bearers to one coffin, there were generally six coffins to one-team. Silently the processions moved, and silently they unloaded their burdens in the lap of mother earth. No minister of God was there to pronounce a last blessing as the clods rattled down, except a few faithful priests who had followed some representatives of their faith to the grave.

All day long the corpses were being hurried below ground. The unidentified bodies were grouped on a high hill west of the doomed city, where one epitaph must do for all, and that the word " unknown."

Almost every stroke of the pick in some portions of the city resulted in the discovery of another victim, and, although the funerals of the morning relieved the morgues of their crush, before night they were as full of the dead as ever. Wherever one turns the melancholy view of a coffin is met. Every train into Johnstown was laden with them, the better ones being generally accompanied by friends of the dead. Men could be seen staggering over the ruins with shining mahogany caskets on their shoulders.

In the midst of this scene of death and desolation a relenting Providence seems to be exerting a subduing influence. Six days have elapsed since the great disaster, and the temperature still remains low and chilly in the Conemaugh valley. When it is remembered that in the ordinary June weather of this locality from two to three days are sufficient to bring an unattended body to a degree of decay and putrefaction that would render it almost impossible to prevent the spread of disease throughout the valley, the inestimable benefits of this cool weather are almost beyond appreciation.

The first body taken from the ruins was that of a boy, Willie Davis, who was found in the debris near the bridge. He was badly bruised and burned. The remains were taken to the undertaking rooms at the Pennsylvania Railroad station, where they were identified. The boy's mother has been making a tour of the different morgues for the past few days, and was just going through the undertaking rooms when she saw the remains of her boy being brought in. She ran up to the body and demanded it. She seemed to have lost her mind, and caused quite a scene by her actions. She said that she had lost her husband and six children in the flood, and that this was the first one of the family that had been recovered. The bodies of a little girl named Bracken and of Theresa and Katie Downs of Clinton Street were taken out near where the remains of Willie Davis were found.

Two hundred experienced men with dynamite, a portable crane, a locomotive, and half a dozen other appliances for pulling, hauling, and lifting, toiled all of Wednesday at the sixty-acre mass of debris that lies above the Pennsylvania Railroad bridge at Johnstown. "As a result," wrote a correspondent, "there is visible, just in front of the central arch, a little patch of muddy water about seventy-five feet long by thirty wide. Two smaller patches are in front of the two arches on each side of this one, but both together would not be heeded were they not looked for especially. Indeed, the whole effect of the work yet done would not be noticed by a person who had never seen the wreck before. The solidity of the wreck and the manner in which it is interlaced and locked together exceeds the expectations of even those who had examined the wreck carefully, and the men who thought that with dynamite the mass could be removed in a week, now do not think the work can be done in twice this time. The work is in charge of Arthur Kirk, a Pittsburg contractor. Dynamite is depended upon for loosening the mass, but it has to be used in small charges for fear of damaging the bridge, which, at this time, would be another disaster for the town. As it is, the south abutment has been broken a little by the explosions.

"After a charge of dynamite had shaken up a portion of the wreck in front of the middle arch, men went to work with long poles, crowbars, axes, saws, and spades. All the loose pieces that could be got out were thrown into the water under the bridge, and then, beginning at the edges, the bits of wreck were pulled, pushed and cut out, and sent floating away. At first the work of an hour was hardly perceptible, but each fresh log of timber pulled out loosened others and made better progress possible. When the space beneath the arch was cleared, and a channel thus made through which the debris could be floated off, a huge portable crane, built on a flat-car and made for raising locomotives and cars, was run upon the bridge over the arch and fastened to the track with heavy chains. A locomotive was furnished to pull the rope, instead of the usual winch with a crank handle. A rope from the crane was fastened by chains or grapnels to a log, and then the locomotive pulled. About once in five times the log came out. Other times the chain slipped or something else made the attempt a failure. Whenever a big stick came out men with pikes pushed off all the other loosened debris that they could get at. Other men shoveled off the dirt and ashes which cover the raft so thickly that it is almost as solid as the ground.

"When a ten-foot square opening had been made back on the arch, the current could be seen gushing up like a great spring from below, showing that there was a large body of it being held down there by the weight of the debris. The current through the arch became so strong that the heaviest pieces in the wreck were carried off readily once they got within its reach. One reason for this is that laborers are filling up the gaps on the railroad embankment approaching the bridge in the north, through which the river had made itself a new bed, and the water thus dammed back has to go through or under the raft and out by the bridge-arches. This both buoys up the whole mass and provides a means of carrying off the wooden part of the debris as fast as it can be loosened.

"Meanwhile an attack on the raft was being made through the adjoining arch in another way. A heavy winch was set up on a small island in the river seventy-five yards below the bridge, and ropes run from this were hitched to heavy timbers in the raft, and then pulled out by workmen at the winch. A beginning for a second opening in the raft was made in this way. One man had some bones broken and was otherwise hurt by the slipping of the handle while he was at work at the winch this afternoon. The whole work is dangerous for the men. There is twenty feet of swift water for them to slip into, and timbers weighing tons are swinging about in unexpected directions to crush them.

"So far it is not known that any bodies have been brought out of the debris by this work of removal, though many logs have been loosened and sent off down the river beneath the water without being seen. There will probably be more bodies back toward the centre of the raft than at the bridge, for of those that came there many were swept over the top. Some went over the arches and a great many were rescued from the bridge and shore. People are satisfied now that dynamite is the only thing that can possibly remove the wreck and that as it is being used it is not likely to mangle bodies that may be in the debris any more than would any other means of removing it. There are no more protests heard against its use."

Bodies continue to be dug out of the wreck in the central portion all day. A dozen or so had been recovered up to nightfall, all hideously burned and mangled. In spite of all the water that has been thrown upon it by fire engines and all the rain that has fallen, the debris is still smouldering in many spots.

Work was begun in dead earnest on Wednesday on the Cambria Iron Works buildings. The Cambria people gave out the absurd statement that their loss will not exceed $100,000. It will certainly take this amount to clean the works of the debris, to say nothing of repairing them. The buildings are nearly a score in number, some of them of enormous size, and they extend along the Conemaugh River for half a mile, over a quarter of a mile in width. Their lonely chimneys, stretching high out of the slate roofs above the brick walls, make them look not unlike a man-of-war of tremendous size. The buildings on the western end of the row are not damaged a great deal, though the torrent rolled through them, turning the machinery topsy-turvy ; but the buildings on the eastern end, which received the full force of the flood, fared badly. The eastern ends are utterly gone, the roofs bent over and smashed in, the chimneys flattened, the walls cracked and broken, and, in some cases, smashed entirely.

Most of the buildings are filled with drift. The workmen, who have clambered over the piles of logs and heavy drift washed in front of the buildings and inside, say that they do not believe that the machinery in the mills is damaged very much, and that the main loss will fall on the mills themselves. Half a million may cover the loss of the Cambria people, but this is a rather low estimate. They have nine hundred men t work getting things in shape, and the manner in which they have had to go to work illustrates the force with which the flood acted. The trees jammed in and before the buildings were so big and so solidly wedged in their places that no force of men could pull them out, and temporary railroad tracks were built up to the mass of debris. Then one of the engines backed down from the Pennsylvania Railroad yards, and the workmen, by persistent effort, managed to get big chains around parts of the drift. These chains were attached to the engine, which rolled off puffing mightily, and in this way the mass of drift was pulled apart. Then the laborers gathered up the loosened material, heaped it in piles a distance from the buildings, and burned them. Sometimes two engines had to be attached to some of the trees to pull them out, and there are many trees which cannot be extricated in this manner. They will have to be sawed into parts, and these parts lugged away by the engines.

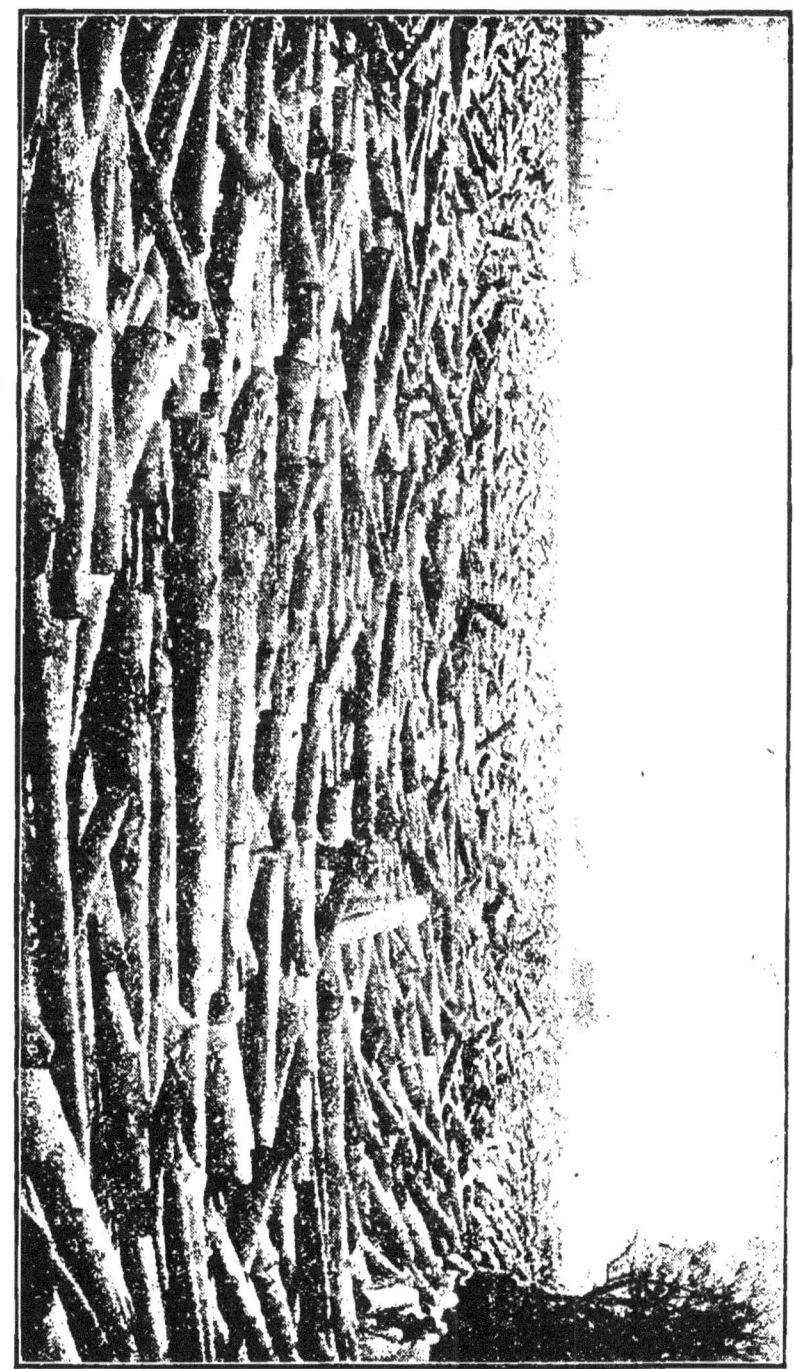

250,000,000 FEET OF LOGS AFLOAT IN THE SUSQUEHANNA.

CHAPTER XXVII

UPON a pretty little plateau two hundred feet above the waters of Stony Creek, and directly in front of a slender foot-bridge which leads into Kernsville, stands a group of tents which represents the first effort of any national organization to give material sanitary aid to the unhappy survivors of Johnstown.

It is the camp of the American National Association of the Red Cross, and is under the direction of that noble woman, Miss Clara Barton of Washington, the President of the organization in this country. The camp is not more than a quarter of a mile from the scene of operations in this place, and, should pestilence attend upon the horrors of the flood, this assembly of trained nurses and veteran physicians will be known all over the land. That an epidemic of some sort will come, there seems to be no question. The only thing which can avert it is a succession of cool days, a possibility which is very remote.

Miss Barton, as soon as she heard of the catastrophe, started preparations for opening head-quarters in this place. By Saturday morning she had secured a staff, tents, supplies, and all the necessary appurtenances of her work, and at once started on the Baltimore and Ohio Road. She arrived here on Tuesday morning, and pitched her tents near Stony Creek. This was, however, a temporary choice, for soon she removed her camp to the plateau upon which it will remain until all need for Miss Barton will have passed. With her came Dr. John B. Hubbell, field agent; Miss M. L. White, stenographer; Gustave Ang-erstein, messenger, and a corps of fifteen physi-cians and four trained female nurses, under the direction of Dr. O'Neill, of Philadelphia.

Upon their arrival they at once established quartermaster and kitchen departments, and in less than three hours these divisions were fully equipped for work. Then when the camp was formally opened on the plateau there were one large hospital tent, capable of accommodating forty persons, four smaller tents to give aid to twenty persons each, and four still smaller ones which will hold ten patients each. Then Miss Barton organized a house-to-house canvass by her corps of doctors, and began to show results almost immediately.

The first part of the district visited was Kerns-ville. There great want and much suffering were discovered and promptly relieved. Miss Barton says that in most of the houses which were visited were several persons suffering from nervous prostration in the most aggravated form, many cases of temporary insanity being discovered, which, if neglected, would assume chronic conditions. There were a large number of persons, too, who were bruised by their battling on the borders of the flood, and were either ignorant or too broken-spirited to endeavor to aid themselves in any particular. The majority of these were not sufficiently seriously hurt to require removal from their homes to the camp, and so were given medicines and practical, intelligent advice how to use them.

There were fifteen persons, however, who were removed from Kernsville and from a district known as the Brewery, on the extreme east of Johnstown. Three of the number were women and were sadly bruised. One man, Caspar Walthaman, a German operative at the Cambria Iron Works, was the most interesting of all. He lived in a little frame house within fifty yards of the brewery. When the flood came his house was lifted from its foundations and was tossed about like a feather in a gale, until it reached a spot about on a line with Washington Street. There the man's life was saved by a great drift, which completely surrounded the house, and which forced the structure against the Prospect Hill shore, where the shock wrecked it. Walthaman was sent flying through the air, and landed on his right side on the water-soaked turf. Fortunately the turf was soft and springy with the moisture, and Walthaman had enough consciousness left to crawl up the hillside, and then sank into unconsciousness.

At ten o'clock Saturday morning some friends found him. He was taken to their home in Kernsville. He was scarcely conscious when found, and before he had been in a place of safety an hour he had lost his mind, the reaction was so great. His hair had turned quite white, and the places where before the disaster his hair had been most abundant, on the sides of his head, were completely denuded of it. His scalp was as smooth as an apple-cheek. The physicians who removed him to the Red Cross Hospital declared the case as the most extraordinary one resulting from fright that had ever come under their observation. Miss Barton declares her belief that not one of the persons who are now under treatment is seriously injured, and is confident they will recover in a few days.

Her staff was reinforced by Mrs. and Dr. Gardner, of Bedford, who, during the last great Western floods, rendered most excellent assistance to the sufferers. Both are members of the Relief Association. The squad of physicians and nurses was further added to by more from Philadelphia, and then Miss Barton thought she was prepared to cope with anything in the way of sickness which might arise.

The appearance of the tents and the surroundings are exceedingly inviting. Everything is exquisitely neat, the boards of the tent-floors being almost as white as the snowy linen of the cots. This contrast to the horrible filth of the town, with its fearful stenches and its dead-paved streets, is so invigorating that it has become a place of refuge to all who are compelled to remain here.

The hospital is an old rink on the Bedford pike, which has been transformed into an inviting retreat. Upon entering the door the visitor finds himself in a small ante-room, to one side of which is attached the general consulting-room. On the other side, opposite the hall, is the apothecary's department, where the prescriptions are filled as carefully as they would be at a first-class druggist's. In the rear of the medical department and of the general consultation-room are the wards. There are two of them—one for males and the other for females. A long, high, heavy curtain divides the wards, and insures as much privacy as the most modest person would wish. Around the walls in both wards are ranged the regulation hospital beds, with plenty of clean and comfortable bed-clothes.

Patients in the hospital said they couldn't be better treated if they were paying the physician for their attendance. The trained nurses of the Red Cross Society carefully look after the wants of the sick and injured, and see that they get everything they wish. People who have an abhorrence of going into these hospitals need have no fear that they will not be well treated.

The orphans of the flood—sadly few there are of them, for it was the children that usually went down first, not the parents—are looked after by the Pennsylvania Children's Aid Society, which has transferred its headquarters for the time being from Philadelphia to this city. There was a thriving branch of this society here before the flood, but of all its officers and executive force two only are alive. Fearing such might be the situation, the general officers of the society sent out on the first available train Miss H. E. Hancock, one of the directors, and Miss H. W. Hinckley, the Secretary. They arrived on Thursday morning, and within thirty minutes had an office open in a little cottage just above the water-line in the upper part of the city. Business was ready as soon as the office, and there were about fifty children looked after before evening. In most cases these were children with relatives or friends in or near Johnstown, and the society's work has been to identify them and restore them to their friends.

As soon as the society opened its office all cases in which children were involved were sent at once to them, and their efforts have been of great benefit in systematizing the care of the children who are left homeless. Besides this, there are many orphans who have been living in the families of neighbors since the flood, but for whom permanent homes must be found. One family has cared for one hundred and fifty-seven children saved from the flood, and nearly as many are staying with other families. There will be no difficulty about providing for these little ones. The society already has offers for the taking of as many as are likely to be in need of a home.

The Rev. Morgan Dix, on behalf of the Leake and Watts Orphan Home in New York, has telegraphed an offer to care for seventy-five orphans. Pittsburg is proving itself generous in this as in all other matters relating to the flood, and other places all over the country are telegraphing offers of homes for the homeless. Superintendent Pierson, of the Indianapolis Natural Gas Company, has asked for two; Cleveland wants some; Altoona would like a few; Apollo, Pa., has vacancies the orphans can fill, and scores of other small places are sending in similar offers and requests. A queer thing is that many of the officers are restricted by curious provisions as to the religious belief of the orphans. The Rev. Dr. Griffith, for instance, of Philadelphia, says that the Angora (Pa.) Home would like some orphans, "especially Baptist ones," and Father Field, of Philadelphia, offers to look after a few Episcopal waifs.

The work of the society here has been greatly assisted by the fact that Miss Maggie Brooks, formerly Secretary of the local society here, but living in Philadelphia at the time of the flood, has come here to assist the general officers. Her acquaintance with the town is invaluable.

Johnstown is generous in its misery. Whatever it has left it gives freely to the strangers who have come here. It is not much, but it shows a good spirit. There are means by which Johnstown people might reap a rich harvest by taking advantage of the necessities of strangers. It is necessary, for instance, to use boats in getting about the place, and men in light skiffs are poling about the streets all day taking passengers from place to place. Their services are free. They not only do not, but will not accept any fee. J. D. Haws & Son own large brick-kilns near the bridge. The newspaper men have possession of one of the firm's buildings and one of the firm spends most of his time in running about trying to make the men comfortable. A room in one of the firm's barns filled with straw has been set apart solely for the newspaper men, who sleep there wrapped in blankets as comfortably as in beds. There is no charge for this, although those who have tried one night on the floors, sand-piles, and other usual dormitories of the place, would willingly pay high for the use of the straw. Food for the newspaper and telegraph workers has been hard to get except in crude form. Canned corned beef, eaten with a stick for a fork, and dry crackers were the staples up to Tuesday, when a house up the hill was discovered were anybody who came was welcome to the best the house afforded. There was no sugar for the coffee, no vinegar for the lettuce, and the apple butter ran out before the siege was raised, but the defect was in the circumstances of Johnstown, and not in the will of the family.

"How much?" was asked at the end of the meal.

They were poor people. The man probably earns a dollar a day.

"Oh!" replied the woman, who was herself cook, waiter, and lady of the house, "we don't charge anything in times like these. You see, I went out and spent ten dollars for groceries at a place that wasn't washed away right after the flood, and we've been living on that ever since. Of course we don't ask any of the relief, not being washed out. You men are welcome to all I can give."

She had seen the last of her ten dollars worth of provisions gobbled up without a murmur, and yet

didn't " charge anything in times like these." Her
scruples did not, however, extend so far as to re-
fusing tenders of coin, inasmuch as without it her
larder would stay empty. She filled it up last
night, and the news of the place having spread,
she has been getting a continual meal from five
in the morning until late at night. Although she
makes no charge, her income would make a regular restaurant keeper dizzy.

So far as the Signal Service is concerned, the
amount of rainfall in the region drained by the
Conemaugh River cannot be ascertained. Mrs.
H. M. Ogle, who had been the Signal Service
representative in Johnstown for several years and
also manager of the Western Union office there,
telegraphed at eight o'clock Friday morning to
Pittsburg that the river marked fourteen feet,
rising; a rise of thirteen feet in twenty-four hours.
At eleven o'clock she wired : " River twenty feet
and rising, higher than ever before ; water in first
floor. Have moved to second. River gauges
carried away. Rainfall, two and three-tenth
inches." At twenty-seven minutes to one P. M.
Mrs. Ogle wired: "At this hour north wind ; very
cloudy ; water still rising."

Nothing more was heard from her by the bureau, but at the Western Union office at Pittsburg
later in the afternoon she commenced to tell an
operator that the dam had broken, that a flood

was coming, and before she had finished the conversation a singular click of the instrument announced the breaking of the current. A moment afterward the current of her life was broken forever.

Sergeant Stewart, in charge of the Pittsburg bureau, says that the fall of water on the Conemaugh shed at Johnstown up to the time of the flood was probably two and five-tenth inches. He believes it was much heavier in the mountains. The country drained by the little Conemaugh and Stony Creek covers an area of about one hundred square miles. The bureau, figuring on this basis and two and five-tenth inches of rainfall, finds that four hundred and sixty-four million six hundred and forty thousand cubic feet of water was precipitated toward Johnstown in its last hours. This is independent of the great volume of water in the lake, which was not less than two hundred and fifty million cubic feet.

It is therefore easily seen that there was ample water te cover the Conemaugh Valley to the depth of from ten to twenty-five feet. Such a volume of water was never known to fall in that country in the same time.

Colonel T. P. Roberts, a leading engineer, estimates that the lake drained twenty-five square miles, and gives some interesting data on the probable amount of water in contained. He says: "The dam, as I understand, was from hill to hill, about one thousand feet long and about eighty-five feet high at the highest point. The pond covered above seven hundred acres, at least for the present I will assume that to be the case. We are told also that there was a waste-weir at one end seventy-five feet wide and ten feet below the comb or top of the dam. Now we are told that with this weir open and discharging freely to the utmost of its capacity, nevertheless the pond or lake rose ten inches per hour until finally it overflowed the top, and, as I understand, the dam broke by being eaten away at the top.

"Thus we have the elements for very simple calculation as to the amount of water precipitated by the flood, provided these premises are accurate. To raise seven hundred acres of water to a height of ten feet would require about three hundred million cubic feet of water, and while this was rising the waste-weir would discharge an enormous volume—it would be difficult to say just how much without a full knowledge of the shape of its side-walls, approaches, and outlets— but if the rise required ten hours the waste-weir might have discharged perhaps ninety million cubic feet. We would then have a total of flood water of three hundred and ninety million cubic feet. This would indicate a rainfall of about eight inches over the twenty-five square miles.

As that much does not appear to have fallen at the hotel and dam it is more than likely that even more than eight inches was precipitated in places farther up. These figures I hold tentatively, but I am much inclined to believe that there was a cloud burst."

Of course, the Johnstown disaster, great as it was, was by no means the greatest flood in history, since Noah's Deluge. The greatest of modern floods was that which resulted from the overflow of the great Houng-Ho, or Yellow River, in 1887. This river, which has earned the title of "China's Sorrow," has always been the cause of great anxiety to the Chinese Government and to the inhabitants of the country through which it flows. It is guarded with the utmost care at great expense, and annually vast sums are spent in repairs of its banks. In October, 1887, a number of serious breaches occurred in the river's banks about three hundred miles from the coast. As a result the river deserted its natural bed and spread over a thickly-populated plain, forcing for itself finally an entire new road to the sea. Four or five times in two thousand years the great river had changed its bed, and each time the change had entailed great loss of life and property.

In 1852 it burst through its banks two hundred and fifty miles from the sea and cut a new bed through the northern part of Shaptung into the

Gulf of Pechili.   The isolation in which foreigners
lived at that time in China prevented their obtain-
ing any information as to the calamitous results
of this change, but in 1887 many of the barriers
against foreigners had been removed and a general idea of the character of the inundation was
easily obtainable.

For several weeks preceding the actual overflow of its banks the Hoang-Ho had been swollen
from its tributaries.   It had been unusually wet
and stormy in northwest China, and all the small
streams were full and overflowing.   The first
break occurred in the province of Honan, of which
the capital is Kaifeng, and the city next in import-
ance is Ching or Cheng Chou.   The latter is forty
miles west of Kaifeng and a short distance above
a bend in the Hoang-Ho. At this bend the stream
is borne violently against the south shore.   For
ten days a continuous rain had been soaking the
embankments, and a strong wind increased the
already great force of the current.   Finally a
breach was made.   At first it extended only for a
hundred yards.   The guards made frantic efforts
to close the gap, and were assisted by the frightened people in the vicinity.   But the beach grew
rapidly to a width of twelve hundred yards, and
through this the river rushed with awful force.
Leaping over the plain with incredible velocity,
the water merged into a small stream called the

Lu-chia. Down the valley of the Lu-chia the torrent poured in an easterly direction, overwhelming
everything in its path.

Twenty miles from Cheng Chou it encountered
Chungmou, a walled city of the third rank. Its
thousands of inhabitants were attending to their
usual pursuits. There was no telegraph to warn
them, and the first intimation of disaster came with
the muddy torrent that rolled down upon them.
Within a short time only the tops of the high walls
marked where a flourishing city had been. Three
hundred villages in the district disappeared utterly,
and the lands about three hundred other villages
were inundated.

The flood turned south from Chungmou, still
keeping to the course of the Lu-chia, and stretched
out in width for thirty miles. This vast body of
water was from ten to twenty feet deep. Several
miles south of Kaifeng the flood struck a large
river which there joins the Lu-chia. The result
was that the flood rose to a still greater height,
and, pouring into a low-lying and very fertile
plain which was densely populated, submerged
upward of one thousand five hundred villages.

Not far beyond this locality the flood passed
into the province of Anhui, where it spread very
widely. The actual loss of life could not be com-
puted accurately, but the lowest intelligent estimate placed it at one million five hundred thou-

sand, and one authority fixed it at seven million. Two million people were rendered destitute by the flood, and the suffering that resulted was frightful. Four months later the inundated provinces were still under the muddy waters. The government officials who were on guard when the Hoang-Ho broke its banks were condemned to severe punishment, and were placed in the pillory in spite of their pleadings that they had done their best to avert the disaster.

The inundation which may be classed as the second greatest in modern history occurred in Holland in 1530. There have been many floods in Holland, nearly all due to the failure of the dikes which form the only barrier between it and the sea. In 1530 there was a general failure of the dikes, and the sea poured in upon the low lands. The people were as unprepared as were the victims of the Johnstown disaster. Good authorities place the number of human beings that perished in this flood at about four hundred thousand, and the destruction of property was in proportion.

In April, 1421, the River Meuse broke in the dikes at Dort, or Dordrecht, an ancient town in the peninsula of South Holland, situated on an island. Ten thousand persons perished there and more than one hundred thousand in the vicinity. In January, 1861, there was a disastrous flood in

LAST TRAINS IN AND OUT OF HARRISBURG.

Holland, the area sweeping over forty thousand acres, and leaving thirty thousand villages destitute, and again in 1876 severe losses resulted from inundations in this country.

The first flood in Europe of which history gives any authentic account occurred in Lincolnshire, England, A. D. 245, when the sea passed over many thousands of acres. In the year 353 a flood in Cheshire destroyed three thousand human lives and many cattle. Four hundred families were drowned in Glasgow by an overflow of the Clyde in 758. A number of English seaport towns were destroyed by an inundation in 1014. In 1483 a terrible overflow of the Severn, which came at night and lasted for ten days, covered the tops of mountains. Men, women, and children were carried from their beds and drowned. The waters settled on the lands and were called for one hundred years after the Great Waters.

A flood in Catalonia, a province of Spain, occurred in 1617, and fifty thousand persons lost their lives. One of the most curious inundations in history, and one that was looked upon at the time as a miracle, occurred in Yorkshire, England, in 1686. A large rock was split assunder by some hidden force, and water spouted out, the stream reaching as high as a church steeple. In 1771 another flood, known as the Ripon flood, occurred in the same province.

In September, 1687, mountain torrents inundated Navarre, and two thousand persons were drowned. Twice, in 1787 and in 1802, the Irish Liffey overran its banks and caused great damsge. A reservoir in Lurca, a city of Spain, burst in 1802, in much the same way as did the dam at Johnstown, and as a result one thousand persons perished. Twenty-four villages near Presburg, and nearly all their inhabitants, were swept away in April, 1811, by an overflow of the Danube. Two years later large provinces in Austria and Poland were flooded, and many lives were lost. In the same year a force of two thousand Turkish soldiers, who were stationed on a small island near Widdin, were surprised by a sudden overflow of the Danube and all were drowned. There were two more floods in this year, one in Silesia, where six thousand persons perished, and the French army met such losses and privations that its ruin was accelerated; and another in Poland, where four thousand persons were supposed to have been drowned. In 1816 the melting of the snow on the mountains surrounding Strabane, Ireland, caused destructive floods, and the overflow of the Vistula in Germany laid many villages under water. Floods that occasioned great suffering occurred in 1829, when severe rains caused the Spey and Findhorn to rise fifty feet above their ordinary level. The following year the •

Danube again ouerflowed its banks and inundated the houses of fifty thousand inhabitants of Vienna. The Saone overflowed in 1840, and poured its turbulent waters iuto the Rhine, causing a flood which covered sixty thousand acres. Lyons was flooded, one hundred houses were swept away at Avignon, two hundred and eighteen at La Guillotiere, and three hundred at Vaise, Marseilles, and Nimes. Another great flood, entailing much suffering, occurred in the south of France in 1856.

A flood in Mill River valley in 1874 was caused by the bursting of a badly constructed dam. The waters poured down upon the villages in the valley much as at Johnstown, but the people received warning in time, and the torrent was not so swift. Several villages were destroyed and one hundred and forty-four persons drowned. The rising of the Garonne in 1875 caused the death of one thousand persons near Toulouse, and twenty thousand persons were made homeless in India by floods in the same year. In 1882 heavy floods destroyed a large amount of property and drowned many persons in the Mississippi and Ohio valleys.

The awful disaster in the Conemaugh Valley calls attention to the fact that there are many similar dams throughout the United States. Though few of these overhang a narrow gorge like the one in which the borough of Johnstown reposed, there is no question that several of the dams now deemed safe would, if broken down by a sudden freshet, sweep down upon peaceful hamlets, cause immense damage to property and loss of life. The lesson taught by the awful scenes at Johnstown should not go unheeded.

Croton Lake Dam was first built with ninety feet of masonry overfall, the rest being earth embankment. On January 7th, 1841, a freshet carried away this earth embankment, and when rebuilt the overfall of the dam was made two hundred and seventy feet long. The foundation is two lines of cribs, filled with dry stone, and ten feet of concrete between. Upon this broken range stone masonry was laid, the down-stream side being curved and faced with granite, the whole being backed with a packing of earth. The dam is forty feet high, its top is one hundred and sixty-six feet above tidewater, and it controls a reservoir area of four hundred acres and five hundred million gallons of water. The Boyd's Corner Dam holds two million seven hundred and twenty-seven thousand gallons, and was built during the years 1866 and 1872. It stands twenty-three miles from Croton dam, and has cut-stone faces filled between with concrete. The extreme height is seventy-eight feet, and it is six hundred and seventy feet long. Although this dam holds a body of water five times greater than that at

Croton Lake, it is claimed by engineers that should it give way the deluge of water which would follow would cause very little loss of life and only destroy farming lands, as below it the country is comparatively level and open. Middle Branch Dam holds four billion four hundred thousand gallons, and was built during 1874 and 1878. It is composed of earth, with a centre of rubble masonry carried down to the rock bottom. It is also considered to be in no danger of causing destruction by sudden breakage, as the downpour of water would spread out over a large area of level land. Besides these there are other Croton water storage basins formed by dams as follows: East Branch, with a capacity of 4,500,-000,000 gallons; Lake Mahopac, 575,000,000 gallons; Lake Kirk, 565,000,000 gallons; Lake Gleneida, 165,000,000 gallons: Lake Gilead, 380,-000,000 gallons; Lake Waccabec, 200,000,0c0 gallons; Lake Lonetta, 50,000,000 gallons; Barrett's ponds, 170,000,000 gallons; China pond, 105,000,000 gallons; White pond, 100,000,000 gallons; Pines pond, 75,000,0c0 gallons; Long pond, 60,000,000 gallons; Peach pond, 230,000,-000 gallons; Cross pond, 110,000.000 gallons, and Haines pond, 125,000,000 gallons, thus completing the storage capacity of the Croton water system of 14,000,000,000 gallons. The engineers claim that none of these last-named could cause loss of life or any great damage to property, because there exist abundant natural outlets.

At Whitehall, N. G., there is a reservoir created by a dam three hundred and twenty feet long across a valley half a mile from the village and two hundred and sixty-six feet above it. A break in this dam would release nearly six million gallons, and probably sweep away the entire town. Norwich, N. Y., is supplied by an earthwork dam, with centre puddle-wall, three hundred and twenty-three feet long and forty feet high. It imprisons thirty million gallons and stands one hundred and eighty feet above the village. At an elevation of two hundred and fifty feet above the town of Olean N. Y., stands an embankment holding in check two million, five hundred thousand gallons. Oneida, N. Y., is supplied by a reservoir formed by a dam across a stream which controls twenty-two million, three hundred and fifty thousand gallons. The dam is nearly three miles from the village and at an altitude of one hundred and ninty feet above it. Such are some of the reservoirs which threaten other communities of our fair land.

CHAPTER XXVIII.

Ir is now the Thursday after the disaster, and amid the ruins of Johnstown people are beginning to get their wits together. They have quit the aimless wandering about amid the ruins, that marked them for a crushed and despairing people. Everybody is getting to work and forgetting something of the horror of the situation in the necessity of thinking of what they are doing. The deadly silence that has prevailed throughout the town is ended, giving place to the shouts of hundreds of men pulling at ropes, and the crash of timbers and roofs as they pull wrecked buildings down or haul heaps of débris to pieces. Hundreds more are making an almost merry clang with pick and shovel as they clear away mud and gravel, opening ways on the lines of the old streets. Locomotives are puffing about, down into the heart of the town now, and the great whistle at the Cambria-Iron Works blew for noon yesterday and to-day for the first time since the flood silenced it.   To lighten the sombre aspect of the ruined area, heightened by the cold gray clouds hanging low about the hills, were acres of flame, where débris is being got rid of.   Down in what was the heart of the city the soldiers have gone into camp, and little flags snap brightly in the high wind from their acres of white tents.

The relief work seems now to be pretty thoroughly organized, and thousands of men are at work under the direction of the committee.   The men are in gangs of about a hundred each, under foremen, with mounted superintendents riding about overseeing the work.

The first effort, aside from that being made upon the gorge at the bridge, is in the upper part of the city and in Stony Creek·Gap, where there are many houses with great heaps of débris covering and surrounding them.   Three or four hundred men were set at work with ropes, chains, and axes upon each of these heaps, tearing it to pieces as rapidly as possible.   Where there are only smashed houses and furniture in the heap the work is easy, but when, as in most instances, there are long logs and tree-trunks reaching in every direction through the mass, the task of getting them out is a slow and difficult one.   The lighter parts of the wreck are tossed into heaps in the nearest clear space and set on fire.   Horses

haul the logs and heavier pieces off to add them
to other blazing piles. Everything of any value
is carefully laid aside, but there is little of it.
Even the strongest furniture is generally in little
bits when found, but in one heap this morning
were found two mirrors, one about six feet by
eight in size, without a crack in it, and with its
frame little damaged ; the other one, about two
feet by three in size, had a little crack at the bottom, but was otherwise all right.

Every once in a while the workmen about these
wreck-heaps will stop their shouting and straining
at the ropes, gather into a crowd at some one
spot in the ruins, and remain idle and quiet for a
little while. Presently the group will stir itself a
little, fall apart, and out of it will come six men
bearing between them on a door or other improvised stretcher a vague form covered with a
canvas blanket. The bearers go off along the
irregular paths worn into the muddy plain, toward the different morgues, and the men go to
work again.

These little groups of six, with the burden between them, are as frequent as ever. One runs
across them everywhere about the place. Sometimes they come so thick that they have to form
in line at the morgue doors. The activity with
which work was prosecuted brought rapidly to
light the dark places within the ruins in which

remained concealed those bodies that the previous desultory searching had not brought to light. Many of the disclosures might almost better have never seen the light, so heart-rending were they. A mother lay with three children clasped in her arms. So suddenly had the visitation come upon them that the little ones had plainly been snatched up while at play, for one held a doll clutched tightly in its dead hand, and in one hand of another were three marbles. This was right opposite the First National Bank building, in the heart of the city, and near the same spot a family of five—father, mother, and three children—were found dead together. Not far off a roof was lifted up, and dropped again in horror at the sight of nine bodies beneath it. There were more bodies, or fragments of bodies, found, too, in the gorge at the bridge, and from the Cambria Iron Works the ghastly burden-bearers began to come in with the first contributions of that locality to the death list. The passage of time is also bringing to the surface bodies that have been lying beneath the river further down, and from Nineveh bodies are continually being sent up to Morrellville, just below the iron works, for identification.

Wandering about near the ruins of Wood, Morrell & Co.'s store a messenger from Morrellville found a man who looked like the pictures of the Tennessee mountaineers in the *Century Maga-*

zinc, with an addition of woe and misery upon his gaunt, hairy face that no picture could ever indicate. He was tall and thin, and bent, and, from his appearance, abjectly poor. He was telling two strangers how he had lived right across from the store, with his wife and eight children. When the high water came and word was brought that the dam was in danger, he told his wife to get the children together and come with him. The water was deep in the streets, and the passage to the bluff would have been difficult. She laughed at him and told him the dam was all right. He urged her, ordered her, and did everything else but pick her up bodily and carry her out, but she would not come. Finally he set the example and dashed out, himself, through the water, calling to his wife to follow. As his feet began to touch rising ground, he saw the wall of water coming down the valley. He climbed in blind terror up the bank, helped by the rising water, and, reaching solid ground, turned just in time to see the water strike his house.

"When I turned my back," he said, "I couldn't look any longer."

Tears ran down his face as he said this. The messenger coming up just then said :—

"Your wife has been found. They got her down at Nineveh. Her brother has gone to fetch her up."

The man went away with the messenger.

" He didn't seem much rejoiced over the good news about his wife," remarked one of the strangers, who had yet to learn that Johnstown people speak of death and the dead only indirectly whenever possible.

It was the wife's body, not the wife, that had been found, and that the messenger was to fetch up. The bodies of this man's eight children have not yet been found. He is the only survivor of a family of ten.

Queer salvage from the flood was a cat that was taken out alive last evening. Its hair was singed off and one eye gone, but it was able to lick the hand of the man who picked it up and carried it off to keep, he said, as a relic of the flood. A white Wyandotte rooster and two hens were also dug out alive, and with dry feathers, from the centre of a heap of wrecked buildings.

The work of clearing up the site of the town has progressed so far that the outlines of some of the old streets could be faintly traced, and citizens were going about hunting up their lots. In many cases it was a difficult task, but enough old landmarks are left to make the determination of boundary lines by a new survey a comparatively easy matter.

The scenes in the morgues are disgusting in the highest degree. The embalmers are at work cut-

ting and slashing with an apathy born of four days
and nights of the work, and such as they never
experienced before. The boards on which the
bodies lie are covered with mud and slime, in
many instances.

Men with dynamite, blowing up the drift at the
Pennsylvania Railroad bridge, people in the drift
watching for bodies, people finding bodies in the
ruins and carrying them away on stretchers or
sheets, the bonfires of blazing débris all over the
town, the soldiers with their bayonets guarding
property or taking thieves into custody, the tin-
starred policemen with their base ball clubs
promenading the streets and around the ruins,
the scenes of distress and frenzy at the relief stations, the crash of buildings as their broken remnants fall to the ground—this is the scene that
goes on night and day in Johnstown, and will go
on for an indefinite time. Still, people have
worked so in the midst of such excitement, with
the pressure of such an awful horror on their
minds that they can get but little rest even when
they wish to. Men in this town are too tired to
sleep. They lie down with throbbing brains that
cannot stop throbbing, so that even the sense of
thinking is intense agony.

The undertakers and embalmers claim that
they are the busiest men in town, and that they
have done more to help the city than any other

workmen. The people who attend the morgues for the purpose of identifying their friends and relatives are hardly as numerous as before. Many of them are exhausted with the constant wear and tear, and many have about made up their minds that their friends are lost beyond recovery, and that there is no use looking for them any longer. Others have gone to distant parts of the State, and have abandoned Johnstown and all in it.

A little girl in a poor calico dress climbed upon the fence at the Adams Street morgue and looked wistfully at the row of coffins in the yard. People were only admitted to the morgue in squads of ten each, and the little girl's turn had not come yet. Her name was Jennie Hoffman. She was twelve years old. She told a reporter that out of her family of fourteen the father and mother and oldest sister were lost. They were all in their home on Somerset Street when the flood came. The father reached out for a tree which went sweeping by, and was pulled out of the window and lost. The mother and children got upon the roof, and then a dash of water carried her and the eldest daughter off. A colored man on an adjoining house took off the little girls who were left—all of them under twelve years of age, except Jennie—and together they clambered over the roofs of the houses near by and escaped.

CHAPTER XXIX.

Day after day the work of reparation goes on. The city has been blotted out. Yet the reeking ruins that mark its site are teeming with life and work more vigorous than ever marked its noisy streets and panting factories. As men and money pour into Johnstown the spirit of the town greatly revives, and the people begin to take a much more favorable view of things. The one thing that is troubling people just now is the lack of ready money. There are drafts here in any quantity, but there is no money to cash them until the money in the vaults of the First National Bank has been recovered. It is known that the vaults are safe and that about $500,000 in cash is there. Of this sum $125,000 belongs to the Cambria Iron Company. It was to pay the five thousand employés of the works. The men are paid off every two weeks, and the last pay-day was to have been on the Saturday after the fatal

flood. The money was brought down to Johnstown, on the day before the flood, by the Adams
Express Company, and deposited in the bank.
After the water subsided, and it was discovered
that the money was safe, a guard was placed
around the bank and has been maintained ever
since.

When the pay-day of the Cambria Iron Company does come it will be an impressive scene.
The only thing comparable to it will be the roll-
call after a great battle. Mothers, wives, and
children will be there to claim the wages of sons,
and husbands, and fathers. The men in the
gloomy line will have few families to take their
wages home to. The Cambria people do not
propose to stand on any red-tape rules about
paying the wages of their dead employés to the
surviving friends and relatives. They will only
try to make reasonably sure that they are paying
the money to the right persons.

An assistant cashier, Thomas McGee, in the
company's store saved $12,000 of the company's
funds. The money was all in packages of bills
in bags in the safe on the ground floor of the
main building of the stores. When the water
began to rise he went up on the second floor of
the building, carrying the money with him.
When the crash of the reservoir torrent came
Mr. McGee clambered upon the roof, and just

before the building tottered and fell he managed
to jump on the roof of a house that went by. The
house was swept near the bank. Mr. McGee
jumped off and fell into the water, but struck out
and managed to clamber up the bank. Then he
got up on the hills and remained out all night
guarding his treasure.

At dawn of Thursday the stillness of the night,
which had been punctured frequently by the pistol and musket shots of vigilant guards scaring
off possible marauders, was permanently fractured
by the arousing of gangs of laborers who had
slept about wherever they could find a soft spot
in the ruins, as well as in tents set up in the centre of where the town used to be. The soldiers
in their camps were seen about later, and the railroad gang of several hundred men set out up the
track toward where they had left off work the
night before. Breakfast was cooked at hundreds
of camp-fires, and about brick-kilns, and wherever
else a fire could be got. At seven o'clock five
thousand laborers struck pick and shovel and saw
into the square miles of débris heaped over the
city's site. At the same time more laborers began to arrive on trains and march through the
streets in long gangs toward the place where they
were needed. Those whose work was to be pulling and hauling trailed along in lines, holding to
their ropes. They looked like gangs of slaves

20

being driven to a market. By the time the fore-noon was well under way, seven thousand labor-ers were at work in the city under the direction of one hundred foremen. There were five hun-dred cars and as many teams, and half a dozen portable hoisting engines, besides regular loco-motives and trains of flat cars that were used in hauling off débris that could not be burned. With this force of men and appliances at work the ruined city, looked at from the bluffs, seemed to fairly swarm with life, wherever the flood had left anything to be removed. The whole lower part of the city, except just above the bridge, re-mained the deserted mud desert that the waters left. There was no cleaning up necessary there. Through the upper part of the city, where the houses were simply smashed to kindling wood and piled into heaps, but not ground to pieces under the whirlpool that bore down on the rest of the city, acres of bonfires have burned all day. The stifling smoke, blown by a high wind, has made life almost unendurable, and the flames have twirled about so fiercely in the gusts as to scorch the workmen some distance away. Citi-zens whose houses were not damaged beyond sal-vation have almost got to work in clearing out their homes and trying to make them somewhere near habitable. In the poorer parts of the city often one story and a half frame cottages are seen completely surrounded by heaps of débris tossed up high above their roofs. Narrow lanes driven through the débris have given the owners entrance to their homes.

With all the work the apparent progress was small. A stranger seeing the place for the first time would never imagine that the wreck was not just as the flood left it. The enormity of the task of clearing the place grows more apparent the more the work is prosecuted, and with the force now at work the job cannot be done in less than a month. It will hardly be possible to find room for any larger force.

The railroads added largely to the bustle of the place. Long freight trains, loaded with food and clothing for the suffering, were continually coming in faster than they could be unloaded. Lumber was also arriving in great quantities, and hay and feed for the horses was heaped up high alongside the tracks. Hundreds of men were swarming over the road-bed near the Pennsylvania station, strengthening and improving the line. Work was begun on frame sheds and other temporary buildings in several places, and the rattle of hammers added its din to the shouts of the workmen and the crash of falling wreckage.

Some sort of organization is being introduced into other things about the city than the clearing away of the débris. The Post-office is established

in a small brick building in the upper part of the
city. Those of the letter carriers who are alive,
and a few clerks, are the working force. The reception of mail consists of one damaged street
letter-box set upon a box in front of the building
and guarded by a carrier, who has also to see
that there is no crowding in the long lines of people waiting to get their turn at the two windows
where letters and stamps are served out. A wide
board, stood up on end, is lettered rudely, "Post-
office Bulletin," and beneath is a slip of paper
with the information that a mail will leave the city
for the West during the day, and that no mail
has been received. There are many touching
things in these Post-office lines. It is a good
place for acquaintances who lived in different parts
of the city to find out whether each is alive or
dead.

"You are through all right, I see," said one
man in the line to an acquaintance who came up
this morning.

"Yes," said the acquaintance.

"And how's your folks? They all right, too?"
was the next question.

"Two of them are—them two little ones sitting
on the steps there. The mother and the other
three have gone down."

Such conversations as this take place every few
minutes. Near the Post-office is the morgue for

that part of the city, and other lines of waiting
people reach out from there, anxious for a glimpse
at the contents of the twenty-five coffins ranged in
lines in front of the school-building, that does duty
for a dead-house. Only those who have business
are admitted, but the number is never a small one.
Each walks along the lines of coffins, raises the
cover over the face, glances in, drops the cover
quickly, and passes on. Men bearing ghastly
burdens on stretchers pass frequently into the
school-house, where the undertakers prepare the
bodies for identification.

A little farther along is the relief headquarters
for that part of the city, and the streets there are
packed all day long with women and children with
baskets on their arms. So great is the demand
that the people have to stand in line for an hour
to get their turn. A large unfinished building is
turned into a storehouse for clothing, and the
people throng into it empty-handed and come out
with arms full of underclothing and other wearing apparel. At another building the sanitary
bureau is serving out disinfectants.

The workmen upon the débris in what was the
heart of the city have now reached well into the
ruins and are getting to where the valuable contents of jewelry and other stores may be expected
to be found, and strict watch is being kept to prevent the theft of any such articles by the work-

men or others. In the ruins of the Wood, Morrell
& Co. general store a large amount of goods,
chiefly provisions and household utensils, has been
found in fairly good order. It is piled in a heap
as fast as gotten out, and the building is being
pulled down.

About the worst heap of wreckage in the centre of the city is where the Cambria Library building stood, opposite the general store. This was
a very substantial and handsome building and offered much obstruction to the flood. It was completely destroyed, but upon its site a mass of
trees, logs, heavy beams, and other wreckage
was left, knotted together into a mass only extri-
cable by the use of the ax and saw. Two hundred men have worked at it for three days and it
is not half removed yet.

The Cambria Iron Company have several acres
of gravel and clay to remove from the upper end
of its yard. Except for an occasional corner of
some big iron machine that projects above the
surface no one would ever suspect that it was not
the original earth. In one place a freight car
brake-wheel lies just on the surface of the ground,
apparently dropped there loosely. Any one who
tries to kick it aside or pick it up finds that it
is still attached to its car, which is buried under
a solid mass of gravel and broken rock. Several
lanes have been dug through this mass down to

the old railroad tracks, and two or three of the little yard engines of the iron company, resurrected with smashed smoke-stacks and other light damage, but workable yet, go puffing about hardly visible above the general level of the new-made ground.

The progress of the work upon the black and still smoking mass of charred ruins above the bridge is hardly perceptible. There is clear water for about one hundred feet back from the central arch, and a little opening before the two on each side of it. When there is a good-sized hole made before all three of these arches, through which the bulk of the water runs, it is expected that the stuff can be pulled apart and set afloat much more rapidly. Dynamiter Kirk, who is overseeing the work, used up the last one hundred pounds of the explosive early this afternoon, and had to suspend operations until the arrival of two hundred pounds more that was on the way from Pittsburgh. The dynamite has been used in small doses for fear of damaging the bridge. Six pounds was the heaviest charge used. Even with this the stone beneath the arches of the bridge is charred and crumbling in places, and some pieces have been blown out of the heavy coping. The whole structure shakes as though with an earthquake at every discharge.

The dynamite is placed in holes drilled in logs

matted into the surface of the raft, and its effect
being downward, the greatest force of the explosion is upon the mass of stuff beneath the water.
At the same time each charge sent up into the
air, one hundred feet or more, a fountain of dirt,
stones, and blackened fragments of logs, many
of them large enough to be dangerous. The
rattling crash of their fall upon the bridge follows
hard after the heavy boom of the explosion. One
of the worst and most unexpected objects with
which the men on the raft have to contend is the
presence in it of hundreds of miles of telegraph
wire wound around almost everything there and
binding the whole mass together.

No bodies have yet been brought to the surface by the operations with dynamite, but indications of several buried beneath the surface are
evident. A short distance back from where the
men are not at work, bodies continue to be taken
out from the surface of the raft at the rate of
ten or a dozen a day. The men this afternoon
came across hundreds of feet of polished copper
pipe, which is said to have come from a Pullman
car. It was not known until then that there was a
Pullman car in that part of the raft. The remnants of a vestibule car are plainly seen at a point
a hundred feet away from this.

CHAPTER XXX.

THE first thing that Johnstown people do in the morning is to go to the relief stations and get something to eat. They go carrying big baskets, and their endeavor is to get all they can. There has been a new system every day about the manner of dispensing the food and clothing to the sufferers. At first the supplies were placed where people could help themselves. Then they were placed in yards and handed to people over the fences. Then people had to get orders for what they wanted from the Citizens Committee, and their orders were filled at the different relief stations. Now the whole matter of receiving and dispensing relief supplies has been placed in the hands of the Grand Army of the Republic men. Thomas A. Stewart, commander of the Department of Pennsylvania, G. A. R., arrived with his staff and established his headquarters in a tent near the headquarters of the Citizens Committee,

and opposite the temporary post-office. Over this
tent floats Commander Stewart's flag, with purple border, bearing the arms of the State of
Pennsylvania. The members of his staff are:
Quartermaster-General Tobin Taylor and his assistant H. J. Williams, Chaplain John W. Sayres,
and W. V. Lawrence, quartermaster-general of
the Ohio Department. The Grand Army men
have made the Adams Street relief station a
central relief station, and all the others, at Kernville, the Pennsylvania depot, Cambria City, and
Jackson and Somerset Street, sub-stations. The
idea is to distribute supplies to the sub-stations
from the central station, and thus avoid the jam
of crying and excited people at the committee's
headquarters.

The Grand Army men have appointed a committee of women to assist them in their work.
The women go from house to house, ascertaining
the number of people quartered there, the number of people lost from there in the flood, and the
exact needs of the people. It was found necessary to have some such committee as this, for
there were women actually starving, who were too
proud to take their places in line with the other
women with bags and baskets. Some of these
people were rich before the flood. Now they are
not worth a dollar. A *Sun* reporter was told of
one man who was reported to be worth $100,000

before the flood, but who now is penniless, and who has to take his place in the line along with others seeking the necessaries of life.

Though the Adams Street station is now the central relief station, the most imposing display of supplies is made at the Pennsylvania Railroad freight and passenger depots. Here, on the platforms and in the yards, are piled up barrels of flour in long rows, three and four barrels high; biscuits in cans and boxes, where car-loads of them have been dumped; crackers, under the railroad sheds in bins; hams, by the hundred, strung on poles; boxes of soap and candles, barrels of kerosene oil, stacks of canned goods, and things to eat of all sorts and kinds. The same is visible at the Baltimore and Ohio road, and there is now no fear of a food famine in Johnstown, though of course everybody will have to rough it for weeks. What is needed most in this line is cooking utensils. Johnstown people want stoves, kettles, pans, knives, and forks. All the things that have been sent so far have been sent with the evident idea of supplying an instant need, and that is right and proper, but it would be well now, if, instead of some of the provisions that are sent, cooking utensils would arrive. Fifty stoves arrived from Pittsburgh this morning, and it is said that more are coming.

At both the depots where the supplies are re-

ceived and stored a big rope-line incloses them
in an impromptu yard, so as to give room to
those having them in charge to walk around and
see what they have got.   On the inside of this
line, too, stalk back and forth the soldiers, with
their rifles on their shoulders, and, beside the
lines pressing against the ropes, there stands
every day, from daylight until dawn, a crowd of
women with big baskets, who make piteous appeals to the soldiers to give them food for their
children at once, before the order of the relief
committee.   Those to whom supplies are dealt
out at the stations have to approach in a line, and
this line is fringed with soldiers, Pittsburgh policemen, and deputy sheriffs, who see that the children and weak women are not crowded out of
their places by the stronger ones.   The supplies
are not given in large quantities, but the applicants are told to come again in a day or so and
more will be given them.   The women complain
against this bitterly, and go away with tears in
their eyes, declaring that they have not been given
enough.   Other women utter broken words of
thankfulness and go away, their faces wreathed
in smiles.

One night something in the nature of a raid
was made by Father McTahney, one of the Catholic priests here, on the houses of some people
whom he suspected of having imposed upon the

relief committee. These persons represented that they were destitute, and sent their children with baskets to the relief stations, each child getting supplies for a different family. There are unquestionably many such cases. Father McTahney found that his suspicions were correct in a great many cases, and he brought back and made the wrong-doers bring back the provisions which they had obtained under false pretenses.

The side tracks at both the Pennsylvania and Baltimore and Ohio Railroad depots are filled with cars sent from different places, bearing relief supplies to Johnstown. The cars are nearly all freight cars, and they contain the significant inscriptions of the railroad officials: "This car is on time freight. It is going to Johnstown, and must not be delayed under any circumstances." Then, there are the ponderous labels of the towns and associations sending the supplies. They read this way: "This car for Johnstown with supplies for the sufferers." "Braddock relief for Johnstown." "The contributions of Beaver Falls to Johnstown." The cars from Pittsburgh had no inscriptions. Some cars had merely the inscription, in great big black letters on a white strip of cloth running the length of the car, "Johnstown." One car reads on it: "Stations along the route fill this car with supplies for Johnstown, and don't delay it."

CHAPTER XXXI.

AT the end of the week Adjutant-General Hastings moved his headquarters from the signal tower and the Pennsylvania Railroad depot to the eastern end of the Pennsylvania freight depot. Here the general and his staff sleep on the hard floor, with only a blanket under them. They have their work systematized and in good shape, though about all they have done or will do is to prevent strangers and others who have no business here from entering the city. The entire regiment which is here is disposed around the city in squads of two or three men each. The men are scattered up and down the Conemaugh, away out on the Pennsylvania and Baltimore and Ohio Railaoad tracks, along Stony Creek on the southern side of the town, and even upon the hills. It is impossible for any one to get into town by escaping the guards, for there is a cordon of soldiers about it. General Hastings rides around on a horse, inspecting the posts, and the men on guard present arms to him in due form, he returning the salute. The sight is a singular one, for General Hastings is not in uniform, and in fact wears a very rusty civilian's dress. He wears a pair of rubber boots covered with mud, and a suit of old, well-stained, black clothes. His coat is a cutaway. His appearance among his staff officers is still more dramatic, for the latter, being ordered out and having time to prepare, are in gold lace and feathers and glittering uniforms.

General Hastings came here right after the flood, on the spur of the moment, and not in his official capacity. He rides his horse finely and looks every inch a soldier. He has established in his headquarters in the freight depot a very much-needed bureau for the answering of telegrams from friends of Johnstown people making inquiries as to the latter's safety. The bureau is in charge of A. K. Parsons, who has done good work since the flood, and who, with Lieutenant George Miller, of the Fifth Infantry, U. S. A., General Hastings' right-hand man, has been with the general constantly. The telegrams in the past have all been sent to the headquarters of the Citizens Committee, in the Fourth Ward Hotel, and have laid there, along with telegrams of every sort, in a little heap on a little side table in one corner of the room. Three-quarters of them were not called for, and people who knew that telegrams were there for them did not have the patience to look through the heap for them. Finally some who were not worried to death took the telegrams, opened them all, and pinned them in separate packages in alphabetical order and then put them back on the table again, and they have been pored over, until their edges are frayed, by all the people who crowded into the little low-roofed room where Dictator Scott and his messengers are. There were something like three thousand telegrams there in all. Occasionally a few are taken away, but in the majority of cases they remain there. The persons to whom they were sent are dead or have not taken the trouble to come to headquarters and see if their friends are inquiring after them. Of course the Western Union Telegraph Company makes no effort to deliver the messages. This would be impossible.

The telegrams addressed to the Citizens Committee headquarters are all different in form, of course, but they all breathe the utmost anxiety and suspense. Here are some samples :—

Is Samuel there? Is there any hope? Answer me and end this suspense. Sarah.

To anybody in Johnstown :

Can you give me any information of Adam Brennan? Mary Brennan.

PENNSYLVANIA AVE., COR. SIXTH ST., WASHINGTON, D. C.

LEYYTYPE CO. PHILA.

Are any of you alive?   JAMES.

Are you all safe? Is it our John Burn that is dead? Is Eliza safe? Answer.

It is worth repeating again that the majority of these telegrams will never be answered.

The Post-office letter carriers have only just begun to make their rounds in that part of the town which is comparatively uninjured. Bags of first-class mail matter are alone brought into town. It will be weeks before people see the papers in the mails. The supposition is that nobody has time to read papers, and this is about right. The letter carriers are making an effort, as far as they can, to distribute mail to the families of the deceased people. Many of the letters which arrive now contain money orders, and while great care has to be taken in the distribution, the postal authorities recognize the necessity of getting these letters to the parties addressed, or else returning them to the Dead Letter Office as proof of the death of the individuals in question. It is no doubt that in this way the first knowledge of the death of many will be transmitted to friends.

It is fair to say that the best part of the energies of the State of Pennsylvania at present are all turned upon Johnstown. Here are the leading physicians, the best nurses, some of the heaviest contractors, the brightest newspaper men, all the military geniuses, and, if not the actual presence,

21

at least the attention, of the capitalists. The newspapers, medical reviews, and publications of all sorts teem with suggestions. Johnstown is a compendium of business, and misery, and despair. One class of men should be given credit for thorough work in connection with the calamity. These are the undertakers. They came to Johnstown, from all over Pennsylvania, at the first alarm. They are the men whose presence was imperatively needed, and who have actually been forced to work day and night in preserving bodies and preparing them for burial. One of the most active undertakers here is John McCarthy, of Syracuse, N. Y., one of the leading undertakers there, and a very public-spirited man. He brought a letter of introduction from Mayor Kirk, of Syracuse, to the Citizens Committee here. He said to a reporter:—

"It is worthy of mention, perhaps, that never before in such a disaster as this have bodies received such careful treatment and has such a wholesale embalming been practiced. Everybody recovered, whether identified or not, whether of rich man or poor man, or of the humblest child, has been carefully cleaned and embalmed, placed in a neat coffin, and not buried when unidentified until the last possible moment. When you reflect that over one thousand bodies have been treated in this way it means something. It is to be regretted that some pains were not taken to keep a record of the bodies recovered, but the undertakers cannot be blamed for that. They should have been furnished with clerks, and that whole matter made the subject of the work of a bureau by itself. We have had just all we could do cleaning and embalming the bodies."

The unsightliest place in Johnstown is the morgue in the Presbyterian Church. The edifice is a large brick structure in the centre of the city, and was about the first church building in the city. About one hundred and seventy-five people took refuge there during the flood. After the first crash, when the people were expecting another every instant, and of course that they would perish, the pastor of the church, the Rev. Mr. Beale, began to pray fervently that the lives of those in the church might be spared. He fairly wrestled in prayer, and those who heard him say that it seemed to be a very death-struggle with the demon of the flood itself. No second crash came, the waters receded, and the lives of those in the church were spared. The people said that it was all due to the Rev. Mr. Beale's prayer. The pews in the church were all demolished, and the Sunday-school room under it was flooded with the angry waters, and filled up to the ceiling with débris. The Rev. Mr. Beale is now general morgue director in Johnstown, and has the au-

thority of a dictator of the bodies of the dead.
In the Presbyterian Church morgue the bodies
are, almost without exception, those which have
been recovered from the ruins of the smashed
buildings. The bodies are torn and bruised in
the most horrible manner, so that identification is
very difficult. They are nearly all bodies of the
prominent or well-known residents of Johnstown.
The cleaning and embalming of the bodies takes
place in the corners of the church, on either side
of the pulpit. As soon as they have a present-
able appearance, the bodies are placed in coffins,
put across the ends of the pews near the aisles,
so that people can pass around through the aisles
and look at them. Few identifications have yet
been made here. In one coffin is the body of a
young man who had on a nice bicycle suit when
found. In his pockets were forty dollars in money.
The bicycle has not been found. It is supposed
that the body is that of some young fellow who
was on a bicycle tour up the Conemaugh River,
and who was engulfed by the flood.

The waters played some queer freaks. A
number of mirrors taken out of the ruins with
the frames smashed and with the glass parts entirely uninjured have been a matter for constant
comment on the part of those who have inspected
the ruins and worked in them. When the waters
went down, the Sunday-school rooms of the Pres-

byterian Church just referred to were found littered with playing cards. In a baby's cradle was found a dissertation upon infant baptism and two volumes of a history of the Crusades. A commercial man from Pittsburgh, who came down to look at the ruins, found among them his own picture. He never was in Johnstown but two or three times before, and he did not have any friends there. How the picture got among the ruins of Johnstown is a mystery to him.

About the only people who have come into Johnstown, not having business there connected with the clearing up of the city, are people from a great distance, hunting up their friends and relatives. There are folks here now from almost every State in the Union, with the exception, perhaps, of those on the Pacific coast. There are people, too, from Pennsylvania and States near by, who, receiving no answer to their telegrams, have decided to come on in person. They wander over the town in their search, at first frantically asking everybody right and left if they have heard of their missing friends. Generally nobody has heard of them, or some one may remember that he saw a man who said that he happened to see a body pulled out at Nineveh or Cambria City, or somewhere, that looked like Jack So-and-So, naming the missing one. At the morgues the inquirer is told that about four hundred unidentified dead have already been buried, and on the fences before the morgues and on the outside house walls of the buildings themselves he reads several hundred such notices as these, of bodies still unclaimed:—

A woman, dark hair, blue eyes, blue waist, dark dress, clothing of fine quality; a single bracelet on the left arm; age, about twenty-three.

An old lady, clothing undistinguishable, but containing a purse with twenty-seven dollars and a small key.

A young man, fair complexion, light hair, gray eyes, dark blue suit, white shirt; believed to have been a guest at the Hurlburt House.

A female; supposed to belong to the Salvation Army.

A man about thirty-five years old, dark-complexioned, brown hair, brown moustache, light clothes, left leg a little shortened.

A boy about ten years old, found with a little girl of nearly same age; boy had hold of girl's hand; both light-haired and fair-complexioned, and girl had long curls; boy had on dark clothes, and girl a gingham dress.

The people looking for their friends had lots of money, but money is of no use now in Johnstown. It cannot hire teams to go up along the Conemaugh River, where lots of people want to go; it cannot hire men as searchers, for all the people in Johnstown not on business of their own are digging in the ruins ; it cannot even buy food, for what little food there is in Johnstown is practically free, and a good square meal cannot be procured for love nor money anywhere. Under these discouragements many people are giving up the search and going home, either giving their relatives up for dead or waiting for them to turn up, still maintaining the hope that they are alive.

Johnstown at night now is a wild spectacle. The major part of the town is enveloped in darkness, and lights of all colors flare out all around, so that the city looks something like a night scene in a railroad yard. The burning of immense piles of débris is continued at night, and the red glare of the flames at the foot of the hills seems like witch-fires at the mouth of caverns. The camp-fires of the military on the hills above the Conemaugh burn brightly. Volumes of smoke pour up all over the town. Along the Pennsylvania Railroad gangs of men are working all night long by electric light, and the engines, with their great headlights and roaring steam, go about continually. Below the railroad bridge stretches away the dark, sullen mass of the drift, with its freight of human bodies beyond estimate. Now and then, from the headquarters of the newspaper men, can be heard the military guards on their posts challenging passers-by.

CHAPTER XXXII.

It is now a week since the flood, and Johnstown is a cross between a military camp and a new mining town, and is getting more so every day. It has all the unpleasant and disagreeable features of both, relieved by the pleasures of neither. Everywhere one goes soldiers are lounging about or standing guard on all roads leading into the city, and stop every one who cannot show a pass. There is a mass of tents down in the centre of the ruins, and others are scattered everywhere on every cleared space beside the railroad tracks and on the hills about. A corps of engineers is laying pontoon bridges over the streams, pioneers are everywhere laying out new camps, erecting mess sheds and other rude buildings, and clearing away obstructions to the ready passage of supply wagons. Mounted men are continually galloping about from place to place carrying orders. At headquarters about the

(370)

Pennsylvania Railroad depot there are dozens of petty officers in giddy gold lace, and General Hastings, General Wiley, and a few others in dingy clothes, sitting about the shady part of the platform giving and receiving orders. The occasional thunder of dynamite sounds like the boom of distant cannon defending some outpost. Supplies are heaped up about headquarters, and are being unloaded from cars as rapidly as locomotives can push them up and get the empty cars out of the way again. From cooking tents smoke and savory odors go up all day, mingled with the odor carbolic from hospital tents scattered about. It is very likely that within a short time this military appearance will be greatly increased by the arrival of another regiment and the formal declaration of martial law.

On the other hand the town's resemblance to a new mining camp is just as striking. Everything is muddy and desolate. There are no streets nor any roads, except the rough routes that the carts wore out for themselves across the sandy plain. Rough sheds and shanties are going up on every hand. There are no regular stores, but cigars and drink—none intoxicating, however—are peddled from rough board counters. Railroads run into the camp over uneven, crooked tracks. Trains of freight cars are constantly arriving and being shoved off onto all sorts of sid-

ings, or even into the mud, to get them out of the
way. Everybody wears his trousers in his boots,
and is muddy, ragged, and unshaven. Men with
picks and shovels are everywhere delving or mining for something that a few days ago was more
precious than gold, though really valueless now.
Occasionally they make a find and gather around
to inspect it as miners might a nugget. All it
needs to complete the mining camp aspect of the
place is a row of gambling hells in full blast under the temporary electric lights that gaudily il-
luminate the centre of the town.

Matters are becoming very well systematized,
both in the military and the mining way. Martial
law could be imposed to-day with very little inconvenience to any one. The guard about the
town is very well kept, and the loafers, bummers,
and thieves are being pretty well cleared out.
The Grand Army men have thoroughly organized
the work of distributing supplies to the sufferers
by the flood, the refugees, and contraband of this
camp.

The contractors who are clearing up the débris
have their thousands of men well in hand, and
are getting good work out of them, considering
the conditions under which the men have to live,
with insufficient food, poor shelter, and other
serious impediments to physical effectiveness.
All the men except those on the gorge above

the bridge have been working amid the heaps
of ruined buildings in the upper part of the
city. The first endeavor has been to open the
old streets in which the débris was heaped as
high as the house-tops. Fair progress has been
made, but there are weeks of work at it yet. Only
one or two streets are so far cleared that the public can use them. No one but the workmen are
allowed in the others.

Up Stony Creek Gap, above the contractors,
the United States Army engineers began work on
Friday under command of Captain Sears, who
is here as the personal representative of the
Secretary of War. The engineers, Captain Berg-
land's company from Willet's Point, and Lieutenant Biddle's company from West Point, arrived
on Friday night, having been since Tuesday on the
road from New York. Early in the morning they
went to work to bridge Stony Creek, and unloaded and launched their heavy pontoons and strung
them across the streams with a rapidity and skill
that astonished the natives, who had mistaken
them, in their coarse, working uniforms of over-
all stuff, for a fresh gang of laborers. The engineers, when there are bridges enough laid,
may be set at other work about town. They have
a camp of their own on the outskirts of the place.
There are more constables, watchmen, special
policemen, and that sort of thing in Johnstown

than in any three cities of its size in the country.
Naturally there is great difficulty in equipping
them. Badges were easily provided by the clip-
ping out of stars from pieces of tin, but every
one had to look out for himself when it came to
clubs. Everything goes, from a broomstick to a
base ball bat. The bats are especially popular.

"I'd like to get the job of handling your paper
here," said a young fellow to a Pittsburgh newspaper man. "You'll have to get some newsman
to do it anyhow, for your old men have gone
down, and I and my partner are the only news-
men in Johnstown above ground."

The newsdealing business is not the only one
of which something like that is true.

There has been a great scarcity of cooking
utensils ever since the flood. It not only is very
inconvenient to the people, but tends to the waste
of a good deal of food. The soldiers are growl-
ing bitterly over their commissary department.
They claim that bread, and cheese, and coffee are
about all they get to eat.

The temporary electric lights have now been
strung all along the railroad tracks and through
the central part of the ruins, so that the place
after dark is really quite brilliant seen from a distance, especially when to the electric display is
added the red glow in the mist and smoke of
huge bonfires.

Anybody who has been telegraphing to Johnstown this week and getting no answers, would understand the reason for the lack of answers if he could see the piles of telegrams that are sent out here by train from Pittsburgh. Four thousand came in one batch on Thursday. Half of them are still undelivered, and yet there is probably no place in the country where the Western Union Company is doing better work than here. The flood destroyed not only the company's offices, but the greater part of their wires in this part of the country. The office they established here is in a little shanty with no windows and only one door which won't close, and it handles an amount of outgoing matter, daily, that would swamp nine-tenths of the city offices in the country. Incoming business is now received in considerable quantities, but for several days so great was the pressure of outgoing business that no attempt was made to receive any dispatches. The whole effort of the office has been to handle press matter, and well they have done it. But there will be no efficient delivery service for a long time. The old messenger boys are all drowned, and the other boys who might make messenger boys are also most of them drowned, so that the raw material for creating a service is very scant. Besides that, nobody knows nowadays where any one else lives.

The amateur and professional photographers who have overrun the town for the last few days came to grief on Friday. A good many of them were arrested by the soldiers, placed under a guard, taken down to the Stony Creek and set to lugging logs and timbers. Among those arrested were several of the newspaper photographers, and these General Hastings ordered released when he heard of their arrest. The others were made to work for half a day. They were a mad and disgusted lot, and they vowed all sorts of vengeance. It does seem that some notice to the effect that photographers were not permitted in Johnstown should have been posted before the men were arrested. The photographers all had passes in regular form, but the soldiers refused even to look at these.

More sightseers got through the guards at Bolivar on Friday night, and came to Johnstown on the last train. Word was telegraphed ahead, and the soldiers met them at the train, put them under arrest, kept them over night, and in the morning they were set to work in clearing up the ruins.

The special detail of workmen who have been at work looking up safes in the ruins and seeing that they were taken care of, reports that none of the safes have been broken open or otherwise interfered with. The committee on valuables reports that quantities of jewelry and money are being daily turned into them by people who have found them in the ruins. Often the people surrendering this stuff are evidently very poor themselves. The committee believes that as a general thing the people are dealing very honestly in this matter of treasure-trove from the ruins.

Three car-loads of coffins was part of the load of one freight train. Coffins are scattered everywhere about the city. Scores of them seem to have been set down and forgotten. They are used as benches, and even, it is said, as beds.

Grandma Mary Seter, aged eighty-three years, a well-known character in Johnstown, who was in the water until Saturday, and who, when rescued, had her right arm so injured that amputation at the shoulder was necessary, is doing finely at the hospital, and the doctors expect to have her around again before long.

One enterprising man has opened a shop for the sale of relics of the disaster, and is doing a big business. Half the people here are relic cranks. Everything goes as a relic, from a horseshoe to a two-foot section of iron pipe. Buttons and little things like that, that can easily be carried off, are the most popular.

CHAPTER XXXIII.

A MANTLE of mist hung low over the Conemaugh Valley when the people of Johnstown rose
on Sunday morning, June 9th; but about the time
the two remaining church bells began to toll, the
sun's rays broke through the fog, and soon the
sky was clear save for a few white clouds which
sailed lazily to the Alleghenies. Never in the
history of Johnstown did congregations attend
more impressive church services. Some of them
were held in the open air, others in half-ruined
buildings, and one only in a church. The cere-
monies were deeply solemn and touching. Early
in the forenoon German Catholics picked their
way through the wreck to the parsonage of St.
Joseph's, where Fathers Kesbernah and Ald said
four masses. Next to the parsonage there was a
great breach in the walls made by the flood, and
one-half of the parsonage had been carried away.
At one end of the pastor's reception-room had

SEVENTH STREET, WASHINGTON, D. C., UNDER THE FLOOD.

been placed a temporary altar lighted by a solitary candle. There were white roses upon it, while from the walls, above the muddy stains, hung pictures of the Immaculate Conception, the Crucifixion, and the Virgin Mary. The room was filled with worshipers, and the people spread out into the lateral hall hanging over the cellar washed bare of its covering. No chairs or benches were in the room. There was a deep hush as the congregation knelt upon the damp floors, silently saying their prayers. With a dignified and serene demeanor, the priest went through the services of his church, while the people before him were motionless, the men with bowed heads, the women holding handkerchiefs to their faces.

Back of this church, on the side of a hill, there gathered another congregation of Catholics. Their church and parsonage and chapel had all been destroyed, and they met in a yard near their cemetery. A pretty arbor, covered with vines, ran back from the street, and beneath this stood their priest, Father Tahney, who had worked with them over a quarter of a century. His hair was white, but he stood erect as he talked to his people. Before him was a white altar. This, too, was lighted with a single candle. The people stood before him and on each side, reverently kneeling on the grass as they prayed. Three masses were said by Father Tahney and by Father Matthews, of

22

Washington, and then the white-haired priest
spoke a few words of encouragement to his list-
eners.   He urged them to make a manful struggle to rebuild their homes, to assist one another
in their distress, and to be grateful to all Americans for the helping hand extended to them.
Other Catholic services were held at the St. Co-
lumba's Church, in Cambria, where Father Trout-
wein, of St. Mary's Church, Fathers Davin and
Smith said mass and addressed the congregation.
Father Smith urged them not to sell their lands
to those who were speculating in men's misery,
but to be courageous until the city should rise
again.

At the Pennsylvania station a meeting was held
on the embankment overlooking the ruined part
of the town.   The services were conducted by the
Rev. Mr. McGuire, chaplain of the 14th Regiment.
The people sang "Come, Thou Fount of Every
Blessing," and then Mr. McGuire read the psalm
beginning "I will bless the Lord at all times."
James Fulton, manager of the Cambria Iron
Works, spoke encouraging words.   He assured
them that the works would be rebuilt, and that
the eight thousand employés would be cared for.
Houses would be built for them and employment
given to all in restoring the works.   There was a
strained look on men's faces when he told them
in a low voice that he held the copy of a report

which he had drawn up on the dam, calling attention to the fact that it was extremely dangerous
to the people living in the valley.

One of the peculiar things a stranger notices
in Johnstown is the comparatively small number of
women seen in the place. Of the throngs who walk
about the streets searching for dead friends, there
is not one woman to ten men. Occasionally a little
group of two or three women with sad faces will
pick their way about, looking for the morgues.
There are a few Sisters of Charity, in their black
robes, seen upon the streets, and in the parts of
the town not totally destroyed the usual number of women are seen in the houses and yards.
But, as a rule, women are a rarity in Johnstown
now. This is not a natural peculiarity of Johnstown, nor a mere coincidence, but a fact with a
dreadful reason behind it. There are so many
more men than women among the living in Johnstown now, because there are so many more women
than men among the dead. Of the bodies recovered there are at least two women for every
man. Besides the fact that their natural weak-
ness made them an easier prey to the flood, the
hour at which the disaster came was one when the
women would most likely be in their homes and
the men at work in the open air or in factory
yards, from which escape was easy.

Children also are rarely seen about the town,

and for a similar reason. They are all dead. There is never a group of the dead discovered that does not contain from one to three or four children for every grown person. Generally the children are in the arms of the grown persons, and often little toys and trinkets clasped in their hands indicate that the children were caught up while at play, and carried as far as possible toward safety.

Johnstown when rebuilt will be a city of many widowers and few children. In turning a school-house into a morgue the authorities probably did a wiser thing than they thought. It will be a long time before the school-house will be needed for its original purpose.

The miracle, as it is called, that happened at the Church of the Immaculate Conception, has caused a tremendous sensation. A large number of persons will testify as to the nature of the event, and, to put it mildly, the circumstances are really remarkable. The devotions in honor of the Blessed Virgin celebrated daily during the month of May were in progress on that Friday when the water descended on Cambria City. The church was filled with people at the time, but when the noise of the flood was heard the congregation hastened to get out of the way. They succeeded as far as escaping from the interior is concerned, and in a few minutes the church was partially submerged, the water reaching fifteen feet up the sides and swirling around the corners furiously. The building was badly wrecked, the benches were torn out, and in general the entire structure, both inside and outside, was fairly dismantled. Yesterday morning, when an entrance was forced through the blocked doorway the ruin appeared to be complete. One object alone had escaped the water's wrath. The statue of the Blessed Virgin, that had been decorated and adorned because of the May devotions, was as unsullied as the day it was made. The flowers, the wreaths, the lace veil were undisturbed and unsoiled, although the marks on the wall showed that the surface of the water had risen above the statue to a height of fifteen feet, while the statue nevertheless had been saved from all contact with the liquid. Every one who has seen the statue and its surroundings is firmly convinced that the incident was a miraculous one, and even to the most skeptical the affair savors of the supernatural.

A singular feature of the great flood was discovered at the great stone viaduct about half way between Mineral Point and South Fork. At Mineral Point the Pennsylvania Railroad is on the south side of the river, although the town is on the north side. About a mile and a half up the stream there was a viaduct built of very solid masonry. It was originally built for the old Portage Road. It was seventy-eight feet above the ordinary surface of the water. On this viaduct the railroad tracks crossed to the north side of the river and on that side ran into South Fork, two miles farther up. It is the general opinion of engineers that this strong viaduct would have stood against the gigantic wave had it not been blown up by dynamite. But at South Fork there was a dynamite magazine which was picked up by the flood and shot down the stream at the rate of twenty miles an hour. It struck the stone viaduct and exploded. The roar of the flood was tremendous, but the noise of this explosion was heard by farmers on the Evanston Road, two miles and a half away. Persons living on the mountain sides, in view of the river, and who saw the explosion, say that the stones of the viaduct at the point where the magazine struck it, were thrown into the air to the height of two hundred feet. An opening was made, and the flood of death swept through on its awful errand.

CHAPTER XXXIV.

IT is characteristic of American hopefulness and energy that before work was fairly begun on clearing away the wreck of the old city, plans were being prepared for the new one that should arise, Phœnix-like, above its grave. If the future policy of the banks and bankers of Johnstown is to be followed by the merchants and manufacturers of the city the prospects of a magnificent city rising from the present ruins are of the brightest. James McMillen, president of the First National and Johnstown Savings Banks, said:

"The loss sustained by the First National Bank will be merely nominal. It did a general commercial business and very little investing in the way of mortgages. When the flood came the cash on hand and all our valuable securities and papers were locked in the safe and were in no way affected by the water. The damage to the building itself will be comparatively small. Our capital was one hundred thousand dollars, while our

387

surplus was upwards of forty thousand dollars.
The depositors of this bank are, therefore, not
worrying themselves about our ability to meet all
demands that may be made upon us by them.
The bank will open up for business within a few
days as if nothing had happened.

"As to the Johnstown Savings Bank it had
probably $200,000 invested in mortgages on
property in Johnstown, but the wisdom of our
policy in the past in making loans has proven of
great value to us in the present emergency. Since
we first began business we have refused to make
loans to parties on property where the lot itself
would not be of sufficient value to indemnify us
against loss in case of the destruction of the
building. If a man owned a lot worth $2,000 and
had on it a building worth $100,000 we would
refuse to loan over the $2,000 on the property.
The result is that the lots on which the buildings
stood in Johnstown, on which $200,000 of our
money is loaned, are worth double the amount,
probably, that we have invested in them.

"What will be the effect of the flood on the
value of lots in Johnstown proper? Well, instead of decreasing, they have already advanced
in value. This will bring outside capital to Johnstown, and a real estate boom is bound to follow
in the wake of this destruction. All the people
want is an assurance that the banks are safe and

will open up for business at once. With that feeling they have started to work with a vim. We have in this bank $300,000 invested in Government bonds and other securities that can be converted into cash on an hour's notice. We propose to keep these things constantly before our business men as an impetus to rebuilding our principal business blocks as soon as possible."

"What do you think of the idea projected by Captain W. R. Jones, to dredge and lower the river bed about thirty feet and adding seventy per cent. to its present width, as a precautionary measure against future washouts?"

"I not only heartily indorse that scheme, but have positive assurance from other leading business men that the idea will be carried out, as it certainly should be, the moment the work of cleaning away the debris is completed. Besides that, a scheme is on foot to get a charter for the city of Johnstown which will embrace all those surrounding boroughs. In the event of that being done, and I am certain it will be, the plan of the city will be entirely changed and made to correspond with the best laid-out cities in the country. In ten years Johnstown will be one of the prettiest and busiest cities in the world, and nothing can prevent it. The streets will be widened and probably made to start from a common centre, something after the fashion of Washington City, with a little more regard for the value of property. With the Cambria Iron Company, the Gautier Steel Works, and other manufactories, as well as yearly increasing railroad facilities, Johnstown has a start which will grow in a short time to enormous proportions. From a real estate standpoint the flood has been a benefit beyond a doubt. Another addition to the city will be made in the shape of an immense water-main to connect with a magnificent reservoir of the finest water in the world to be located in the mountains up Stony Creek for supplying the entire city as contemplated in the proposed new charter. This plant was well under way when the flood came, and about ten thousand dollars had already been expended on it which has been lost."

Mr. John Roberts, the surviving partner of the banking-house of John Dibert & Company, said:

" Aside from the loss to our own building we have come out whole and entire. We had no money invested in mortgages in Johnstown that is not fully indemnified by the lots themselves. Most of our money is invested in property in Somerset County, where Mr. Dibert was raised. We will exert every influence in our power to place the city on a better footing than was ever before. The plan of raising the city or lowering the bed of the river as well as widening its banks will surely be carried out. In addition, I think the idea of changing the plan of the city and embracing Johnstown and the surrounding buroughs in one large city will be one of the greatest benefits the flood could have wrought to the future citizens of Johnstown and the Conemough Valley.

"I have been chairman of our Finance Committee of Councils for ten years past, and I know the trouble we have had with our streets and alleys and the necessity of a great change. In order to put the city in the proper shape to insure commercial growth and topographical beauty, we will be ready for business in a few days, and enough money will be put into circulation in the valley to give the people encouragement in the work of rebuilding."

CHAPTER XXXV

AMONG the travelers who were in or near the Conemaugh Valley at the time of the flood, and who thus narrowly escaped the doom that swallowed up thousands of their fellow-mortals, was Mr. William Henry Smith, General Manager of the Associated Press. He remained there for some time and did valuable work in directing the operations of news-gatherers and in the general labors of relief.

The wife and daughter of Mr. E. W. Halford, private secretary to President Harrison, were also there. They made their way to Washington on Thursday, to Mr. Halford's inexpressible relief, they having at first been reported among the lost. On their arrival at the Capital they went at once to the Executive Mansion, where the members of the Executive household were awaiting them with great interest. The ladies lost all their baggage, but were thankful for their almost miraculous delivery from the jaws of death. Mrs. Harrison's eyes were suffused with tears as she listened to the dreadful narrative. The President was also deeply moved. From the first tidings of the dire calamity his thoughts have been absorbed in sympathy and desire to alleviate the sufferings of the devastated region. The manner of the escape of Mrs. Halford and her daughter has already been told. When the alarm was given, she and her daughter rushed with the other passengers out of the car and took refuge on the mountain side by climbing up the rocky excavation near the track. Mrs. Halford was in delicate health owing to bronchial troubles. She has borne up well under the excitement, exposure, fatigue, and horror of her experiences.

Mrs. George W. Childs was also reported among the lost, but incorrectly. Mr. Childs received word on Thursday for the first time direct from his wife, who was on her way West to visit Miss Kate Drexel when detained by the flood. Indirectly he had heard she was all right. The telegram notified him that Mrs. Childs was at Altoona, and could not move either way, but was perfectly safe.

George B. Roberts, President of the Pennsylvania Railway Company, was obliged to issue the following card: "In consequence of the terrible calamity that has fallen upon a community which has such close relations to the Pennsylvania Railway Company, Mr. and Mrs. George B. Roberts feel compelled to withdraw their invitations for Thursday, June 6th." Mr. and Mrs. Charles E. Pugh also felt obliged to withdraw their invitations for Wednesday, June 5th.

The Rev. J. A. Ranney, of Kalamazoo, Mich., and his wife were passengers on one of the trains wrecked by the Conemaugh flood. Mr. Ranney said :

"Mrs. Ranney and I were on one of the trains at Conemaugh when the flood came. There was but a moment's warning and the disaster was upon us. The occupants of our car rushed for the door, where Mrs. Ranney and I became separated. She was one of the first to jump, and I saw her run and disappear behind the first house in sight. Before I could get out the deluge was too high, and, with a number of others, I remained in the car. Our car was lifted up and dashed against a car loaded with stone and badly wrecked, but most of the occupants of this car were rescued. As far as I know all who jumped from the car lost their lives. The remainder of the train was swept away. I searched for days for Mrs. Ranney, but could find no trace of her. I think she perished. The mind cannot conceive the awful sight presented when we first saw the danger. The approaching wall of water looked like Niagara, and huge engines were caught up and whirled away as if they were mere wheel-barrows."

D. B. Cummins, of Philadelphia, the President
of the Girard National Bank, was one of the party
of four which consisted of John Scott, Solicitor-
General of the Pennsylvania Railroad ; Edmund
Smith, ex-Vice-President of the same company ;
and Colonel Welsh himself, who had been stopping in the country a few miles back of Williamsport.

Mr. Cummins, in talking of the condition of
things in that vicinity and of his experience, said :
"We were trout-fishing at Anderson's cabin,
about fourteen miles from Williamsport, at the time
the flood started. We went to Williamsport, in-
tending to take a train for Philadelphia. Of course,
when we got there we found everything in a frightful condition, and the people completely disheart-
ened by the flood. Fortunately the loss of life
was very slight, especially when compared with
the terrible disaster in Johnstown. The loss, from
a financial standpoint, will be very great, for the
city is completely inundated, and the lumber
industry seriously crippled. Besides, the stag-
nation of business for any length of time produces
results which are disastrous."

The first passengers that came from Altoona
to New York by the Pennsylvania Railroad since
the floods included five members of the " Night
Off " Company, which played in Johnstown on
Thursday night, about whom considerable anxiety
was felt for some time, till E. A. Eberle received

telegrams from his wife, the contents of which he at once gave to the press. Mrs. Eberle was among the five who arrived.

" No words can tell the horrors of the scenes we witnessed," she said in answer to a request for an account of her experiences, " and nothing that has been published can convey any idea of the awful havoc wrought in those few but apparently never-ending minutes in which the worst of the flood passed us.

" Our company left Johnstown on Friday morning. We only got two miles away, as far as Conemaugh, when we were stopped by a landslide a little way ahead. About noon we went to dinner, and soon after we came back some of our company noticed that the flood had extended and was washing away the embankment on which our train stood. They called the engineer's attention to the fact, and he took the train a few hundred feet further. It was fortunate he did so, for a little while after the embankment caved in.

" Then we could not move forward or backward, as ahead was the landslide and behind there was no track. Even then we were not frightened, and it was not till about three o'clock, when we saw a heavy iron bridge go down as if it were made of paper, that we began to be seriously alarmed. Just before the dam broke a gravel train came tearing down, with the engine giving out the most awful shriek I ever heard. Every

FOURTEENTH STREET, WASHINGTON, D. C., IN THE FLOOD.

one recognized that this was a note of warning. We fled as hard as we could run down the embankment, across a ditch, and for a distance equal to about two blocks up the hillside. Once I turned to look at the vast wall of water, but was hurried on by my friends. When I had gone about the distance of another block the head of the flood had passed far away, and with it went houses, cars, locomotives, everything that a few minutes before had made up a busy scene. The wall of water looked to be fifty feet high. It was of a deep yellow color, but the crest was white with foam.

" Three of us reached the house of Mrs. William Wright, who took us in and treated us most kindly. I did not take any account of time, but I imagine it was about an hour before the water ceased to rush past the house. The conductor of our train, Charles A. Wartham, behaved with the greatest bravery. He took a crippled passenger on his back in the rush up the hill. A floating house struck the cripple, carried him away and tore some of the clothes off Wartham's back, and he managed to struggle on and save himself. Our ride to Ebensburg, sixteen miles, in a lumber wagon without springs, was trying, but no one thought of complaining. Later in the day we were sent to Cresson and thence to Altoona."

23

CHAPTER XXXVI.

NO travelers in an upheaved and disorganized land push through with more pluck and courage than the newspaper correspondents. Accounts have already been given of some of their experiences. A writer in the New York *Times* thus told of his, a week after the events described :

"A man who starts on a journey on ten minutes' notice likes the journey to be short, with a promise of success and of food and clothes at its end. Starting suddenly a week ago, the *Times's* correspondent has since had but a small measure of success, a smaller measure of food, and for nights no rest at all ; a long tramp across the Blue Hills and Allegheny Mountains, behind jaded horses ; helping to push up-hill the wagon they tried to pull or to lift the vehicle up and down bridges whose approaches were torn away, or in and out of fords the pathways to which had disappeared ; and in the blackness of the night, scrambling through gullies in the pike road made by the storm, paved

400

with sharp and treacherous rocks and traversed
by swift-running streams, whose roar was the only
guide to their course. All this prepared a weary
reporter to welcome the bed of straw he found in
a Johnstown stable loft last Monday, and on which
he has reposed nightly ever since.

"And let me advise reporters and other persons
who are liable to sudden missions to out-of-the-
way places not to wear patent leather shoes.
They are no good for mountain roads. This is
the result of sad experience. Wetness and stone
bruises are the benisons they confer on feet that
tread rough paths.

"The quarter past twelve train was the
one boarded by the *Times's* correspondent and
three other reporters on their way hither a week
ago Friday night. It was in the minds of all that
they would get as far as Altoona, on the Pennsylvania Road, and thence by wagon to this place.
But all were mistaken. At Philadelphia we were
told that there were wash-outs in many places and
bridges were down everywhere, so that we would
be lucky if we got even to Harrisburg. This was
harrowing news. It caused such a searching of
time-tables and of the map of Pennsylvania as
those things were rarely ever subjected to before.
It was at last decided that if the Pennsylvania
Railroad stopped at Harrisburg an attempt would
be made to reach the Baltimore and Ohio Rail-

road at Martinsburg, West Virginia, by way of
the Cumberland Railroad, a train on which was
scheduled to leave Harrisburg ten minutes after
the arrival of the Pennsylvania train.

"It was only too evident to us, long before we
reached Harrisburg, that we would not get to the
West out of that city. The Susquehanna had
risen far over its banks, and for miles our train
ran slowly with the water close to the fire-box of
the locomotive and over the lower steps of the car
platform. At last we reached the station. Several energetic Philadelphia reporters had come on
with us from that lively city, expecting to go
straight to Johnstown. As they left the train one
cried : 'Hurrah, boys, there's White. He'll know
all about it.' White stood placidly on the steps,
and knew nothing more than that he and several
other Philadelphia reporters, who had started Friday night, had got no further than the Harrisburg
station, and were in a state of wonderment, leaving them to think our party caught.

"As the Cumberland Valley train was pulling
out of the station, its conductor, a big, genial fellow, who seemed to know everybody in the valley,
was loth to express an opinion as to whether we
would get to Martinsburg. He would take us as
far as he could, and then leave us to work out our
own salvation. He could give us no information
about the Baltimore and Ohio Road. Hope and

fear chased one another in our midst; hope that trains were running on that road, and fear that it, too, had been stopped by wash-outs. In the latter case it seemed to us that we should be compelled to return to Harrisburg and sit down to think with our Philadelphia brethren.

The Cumberland Valley train took us to Hagerstown, and there the big and genial conductor told us it would stay, as it could not cross the Potomac to reach Martinsburg. We were twelve miles from the Potomac and twenty from Martinsburg. Fortunately, a construction train was going to the river to repair some small wash-outs, and Major Ives, the engineer of the Cumberland Valley Road, took us upon it, but he smiled pitifully when we told him we were going across the bridge.

"'Why, man,' he said to the *Times's* correspondent, 'the Potomac is higher than it was in 1877, and there's no telling when the bridge will go.'

"At the bridge was a throng of country people waiting to see it go down, and wondering how many more blows it would stand from foundering canal-boats, washed out of the Chesapeake and Ohio Canal, whose lines had already disappeared under the flood. A quick survey of the bridge showed that its second section was weakening, and had already bent several inches, making a slight concavity on the upper side.

" No time was to be lost if we were going to Martinsburg. The country people murmured disapproval, but we went on the bridge, and were soon crossing it on the one-foot plank that served for a footwalk. It was an unpleasant walk. The river was roaring below us. To yield to the fascination of the desire to look between the railroad ties at the foaming water was to throw away our lives. Then that fear that the tons of drift stuff piled against the upper side of the bridge, would suddenly throw it over, was a cause of anything but confidence. But we held our breath, balanced ourselves, measured our steps, and looked far ahead at the hills on the Western Virginia shore. At last the firm embankment was reached, and four reporters sent up one sigh of relief and joy.

" Finding two teams, we were soon on our way to Martinsburg.

" The Potomac was nine feet higher than it was ever known to be before, and it was out for more than a mile beyond the tracks of the Cumberland Valley Railroad at Falling Waters, where it had carried away several houses. This made the route to Martinsburg twice as long as it otherwise would have been. To weary, anxious reporters it seemed four times as long, and that we should never get beyond the village of Falling Waters. It confronted us at every turn of the crooked way, until it became a source of pain. It is a pretty place, but we were yearning for Johnstown, not for rural beauty.

" All roads have an end, and Farmer Sperow's teams at last dragged us into Martinsburg. Little comfort was in store for us there. No train had arrived there for more than twenty-four hours. Farmer Sperow was called on to take us back to the river, our instructions being to cross the bridge again and take a trip over the mountains. Hope gave way to utter despair when we learned that the bridge had fallen twenty minutes after our passage. We had put ourselves into a pickle. Chief Engineer Ives and his assistant, Mr. Schoonmaker joined us a little while later. They had followed us across the bridge and been cut off also. They were needed at Harrisburg, and they backed up our effort to get a special train to go to the Shenandoah Valley Road's bridge, twenty-five miles away, which was reported to be yet standing.

" The Baltimore and Ohio officials were obdurate. They did not know enough about the tracks to the eastward to experiment with a train on them in the dark. They promised to make up a train in the morning. Wagons would not take us as soon. A drearier night was never passed by men with their hearts in their work. Morning came at last and with it the news that the road to

the east was passable nearly to Harper's Ferry.
Lots of Martinsburg folks wanted to see the
sights at the Ferry, and we had the advantage of
their society on an excursion train as far as Shenandoah Junction, where Mr. Ives had telegraphed
for a special to come over and meet us if the
bridge was standing.

"The telegraph kept us informed about the
movement of the train. When we learned that
it had tested and crossed the bridge our joy was
modified only by the fear that we had made fools
of ourselves in leaving Harrisburg, and that the
more phlegmatic Philadelphia reporters had
already got to Johnstown. But this fear was soon
dissipated. The trainman knew that Harrisburg
was inundated and no train had gone west for
nearly two days. A new fear took its place. It
was that New York men, starting behind us, had
got into Johnstown through Pittsburg by way of
the New York Central and its connections. No
telegrams were penned with more conflicting
emotions surging through the writer than those
by which the *Times's* correspondent made it known
that he had got out of the Martinsburg pocket
and was about to make a wagon journey of one
hundred and ten miles across the mountains, and
asked for information as to whether any Eastern
man had got to the scene of the flood.

"The special train took us to Chambersburg,

where Superintendent Riddle, of the Cumberland Valley Road, had information that four Phila-. delphia men were on their way thither, and had engaged a team to take them on the first stage of the overland trip. A wild rush was made for Schiner's livery, and in ten minutes we were howling over the pike toward McConnellsburg, having already sent thither a telegraphic order for fresh teams. The train from Harrisburg was due in five minutes when we started. As we mounted each hill we eagerly scanned the road behind for pursuers. They never came in sight.

"In McConnellsburg the entire town had heard of our coming, and were out to greet us with cheers. They knew our mission and that a party of competitors was tracking us. Landlord Prosser, of the Fulton Hotel, had his team ready, but said there had been an enormous wash-out near the Juniata River, beyond which he could not take us. We would have to walk through the break in the pike and cross the river on a bridge tottering on a few supports. Telegrams to Everett for a team to meet us beyond the river and take us to Bedford, and to the latter place for a team to make the journey across the Alleghenies to Johnstown settled all our plans.

"As well as we could make it out by telegraphic advices, we were an hour ahead of the Philadelphians. Ten minutes was not, therefore, too long for supper.   Landlord Prosser took the reins himself and we started again, with a hurrah from the populace.   As it was Sunday, they would sell us nothing, but storekeeper Young and telegraph operator Sloan supplied us with tobacco and other little comforts, our stock of which had been exhausted.   It will gratify our Prohibition friends to learn that whisky was not among them.   McConnellsburg is, unfortunately, a dry town for the time being.   It was a long and weary pull to the top of Sidling Hill.   To ease up on the team, we walked the greater part of the way.   A short descent and a straight run took us to the banks of Licking Creek.

" Harrisonville was just beyond, and Harrisonville had been under a raging flood, which had weakened the props of the bridge and washed out the road for fifty feet beyond it.   The only thing to do was to unhitch and lead the horses over the bridge and through the gully.   This was difficult, but it was finally accomplished.   The more difficult task was to get the wagon over.   A long pull, with many strong lifts, in which some of the natives aided, took it down from the bridge and through the break, but at the end there were more barked shins and bruised toes than any other four men ever had in common.

" It was a quick ride from Everett to Bedford, for our driver had a good wagon and a speedy team. Arriving at Bedford a little after two o'clock in the morning, we found dispatches that cheered us, for they told us that we had made no mistake, and might reach the scene of disaster first. Only a reporter who has been on a mission similar to this can tell the joy imparted by a dispatch like this:

" ' NEW YORK—Nobody is ahead of you. Go it.'

" At four o'clock in the morning we started on our long trip of forty miles across the Alleghenies to Johnstown. Pleasantville was reached at half-past six A. M. Now the road became bad, and everybody but the driver had to walk. Footsore as we were, we had to clamber over rocks and through mud in a driving rain, which wet us through. For ten miles we went thus dismally. Ten miles from Johnstown we got in the wagon, and every one promptly went to sleep, at the risk of being thrown out at any time as the wagon jolted along. Tired nature could stand no more, and we slumbered peacefully until four half-drunken special policemen halted us at the entrance to Johnstown. Argument with them stirred us up, and we got into town and saw what a ruin it was."

CHAPTER XXXVII.

Nor was the life of the correspondents at Johnstown altogether a happy one. The life of a newspaper man is filled with vicissitudes. Sometimes he feeds on the fat of the land, and at others he feeds on air; but as a rule he lives comfortably, and has as much satisfaction in life as other men. It may safely be asserted, however, that such experiences as the special correspondents of Eastern papers have met with in Johnstown are not easily paralleled. When a war correspondent goes on a campaign he is prepared for hardship and makes provision against it. He has a tent, blankets, heavy overcoat, a horse, and other things which are necessaries of life in the open air. But the men who came hurrying to Johnstown to fulfill the invaluable mission of letting the world know just what was the matter were not well provided against the suffering set before them.

The first information of the disaster was sent

out by the Associated Press on the evening of its occurrence. The destruction of wires made it impossible to give as full an account as would otherwise have been sent, but the dispatches convinced the managing editors of the wide-awake papers that a calamity destined to be one of the most fearful in all human history had fallen upon the peaceful valley of the Conemaugh. All the leading Eastern papers started men for Philadelphia at once. From Philadelphia these men went to Harrisburg. There were many able representatives in the party, and they are ready to wager large amounts that there was never at any place a crowd of newspaper men so absolutely and hopelessly stalled as they were there. Bridges were down and the roadway at many places was carried away.

Then came the determined and exhausting struggle to reach Johnstown. The stories of the different trips have been told. From Saturday morning till Monday morning the correspondents fought a desperate battle against the raging floods, risking their lives again and again to reach the city. At one place they footed it across a bridge that ten minutes later went swirling down the mad torrent to instant destruction. Again they hired carriages and drove over the mountains, literally wading into swollen streams and carrying their vehicles across. Finally one party caught a Baltimore and Ohio special train and got into Johnstown.

It was Monday. There was nothing to eat. The men were exhausted, hungry, thirsty, sleepy. Their work was there, however, and had to be done. Where was the telegraph office? Gone down the Conemaugh Valley to hopeless oblivion. But the duties of a telegraph company are as imperative as those of a newspaper. General Manager Clark, of Pittsburgh, had sent out a force of twelve operators, under Operator Munson as manager *pro tem.*, to open communications at Johnstown. The Pennsylvania Railroad rushed them through to the westerly end of the fatal bridge. Smoke and the pall of death were upon it. Ruin and devastation were all around. To get wires into the city proper was out of the question. Nine wires were good between the west end of the bridge and Pittsburgh. The telegraph force found, just south of the track, on the side of the hill overlooking the whole scene of Johnstown's destruction, a miserable hovel which had been used for the storage of oil barrels. The interior was as dark as a tomb, and smelled like the concentrated essence of petroleum itself. The floor was a slimy mass of black grease. It was no time for delicacy. In went the operators with their relay instruments and keys; out went the barrels. Rough shelves were thrown up to take copy on, and some old chairs were subsequently secured. Tallow dips threw a fitful red glare upon the scene. The operators were ready.

Toward dusk ten haggard and exhausted New York correspondents came staggering up the hillside. They found the entire neighborhood infested with Pittsburgh reporters, who had already secured all the good places, such as they were, for work, and were busily engaged in wiring to their offices awful tales of Hungarian depredations upon dead bodies, and lynching affairs which never occurred. One paper had eighteen men there, and others had almost an equal number. The New York correspondents were in a terrible condition. Some of them had started from their offices without a change of clothing, and had managed to buy a flannel shirt or two and some footwear, including the absolutely necessary rubber boots, on the way. Others had no extra coin, and were wearing the low-cut shoes which they had on at starting. One or two of them were so worn out that they turned dizzy and sick at the stomach when they attempted to write. But the work had to be done. Just south of the telegraph office stands a two-story frame building in a state of dilapidation. It is flanked on each side by a shed, and its lower story, with an earth floor, is used for the storage of fire bricks. The second-story floor is full of great gaps, and the entire building is as draughty as a seive and as dusty as a country road in a drought. The Associated Press and the *Herald* took the second floor, the *Times, Tribune, Sun, Morning Journal, World*, Philadelphia *Press*, Baltimore *Sun*, and Pittsburgh *Post* took possession of the first floor, using the sheds as day outposts. Some old barrels were found inside. They were turned up on end, some boards were picked up outdoors and laid on them, and seats were improvised out of the fire-bricks. Candles were borrowed from the telegraph men, who were hammering away at their instruments and turning pale at the prospect, and the work of sending dispatches to the papers began.

Not a man had assuaged his hunger. Not a man knew where he was to rest. All that the operators could take, and a great deal more, was filed, and then the correspondents began to think of themselves. Two tents, a colored cook, and provisions had been sent up from Pittsburgh for the operators. The tents were pitched on the side of the hill, just over the telegraph "office," and the colored cook utilized the natural gas of a brick-kiln just behind them. The correspondents procured little or nothing to eat that night. Some of them plodded wearily across the Pennsylvania bridge and into the city, out to the Baltimore and Ohio tracks, and into the car in which they

SEVENTH STREET, WASHINGTON, DURING THE FLOOD.

had arrived. There they slept, in all their clothing, in miserably-cramped positions on the seats.
In the morning they had nothing to wash in but
the polluted waters of the Conemaugh. Others,
who had no claim on the car, moved to pity a
night watchman, who took them to a large barn
in Cambria City. There they slept in a hay-loft,
to the tuneful piping of hundreds of mice, the
snorting of horses and cattle, the nocturnal dancing of dissipated rats, and the solemn rattle of
cow chains.

In the morning all hands were out bright and
early, sparring for food. The situation was desperate. There was no such thing in the place as
a restaurant or a hotel; there was no such thing
as a store. The few remaining houses were overcrowded with survivors who had lost all. They
could get food by applying to the Relief Committee. The correspondents had no such privilege. They had plenty of money, but there was
nothing for sale. They could not beg nor borrow; they wouldn't steal. Finally, they prevailed upon a pretty Pennsylvania mountain
woman, with fair skin, gray eyes, and a delicious
way of saying "You un's," to give them something to eat. She fried them some tough pork,
gave them some bread, and made them some
coffee without milk and sugar. The first man
that stayed his hunger was so glad that he gave

24

her a dollar, and that became her upset price. It cost a dollar to go in and look around after that.

Then Editor Walters, of Pittsburgh, a great big man with a great big heart, ordered up $150 worth of food from Pittsburgh. He got a German named George Esser, in Cambria City, to cook at his house, which had not been carried away, and the boys were mysteriously informed that they could get meals at the German's. He was supposed to be one of the dread Hungarians, and the boys christened his place the Café Hungaria. They paid fifty cents apiece to him for cooking the meals, but it was three days before the secret leaked out that Mr. Walters supplied the food. If ever Mr. Walters gets into a tight place he has only to telegraph to New York, and twenty grateful men will do anything in their power to repay his kindness.

Then the routine of Johnstown life for the correspondents became settled. At night they slept in the old car or the hay-mow or elsewhere. They breakfasted at the Café Hungaria. Then they went forth to their work. They had to walk everywhere. Over the mountains, through briers and among rocks, down in the valley in mud up to their knees, they tramped over the whole district lying between South Fork and New Florence, a distance of twenty-three miles, to gather the details of the frightful calamity. Luncheon was a rare and radiant luxury. Dinner was eaten at the café. Copy was written everywhere and anywhere.

Constant struggles were going on between correspondents and policemen or deputy sheriffs. The countersign was given out incorrectly to the newspaper men one night, and many of them had much trouble. At night the boys traversed the place at the risk of life and limb. Two *Times* men spent an hour and a half going two miles to the car for rest one night. The city— or what had been the city—was wrapped in Cimmerian darkness, only intensified by the feeble glimmer of the fires of the night guards. The two correspondents almost fell through a pontoon bridge into the Conemaugh. Again they almost walked into the pit full of water where the gas tank had been. At length they met two guards going to an outlying post near the car with a lantern. These men had lived in Johnstown all their lives. Three times they were lost on their way over. Another correspondent fell down three or four slippery steps one night and sprained his ankle, but he gritted his teeth and stuck to his work. One of the *Times* men tried to sleep in a hay-mow one night, but at one o'clock he was driven out by the rats. He wandered about till he found a night watchman, who escorted him to a brick-kiln. Attired in all his clothing, his mackintosh, rubber boots, and hat, and with his handkerchief for a pillow, he stretched himself upon a plank on top of the bricks inside the kiln and slept one solitary hour. It was the third hour's sleep he had enjoyed in seventy-two hours. The next morning he looked like a paralytic tramp who had been hauled out of an ash-heap.

Another correspondent fell through an opening in the Pennsylvania bridge and landed in a culvert several feet below. His left eye was almost knocked out, and he had to go to one of the hospitals for treatment. But he kept at his work. The more active newspaper men were a sight by Wednesday. They knew it. They had their pictures taken. They call the group "The Johnstown Sufferers." Their costumes are picturesque. One of them—a dramatically inclined youth sometimes called Romeo—wears a pair of low shoes which are incrusted with yellow mud, a pair of gray stained trousers, a yellow corduroy coat, a flannel shirt, a soft hat of a dirty greenish-brown tint, and a rubber overcoat with a cape. And still he is not happy.

CHAPTER XXXVIII.

THE storm that filled Conemaugh Lake and burst its bounds also wrought sad havoc elsewhere. Williamsport, Pa., underwent the experience of being flooded with thirty-four feet of water, of having the Susquehanna boom taken out with two hundred million feet of logs, over forty million feet of sawed lumber taken, mills carried away and others wrecked, business and industrial establishments wrecked, and a large number of lives lost. The flood was nearly seven feet higher than the great high water of 1865.

Early on Friday news came of the flood at Clearfield, but it was not before two o'clock Saturday morning that the swelling water began to become prominent, the river then showing a rise averaging two feet to the hour. Steadily and rapidly thereafter the rise continued. The rain up the country had been terrific, and from Thurs-

(421)

day afternoon, throughout the night, and during Friday and Friday night, the rain fell here with but little interruption. After midnight Friday it came down in absolute torrents until nearly daylight Saturday morning. As a result of this rise, Grafins Run, a small stream running through the city from northwest to southeast, was raised until it flooded the whole territory on either side of it.

Soon after daylight, the rain having ceased, the stream began to subside, and as the river had not then reached an alarming height, very few were concerned over the outlook. The water kept getting higher and higher, and spreading out over the lower streets. At about nine o'clock in the forenoon the logs began to go down, filling the stream from bank to bank. The water had by this time reached almost the stage of 1865. It was coming up Third Street to the Court-house, and was up Fourth Street to Market. Not long after it reached Third Street on William, and advanced up Fourth to Pine. Its onward progress did not stop, however, as it rose higher on Third Street, and soon began to reach Fourth Street both at Elmira and Locust Streets. No one along Fourth between William and Hepburn had any conception that it would trouble them, but the sequel proved they were mistaken.

Soon after noon the water began crossing the railroad at Walnut and Campbell Streets, and soon all the country north of the railroad was submerged, that part along the run being for the second time during the day flooded. The rise kept on until nine o'clock at night, and after that hour it began to go slowly the other way. By daylight Sunday morning it had fallen two feet, and that receding continued during the day. When the water was at its highest the memorable sight was to be seen of a level surface of water extending from the northern line of the city from Rural Avenue on Locust Street, entirely across the city to the mountain on the south side. This meant that the water was six feet deep on the floors of the buildings in Market Square, over four feet deep in the station of the Pennsylvania Railroad and at the Park Hotel. Fully three-quarters of the city was submerged.

The loss was necessarily enormous. It was heaviest on the lumbermen. All the logs were lost, and a large share of the cut lumber.

The loss of life was heavy.

A general meeting of lumbermen was held, to take action on the question of looking after the lost stock. A comparison as to losses was made, but many of those present were unable to give an estimate of the amount they had lost. It was found that the aggregate of logs lost from the boom was about two hundred million feet, and the aggregate of manufactured lumber fully forty million feet. The only saw-mill taken was the Beaver mill structure, which contained two mills, that of S. Mack Taylor and the Williamsport Lumber Company. It went down stream just as it stood, and lodged a few miles below the city.

A member of the Philadelphia *Times'* staff telegraphed from Williamsport :—

"Trusting to the strong arms of brave John Nichol, I safely crossed the Susquehanna at Montgomery in a small boat, and met Superintendent Westfall on the other side on an engine. We went to where the Northern Central crosses the river again to Williamsport, where it is wider and swifter. The havoc everywhere is dreadful. Most of the farmers for miles and miles have lost their stock and crops, and some their horses and barns. In one place I saw thirty dead cattle. They had caught on the top of a hill, but were drowned and carried into a creek that had been a part of a river. I could see where the river had been over the tops of the barns a quarter of a mile from the usual bank. A man named Gibson, some miles below Williamsport, lost every animal but a gray horse, which got into the loft and stayed there, with the water up to his body.

"A woman named Clark is alive, with six cows that she got upstairs. Along the edges of the washed-out tracks families with stoves and a few things saved are under board shanties. We

passed the saw-mill that, by forming a dam, is
responsible for the loss of the Williamsport
bridges. The river looked very wild, but Superintendent Westfall and I crossed it in two boats.
It is nearly half a mile across. Both boats were
carried some distance and nearly upset. It was
odd, after wading through mud into the town, to
find all Williamsport knowing little or nothing
about Johnstown or what had been happening
elsewhere. Mr. Westfall was beset by thousands
asking about friends on the other side, and inquiring when food can be got through.

"The loss is awful. There have not been
many buildings in the town carried off, but there
are few that have not been damaged. There is
mourning everywhere for the dead. Men look
serious and worn, and every one is going about
splashed with mud. The mayor, in his address,
says: 'Send us help at once—in the name of
God, at once. There are hundreds utterly destitute. They have lost all they had, and have
no hope of employment for the future. Philadelphia should, if possible, send provisions. Such
a thing as a chicken is unknown here. They
were all carried off. It is hard to get anything to
eat for love or money. Flour is needed worse
than anything else.'

"I gave away a cooked chicken and sandwiches
that I had with me to two men who had had noth-

ing to eat since yesterday morning. The flood having subsided, all the grim destitution is now uncovered. Last night a great many grocery and other stores were gutted, not by the water, but by hungry, desperate people. They only took things to eat.

"A pathetic feature of the loss of life is the great number of children drowned. In one case two brothers named Youngman, up the river, who have a woolen mill, lost their wives and children and their property, too, by the bursting of the dam. Everything was carried away in the night. They saved themselves by being strong. One caught in a tree on the side of the mountain across the river and remained there from Saturday night until late Sunday, with the river below him."

Among the many remarkable experiences was that of Garrett L. Crouse, proprietor of a large kindling-wood mill, who is also well known to many Philadelphia and New York business men. Mr. Crouse lives on the north side of West Fourth Street, between Walnut and Campbell. On Saturday he was down town, looking after his mill and wood, little thinking that there was any flood in the western part of the city. At eleven o'clock he started to go home, and sauntered leisurely up Fourth Street. He soon learned the condition of things and started for Lycoming Street, and was soon in front of the Rising Sun Hotel, on Walnut Street, wading in the water, which came nearly to his neck. Boats passing and repassing refused to take him in, notwithstanding that he was so close to his home. The water continued to rise and he detached a piece of board-walk, holding on to a convenient tree. In this position he stayed two hours in the vain hope that a boat would take him on.

At this juncture a man with a small boat hove in sight and came so close that Mr. Crouse could touch it. Laying hold of the boat he asked the skipper how much he would take to row him down to Fourth Street, where the larger boats were running.

"I can't take you," was the reply; "this boat only holds one."

"I know it only holds one, but it will hold two this time," replied the would-be passenger. "This water is getting unpleasantly close to my lower lip. It's a matter of life and death with me, and if you don't want to carry two your boat will carry one; but I'll be that one."

The fellow in the boat realized that the talk meant business, and the two started down town. At Pine Street Mr. Crouse waited for a big boat another hour, and when he finally found one he was shivering with cold. The men in the boat engaged to run him for five dollars, and they started.

It was five o'clock when they reached their destination, when they rowed to their passenger's stable and found his horses up to their necks in the flood.

" What will you charge to take these two horses to Old Oaks Park ? " he asked.

"Ten dollars apiece," was the reply.

" I'll pay it."

They then rowed to the harness room, got the bridles, rowed back to the horses and bridled them. They first took out the brown horse and landed her at the park, Mr Crouse holding her behind the boat. They returned for the gray and started out with her, but had scarcely left the stable when her head fell back to one side. Fright had already exhausted her. They took her back to the house porch, when Mr. Crouse led her upstairs and put her in a bed-room, where she stayed high and dry all night. On Sunday morning the folks who were cleaning up were surprised to see a gray horse and a man backing down a plank out of the front door of a Fourth Street residence.

It was Garrett Crouse and his gray horse, and when the neighbors saw it they turned from the scene of desolation about them and warmly applauded both beast and master. This is how a Williamsport man got home during the flood and saved his horses. It took him five hours and cost him twenty-five dollars.

Mr. James R. Skinner, of Brooklyn, N. Y., arrived home after a series of remarkable adventures in the floods at Williamsport.

"I went to Williamsport last Thursday," said Mr. Skinner, "and on Friday the rain fell as I had never seen it fall before. The skies seemed simply to open and unload the water. The Susquehanna was booming and kept on rising rapidly, but the people of Williamsport did not seem to be particularly alarmed. On Saturday the water had risen to such a height that the people quit laughing and gathered along the sides of the torrent with a sort of awe-stricken curiosity.

"A friend of mine, Mr. Frank Bellows, and myself went out to see the grand spectacle, and found a place of observation on the Pennsylvania Railroad bridge. Great rafts of logs were swept down the stream, and now and then a house would be brought with a crash against the bridge. Finally, one span gave way and then we beat a hasty retreat. By wading we reached the place of a man who owned a horse and buggy. These we hired and started to drive to the hotel, which is on the highest ground in the city. The water was all the time rising, and the flood kept coming in waves. These waves came with such frequency and volume that we were forced to abandon the horse and buggy and try wading. With the water up to our armpits we got to an out-

house, and climbing to the top of it made our
way along to a building.   This I entered through
a window, and found the family in the upper
stories.   Floating outside were two canoes, one
of which I hired for two dollars and fifty cents.   I
at once embarked in this and tried to paddle for
my hotel.   I hadn't gone a hundred feet when I
capsized.   Going back, I divested myself of my
coat, waistcoat, shoes, and stockings.   I tried
again to make the journey, and succeeded very
well for quite a distance, when the canoe suddenly struck something and over it went.   I managed to hold the paddle and the canoe, but everything else was washed away and lost.   After a
struggle in the water, which was running like a
mill-race, I got afloat again and managed to lodge
myself against a train of nearly submerged freight
cars.   Then, by drawing myself against the
stream, I got opposite the hotel and paddled
over.   My friend Bellows was not so fortunate.
The other canoe had a hole in it, and he had to
spend the night on the roof of a house.

"The trainmen of the Pennsylvania road
thought to sleep in the cars, but were driven out,
and forced to take refuge in the trees, from which
they were subsequently rescued.   The Beaver
Dam mill was moved from its position as though
it was being towed by some enormous steam
tug.   The river swept away everything that

offered it any resistance. Saturday night was the most awful I ever experienced. The horrors of the flood were intensified by an inky darkness, through which the cries of women and children were ceaselessly heard. Boatmen labored all night to give relief, and hundreds were˜ brought to the hotel for safety.

"On Sunday the waters began to subside, and then the effects were more noticeable. All the provision stores were washed out completely, and one of the banks had its books, notes, and greenbacks destroyed. I saw rich men begging for bread for their children. They had money, but there was nothing to be bought. This lack of supplies is the greatest trouble that Williamsport has to contend with, and I really do not see how the people are to subsist.

"Sunday afternoon Mr. C. H. Blaisdell, Mr. Cochrane, a lumberman and woodman, a driver, and myself started in a wagon for Canton, with letters and appeals for assistance. The roads were all washed away, and we had to go over the mountains. We had to cut our way through the forests at times, hold the wagon up against the sides of precipices, ford streams, and undergo a thousand hardships. After two days of travel that even now seems impossible, we got into Canton more dead than alive. The soles were completely gone from my boots, and I had on

only my night-shirt, coat, and trousers, which I
had saved from the flood.   A relief corps was at
once organized, and sent with provisions for the
sufferers.   But it had to take a roundabout way,
and I do not know what will become of those poor
people in the meantime."

Mr. Richard P. Rothwell, the editor of the New
York *Engineering and Mining Journal*, and Mr.
Ernest Alexander Thomson, the two men who
rowed down the Susquehanna River from Williamsport, Pa., to Sunbury, and brought the first
news of the disaster by flood at Williamsport,
came through to New York by the Reading road.
The boat they made the trip in was a common
flat-bottom rowboat, about thirteen feet long, fitted
for one pair of oars.   There were three men in
the crew, and her sides were only about three
inches above the water when they were aboard.
The third was Mr. Aaron Niel, of Phœnixville,
Pa.   He is a trotting-horse owner.

Mr. Thomson is a tall, athletic young man, a
graduate of Harvard in '87.   He would not ac-
knowledge that the trip was very dangerous, but
an idea of it can be had from the fact that they
made the run of forty-five miles in four and one-
half hours.

"My brother, John W. Thomson, myself, and
Mr. Rothwell," he said, "have been prospecting
for coal back of Ralston.   It began to rain on

Friday just after we got into Myer's Hotel, where we were staying. The rain fell in torrents for thirty-two hours. The water was four or five feet deep in the hotel when the railroad bridge gave way, and domestic animals and outhouses were floating down the river by scores. The bridge swung around as if it were going to strike the hotel. Cries of distress from the back porch were heard, and when we ran out we found a parrot which belonged to me crying with all his might, ' Hellup ! hellup ! hellup !' My brother left for Williamsport by train on Friday night. We followed on foot. There were nineteen bridges in the twenty-five miles to Williamsport, and all but three were gone.

"In Williamsport every one seemed to be drinking. Men waited in rows five or six deep in front of the bars of the two public houses, the Lush House and the Concordia. We paid two dollars each for the privilege of sleeping in a corner of the bar-room. Mr. Rothwell suggested the boat trip when we found all the wagons in town were under water. The whole town except Sauerkraut Hill was flooded, and it was as hard to buy a boat as it was to get a cab during the blizzard. It was here we met Niel. 'I was a raftsman,' he said, 'on the Allegheny years ago, and I may be of use to you,' and he was. He sat in the bow, and piloted, I rowed, and Mr. Rothwell

25

steered with a piece of board. Our danger was from eddies, and it was greatest when we passed the ruins of bridges. We started at 10.15, and made the run to Montgomery, eighteen miles, in one and a quarter hours. In places we were going at the rate of twenty miles an hour. There wasn't a whole bridge left on the forty-five miles of river. As we passed Milton we were in sight of the race-track, where Niel won a trot the week before. The grand stand was just toppling into the water.

"I think I ought to row in a 'Varsity crew now," Mr. Thomson concluded. "I don't believe any crew ever beat our time"

CHAPTER XXXIX.

THERE was terrible destruction to life and property throughout the entire Juniata Valley by the unprecedented flood. Between Tyrone and Lewistown the greatest devastation was seen and especially below Huntingdon at the confluence of the Raystown branch and the Juniata River. During the preceding days of the week the rain-filled clouds swept around the southeast, and on Friday evening met an opposing strata of storm clouds, which resulted in an indescribable downpour of rain of twelve hours' duration.

The surging, angry waters swept down the river, every rivulet and tributary adding its raging flood to the stream, until there was a sea of water between the parallel hills of the valley. Night only added to the terror and confusion. In Huntingdon City, and especially in the southern and eastern suburbs, the inhabitants were forced to flee for their lives at midnight on Thursday, and by daybreak the chimneys of their houses were visible above the rushing waters. Opposite the city the people of Smithfield found safety within the walls of the State Reformatory, and for two days they were detained under great privations.

Some conception of the volume of water in the river may be had from the fact that it was thirty-five feet above low-water mark, being eight feet higher than the great flood of 1847. Many of the inhabitants in the low sections of Huntingdon, who hesitated about leaving their homes, were rescued, before the waters submerged their houses, with great difficulty.

Huntingdon, around which the most destruction is to be seen of any of the towns in the Juniata Valley, was practically cut off from all communication with the outside world, as all the river bridges crossing the stream at that point were washed away. There was but one bridge standing in the county, and that was the Huntingdon and Broad Top Railroad bridge, which stood isolated in the river, the trestle on the other end being destroyed. Not a county bridge was left, and this loss alone approximated $200,000.

The gas works were wrecked on Thursday night and the town was left in darkness.

Just below where the Juniata and Raystown branch meet, lived John Dean and wife, aged seventy-seven each, and both blind. With them resided John Swaner and wife. Near by lived John Rupert, wife and three small children. When the seething current struck these houses they were carried a half mile down the course of the stream and lodged on the ends amid stream.

The Ruperts were soon driven to the attic, and finally, when it became evident that they must perish, the frantic mother caught up two bureau drawers, and placed her little children in them upon the angry waves, hoping that they might be saved; but all in vain.

The loss of life by the flood in Clinton County, in which Lock Haven is situated, was heavy. Twenty of those lost were in the Nittany Valley, and seven in Wayne Township. Lock Haven was very fortunate, as the inhabitants there dwelling in the midst of logs on the rivers are accustomed to overflows. There were many sagacious inhabitants who, remembering the flood of 1865, on Saturday began to prepare by removing their furniture and other possessions to higher ground for safety. It was this full and realizing sense of the danger that gave Lock Haven such immunity from loss of life.

The only case of drowning in Lock Haven was of James Guilford, a young man who, though warned not to do so, attempted to wade across the main street, where six feet of the overflowed river was running, and was carried off by the swift current. The other dead include William Confur and his wife and three children, all carried off and drowned in their little home as it floated away, and the two children of Jacob Kashne.

Robert Armstrong and his sister perished at Clintondale under peculiarly dreadful circumstances. At Mackeyville, John Harley, Andrew R. Stine, wife and two daughters, were drowned, while the two boys were saved. At Salona, Alexander M. Uting and wife, Mrs. Henry Snyder were drowned. At Cedar Springs, Mrs. Luther S. Eyler and three children were drowned. The husband was found alive in a tree, while his wife was dead in a drift-pile a few rods away. At Rote, Mrs. Charles Cole and her two children were drowned, while he was saved. Mrs. Charles Barner and her children were also drowned, while the husband and father was saved. This is a queer coincidence found all through this section, that the men are survivors, while the wives and children are victims.

The scenes that have been witnessed in Tyrone City during the time from Friday evening, May 31st, to Monday evening, June 3d, are almost indescribable. On Friday afternoon, May 31st, telephone messages from Clearfield gave warning of a terrible flood at that place, and preparations were commenced by everybody for high water, although no one anticipated that it would equal in height that of 1885, which had always in the past served as high-water mark in Lock Haven.

All of that Friday rain descended heavily, and when at eight o'clock in the evening the water commenced rising, the rain was falling in torrents. The river rose rapidly, and before midnight was over the top of the bank. Its rapid rising was the signal for hasty preparations for higher water than ever before witnessed in the city. As the water continued rising, both the river and Bald Eagle Creek, the vast scope of land from mountain to mountain was soon a sea of foaming water.

The boom gave away about two o'clock Saturday morning, and millions of feet of logs were taken away. Along Water Street, logs, trees, and every conceivable kind of driftwood went rushing by the houses at a fearful rate of swiftness. The night was one to fill the stoutest heart with dread, and the dawn of day on Saturday morning was anxiously awaited by thousands of people.

In the meantime men in boats were busy during the night taking people from their houses in the lower portions of the city, and conveying them to places of imagined security.

When day dawned on June 1st, the water was still rising at a rapid rate. The city was then completely inundated, or at least all that portion lying east of the high lands in the Third and Fourth Wards. It was nearly three o'clock Saturday afternoon before the water reached the highest mark. It then was about three feet above the high-water mark of 1885.

At four o'clock Saturday evening the flood began to subside, slowly at first, and it was nearly night on Sunday before the river was again within its banks. Six persons are reported missing at Salona, and the dead bodies of Mrs. Alexander Whiting and Mrs. William Emenheisen were recovered at Mill Hall and that of a six-year old child near by. The loss there is terrible, and the community is in mourning over the loss of life.

G. W. Dunkle and wife had a miraculous escape from drowning early Saturday A. M. They were both carried away on the top of their house from Salona to Mill Hall, where they were both rescued in a remarkable manner. A window in the house of John Stearn was kicked out, and Mr. and Mrs. Dunkle taken in the aperture, both thus being rescued from a watery grave.

Near by a baby was saved, tied in a cradle. It was a pretty, light-haired light cherub, and seemed all unconscious of the peril through which it passed on its way down the stream. The town of Mill Hall was completely gutted by the flood, entailing heavy loss upon the inhabitants.

The town of Renovo was completely wrecked. Two spans of the river bridge and the opera-house were swept away. Houses and business places were carried off or damaged and there was some loss of life. At Hamburg seven persons were drowned by the flood, which carried away almost everything in its path.

Bellefonte escaped the flood's ravages, and lies high and dry. Some parts of Centre County were not so fortunate, however, especially in Co-burn and Miles Townships, where great destruction is reported. Several persons were drowned at Coburn, Mrs. Roust and three children among the number. The bodies of the mother and one child were recovered.

James Corss, a well-known resident of Lock Haven, and Miss Emma Pollock, a daughter of ex-Governor Pollock of Philadelphia, were married at the fashionable Church of the Holy Trinity, Philadelphia, at noon of Wednesday, June 5th. The cards were sent out three weeks before, but when it was learned that the freshet had cut off Lock Haven from communication with the rest of the world, and several telegrams to the groom had failed to bring any response, it was purposed to postpone the wedding. The question of post-ponement was being considered on Tuesday even-ing, when a dispatch was brought in saying that the groom was on his way overland. Nothing further was heard from him, and the bride was dressed and the bridal party waiting when the groom dashed up to the door in a carriage at almost noon.

After an interchange of joyful greetings all around, the bride and groom set out at once for the church, determined that they should not be late. On the way to the church the bride fainted. As the church came into view she fainted again, and she was driven leisurely around Rittenhouse Square to give her a chance to recover. She got better promptly. The groom stepped out of the carriage and went into the church by the vestry way. The carriage then drove round to the main entrance, and the bride alighted with her father and her maids, and, taking her proper place in the procession, marched bravely up the aisle, while the organ rang out the well-remembered notes of Mendelssohn's march. The groom met her at the chancel, the minister came out, and they were married. A reception followed.

The bride and groom left on their wedding-journey in the evening. Before they went the groom told of his journey from Lock Haven. He said that the little lumber town had been shut out from the rest of the world on Friday night. He is a widower, and, accompanied by his grown daughter, he started on his journey on Monday at two o'clock. They drove to Bellefonte, a distance of twenty-five miles, and rested there on Monday night. They drove to Leedsville on Tuesday morning. There, by hiring relays of horses and engaging men to carry their baggage and row them across streams, they succeeded in reaching Lewistown, a distance of sixty-five miles, by Tuesday night. At Lewistown they found a direct train for Philadelphia, and arrived there on Wednesday forenoon.

CHAPTER XL

The opening of the month of June will long be remembered with sadness and dismay by thousands of people in New York, Pennsylvania, Maryland and the two Virginias. In the District of Columbia, too, it was a time of losses and of terror. The northwestern and more fashionable part of Washington, D. C., never looked more lovely than it did on Sunday, but along a good part of the principal business thoroughfare, Pennsylvania avenue, and in the adjacent streets to the southward, there was a dreary waste of turbid, muddy water, that washed five and six feet deep the sides of the houses, filling cellars and basements and causing great inconvenience and considerable loss of property. Boats plied along the avenue near the Pennsylvania Railroad station and through the streets of South Washington. A carp two feet long was caught in the ladies' waiting-room at the Baltimore and Potomac station, and several others were caught in the streets by boys. These fish came from the Government Fish Pond, the waters of the Potomac having covered the pond and allowed them to escape.

Along the river front the usually calm Potomac was a wide, roaring, turbulent stream of dirty

444

water, rushing madly onward, and bearing on its swift-moving surface logs, telegraph poles, portions of houses and all kinds of rubbish. The stream was nearly twice its normal width, and flowed six feet and more deep through the streets along the river front, submerging wharves, small manufacturing establishments, and lapping the second stories of mills, boat-houses and fertilizing works in Georgetown. It completely flooded the Potomac Flats, which the Government had raised at great expense to a height in most part of four and five feet, and inundated the abodes of poor negro squatters, who had built their frame shanties along the river's edge. The rising of the waters has eclipsed the high-water mark of 1877. The loss was enormous.

The river began rising early on Saturday morning, and from that time continued to rise steadily until five o'clock Sunday afternoon, when the flood began to abate, having reached a higher mark than ever before known. The flood grew worse and worse on Saturday, and before noon the river had become so high and strong that it overflowed the banks just above the Washington Monument, and backing the water into the sewer which empties itself at this point, began to flow along the streets on the lower levels.

By nightfall the water in the streets had increased to such an extent as to make them

impassable by foot passengers, and boats were
ferrying people from the business part of the
town to the high grounds in South Washington.
The street cars also continued running and did a
thriving business conveying pleasure-seekers, who
sat in the windows and bantered one another as
the deepening waters hid the floor. On Louisiana
avenue the produce and commission houses are
located, and the proprietors bustled eagerly about
securing their more perishable property, and
wading knee-deep outside after floating chicken-
coops. The grocery merchants, hotel men and
others hastily cleared out their cellars and worked
until the water was waist-deep removing their
effects to higher floors.

Meanwhile the Potomac, at the Point of Rocks,
had overflowed into the Chesapeake and Ohio
Canal, and the two became one. It broke open
the canal in a great many places, and lifting the
barges up, shot them down stream at a rapid rate.
Trunks of trees and small houses were torn from
their places and swept onward.

The water continued rising throughout the
night, and about noon of Sunday reached its
maximum, three feet six inches above high-water
mark of 1877, which was the highest on record.
At that time the city presented a strange spectacle.
Pennsylvania avenue, from the Peace monument,
at the foot of the Capitol, to Ninth street, was

flooded with water, and in some places it was up to the thighs of horses. The cellars of stores along the avenue were flooded, and so were some of the main floors. In the side streets south of the avenue there was six to eight feet of water, and yawls, skiffs and canoes were everywhere to be seen. Communication except by boat was totally interrupted between North and South Washington. At the Pennsylvania Railroad station the water was up to the waiting-room.

Through the Smithsonian and Agricultural Department grounds a deep stream was running, and the Washington Monument was surrounded on all sides by water.

A dozen lives lost, a hundred poor families homeless, and over $2,000,000 worth of property destroyed, is the brief but terrible record of the havoc caused by the floods in Maryland. Every river and mountain stream in the western half of the State has overflowed its banks, inundating villages and manufactories and laying waste thousands of acres of farm lands. The losses by wrecked bridges, washed-out roadbeds and landslides along the western division of the Baltimore and Ohio Railroad, from Baltimore to Johnstown, reach half a million dollars or more. The Chesapeake and Ohio Canal, that political bone of contention and burden to Maryland, which has cost the State many millions, is a total wreck. The

Potomac river, by the side of which the canal runs, from Williamsport, Md., to Georgetown, D. C., has swept away the locks, towpaths, bridges, and, in fact, everything connected with the canal. The probability is that the canal will not be restored, but that the canal bed will be sold to one of the railroads that have been trying to secure it for several years. The concern has never paid, and annually has increased its enormous debt to the State.

The Western Maryland Railroad Company and the connecting lines, the Baltimore and Harrisburg, and the Cumberland Valley roads, lose heavily. On the mountain grades of the Blue Ridge there are tremendous washouts, and in some sections the tracks are torn up and the road-bed destroyed. Several bridges were washed away. Dispatches from Shippensburg, Hagerstown and points in the Cumberland Valley state that the damage to that fertile farming region is incalculable. Miles of farm lands were submerged by the torrents that rushed down from the mountains. Several lives were lost and many head of cattle drowned. At the mountain town of Frederick, Md., the Monocacy river, Carroll creek and other streams combined in the work of destruction.

Friday night was one of terror to the people of that section. The Monocacy river rose rapidly from the time the rain ceased until last night, when the waters began to fall. The back-water of the river extended to the eastern limit of the city, flooding everything in its path and riding over the fields with a fierce current that meant destruction to crops, fences and everything in its path. At the Pennsylvania Railroad bridge the river rose thirty feet above low-water mark. It submerged the floor of the bridge and at one time threatened it with destruction, but the breaking away of 300 feet of embankment on the north side of the bridge saved the structure. With the 300 feet of embankment went 300 feet of track. The heavy steel rails were twisted by the waters as if they had been wrenched in the jaws of a mammoth vise. The river at this point and for many miles along its course overflowed its banks to the width of a thousand feet, submerging the corn and wheat fields on either side and carrying everything before it. Just below the railroad bridge a large wooden turnpike bridge was snapped in two and carried down the tide. In this way a half-dozen turnpike bridges at various points along the river were carried away. The loss to the counties through the destruction of these bridges will foot up many thousand dollars.

Mrs. Charles McFadden and Miss Maggie Moore, of Taneytown, were drowned in their carriage while attempting to cross a swollen stream.

26

The horse and vehicle were swept down the stream, and when found were lodged against a tree. Miss Moore was lying half-way out of the carriage, as though she had died in trying to extricate herself. Mrs. McFadden's body was found near the carriage. At Knoxville considerable damage was done, and at Point of Rocks people were compelled to seek the roofs of their houses and other places of safety. A family living on an island in the middle of the river, opposite the Point, fired off a gun as a signal of distress. They were with difficulty rescued. In Frederick county, Md., the losses aggregate $300,000.

The heaviest damage in Maryland was in the vicinity of Williamsport, Washington county. The railroads at Hagerstown and Williamsport were washed out. The greatest loser is the Cumberland Valley Railroad. Its new iron bridge across the Potomac river went down, nothing being left of the structure except the span across the canal. The original cost of the bridge was $70,000. All along the Potomac the destruction was great. At and near Williamsport, where the Conococheague empties into the Potomac, the loss was very heavy.

At Falling Waters, where only a few days before a cyclone caused death and destruction, two houses went down in the angry water, and the little town was almost entirely submerged. In Carroll County, Md., the losses reached several hundred thousand dollars. George Derrick was drowned at Trevanion Mills, on Pipe creek. Along the Patapsco river in Howard county great damage was done to mills and private property. Near Sykesville the water undermined the Baltimore and Ohio Railroad track and a freight train was turned over an embankment. William Hudson was standing on the Suspension Bridge, at Orange Grove, when the structure was swept away, and he was never seen again.

Port Deposit, near the mouth of the Susquehanna river, went under water. Residents along the river front left their homes and took refuge on the hills back of the town. The river was filled with thousands of logs from the broken booms up in the timber regions. From the eastern and southern sections of the State came reports of entire fruit farms swept away. Two men were drowned in the storm by the capsizing of a sloop near Salisbury.

A number of houses on the Shenandoah and Potomac rivers near Harper's Ferry were destroyed by the raging waters which came thundering down from the mountains, thirty to forty feet higher than low-water mark. John Brown's fort was nearly swept away. The old building has withstood a number of floods. There is only a rickety portion of it standing, anyhow, and that is now covered with mud and rubbish. While the

crowds on the heights near Harper's Ferry were
watching the terrible work of destruction, a house
was seen coming down the Potomac. Upon its
roof were three men wildly shouting to the people
on the hills to save them. Just as the structure
struck the railroad bridge, the men tried to catch
hold of the flooring and iron work, but the swift
torrent swept them all under, and they were seen
no more. What appeared to be a babe in a cradle
came floating down behind them, and a few
moments later the body of a woman, supposed to
be the mother of the child, swept by. Robert
Connell, a farmer living upon a large island in the
Potomac, known as Herter Island, lost all his
wheat crop and his cattle. His family was rescued
by Clarence Stedman and E. A. Keyser, an artist
from Washington, at the risk of their lives. The
fine railroad bridge across the Shenandoah, near
Harper's Ferry, was destroyed. The Ferry Mill
Company sustained heavy losses.

Along the South Mountains, in Washington
and Alleghany counties, Md., the destruction was
terrible. Whole farms, including the houses and
barns, were swept away and hundreds of live stock
killed. Between Williamsport, Md., and Dam No.
6 on the Chesapeake and Ohio Canal twenty-six
houses were destroyed, and it is reported that
several persons were drowned. The homeless
families are camping out on the hills, being sup-

plied with food and clothing by the citizens of Williamsport.

Joseph Shifter and family made a narrow escape. They were driven to the roof of their house by the rising waters, and just a minute before the structure collapsed the father caught a rowboat passing by, and saved his wife and little ones.

The town of Point of Rocks, on the Potomac river, twelve miles eastward of Harper's Ferry, was half-submerged. Nearly $100,000 worth of property in the town and vicinity was swept away. The Catholic Church there is 500 feet from the river. The extent of the flood here may be imagined when it is stated that the water was up to the eaves of the church.

The Chesapeake and Ohio Canal has been utterly lost, and what formerly was the bed of the canal is now part of the Potomac river. There were but few houses in Point of Rocks that were not under water. The Methodist Church had water in its second story. The two hotels of which the place boasts, the American and the St. Charles, were full of water, and any stranger in town had to hunt for something to eat.

Every bridge in Frederick county, Md., was washed away. Some of these bridges were built as long ago as 1834, and were burned by the Confederate and Union forces at various times in 1864, afterward being rebuilt. At Martinsburg,

W. Va., a number of houses were destroyed. Little Georgetown, a village on the Upper Potomac, near Williamsport, Md., was entirely swept away.

Navigation on Chesapeake Bay was seriously interrupted by the masses of logs, sections of buildings and other ruins afloat. Several side-wheel steamers were damaged by the logs striking the wheels. Looking southward for miles from Havre de Grace, the mouth of the Susquehanna, and far out into the bay the water was thickly covered with the floating wood. Crowds of men and boys were out on the river securing the choicest logs of hard wood and bringing them to a safe anchorage. By careful count it was estimated that 200 logs, large and small, were swept past Havre de Grace every minute. At that rate there would be 12,000 logs an hour. It is estimated that over 70,000,000 feet of cut and uncut timber passed Havre de Grace within two days. Large rafts of dressed white pine boards floated past the city. The men who saved the logs got from 25 cents to $1 for each log for salvage from the owners, who sent men down the river to look after the timber. Enough logs have been saved to give three years' employment to men, and mills will be erected to saw up the stuff.

Not within the memory of the oldest inhabitants had Petersburg, Virginia, been visited by a flood as fierce and destructive as that which surprised it on Saturday and Sunday. The whole population turned out to see the sight.

The storm that did such havoc in Virginia and West Virginia on Thursday reached Gettysburg on Saturday morning. The rain began at 7 o'clock Friday morning and continued until 3 o'clock Saturday. It was one continuous down-pour during all that time. As a result, the streams were higher than they had been for twenty-five years. By actual measurement the rain-fall was 4.15 inches between the above hours. Nearly every bridge in the county was either badly damaged or swept away, and farmers who lived near the larger streams mourn for their fences carried away and grain fields ruined. Both the railroads leading to the town had large portions of their embankments washed out and many of their bridges disturbed. On the Baltimore and Harrisburg division of the Western Maryland Railroad the damage was great. At Valley Junction 1000 feet of the embankment disappeared, and at Marsh creek, on the new branch of the road to Hagerstown, four divisions of the bridge were swept away.

But at Pine Grove and Mount Holly perhaps the greatest damage was done. The large Laudel dam, which supplies the water to run the forge at Pine Grove furnace, and which covers thirty acres of land, burst. It swept away part of the furnace and a house. The occupants were saved by men wading in water up to their waists. Every bridge, with one exception, in Mount Holly was swept away by the flood occasioned by the breaking of the dam which furnished water for the paper mills at that place.

The water at Elmira, N. Y., on Saturday night was from a foot to a foot and a half higher than ever before known. The Erie Railroad bridge was anchored in its place by two trains of loaded freight cars. The water rose to the cars, which, with the bridge, acted as a dam, and forced the water back through the city on the north side of the Chemung river, where the principal business houses are located. The water covered the streets to a depth of two or three feet, and the basements of the stores were quickly flooded, causing thousands of dollars of damage. The only possible way of entering the Rathbone House, the principal hotel of the city and on the chief business street, was by boats, which were rowed directly into the hotel office. On the south side of the river the waters were held in check for several hours by the ten-foot railroad embankment, but hundreds of families were driven into the upper stories of their houses. Late in the evening, two thousand feet of the embankment was forced away, and the water carried the railroad tracks and everything else before it. An extensive lumber yard in the path of the rushing water was swept away. Many horses were drowned, and the people living on the flats were rescued with great difficulty by the police and firemen.

A terrible rain-storm visited Andover, N. Y. All the streams were swollen far above high-water mark, and fields and roads were overflowed. No less than a dozen bridges in this town were carried away, and newly planted crops were utterly ruined. The water continued to rise rapidly until 4 o'clock. At that hour the two dams at the ponds above the village gave away, and the water rushed wildly down into the village. Nearly every street in the place was overflowed, and in many cases occupants of houses were driven to the upper floors for safety. Owen's large tannery was flooded and ruined. Almost every rod of railroad track was covered and much of it will have to be rebuilt. The track at some points was covered fifteen feet with earth.

At Wellsville, N. Y., the heavy rain raised creeks into rivers and rivers into lakes. Never, in the experience of the oldest inhabitant, had Wellsville been visited with such a flood. Both ends of the town were submerged, water in many cases standing clear to the roofs of houses.

Canisteo, N. Y., was invaded by a flood the equal of which had never been known or seen in that vicinity before. Thursday afternoon a drizzling rain began and continued until it became a perfect deluge. The various creeks and mountain rills tributary to the Caniesto river became swollen and swept into the village, inundating many of the streets to the depth of three feet and others from five to seven feet. The streets were scarcely passable, and all stores on Main and the adjacent streets were flooded to a depth of from one to two feet and much of the stock was injured or spoiled. Many houses were carried away from their foundations, and several narrow escapes from death were made.

One noble deed, worthy of special mention, was performed by a young man, who waded into the water where the current was swift and caught a baby in his arms as it was thrown from the window of a house that had just been swept from its foundation.

The Fire Department Building, one of the most costly blocks in town, was undermined by the flood and the greater part fell to the ground with a crash. The town jail was almost destroyed.

The inundation in the coal, iron and lumber country around Sunbury, Penn., occasioned much destruction and suffering, while no less than fifty lives were lost. The Susquehanna, Allegheny, Bald Eagle, Sinnamahoning and Huntingdon Railways suffered greatly, and the losses incurred reach, in round numbers, $2,000,000. In Clearfield, Clinton, Lycoming, Elk, Cameron, Northumberland, Centre, Indiana, McKean, Somerset, Bedford, Huntingdon, Blair and Jefferson counties the rain-storm was one of unprecedented severity. The mountain streams grew into great rivers, which swept through the country with irresistible fury and force, and carried devastation in all directions.

The destruction in the Allegheny Valley at and near Dubois, Red Bank, New Bethlehem and Driftwood was immense, hardly a saw-mill being left standing.

www.ingramcontent.com/pod-product-compliance
Lightning Source LLC
Chambersburg PA
CBHW022020110726
47901CB00006B/1604